PROTECTION DETAIL

BY
JULIE MILLER

D1331610

MILLS &
BOON

First Published in Great Britain 2017
By Mills & Boon, an imprint of HarperCollins*Publishers*
1 London Bridge Street, London, SE1 9GF

© 2017 by Julie Miller

ISBN: 978-0-263-92907-2

46-0817

Our policy is to use papers that are natural, renewable and recyclable products and made from wood grown in sustainable forests. The logging and manufacturing processes conform to the legal environmental regulations of the country of origin.

Printed and bound in Spain
by CPI, Barcelona

Julie Miller is an award-winning *USA TODAY* bestselling author of breathtaking romantic suspense—with a National Readers' Choice Award and a Daphne du Maurier Award, among other prizes. She has also earned an *RT Book Reviews* Career Achievement Award. For a complete list of her books, monthly newsletter and more, go to www.juliemiller.org.

For the Dixons and their Ruby, who taught our Maggie
that not all big dogs are scary.

Thanks for always saying hi to your shy neighbor.

I've loved all our conversations about the dogs.

the past. A late-night in the from a drunk fellow officer in a bar had led to their taking each other, a first
love and a true love. A month later he and Mary were
married and what she should have been—a traditional wedding
begun. Lieutenant...own his wife anymore, but he
missed her. There were no...of life moments as we had
he could have shared with...Like the wedding
of their youngest child...daughter. He clasped
Olivia's hand. "She would have loved to have been here
today, I know she's with us...forever us."

Prologue

Thomas Watson's face hurt from the effort it took not
to cry when he saw his daughter in her wedding gown.

"It's okay, Dad." Olivia Mary Watson had packed up
all her tomboy clothes, her gun and her badge and put
on a beaded ivory gown that made her look every inch
the grown woman he reluctantly admitted she had become. She reached up to cup his cheek and smiled, reminding Thomas of the wife he'd lost to a drugged-up
thief's bullet when Olivia was a toddler. "I will always
be your little girl."

She'd stopped being his little girl the day she'd become a Kansas City cop, like him, his father and her
three older brothers. But a daddy was entitled to indulge
his sentimental side on a day like this. They stood in the
doorway of the changing room at the church while the
pre-ceremony music played, but Thomas was remembering skinned knees, annoying big brothers and broken
hearts that had required his advice, his patience and a hug.

"You're beautiful. You look so like your mother."
He fingered the veil of Irish lace his bride had worn
thirty-five years earlier when he'd been a raw lieutenant stationed in the UK on his first overseas assignment. Mary Kilcannon had been a civilian working on

the base. A late-night rescue from a drunk fellow officer in a bar had led to them talking until dawn, a first kiss and true love. A month later he and Mary were married, and what should have been a lifetime together began. Thomas didn't mourn his wife anymore, but he missed her. There were a lot of life moments he wished he could have shared with Mary. Like the wedding of their youngest child and only daughter. He kissed Olivia's cheek. "She would have loved to have been here today. I know she's watching over us."

"It's been twenty years. You've done your duty by us. We never wanted for anything with you and Grandpa and Millie to take care of us. But Mom would want you to find someone and be happy again."

"I date," he insisted.

"Escorting a female work friend to the annual police officer's ball does not constitute dating." She straightened his red silk tie, an homage to the February 14 date that all the men in the bridal party except for the groom himself were wearing. "You're a handsome man. You're fit. You're smart, a rock of dependability and caring. Maybe you could ease up on the whole alpha male of the pack thing you've got going on. But that's SOP for any senior detective I know, and besides, you probably needed that to raise the four of us. You have a nice house and a good job consulting with KCPD. The right woman is out there waiting to snatch you up if you'd let her."

Thomas laughed. "Let your old dad get through marrying off my baby girl today before you start matchmaking for me."

"*Old dad*, nothing. You're a catch." Thomas gave her a stern look he couldn't sustain in the glow of that bemused smile. "All right. I'll allow you today."

Thomas walked her to the foyer outside the church's sanctuary. "Gabe makes you happy?"

"You know he does."

"I'd be pitchin' a fit if I thought you were marrying a man who didn't love you as much as you love him."

Olivia grinned. "You would not. You have never in your life pitched a fit."

Thomas paused when they reached the center archway at the end of the long aisle, waiting for the music to change. He looked up the aisle as his youngest son, Keir, stepped into his place at the altar beside his firstborn, Duff, and his middle son, Niall. Being a single father hadn't been easy. After Mary's death, he'd needed the help of his father, Seamus, and the older woman he'd hired to run the household, Millie Leighter, to help him raise four kids.

Olivia had grown into a smart, courageous woman. And his boys, lined up as best man and groomsmen at the altar, had turned into three good men, three good cops—a streetwise detective who'd nearly given his life on one of his undercover assignments, a medical examiner with the crime lab with more brains than social acumen and a hotshot young detective who was probably going to be his boss at KCPD one day.

Thomas's smile thinned. "I might pitch one now." Even as adults his sons could sometimes become the Three Stooges. Duff and Keir were trading one-liners under their breaths, and Niall was caught in the middle, trying to shush them both. His middle son adjusted his glasses and said something to both his older and younger brothers that snapped them to attention. "Did you put Niall in charge of corralling Duff and Keir today?"

Olivia nodded. "You taught me to be prepared for any contingency. I figured Niall was the most reliable."

"Smart girl." Now that her older brothers had gotten a look at their baby sister in a wedding dress, their whole demeanor changed. Their fidgeting stopped, and Thomas saw the love and pride on their faces. Thomas was surprised to see he wasn't the only Watson man struggling today. "Your oldest brother is crying."

"Duff's not as tough as he tries to be."

"Neither am I." As Niall slipped Duff a handkerchief, Thomas wiped away his own tear. "I love you, Olivia Mary. You know that?"

Olivia leaned against his shoulder for a moment. "I know, Dad. I love you, too."

The organist in the balcony over their heads started the processional music and the guests filling the pews stood. Thomas pulled his shoulders back to attention, squeezing Olivia's fingers where they rested on his arm. "Let's do this."

Thomas walked down the aisle, honoring his daughter and her marriage, ignoring the twinge of pain shooting through his stiff knee. Almost every bit of that leg had been blown out, torn up, scarred and rebuilt. He was lucky to still have his leg after that fiery wreck he and his partner, Al Junkert, had had in pursuit of a fugitive. That accident had taken him off the front line of law enforcement, but he'd eventually come back to earn his detective's badge and lieutenant's rank, working special cases and mentoring new detectives. So he was a veteran with a desk job, focusing on teaching and behind-the-scenes investigative duties now. He was still a proud man, and he'd be damned if he was going to limp down the aisle like some washed-up hero on this happy day.

When they reached the altar, Thomas winked at his future son-in-law, Gabriel Knight, and succinctly answered the minister's question about giving his daughter away. He caught Olivia in a bear hug before stepping back, marveling again at how much she reminded him of Mary in both looks and personality. As she exchanged silent greetings with her big brothers, Thomas saw parts of his long-dead wife in each of his children—Duff's strength of will and tender heart, Niall's smarts, Keir's gift of the Irish gab as well as Mary's tenacity. He hoped they got some good stuff from him, too, and that he'd done right by them all.

Heading to his seat, Thomas traded a salute with Al, who sat a couple of rows back. Even after the accident that had taken their lives and careers down different paths, they'd remained good friends. He smiled at the silver-haired woman in the second pew. Millie Leighter was sniffling bravely into her lace hankie, losing the battle with her tears. As dear to him as a treasured aunt, Millie had been a godsend from the day he'd hired her to cook and clean and help him raise his children. Even with the kids grown and out of the house, she remained a vital part of the family. So when the next sniffle turned into a quiet sob, he leaned down and wrapped her plump frame up in a hug. Slipping her his own handkerchief, Thomas whispered, "You and I will both get through today okay. I promise."

Millie's tears turned into a sweet smile and she nodded. Thomas straightened and slipped into the first pew beside his father. Seamus Watson moved his cane to the other side and tapped Thomas's leg. When he looked down, he saw his father was handing him his handkerchief. "You're going to need one, too, son."

Thomas arched his eyebrow, daring his father to be honest.

The white-haired man put up a hand in mock surrender, then reached inside his black jacket to pull out a second handkerchief. "I brought two."

Thomas grinned as the minister spoke to Gabe. Yeah, they were all a bunch of tough guys.

They'd survived tragedy. Their hearts had mended. He couldn't be prouder of following his father into a career at KCPD, or seeing his children follow him into the same job. Thomas's family was happy. Secure. The guilt over Mary's death was a little less sharp than it had once been, and he'd done right by her memory. He'd done right by them. Maybe Olivia had a point. Maybe it was time he stopped being a dad and a cop 24/7 and thought about finding that woman Olivia had mentioned. Man, wasn't that a scary thought—putting himself back out there after all these years. He wasn't even sure he knew how to be in a relationship anymore. Maybe he should just sit back and watch the ceremony, and be content surrounded by the love of his family.

"You may now kiss the bride."

Thomas smiled through teary eyes as the minister wrapped up the wedding vows.

"Love you," Olivia whispered.

Gabe kissed her again. "Love you more."

"I now present Mr. and Mrs. Gabriel Knight."

THOMAS BEAMED FROM ear to ear as Gabe and Olivia walked past. He looked back toward the altar to watch Duff, Niall and Keir escort the maid of honor and bridesmaids to the center aisle. His smile vanished and his eyes narrowed when he saw their steps hesitate, saw their jaws go rigid, saw their gazes turn up to the balcony.

His own muscles clenched in that split second and he knew something was terribly wrong.

"Gun!" Niall shouted. His sons were already scrambling when Thomas heard the first shots. "Get down!"

The organ music clashed on a toxic chord and went silent.

Niall touched his arm and Thomas nodded that he was taking cover. Flying like shrapnel, wood splintered over his head as he ducked. A vase at the altar shattered. Explosions of marble dust filled the air.

Thomas's entire world flashed between heartbeats.

Duff was pulling a gun from behind his back. "Everybody down!"

Keir was hugging his arms around Millie and his bridesmaid, tugging them down between the pews. "I'm calling SWAT."

Gabe was shoving Olivia to the floor and shielding her with his body, even as his daughter tried to reverse positions to protect him.

Thomas hadn't protected Mary all those years ago. He should have been the one at that convenience store when the bullets had taken down every customer and cashier in the building. He should have saved her.

People were shouting, ducking for cover, running to save loved ones, running toward the threat raining terror down on the guests in the sanctuary. His gun and badge were locked up at home. He was helpless to protect his children, to save his friends. Helpless to do anything but reach for his elderly father.

Blood spattered his cheek a split second before his father's cane clattered against the marble tiles. Thomas caught Seamus as he fell, cradling him in his arms as he lowered his limp body to the floor.

"Niall!" He shouted for the closest doctor at hand. "Help me, son. Dad's been shot."

Chapter One

September

If anyone had to suffer a stroke after a traumatic brain injury like being shot in the head, Thomas hoped he or she possessed the same stubborn cussedness Seamus Watson did. There were bound to be a lot of arguments, setbacks and hurt feelings along the road to recovery, but apparently, it was the only way to survive.

He just wished there weren't so many casualties along the way.

Thomas looked from his father's red face to Millie's pale, gaping expression to the retreating backside of the young speech-therapy intern who was running out the door of the Saint Luke's Hospital rehab center in tears. Although the young woman barely looked old enough to have graduated from high school, much less college, her youthful enthusiasm, pretty face and obvious competence hadn't spared her from Seamus's wrathful outburst at the end of a long afternoon of medical evaluations.

While he went down on his good knee to gather up the flash cards his father had knocked to the ground, Thomas spared a glance at the fourth person in the room, the private nurse he'd hired to aid in Seamus's recovery, Jane Boyle. How was Battle-Ax Boyle, as his three sons had secretly nicknamed her, going to handle his father's refusal to do the speech test since she was taking point on Seamus's health and physical rehabilitation?

Although her rigid professionalism and terse, almost-awkward personal skills had earned her the teasing, never-to-her-face nickname, Thomas had spent enough time with Jane over the past several months to have a slightly different take on the resident battle-ax. No one could question her devotion to her duty, a fact that all of them, as a three-generation family of cops, could understand and respect. As for the I'm-not-interested-in-making-friends vibe she put off? He wished he wasn't so intrigued by a challenge like that.

Thomas Watson solved mysteries. He'd done it so well for so long that he taught other cops how to solve them. And Jane Boyle was the biggest mystery to cross his path in a long while.

The nurse's honey-brown ponytail hung in a straight line down to the high collar of the pink mock turtleneck she wore. She stood with her arms crossed in front of her, her stance emphasizing feminine curves beneath the shapeless blue scrubs. About the only time she wasn't wearing boxy scrubs and a jacket of one pastel hue or another was in the mornings when she went for a run before breakfast. Or late at night, when she roamed the upstairs hallway between the guest room and the shower in a sweetly sensible pair of pajamas that usually consisted of a T-shirt and cotton pants that never quite met at the waist, exposing a thin strip of bare skin that he'd glimpsed more than once as she hurried into one room or the other and closed the door.

Really? He was a grown man, crawling on the floor of a major metropolitan hospital, cleaning up after his eighty-year-old father's tantrum and picturing the woman who worked for him in her pj's?

Man, he needed to stop noticing details like that. It wasn't like he could do anything about that little hum of awareness that seemed to excite his blood every time he cataloged another observation about Jane. After six months living under his roof, sharing meals and a few family evenings together, he couldn't seem to help himself from noting the sleek arch of her hips, the flawless skin hugging the angles of her oval face, the soft pink mouth that rarely smiled. She worked for him. He needed her to focus on his father's recovery. *He* needed to focus on his father's recovery, too.

He might have a few gray hairs at the temples of his dark brown hair, but he wasn't dead. Yet he needed to act as if all the male parts of his body were too old to care about the pretty in a woman in order to maintain the professional relationship between them.

Thomas set the cards on the table and pushed to his feet, ignoring the inevitable protest in his left leg. "Dad, you can't talk to people that way. Stephanie was doing her job. She was trying to help you."

Seamus's blue eyes stared straight ahead, ignoring both Jane's thinning mouth and his own voice of reason. He'd seen his dad bleeding and unconscious; still and pale in a hospital bed after surgery; unable to speak or use his legs and right arm; fighting to stand and pick up his feet and relearn how to hold a fork; working his lips and teeth and tongue so hard to form a coherent word that a lesser man would have given up months ago. It felt wrong to be wishing for even one moment that the old man couldn't talk.

"I'm not doing da tupid eckertise again." Seamus's slurred words were articulate enough to make his frustration and fatigue clear.

Jane sat her hip on the edge of the table, facing Seamus. "Yesterday in our therapy session at home, you handled the tongue rolls and language exercises just fine."

"I'm too tlow. Tink faster dan I talk. Make mi-takes."

Although her words were a little less peppered than Seamus's tirade had been, Jane's tone seemed as reprimanding as his father had been with the intern. "Speed doesn't matter. How many times have I told you that getting back to the man you were before the shooting isn't going to happen overnight? You're giving up."

Whoa. That was going a step too far. "He's tired. He's been testing for two hours."

Jane tilted her chin toward Thomas, her hazel eyes glittering with angry specks of gold that he shouldn't have noticed, either. "Don't you defend him. He was rude and he knows it." She looked back to Seamus. "You have worked your butt off all month to improve your performance on this evaluation. Now, are you being lazy, or do you just enjoy making women cry?"

"Jane…" Rising to her feet, she put a hand on the middle of Thomas's chest and stiff-armed him away from intervening between her and Seamus. Not that he couldn't have easily overpowered her claim of authority over his own family if he wanted to seize her wrist or push against her hand. But the moment of ire quickly gave way to an ill-timed rush of awareness that heated the spot where she touched him, and Thomas retreated a step from the contact.

Nope. Definitely not dead.

"Seamus?" Jane pressed his father for a reply with the stern tone of a mother dealing with a child. "I know you can do this."

After a few silent moments, Seamus nodded. "I chould 'pologize."

"Yes, you should." Although it burned in his gullet to let someone else take charge of his father, to take charge of the entire room, Thomas retreated another step as Jane turned to the silver-haired woman still clutching her hands and keeping her distance on the opposite side of the table. "Millie, would you see if you can get Stephanie to come back? Tell her Seamus is feeling more cooperative now."

The older woman seemed relieved to have a task to perform. "Of course."

Once the office door at the end of the room had closed behind the Watsons' longtime housekeeper, Jane moved behind Seamus's chair, squaring it in front of the table. She squeezed his shoulder before moving around him to straighten the therapy items on the table. "You should apologize to Millie, too, for using language like that. And your son. And me. I thought you were this infamous Irish charmer who had a way with the ladies. Did you think you were working the streets again? That Stephanie was some perp avoiding arrest you had to yell at?" Thomas propped his hands at his waist, letting his fingers settle near the gun and badge he'd worn on the belt of his jeans every day since his family had been attacked at Olivia's wedding, even on days like this when he wasn't teaching a seminar at the police academy or assisting with an investigation at precinct headquarters. He shook his head as Jane worked her magic on his father. She was tough, almost abrasive at times. But he had to give the woman props for earning his dad's—and his—respect. She understood the way a family of law enforcement professionals worked, the sense of duty that ran through their veins, and often used Seamus's career with KCPD as a motivator. "I'm not happy to have all my hard work be for nothing when we come to see Dr. Koelus." She softened her tone as she slipped into the chair on the opposite side of the table. "I bet you're not happy, either."

"I walked," Seamus reminded her. "Koelus ted I could get rid of de walker and use my cane. I did de finger eckertises. I'm better."

"Yes, you are. And those are wonderful accomplishments you should be proud of. But if you want that peach cobbler at the restaurant for dessert, then you're either going to have to do another half mile on the treadmill with me when we get home, or you're going to have to apologize to Stephanie and repeat the vocal exercises one more time."

Seamus pointed a bony finger at her. "Dat's bwackmail."

"Yes, it is." Jane waited a couple of beats before smiling. "Is it working?"

The undamaged corner of Seamus's mouth crooked up in an answering smile.

Thomas hid his own grin. That woman had his father's number. She might challenge his own authority and rub him the wrong way at times, but she certainly knew the right mix of tough love, teasing and unflinch-

ing faith in her patient that Seamus had been responding to for months now.

A moment later, Millie returned with the speech
therapist. The young woman's eyes and nose were red
from crying, but she smiled to the woman who was old
enough to be her grandmother. "Thank you."

Millie had probably given her a pep talk. The older
woman's smile faded when she chided Seamus. "Now
you be nice to her."

Millie tried to back away from the table, but Seamus
snagged her hand. "I'm torry, my ol' friend. It been long
time tince you heard lang-ege like dat." He struggled to
spit the words out, even growling with frustration, just
as he had a moment before losing his temper. With a
glance at Jane, as if seeking her approval, he folded his
weaker hand around Millie's fingers, too. "I raise my
boy and grand-tons to be gentlemen. I chould be, too."

Twin dots of pink colored Millie's cheeks and her
smile reappeared. "It's all right, Seamus. They weren't
any words I hadn't heard before."

"I chouldn't have taid to you. You lady." He released
her hand and tapped his chest. "Better man dan dat."

"I know you are." To Thomas's surprise, Millie
leaned down and kissed his cheek. Seamus's face was
as rosy as hers as Millie picked up her purse from a
nearby chair and bustled off to the hallway. "I'm going
to find the ladies' room. Excuse me."

The hallway door was swinging shut before the blush
left Seamus's cheeks. He turned to the intern, raising a
snowy white eyebrow in a shrug of apology. "Tefanie?
Forgive a fwustwated ol' man. I have college degree
and worked long time with public. Front dek at KT...
KCPD. But I tound like baby now. Embarashes me."

Jane winked encouragement as she gave up the chair and moved toward Thomas. "I twy again."

Stephanie sat and picked up flash cards again. "Thank you for saying that. You were so sweet with me last time—I guess it surprised me when you got so upset. I will say that you articulated each and every one of those cuss words very clearly." Seamus grinned at her teasing and shook his head. "I'm sorry I ran out on you. I can't be anywhere near as tired as you must be. We'll skip the tongue exercises this time and just do the reading so I have a score to report to Dr. Koelus."

Thomas heard the buzz of the cell phone vibrating in Jane's pocket. Again? That was the fourth text she'd gotten since they'd arrived at the hospital, and she'd ducked out of the evaluation sessions with Dr. Koelus and the physical therapists marking the monthly progress in Seamus's recovery each time. Jane pulled her phone from the pocket of her scrub jacket and read the message. Her forehead knit deeply enough to make a dimple between her brows before she straightened and headed for the door. "Excuse me."

Thomas made sure his dad would be on his best behavior before he caught the swinging door and followed Jane into the hallway to find her furiously typing away on her cell. "You can't let your boyfriend wait for a few more minutes until we're done here?"

"My boyfriend?" Jane stopped with her thumb hovering over the screen. "I haven't been with anyone since my…" When Thomas moved around her to clear the hallway for a doctor and his assistant walking past with some diagnostic equipment, she punched a button and cleared the screen, hiding both the message and her reply from him. "It's none of your business. This is personal."

"Not when you're on the clock with Dad and me."

Her mouth opened with a retort, but snapped shut just as quickly when she saw the custodian with his mop and cart stepping off the elevator at the end of the hall, along with a family walking out with a teenager who was on crutches. She crossed the tile floor to look out the bank of windows overlooking the parking lot below them, avoiding him. Or... Hell. Was she scanning the lot? Looking for a particular vehicle or person? And now he realized she'd scoped out the face of every person who'd gotten off that elevator.

He knew the woman was a runner. From her job application, he knew Jane was thirty-eight, but she worked out and kept in shape like a woman half her age. She probably had to in order to keep up with headstrong patients like his father. He couldn't be the only man in Kansas City noticing her. She didn't wear a ring. So if there wasn't a current boyfriend, there had to be an ex.

A gut-check transformed his irritation into concern. Maybe that was the explanation—the calls, the texts, the dimpled brow. Maybe this was some type of harassment campaign. Could be the messages were more than a distraction from her job—maybe she was in some kind of trouble that could explain being so upset one moment, defensive the next, and guarded as she watched the people below in the parking lot. Thomas crossed the hallway. Since the woman didn't talk about herself much beyond family recipes she shared with Millie and her medical training, he had to ask. "Did you two have a fight?"

Jane startled at the sound of his voice at her shoulder. "No."

Thomas stepped up beside her and looked into the parking lot, scanning for anything that looked out of place. "So he is your boyfriend."

Her ponytail bounced as she whipped her face up to his. "Don't play your interrogation games on me, Detective. I work for you. I'm too old to be your daughter and I'm sure not your wife. You don't have to know about my personal life."

"I do when it interferes with your job."

"How does this…?" She held up the phone and used it to gesture back to the physical and occupational therapy room. "Seamus doesn't need me right now. I can take two seconds to answer a stupid text."

Thomas had years of experience keeping his tone calm in the face of uncooperative witnesses or panicked rookies facing a dangerous or difficult call. "A text that clearly upsets you. Like the other texts and calls that you've been receiving these past few weeks? You've skipped out of meals, left in the middle of conversations. You're about to jump out of your skin right now." He pointed to the cell phone now clasped to her chest like some kind of lifeline. "Every decision you make seems to be centered around whatever is happening on that phone."

"It doesn't… It's some business I need to take care of." With a brush of her fingers over the neat simplicity of her hair, Jane's cool facade returned. She pocketed her phone and resumed the clinically professional tone he was used to hearing. "I'm sorry if you think the calls are affecting my work. After dinner, once I

get Seamus settled in his room and I'm off the clock,
I'll deal with them."

"It'll be after dark by then. What kind of business
do you take care of at night?"

"None of yours."

"None of my what?"

"None of your business," she groaned and touched
her hair again, this time actually pulling a few strands
loose. "I was trying to be clever and shut you up." She
glared at the caramel-colored hair falling over her cheek
and shoved it back behind her ear. "Never mind."

Thomas heard the words coming out of his mouth before he rationally evaluated the impact of saying them.
"I know the signs of someone in trouble. Is there anything I can do to help?"

"No." Her response was a little too vehement for him
to accept that something wasn't bothering her. Jane inhaled a deep breath and spoke in a softer tone. "I'll be
fine. Thank you, Detective."

"Technically, it's Detective Lieutenant. Or Lieutenant. Or just Thomas." Thomas propped his hands at his
belt and dropped his chin so he wouldn't tower over her
quite so much. "We've talked about this. You've been
working for me and living at the house since the first
of March. I think we can call each other by our names."

"Thank you for your concern, *Thomas*. But I'm fine."

"Is it an ex who's giving you trouble?"

"There's no trouble." She could see he wasn't buying her answers. She glanced out the window one more
time before tilting her gaze, which was more green than
gold now, to his. "Not that it's any of your business, but
if you must know—I'm a widow. I have been for three
years, before I ever moved to Kansas City. There's been

no boyfriend since my late husband, so there's no ex, either. Now let it go. Please. And I'll do my best not to let this situation interfere with my work performance."

She'd lost the man she loved? Although her loss was more recent than the years he'd been without Mary, he remembered the gutted feeling that had stayed with him for a long time, the way he'd buried most of his emotions so he could get through the demands of the day, that habit of second-guessing and overanalyzing every decision because the teammate who'd always been his sounding board and ally was no longer there to back him up. Maybe her husband had phoned or texted her often, and each time she received a message, it reminded her of the love she'd lost. That could explain the secretive behavior and testy reaction to his prying.

Thomas didn't want to have something so visceral and private in common with Jane. Lumped on top of the intellectual curiosity and sexual awareness that had been buzzing through his system from the moment she'd moved into the spare bedroom of his house, he did not need to feel this emotional empathy. It felt as though they belonged to an exclusive club, and *exclusive* was an entirely inappropriate connection to feel about someone who worked for him. But it was the most personal information she'd ever revealed to him, and he felt himself worrying about her well-being, anyway. He laid his hand over her fingers, which were still resting on the windowsill. "I'm sorry about your husband. But you said *situation*. If there's some other issue that we need to deal with—"

"*We* do not need to deal with anything." He felt her hand tremble beneath his, as if she was fighting some sort of internal battle—maybe whether or not to slap his face for overstepping the bounds of employer-employee concern? She surprised him by turning her palm into his and lacing their fingers together, accepting the strength, comfort and understanding he offered. Her hand felt small in his, but her grip was strong. "I'll be fine."

Thomas tightened his hold around hers. "Jane—"

The door swung open across the hall and Stephanie came out smiling, hurrying around the slow-moving Seamus with his walker. "He passed with flying colors."

Seamus's face was wan with fatigue, but he was smiling, too. "On to de next s-tage of terapy."

Jane pulled away from Thomas's touch, wiping her fingers against her pant leg as if erasing the heat he could still feel in his own hand. Although the effort seemed to cost her, Jane returned her patient's grin. "That's my guy."

She kissed Seamus on the cheek and patted his arm, studiously ignoring Thomas and the unexpected moment of human connection that had passed between them.

Chapter Two

Why had she reached for Thomas's hand?

Jane scooted the au gratin potatoes around in their dish, wondering if she could stomach another bite to justify ordering the special side with her barbecue brisket. At least she'd had the good sense to pass on the dessert that everyone else at the table had ordered.

She'd turned her hand into Thomas's this afternoon because she was a frightened fool who'd dealt with the past three years on her own for so long that clinging to the strength and compassion he'd offered had given her a rare respite, and the first taste of normal relations with a man she'd known since her life had been turned so completely upside down that it wasn't her own anymore.

But *normal* wasn't truly an option for her since she'd been put into WITSEC and transferred to Kansas City. Until the man who'd murdered her federal agent husband—and believed he'd murdered her, too—could be captured and she could finally testify against what she'd witnessed that horrible night her home had been invaded and Freddie had been taken from her, she needed to remain unattached, alert, able to stand on her own two feet. She had to be strong enough to stand alone.

Most of the time, she was. Her training as a critical-care nurse required her to be able to make quick decisions and handle problems that arose on her own. She no longer worked in a hospital setting as she had back in DC, but her new career as a private nurse demanded she function independently—that she rely on her own experience and skill set to deal with whatever her patient needed. She kept contact with coworkers to a minimum, and with friends even less. She wasn't going to risk the man who carved up her husband finding her through even a casual conversation or picture that could end up posted online. She was already on emotional thin ice by developing a bond with Seamus. He reminded her so much of her own grandfather that she knew she hadn't kept herself as professionally distant as she should, and that gave her a weakness, leverage that sociopath wouldn't hesitate to use against her if he ever found her. It would be far too easy to lean against a man like Thomas and surrender to his strength and authority. Once she did that, however, she'd be completely vulnerable. Easy prey for the stalking skills her husband's killer possessed.

She couldn't drop her guard like that again. Ever. No matter how the fear and loneliness wore her down.

She'd have to be more careful. Jane slipped a glance over at the tall, powerfully built man sitting across the table from her, forcing herself to take another bite of the cold potatoes when she saw him watching her, his eyes narrowed with an unspoken question. Thomas Watson seemed gentle and unassuming at first, a mature man at ease in his own skin—a police officer, former military man and single father used to command, used to taking action and fixing problems, even if they weren't his own.

That man had eyes in the back of his head. Or ESP. Or the training to read people and know when something was off, just as her late husband had when he'd worked with the violent crimes unit at the FBI. She curled her fingers into her palm beneath the table, remembering how the simple touch of his hand had grounded her, calmed her for a few precious seconds. Thomas generated the kind of heat she hadn't felt since that last morning she and Fred had embraced and each had gone off to their respective jobs in Washington, DC. She missed that kind of contact—a hug, holding hands, a kiss. But she couldn't give in to that kind of need anymore. She had to stay strong. She had to survive. She owed Freddie that much.

Even as Thomas ordered four decaf coffees from the waitress, his moss-colored eyes managed to make contact with hers, silently asking for the umpteenth time if anything was wrong. Jane gave up the pretense of having any appetite and set down her fork.

Fortunately, they had the buffer of Millie's chatting and Seamus's determined responses to keep Thomas from following up with any more pointed questions about the messages she'd been receiving. Some of the calls were friendly checkups from one of her husband's friends at the Bureau back in Washington, DC. Levi Hunt wasn't supposed to know where she'd relocated after leaving DC. She supposed he had the reputation as a skilled investigator for a reason. And as a member of her husband's former violent crimes team, he felt personally responsible for making sure she was okay. But her goal had been to leave that whole life, and the dreadful night it had ended, behind her. The fact that he was able to contact her might mean others from that period in her life—when she'd been Fred Davis's wife—would try to contact her, too. More of the messages had been routine checkups from the one man who *was* supposed to know about her new life in Kansas City.

And it was that last text from Conor Wildman that had her delicious barbecue dinner sitting like a rock in her stomach. Had something broken on the investigation? Had her new identity been compromised? Had the killer left another victim with a badge carved in his chest?

At your old house. Come see me. Urgent.

She'd texted back when she'd left the hospital and gotten into the back seat of Thomas's crew cab truck. With the family. At work. Can't get away.

Conor had been quick to answer. He's surfaced. Can't go into detail on phone. Must meet.

WITSEC had a code word and a visual signal to alert her to a sighting of a man matching the suspect's description near her location. Then there was an escape protocol in place. Since Marshal Wildman hadn't used the coded alert in his text, that meant she wasn't in imminent danger of being discovered. Typically, she'd been taught to lie low and not draw any attention to herself, even when there was a new development on the case. The whole idea behind witness protection was for her to disappear off the world's radar. But words like *urgent* and *must meet* indicated the threat level had increased for some reason. That meant she needed to be more on guard, too. But against what? Who?

A deep-pitched laugh from Seamus pulled Jane from

her troubling thoughts. He held up a forkful of cobbler and toasted Millie. "Not as good as yours. But good."

Millie's cheeks turned a deep shade of pink as he stuffed the peach cobbler into his mouth. Jane felt the beginnings of a smile relax the strain around her mouth. Her patient was an unapologetic flirt. When he was feeling good. When he wasn't—either physically or mentally—Seamus could be a pain in the behind. And dear, sweet Millie—she ate up the attention when offered, and didn't put up with any guff from Seamus when it wasn't. One trait she'd noticed about all of the Watson family: the strength of their commitment—to the people they loved, to a cause they believed in. She believed that, despite his age, given enough time, Seamus would make a significant recovery. Some of the damage the bullet and stroke had done to his brain would never heal, but eventually he'd be able to live independently, and he'd have a good quality of life.

She was certain Thomas would see to it.

Personality-wise, father and son couldn't be more different. While Seamus liked to tease, Thomas was as serious as a heart attack. She supposed some women might describe him as stodgy or maybe even boring, compared with his outgoing dad. But she couldn't imagine anything more attractive than a man who put his family first, a man who was rock solid in his strength and demeanor, a man who noticed much, said little, did whatever needed to be done without much of a fuss. Such masculine traits. Maybe that's what she found most attractive about Detective Lieutenant Thomas Watson—despite a few shots of silver in his close-cropped hair, there was no mistaking that he was anything but a seasoned, savvy, sexy man.

All the more reason not to give in to the temptation of sharing her secrets with her employer. He wasn't hers to lean on. Seamus needed him. His family needed him. Kansas City needed him. She couldn't.

The sun had set and the lights had come on in the parking lot by the time they'd finished their coffee and Thomas had paid the bill. She noticed how Thomas's limp was more pronounced at the end of the day as he strode across the parking lot to retrieve his pickup truck. Not for the first time, she wondered what injury he'd sustained to leave him with that chronic pain she sometimes saw on his face, but he never once complained about. She wondered what medicine and treatments he used to combat the pain, or if he even did more than simply tough it out.

Not your problem. He's not your patient.

Concern for her boss wasn't allowed. Concern implied caring. Involvement. Maintaining a professional working relationship and keeping her personal distance meant no concern, no magnetic draw to body heat and strength, and no hand-holding. Period.

Focusing her attention on the man she was supposed to be taking care of, Jane walked with Millie beside Seamus to the edge of the parking lot and waited. While Millie sat on a nearby bench and Seamus braced himself against his walker and stretched out some of the kinks in his shoulders and back, Jane scanned the parking lot.

So the nameless killer known to the FBI simply as Badge Man for the emblem he carved into the chest of each of his victims had surfaced. Where? How? The profile on him said he shadowed his victims, mostly law enforcement professionals or collateral damage as she'd nearly been. He'd watch for days, weeks even, as if he were a cop on a stakeout. Then he'd up his game like he had with Freddie, inserting himself into their lives to learn more about them, playing a dangerous game of cat and mouse—finally cornering his targets like prey, forcing them to either run or fight before he collected them, killed them and left his mark on them.

Was he watching her right now? Following her? Jane couldn't stop the shiver that raised goose bumps across her skin, even on this warm September night. If Conor Wildman suspected the killer was on her trail, he'd have alerted her with the code word and she'd already be gone. She'd had the extraction scenario drilled into her time and time again. He'd call or text her the code word. She'd drop everything instantly and either make her way to the appointed safe house or he'd pick her up and move her to a secure location outside the city. But Badge Man must be somewhere in the country watching, tracking, toying with his next intended victim.

The restaurant near Union Station was immensely popular. There was a rehearsal dinner going on outside on the patio behind them, with clinking glasses and cutlery, loud laughter and enough overlapping conversations to make talking to Millie and Seamus difficult. So Jane stood silently beside the bench, studying the parking lot for any signs of something or someone out of place. The cars in the lot were parked close together, as the business tried to fit as many customers into the fixed space between the railroad tracks and remodeled old buildings as possible. The cars were packed tightly enough that it was difficult to see between them. Plus, the decorative train signal lights overhead cast impenetrable shadows that masked the traffic beyond the second row of vehicles.

Her late husband had taught her to always be aware of her surroundings. It was safety rule number one for living in a metropolitan area as heavily populated as DC. Of course, she hadn't counted on the threat coming right into her own home. Since Freddie's death, she'd gotten into tip-top physical shape, taken self-defense courses and become hypervigilant to the dangers that lurked out there in the world.

That's why she was frowning at the noise of squealing tires and the smell of burned rubber wafting across the parking lot as Thomas pulled his truck up in front of the sidewalk. But she couldn't pinpoint the source at this distance through all the cars and shadows.

Thomas had noticed something suspicious, too. When he climbed out of his truck on the side away from the curb, he was slow to close the door. He turned his head to the right and to the left before heading toward the back of the truck. Seamus had noticed something, too. He'd gone over to stand with his hand on Millie's shoulder.

"What is it?" Millie asked.

Urgent. Conor's text had been trying to warn her. No! Danger wasn't supposed to find her here.

A powerful engine revved and a beat-up white van raced out of the shadows, barreling straight toward the truck.

"Thomas!" Seamus shouted.

"Look out!" Jane ran toward Thomas. He was standing right in the van's path. "Move!"

"Everybody back!" Thomas snapped his arm around her waist as she reached for him. "Get down!"

Thomas lifted her off her feet and dived for the sidewalk. Jane caught a brief glimpse of an open passenger-side window and several small flashes of light a split second before she heard an explosion of gunshots. Thomas grunted against her ear and they were falling, rolling. The points of her knee and elbow burned as she hit concrete. She heard people screaming. Maybe she was one of them. She slammed into Thomas's chest when he came to an abrupt stop against the curb.

Then he was on his feet, pulling his gun, running after the car in his awkward, rolling gait. "KCPD! Stop the vehicle!"

He fired one shot, but the van skidded around the corner of the building into the street and sped away into the night.

Shouts of panic and crashes of dishes and furniture echoed in her ears as Jane pushed to her feet. Ignoring her own voice of panic screaming inside her head, she stumbled over the fallen walker and hurried to the bench where Seamus had collapsed on top of Millie. "Are you two all right?" She touched Seamus's shoulder. Had he fallen? Had he been shot? Freddie's killer had tormented him for weeks before the home invasion, threatening the people around him. Threatening her. "Seamus?"

"I'm all right." He leaned heavily against her as she helped him turn and sit on the bench beside Millie. "We're all right."

Jane swept her gaze over them both to confirm his claim. "Millie?"

"It's happening again, isn't it? Why does someone want to hurt this family?" She sobbed once, but quickly pinched her nose and held off the threat of tears. Seamus pulled a handkerchief from his pocket and pushed it into her fingers. "I'm all right. I don't understand, but I'm all right." She pushed to her feet and swayed. "Where's Thomas?"

"Millie?" Jane caught the older woman by the arm and urged her to sit before she fainted.

"Thomas?"

"I'm right here." Jane turned at the deep voice behind her. His chest and shoulders expanding with deep breaths, Thomas strode up to them, pulling his badge off his belt as he stuffed his phone into his pocket. "Are they okay?"

"Yes. Frightened out of their minds. Millie is a little shocky, but no one was hurt."

"Good." He held his badge over his head and shouted to the crowd. "I'm KCPD. Detective Lieutenant Watson. I need it quiet."

Except for a few lingering whimpers, everyone in the doorway or on the patio stopped talking to listen. Even Jane's panic stopped. For a split second.

"I've already called the incident in. Officers are on their way. Is anyone hurt?"

There was a smattering of conversations as friends and family checked in with each other, but then the group quieted again. Thank goodness. No one had been shot.

"That's good. I need everybody to take a seat." While chairs were righted and people got up off the ground where they'd taken cover, Thomas spoke to one of the waiters. "I need everyone to stay put inside the restaurant, as well. Let me know ASAP if anyone in there is injured. And I need to talk to your manager."

While the young man hurried inside to do Thomas's bidding, Jane turned to inspect Millie again. She caught the older woman's wrist and timed her pulse. Her heart was still racing, or maybe that was her own, but Millie's color was better. Jane picked up Seamus's walker and set it in front of him. She appealed to the cop in him. "I need you to make sure she stays seated. She's a little light-headed and I don't want her to pass out. Can you do that for me?" He took Millie's hand and nodded. She wanted him to stay put, too, so he wouldn't fall and injure himself, either. "I'm going to check around to see if anyone needs medical attention."

She barely had time to finish her sentence when a strong hand clamped around her arm and pulled her away. "What are you...? Thomas."

Without releasing her, he backed her against the door of his truck, his broad shoulders blocking out the lights and chatter of the restaurant behind him. "What the hell were you doing, running into the path of that van? I told you to stay back."

"He was going to run you over!" She tugged her arm free of his grip and pushed him back a step. Into the light. Where she saw the red streak of blood seeping into the forearm of his soiled shirt. "You've been shot." She unbuttoned his cuff and gently pushed the plaid chambray up his arm to inspect the graze across his skin. It wouldn't need stitches, but it could still get infected if the wound wasn't treated. The cloth at his elbow was torn and bloody, too, indicating he'd scraped up a chunk of skin when they'd hit the concrete. "I'm so sorry you got hurt. I never meant—"

As she turned the wounds into the light, their heated words topped each other's. "You could have been run down. You could have been shot. When I give you an order, I expect you to—"

"Screw your order. I won't let anyone else get hurt. He was after me."

"—do what I say and stay safe. He was after me."

Jane froze as they blurted the exact same words. She tipped her chin up to see the shocked look in his eyes that she imagined mirrored her own.

Of course. Duh. She'd overreacted. She'd nearly given her secret away.

This could have been a random drive-by shooting.

Anyone in this crowded restaurant could have been the target.

Tragic as any senseless violence might be, Freddie's killer hadn't found her. This incident wasn't part of his sick game.

She covered the slip of the tongue induced by panic by falling back on the thing she did best. Healing people. She spun around to open the truck door and pull out the first-aid kit from the glove compartment. She opened the contents on the seat and ripped open a couple of gauze pads, buying herself a few seconds to regain her composure. Her voice sounded surprisingly normal when she turned back to press the gauze against Thomas's open wound. "I'll need to debride that gash on your elbow before infection sets in. But I'm more concerned about the blood loss with this graze. Millie's right. This could be related to the shooting at your daughter's wedding. Or could it be related to one of the cases you're working? I know you've been consulting—"

"I'm a cop. Bad guys don't like me." Thomas spread his fingers over hers, stopping her work. He dipped his head to put his face in front of hers and demand she look him in the eye. "But why would someone want to hurt you?"

Chapter Three

Thomas had never met a woman who could lock down as fast or as tight as Jane Boyle. The fear that had darkened her eyes, the confusion and concern dimpling her forehead, had suddenly gone blank. She wasn't about to tell him anything. Fine. He didn't need her sure fingers dancing over his skin, distracting him from getting the answers she refused to give, so he'd sent her over to have her own injuries checked at the second ambulance to arrive on the scene while paramedics from the first bandaged his wounds and cleared him to report to the officers taking charge of the incident.

Although he was the senior officer on the scene, he was also a witness to the drive-by shooting. He and the scene commander had agreed that a third party would be able to process his account more objectively than if he started listening to witness statements from the other patrons and restaurant staff who were still milling about the scene. So Thomas stood off to the side with the onlookers and flashing lights while other detectives conducted interviews, criminologists processed the parking lot and patio and uniformed officers directed traffic.

It didn't stop his favorites of Kansas City's finest from reporting to him, though.

His youngest son, Keir, was waiting to speak to him and hurried over as soon as the scene commander had left. "How's the arm, Dad?" He nodded toward the white gauze bandages on his forearm and elbow. "Other than a panic attack leading to hyperventilation, you're the only casualty." Keir glanced over at the ambulance parked beyond the crime-scene tape to the hazel-eyed woman sitting on the back bumper, stoically turning her head away from the medic cutting off part of her sleeve to inspect the scrape on her elbow. "Well, you and Jane."

"Is she okay?"

"Okay enough, I suppose. Superficial injuries. Main concern is infection."

"That's what she told me."

"That's what she told the medic, too." Keir grinned. "I think she's struggling to sit back and allow someone else to take care of her."

She'd made that abundantly clear to him. Thomas must have been staring too hard at the woman in question, because she suddenly turned her head. Their gazes met across the parking lot before Jane visibly straightened and shifted her attention back to the EMT. She couldn't avoid him and his questions forever, not when whatever the answers were had stamped that look of terror on her face. Jane was his responsibility. She'd become one of his own the moment he'd realized how much his father needed her—and Thomas Watson protected his own. If there was anything more to this concern for her that made his belly ache, he chose to ignore it and focus on someone who was willing to talk to him. He and Keir stood by the hood of his truck while a pair of criminologists documented the bullet lodged in the left rear tire. "What about Dad and Millie? I haven't had a chance to check in with them."

"They're good. They've already given their statements and have been dismissed." Keir must have just come off his shift before responding to the all-points call of shots fired. He'd unbuttoned his collar and loosened his tie, but still wore the tailored gray suit that would have allowed him to pass as an executive in the financial district if it hadn't been for the badge and Glock holstered to his belt. "Grandpa's still got blue running through his veins. He got a partial on the license plate and the scene commander will run it. I'll give them a ride home. Millie's keeping it together, but she's scared. And Grandpa seems pretty tired."

Thomas appreciated being able to trust his father's care to someone else. "It's been a long day for him."

"You, too, I imagine." With blue eyes like his mother's, and that same driving intensity that had guided Mary Watson throughout their marriage until her death, Keir commanded authority, even though Thomas outranked him in both age and chevrons on his badge. "I was analyzing the shot pattern. Either that driver was nearsighted and couldn't hit the side of a barn, or he was intentionally missing."

Didn't that sound eerily familiar. He glanced over at Seamus, now chatting amicably with Millie and a young uniformed officer. Probably regaling him with some story about how they did police work back in his day. Out of all the people at Olivia's wedding, with all that gunfire, only one person had been hit. There had to be a reason Seamus had been targeted specifically that day. Or maybe the shooter had been targeting him, and his dad seated beside him had been collateral damage. If whoever had hired the hit man that day wanted to hurt Thomas, he'd inflicted far more pain by attacking his family than by putting the bullet in him. Maybe that had been the plan all along. But who hated him enough to want to come after his family like that? Had that man made a second attempt to hurt the people he cared about tonight?

"I noticed the same thing. The driver swerved at the last second when he could have hit us. And his shots were aimed down at my tires, not up into the crowd." He lifted the sleeve the paramedic had cut up to the elbow. "In fact, I think the bullet that caught me was a ricochet. Janie could have been hit someplace a lot more vital if it hadn't deflected off me first."

"Janie?" Keir's eyes narrowed as he geared up to ask another question.

But Thomas's oldest son, Duff, walked up, stuffing his detective's notebook into the pocket of his jeans. He grinned at his brother. "Hey, Pipsqueak."

"Muscle-head," Keir deadpanned. The two had been teasing each other from the time Keir was old enough to toddle after his older siblings. And he'd never once let his bigger, brawnier brother intimidate him. The normalcy of the exchange elicited a smile Thomas hadn't felt all evening. Keir answered with a grin of his own. "Call me as soon as you know anything, Dad. Kenna and I will stay at the house with Grandpa and Millie until you get home."

If Thomas didn't know better, he'd think Seamus was a little sweet on Keir's fiancée. Certainly, the high-powered attorney Keir had rescued from a stalker was sweet on Keir's grandpa. "He'll like that. Thanks, son."

Keir nodded to the older man walking beside Duff

before turning away to escort Seamus and Millie to his car.

Duff patted the shoulder of the old family friend Thomas recognized, and pulled him into the conversation. "Look who I ran into while I was canvassing."

"Al." Thomas reached out to shake the man's hand and was immediately pulled in for a backslapping hug.

"Long time, no see, Tommy boy."

That had been Al Junkert's nickname for him since the two had been young hotshots fresh out of the academy. He and Al had started in patrol together, made detective the same year and were well on their way to running their own precinct when the tragic end of a high-speed chase had put Thomas in the hospital, fighting to keep his leg, and scared Al into leaving the investigations bureau of the department and going back to school to earn his business degree. He'd been a fixture in the KCPD administrative offices for years now, working in public relations. Al had been there when Mary died. He was Olivia's godfather and a Dutch uncle to all his children. His graying hair looked white against the deeply tanned skin at his receding hairline, earned from too many hours out on the golf course.

When Al pulled away, he was frowning. "Sorry to reconnect under these circumstances, though. I thought you were safe teaching seminars at the academy. The bad guys are still taking shots at you, huh?"

Thomas propped his hands at his waist, shaking his head at the clear lack of a motive here. "I've made a few enemies over the years, but I can't explain this one yet. Were you at the restaurant? I didn't see you. Shirley with you?"

"Yes and no. I was in the mood for Kansas City barbecue. But unfortunately, Shirley and I didn't work out. I'm on date number two with a gal I met at one of those charity fund-raisers." Al nodded toward the black-and-whites and flashing lights beyond the yellow crime-scene tape. "I may not make it to date number three. Hearing all the gunshots rattled her. When I told her my old partner was the target, she visibly scooted her chair away from mine, like she thought whatever happened to you was catching."

Thomas laughed along with Duff, but his gaze slid over to the ambulance again. The medic was bandaging Jane's arm now. He couldn't forget the frantic insistence in her voice when they'd argued about who was saving whom. *He was after me.* Maybe *his* injuries were the collateral damage instead of the other way around.

That woman was afraid of something. He could feel it in his bones. And he intended to find out what or who could make a strong, independent woman like Jane shut down and pretend she hadn't blurted out that fear.

He reached out to shake Al's hand and thank his buddy for checking on him, eager to get to work on finding out the truth about something tonight. "Sorry about the date. Show her that fancy office of yours and remind her that you and I don't work together anymore. She should be safe from any fallout."

Al grinned. "I don't know. This one's skittish. She's not like Mary was. Your Mary was a strong one—handled any crisis life threw at her. Except for that last one, of course." His grin faded and he swiped his hand over the top of his deep forehead. "I'm sorry, Thomas. That didn't come out right. I just meant that was the one fight she couldn't win."

"It's okay, Al. It's been a long time. We can talk about Mary."

"Seems like yesterday that you and me, Mary and my first wife would all hang out."

"A lot has changed since those days."

"Your kids are all grown up. I'm looking for wife number four. Well, I'd better get back to, um…" He snapped his fingers, trying to come up with a name. "Renee. I'd better get back to Renee." He patted Duff on the shoulder of his black Henley shirt and nodded to Thomas. "Don't be such a stranger. Let's meet up at the Shamrock some night and catch up." He glanced over at the bench where Keir was helping Seamus stand and find his balance. "I'm going to say hi to your old man before I take off. Good luck catching this one, boys."

"Sounds like a plan." Thomas waited for Al to head back down the sidewalk before turning to Duff. "What did you find? Did anybody in one of the other restaurants or bars see anything? I know this neighborhood is packed with traffic and pedestrians on a Friday night."

Duff adjusted the strap of his shoulder holster and tugged down the sleeves of the cotton knit shirt. The days might still be heating up with the dregs of summer, but fall was creeping into the September nights. "We're damn lucky we didn't have a hit-and-run. About the only thing anybody on the street out front can agree on is that the driver was going fast. But I've got reports of a white SUV, a navy-blue sedan and a red convertible with the top up. The driver was Latino, a man with a stocking mask or a woman with long black hair."

"It was a white van. At least a decade old and driven pretty hard, judging by the rust on the chrome trim and dent in the passenger door. The shooter was white, a man from the size of the hand on the steering wheel. The gun was a—"

"Forty-five mil." His middle son, Niall, walked up with an evidence bag in his hand. Although he was a medical examiner with the crime lab and he didn't report to crime scenes unless there was a dead body, like all Thomas's sons, he'd shown up shortly after the all-points broadcast that had mentioned his name. The only reason Olivia wasn't here, too, was because she was attending a profile training seminar in Saint Louis. "The driver wasn't interested in cleaning up his rounds." Niall handed the bag with the bullet to Thomas, who inspected it through the clear plastic window before handing it off to Duff. "He was also a lousy shot, judging by the fact that he didn't hit anybody but you and your truck."

They'd all noticed the same thing. A drive-by shooting with no dead bodies didn't add up. This wasn't a gang neighborhood, but even if it was, a gang member would be aiming for a particular target or targets. Duff handed the evidence bag back to Niall, to assure the chain of custody. "Richard Lloyd, the hired gun who shot up Liv's wedding, didn't hit anything but Grandpa, either. I don't like coincidences like that."

"Neither do I. And you could be right about the mask," Thomas speculated. "I didn't see his face. Just the hand holding the gun through the open window. Do you think whoever hired Lloyd has got someone new on his payroll?"

"If one of us figures that out, we share the intel, right?"

"Right," Niall agreed.

"Right." Thomas inhaled a deep breath. The graze

and scrapes on his arm were stinging, and his head was starting to throb with too many clues and no sensible way to organize them. The only thing that seemed to give him any relief was to turn his attention to the woman with the honey-brown ponytail. Jane was on her feet now, holding a gauze pad beneath her elbow while the paramedic cleaned the grit and debris from her injury. Although Thomas had tried to take the brunt of their tumble, they'd skidded over enough pavement that she could be more banged up than she'd let on, or maybe even realized.

He was marginally aware of Duff continuing the conversation. "You need anything else from me? I have to pick Melanie up from the campus library. She's studying for her anatomy test."

Niall answered. "How's her first semester in premed going? She's not pushing too hard, is she?"

Earlier that summer, Duff's fiancée had nearly been killed when she'd been stabbed. Fortunately, Duff had gotten to her in time to save her life, and had the sense to propose in the hospital. Thomas liked the young woman who'd finally taught his oldest to trust a woman with his heart again. "Sorry, I forgot to ask. How is Mel doing?"

"She's eatin' up college life. I'm glad she has the chance to finally go back to school." Duff grinned. "I always wanted to date a coed."

Niall frowned. "You're not distracting her from her studies, are you? If she has any questions about the material, tell her to call me."

"She knows that. She also knows that you're getting married later this month and doesn't want to bother you. Jane said she'd field any questions Melanie might have while you're busy with your nuptials." Duff nudged Niall with his elbow. "By the way. I had my tux fitting this afternoon. I might look handsomer than you do on the twenty-fifth."

Niall adjusted his glasses on his nose. "I am quite certain that Lucy will only be looking at me. You make her laugh. But she sleeps with me."

Duff laughed out loud. "Seriously, Poindexter? Did you just make a joke? Lucy has been so good for you." When Thomas became aware of the laughter and teasing stopping, he turned to find both his sons staring at him with curious expressions. Neither had missed the woman he'd been watching across the parking lot. "Dad? Something going on with you and Battle-Ax Boyle?"

"I wish you wouldn't call her that, son. She's professional and efficient, not mean-spirited."

"O-kay. You didn't answer my question."

"I appreciate you boys coming out to check up on us. We've got plenty of officers on the scene. We also need to investigate the possibility that I wasn't the target."

A tall, lanky man in a tan suit and brown tie walked up to the ambulance and said something to Jane. She startled at first, but then she chased the paramedic away and turned to exchange heated words with the suit.

Niall wasn't one to miss details, either. "Who is that guy talking to Jane?"

"I don't know. Yet." When he saw her hug her middle, rubbing her hand up and down her uninjured arm, Thomas opened the back door of his truck and pulled out the black KCPD windbreaker he stored there. "You boys follow up with the lead detective and keep me in the loop. I'm going to pursue a different angle."

With the nerve damage in his bum leg sending out dozens of electric shocks through his thigh and calf, he couldn't exactly stride across the parking lot. But his determined pace got him to the ambulance quickly enough to hear the tall blond man mutter an accusation at Jane. "What the hell am I supposed to think when you don't call me?"

Was this who'd been threatening her? Or at the very least, upsetting her with his barrage of messages on her phone?

Thomas had no intention of making her jump the way the tan-suit guy had. "Jane?" he called, waiting for her to turn her head and identify him before he slipped the windbreaker over her shoulders. And yes, his hands lingered on her arms a split second longer than they needed to. "You looked like you were getting cold."

"I…" She glanced up at the blond guy and shivered. Then she was shoving her arms into the sleeves of Thomas's jacket and going all Chatty Cathy on him. "A little. It might be a bit of shock wearing off. My scrub jacket was pretty much shredded. I had the EMT throw it away. You don't need this, do you? Of course not. You wouldn't have offered if you did. Thank you."

Then just like that, she fell silent, as if she'd summoned whatever energy she had left in her and used it all up. Her gaze hovered somewhere near the point of Thomas's chin. Not making eye contact? Running out of words to argue with him? This confusion was so unlike the woman he knew that Thomas was reaching for her when the tan-suit guy extended his hand and a salesman's smile. "Conor Wildman. I'm a friend of Jane's."

What kind of *friend* made her stiffen up like that? Maybe he was the one making her uncomfortable. After all, she worked hard to keep her private life private. Maybe having her boss and her personal life mix was the conflict that made her jaw clench so tightly.

Until he understood the situation better, Thomas decided it couldn't hurt to get to know this guy. He shook Wildman's hand. "Thomas Watson. Jane works for me."

"She's told me. Nice to finally meet you." Wildman's dark gaze bobbed from the badge and gun on Thomas's belt to the letters on the black nylon jacket. "You're with KCPD?"

Rocket scientist, eh? "I am. What do you do?"

"Accountant. Own my own firm. Work my own hours." The golden boy widened his stance and folded his arms across his chest, assuming a more relaxed posture. But the subtle shift tugged at his clothes and Thomas noticed the gun strapped to his ankle beneath his tan slacks. What kind of accountant needed to arm himself? "When I heard Jane had been involved in a drive-by shooting, I had to come and check on her. Now that she's done with the police and the EMT, I'm here to drive her home."

Was that an offer or an order? Relaxed posture or not, Conor Wildman's dark eyes sent the message that he wasn't taking no for an answer, no matter what choice Jane made. Thomas turned his focus from the younger man's smile to Jane and asked a pointed question. "You're okay with that?"

She frowned as she kicked her gaze up to his. "Of course."

"Is he the guy who's been texting you?" *He was after me.* Thomas still hadn't gotten a satisfactory explanation for that frantic assertion when the bullets had been flying. She did understand she had options, didn't she? "You don't have to go with him if you don't want to."

The dimple that marred her forehead disappeared. She didn't exactly give him a reassuring smile, but she did seem to be making a conscious choice when she laid her hand on his arm. "It's okay. It's business. Conor and I need to have a conversation. Thank you for the loan of the jacket. I'll return it as soon as I get home. I'll be fine."

Thomas couldn't shake his suspicion about the man. But unless Jane filed a complaint or he had concrete evidence to say this man was a danger to her, there wasn't anything he could do, legally. Still, it wasn't any concern about legalities that was twisting his gut with a sense that something was off here. Something about that friendly smile and ankle holster felt like Jane was risking more than she should with this guy.

Well, Thomas was about to surprise Conor Wildman. He was certain he'd surprise Jane. Maybe he even surprised himself when he cupped the side of her neck, sliding his fingertips into the silky base of her ponytail before leaning in to kiss her cheek. Her skin was cool and smooth but 100 percent softer than the ivory porcelain it resembled. He lingered for a few seconds, feeling the spot warm beneath his lips before he pulled away.

Her eyes were wide, searching his as he straightened the collar of his jacket and tugged it together at her neck before breaking contact entirely. He wouldn't admit to a stab of jealousy that she was choosing this *friend* over a ride straight to the house in his truck. Thomas had no proprietary claim on this woman. And it was pretty inappropriate for him to be kissing a woman who worked for him. But his gut was telling him it was damn important that Conor Wildman understood Jane wasn't alone here. She had someone looking out for her. Someone would have to answer to him if anything happened to her.

The message was for her as much as Wildman to understand.

"Call me if you need anything. A ride. Whatever. I'll see you at home."

THE UNHAPPY MAN watched Thomas Watson's mouth flatten into a grim expression as the nurse and the suit walked away into the shadows of the parking lot. The Detective Lieutenant Yeah-I'm-a-Legend-in-My-Own-Mind didn't move until the suit's car pulled out of the parking lot and drove away into the night.

Well, now, wasn't that sweet? Thomas had gone old school and marked his territory in front of that other man.

With a family full of well-trained cops who carried guns and were hypervigilant about their surroundings, he'd thought the Watson family's most vulnerable weakness—the one they'd all do anything to protect—had been that white-haired has-been, Seamus. He'd known for years that family was the most important thing in Thomas Watson's world, that hurting his family would be the surest, cruelest way to hurt him.

But now he was rethinking his plan. The aging father wasn't the big guy's only weakness anymore. As he'd begun to suspect over the past couple of months, Watson had developed feelings for the woman. After all these years, the loneliness must be getting to him. Did he want to get into Nurse Boyle's pants? Did he fancy himself in love with her? She'd been living in Thomas's house for six and a half months now. Maybe they were secretly screwing each other every night.

The man's blood burned at the thought. His breath hitched, then came in shorter, deeper gasps as the familiar injustice that Thomas Watson had gone unpunished for far too long raged inside him. The thought of terrorizing Jane Boyle, killing her with his bare hands while Thomas watched—weak, helpless, in the same kind of pain he'd lived with for all these years—almost made him euphoric. That was the kind of pain he wanted to inflict on the man. He inhaled a deep breath, calming himself. Yes. There was another vulnerability he could prey upon to keep Thomas's life in a state of upheaval. Keep him off guard. Keep him focused on Jane until he could...

Wait. From his vantage point in the shadows, the Unhappy Man's gaze was drawn to someone else who'd been watching the interchange at the rear of the ambulance, someone who watched Thomas limp back to his truck and climb inside before darting off through the crowd and disappearing. Curious.

Almost all the Nosy Nellies standing outside the yellow tape were watching the police officers or the CSIs with their badges and guns and crime-scene kits *inside* the tape. That was the show they couldn't resist. But that guy, nondescript with dark hair and his face hidden by sunglasses and the upturned collar of his denim jacket, had been watching the two men and woman and their standoff at the back of the ambulance. He'd watched that kiss.

The Unhappy Man smiled.

Looked like he wasn't the only one who didn't enjoy seeing Thomas Watson safe and happy.

Maybe he could use that to his advantage somehow. Or maybe he'd have to be careful not to let Blue Jean Boy interfere with his end game.

He started the engine of his own car and pulled out, waving to the uniformed officer directing traffic as he drove past. Two hours ago, the two hundred dollars he'd spent to hire that gangbanger to spray bullets at Thomas and the people he cared about had been worth it at ten times the price. But he now knew that he needed to fine-tune his approach to Thomas's downfall. He needed to focus his attack on where it would hurt the most.

The detective lieutenant was worried about the safety of his family and that skinny, shapeless nurse he had the hots for.

The man squeezed his fists around the steering wheel until his knuckles turned white. Mary Watson had been tall and willowy, with hair like sable fur and eyes as blue as the clear Irish sky after a rainstorm. Compared to a beauty like that, what could he possibly see in that beige woman who played down her looks and personality so much that she faded into the background?

Thomas had let Mary die. Watson had taken Mary from him and let her die. He wasn't allowed to be happy with any other woman. He wasn't allowed to be happy, period. But if Jane Beige Boyle made him happy, then he'd be only too happy to relieve him of that burden. An eye for an eye. One dead love for another.

His nostrils flared as he eased out a steadying breath and loosened his grip on the wheel. Patience and invisibility were his allies. The Watsons had no idea of the pain and rage he carried in his heart.

And they wouldn't until the moment he destroyed them all.

Chapter Four

"You think Watson suspects I'm your WITSEC handler?" Marshal Conor Wildman stepped around the corner of the kitchen peninsula in the house where she'd lived before accepting the job as Seamus Watson's home-care nurse and moving into one of the upstairs bedrooms at the Watson house.

Jane took a seat on one of the stools furnished—just like the house itself—for her by the US Marshals Witness Security Program. "I think he thinks you're my ex-boyfriend—and maybe not a very nice one."

Conor grinned, unbuttoning his shirt collar and loosening his tie as he pulled coffee from the cabinet and started brewing a pot. Although the house off Thirty-Ninth Street was still listed under her Jane Boyle identity, Conor had probably spent more time here over the past few months, checking security or planning meetings with her. It was an easy cover to have to return to her own house to pick up clothing or supervise yard work or home repair, and then meet with the man whose job it was to maintain her identity and make sure she was safe. "Well, that would explain that goodbye peck on the cheek before we left the restaurant. The big guy's jealous of you leaving the scene with another man."

Thomas's strong fingers sifting into her hair and the warm press of his lips against her chilled skin had felt like more than a peck on the cheek. It had felt like, if she'd turned her head a fraction, those firm, gentle lips would have been kissing her mouth instead. Jane's breath caught in her chest as she remembered the heat that had suddenly suffused her at the older man's touch. And now, for some inexplicable reason, she felt cheated that she hadn't turned that fraction of an inch. "I don't mean anything to him."

Conor was still amused as he pulled two mugs from the dishwasher. "He's very protective of you."

"Thomas is protective of everybody. It's in his blood. He's been a cop for a long time. You said the Watson house was a good place for me to be because they'd be more alert to their surroundings than the average family."

Nodding, Conor poured them each a mug of coffee, then went to the fridge to pull out a carton of half-and-half. "It's helpful to have an extra set of eyes watching out for you. Even if the lieutenant doesn't know he's assisting with a WITSEC project."

Jane added the half-and-half to her mug, trying to forget for a few seconds that she was considered a "project" by the FBI and US Marshals offices after witnessing her husband's murder at the hands of a serial killer known only as Badge Man. *Think about something else. Anything else.*

Her thoughts instantly turned to the memory of how her skin had tingled and all the blood had rushed to the spot where Thomas had kissed her. She hadn't been kissed in three years. Hadn't been held in strong arms.

Hadn't had any man looking out for her unless he was being paid to do so. Not since Freddie's death.

She rolled up the sleeves of the black nylon jacket she still wore. The creamy coffee she sipped was warming her up, but she wanted to keep the jacket on. Thomas's straightforward scent, a blend of spicy soap and laundry detergent, might be the most masculine smell she'd ever inhaled, and having it surround her reminded her of his strength and calmed nerves that had been frayed to the point of snapping lately. She hadn't had a man offer her his jacket in years, and for a little while at least, the gallant gesture made her feel normal, as if someone cared about her. Not as a valuable witness, a tool the FBI wanted to use to help them bring a dangerous man to justice—but just as her, a woman, a human being who hadn't had anyone care about her on a personal level for a very long time.

Her thoughts took her into some dangerous territory as she considered her employer. Like the finely aged wines she used to drink after dinner with Freddie— before his murder, before she'd stopped drinking altogether to keep her senses clear and alert to the danger she feared could strike again at any given moment— Thomas was mature perfection. Sure of himself, but not arrogantly so. Handsome in a rugged sort of way. The lines beside his rich green eyes bespoke wisdom and life experience, laughter as much as heartbreak. And she'd known young bucks, maybe about the same age as Marshal Wildman, whose toothy smiles and perfect bodies and charming flirtations couldn't ignite a fraction of the heat inside her that a single, purposeful look from Thomas Watson did.

"You're thinking about Lieutenant Watson right now,

aren't you?" Conor braced his elbows on the counter across from her and leaned forward. "You know, Boyle, as long as you don't reveal your real identity or mine, you're allowed to have relationships in this program."

A relationship? She'd scratched that off her future wish list, first out of grief, then out of necessity. "Is that why you're not married? Because opening your heart to someone when some creeper wants you dead is so easy? My life is a sham. And the moment I give up that sham, I and the people I care about become targets of a dangerously sick serial killer. I don't see any happily-ever-after in that scenario."

He laughed. "Touché. I guess it's hard to have an honest relationship with someone when you have to lie about who you are every day. I know that's why my fiancée broke off our engagement. She wanted complete honesty—she deserved it. But the job wouldn't let me do it."

Her heart beat with a compassionate thump. Conor shared very little about himself with her. After all, she was a job more than she was a friend. But she suddenly felt a little more like a kindred spirit to hear he'd lost someone he'd loved, too. "I'm sorry."

"Me, too." He grinned again. "But you could still, you know, fool around."

"With my boss?"

"I saw how you looked at him. You think the ol' boy's still got it." Jane snapped her mouth shut, realizing she was still gaping at the suggestion she have a fling with her attractive employer. "Hey, I imagine what he lacks in speed, he more than makes up for in experience. From everything you've told me about him, Watson seems like a good guy."

"I don't think he's the kind of man to do anything casual." She didn't think she was the kind of woman who'd do that, either. Freddie Davis had been her college sweetheart, her first lover, her only lover. Thomas was a serious-relationship kind of man. And she... Jane swallowed another drink of her coffee. She shouldn't even be thinking about loneliness and flings and relationships she couldn't have right now.

Conor topped off his coffee, and for the first time, she noticed the shadows under his eyes and realized he'd probably been up a long time now, staying on top of the new developments on Badge Man's reappearance. Conor wasn't a threat to her, as Thomas suspected, but the fact that he'd asked to see her apart from their scheduled check-ins meant he believed there was some other kind of threat out there she needed to be on guard against.

"I'm not here to get advice about my nonexistent love life. Or to critique yours." The hour was late and she wanted to get down to business. "Tell me what all these cryptic texts have been about. You didn't say *Andromeda* so I knew I wasn't in imminent danger. But you scared me, anyway. What's happened? What's going on with Badge Man?"

"A victim with the outline of a badge carved into his chest was found in a culvert in Indianapolis three days ago. It took a while to ID the victim, but the report came in this morning. Alonzo Garcia. He was an Indiana state trooper." Jane hugged her arms around her waist and covered her mouth with her fingers to stifle the sob that wanted to come out. Conor glossed over the gruesome details, but she'd already seen an example firsthand. Taser the victim or knock him out with a blow to the head. Bind him. Wait for him to come to before strangling him to death and desecrating the body with his bloody mark. "Investigators believe he pulled over Badge Man for speeding. The license plate he reported hasn't turned up anywhere. They haven't been able to trace Garcia's last known location to the dump site."

"Did Garcia have a family?"

"You know not to ask that." That meant Trooper Garcia did leave someone behind. A wife? Children? Parents? And she was the only one who could stop that man from tearing apart more families. She blinked away the tears that ground like salt in her eyes and listened to Conor spell out his concerns for her. "He's not hunting in the DC area anymore. All his other victims have been back East, but if he's changed his kill zone—"

"Then he might be looking for me."

"Exactly." The flirty kid brother personality vanished and a steely US Marshal took over. "Indianapolis is halfway between DC and here. It might not mean anything, but then again… Maybe there was too much heat on him in the DC area. Maybe he's returned to his hometown. We don't know yet."

"Any chance it's a copycat?"

Conor shook his head. "There are certain details to his MO that were never released to the public. It's his work."

"So what do I do?"

"I need you to start varying your routine. This guy likes to track, and if he's on his way to Kansas City, it'll make it a lot harder to find you if you're not in the same place at the same time every day."

"But I don't look the same as I did three years ago. I've lost weight and stopped coloring my hair. I've let it grow out. How can he find me if I've changed my name and location?"

"On paper, he shouldn't be able to. But it's not my job to take chances with your security."

The coffee blended with stress and fear to burn a hole in her stomach. Jane paced to the kitchen sink to dump out the remnants and rinse her mug. "Seamus has scheduled appointments, daily therapy sessions I'm responsible for. I can't change those or it'll impact his recovery."

"Fine. But take different routes when you drive him to the doctors' offices. I know you like to get him out to the park when the weather's nice—don't go to the same place each time. Use different streets when you drive somewhere. Those morning runs—"

"I'll take a different route. Check out some different parks." Jane set the mug in the drainer beside the sink and faced Conor. "Seamus is a sharp cookie. He'll notice if I change up his routine. What do I tell him?"

"Make up an excuse. You want to see more of the city, you're running an errand, visiting a friend—"

"I don't have friends to visit."

"We have to sharpen your acting skills. Three years in WITSEC without an incident could make you lax. Once Badge Man found out you could identify him…"

"It was only a matter of time before he'd try to come after me again."

"We don't know that he's found you yet," Conor reminded her. "But if you get the sense that anyone's following you, you see a face you don't know popping up in more than one location, anything that makes you uncomfortable, you call me. Also, I want to up our contact to daily check-ins until we're certain Badge Man isn't headed to KC."

She understood. She hated that her entire life revolved around evading a killer, but she understood. Maybe survival was all her life would ever entail—no husband, no children, no long-term friends…just her, staying one step ahead of a man who wanted her dead. But maybe if she was smart enough, strong enough, brave enough, she could survive long enough to see Badge Man captured and put away for the rest of his life. Maybe by that time she wouldn't be too old and frail or senile to enjoy a little bit of normalcy in her own life.

She wasn't even aware that she'd pulled the collar of Thomas's jacket up around her chin until she inhaled his comforting scent. Oh, no. She dropped her hands and moved toward Conor. "Do you think KCPD has been alerted to Badge Man being on the move?"

"He's murdered cops, government agents and a sheriff's deputy. Every law enforcement group in the country knows about him. Now that he's struck again, the FBI is throwing a lot of investigative power behind their manhunt. Fred Davis was one of their own. They won't give up until they have a name and he's behind bars." Conor poured himself one last cup and turned off the coffeemaker. "In fact, I've been alerted that they're sending an agent out to reinterview you. I've notified Marshal Broz, my supervisor. We'll set up a secure meeting place to have that conversation."

"I meant, will the Watsons know?"

"Most likely. But they won't know you're the only surviving witness. Unless you tell them. And you can't do that."

"I know. But…are they in danger because of me?"

"Anyone in the country with a badge could be a target. Having you with a family of cops is another layer of good protection. They'll be on guard against him. And if Lieutenant Watson is already keeping an eye on you, then I don't see any need for a big move that could draw attention to you and get him to asking too many questions."

Jane shook her head. Thomas was already asking too many questions. He knew something was wrong. And while she had a feeling he'd be a good man to confide in—that he'd keep her secrets—she couldn't. "I understand."

Conor must have an iron stomach. He downed the last of the coffee before rinsing out his mug and the carafe. Then he escorted her to the door, pulled his weapon and checked outside before walking her to his car. He set his weapon on the seat between them before starting the engine. "You think you'll still be able to identify him once we catch him?"

Even with the blood thundering in her ears as her consciousness dimmed, that cold, almost breathless voice had imprinted itself in her brain. *There's nothing like the rush of seeing the light go out in someone's eyes.* She sank back against the seat, remembering the blue cord he'd tightened around her neck, and her belief that those would be the last words she'd hear before she died.

Jane clutched Thomas's jacket around her, recalling other details of that real-life nightmare.

She'd come home unexpectedly early from her night shift at the hospital. A nurse with a bad head cold wasn't especially helpful around critical-care patients. The front door was unlocked. Since that was unusual, she hadn't even bothered to take off her gloves and coat before checking to see if Freddie was okay. She'd walked into her bedroom to find her husband dead and that monster carving that grotesque symbol. Jane had held in her scream and had run, but something must have given her away. He caught her before she made it out the door. Her struggle had been brief. The twin pricks of a Taser in her shoulder had rendered her helpless long enough to be dragged into the bedroom to lie beside Freddie while the bastard cut free the noose that was tied around her husband's lifeless neck. Then he wrapped the same blue cord around her throat and choked her until she passed out. If she'd been a man and an agent like her husband, Badge Man would have spent more time on her. But she was only a witness he wanted to silence, and once she'd fallen unconscious and he assumed she was dead, he went back to finish his work and then disappeared.

But those few seconds she'd struggled with him had told her enough.

Her attacker was heterochromatic. Since his eyes were the only part of his face she could see behind the stocking mask he wore, it had been impossible to miss that one iris was brown while the other was such a light blue that it was almost colorless.

An odd scent clung to his clothes and body. He didn't smell like a man. He'd been sweet, like cookie dough or banana bread. To this day, she couldn't eat cinnamon rolls or Danish for breakfast.

And that tattoo on his neck that she'd uncovered when she'd clawed at the mask, making one last attempt to fight for her life as he crushed her larynx, was as crystal clear as if it marked her own skin. Two lines of words, tucked beneath his collar, ironically inspired by

Winston Churchill. *Don't take no for an answer. Never submit to failure.*

Jane's fingers drifted to the tracheotomy scar at the base of her own neck, the only lingering physical reminder of that horrible night. "I won't forget him. I may not recognize his face, but there are too many other details that are etched in my memory. I'll be able to identify him as the man who murdered my husband."

"Good. I wanted you to be aware of the escalation in the situation. Don't let your guard down. But as long as we continue to fly under everybody's radar, you'll be safe. The extra precautions will only help. And I'll be watching. All you have to do is stay alive."

Right. No problem. "I'll do my best."

Why didn't that feel like it was enough?

THOMAS PULLED OFF his reading glasses and glanced over at the clock beside the bed. One a.m.

He could hear her again, pacing the hallway between her bedroom, the guest bathroom and the top of the stairs. He imagined if the hour wasn't so late, Jane would be outside running to burn off that excess energy. Instead, she was quietly walking the tight space outside his door like a caged animal. What had Conor Wildman said to her that upset her like this? Or was her restlessness related to the shooting at the restaurant earlier tonight? Although the spray of bullets had felt personal to him, could Wildman have anything to do with that bizarre drive-by that had elicited more fear than actual injury or damage? The guy had certainly pinged on Thomas's suspicion radar.

He bit back a groan as he dropped his legs off the side of the bed and planted his feet on the soft area rug there. The tank-sized chocolate Lab mix stretched out on the dog bed lifted her head in anticipation. Thomas forced a smile for the big galoot he'd rescued from the pound. "It's okay, Ruby. Daddy wants to check something out." Seeming to understand his words, Ruby lowered her head and went back to quietly eviscerating the dog toy she was chewing on. "At least, I think I am."

His left leg was protesting the beating his body had taken today, diving and rolling over concrete, and chasing after that white van. Three ibuprofen and a hot shower had helped, but there was little more he could do besides try to distract himself from the perpetual ache that had flared into shards of pain shooting through the nerve damage from his thigh down to his ankle.

He set down his glasses and the newsletter inviting him to his air force training class reunion on the lamp table and waited for Jane's shadow to pass by the crack beneath his door again. He had been interested in catching up on news of the men he'd once served with. The reunion was more of a sixtieth birthday party for his buddy Jeff Fraser, put together by their pal Murray Larkin, or "Mutt" as their class of Butter Bars—aka second lieutenants with gold bars on their collars—had called him. Mutt was organizing the event to happen right here in Kansas City since so many of their military police and OSI buddies had trained over at Whiteman AFB, an hour east of KC, before they'd shipped to England together. A lot of the men he'd served with in the Office of Special Investigations either lived in the area or were coming back in a week for a visit, turning one man's birthday into a unit celebration. But as much as he'd loved his air force brothers, the men who'd been his partners in arms before he'd found a new job in a different uniform, Thomas wasn't really in the mood to party.

Jane's shadow blipped by his door again and he turned his gaze to the laptop sitting beside him on the king-size bed. Before he'd picked up Mutt Larkin's newsletter to read through, he'd been online with KCPD and the DMV, running a data search, trying to locate Conor Wildman in the Kansas City area. He hadn't found much. Wildman's home and business were at the same address, a spot he'd occupied for the past three years. But before that three-year mark? Thomas hadn't found an accountant named C. Wildman in any search. Grown men didn't suddenly appear out of nowhere. Discovering that Conor Wildman had no past was as disconcerting as if he'd found out the fair-haired boy had a record of domestic violence or other criminal history.

And this guy was involved in Jane's life?

The footsteps padded by his door again. Thomas had had enough of sitting back and not doing anything to help. Assuming he was well enough covered in his T-shirt and sweatpants so he wouldn't embarrass her, he crossed the room and opened the door.

Jane gasped and spun around at the top of the stairs leading down to the first floor. He blocked most of the light from the glow of his lamp, but illumination from the bedside lamp in her room gave enough light for him to see the startled expression on her face, her golden-brown hair hanging loose and straight to her shoulders, his black KCPD jacket still clutched tightly around her.

Thomas's pulse rate shouldn't have kicked up a notch at seeing a pretty woman in her pajamas cuddled up inside *his* jacket, wandering through the hushed shadows outside his bedroom door. But it did. Something intimate and possessive thrummed through his veins as he studied her from the bare toes curled into the polished wood floor, up the pink plaid pajama pants, over the black nylon jacket that hid most of the interesting bits from his perusal, to the tight pinch of her lips and wide eyes, staring at him expectantly.

"Sorry," he apologized for startling her. His voice was little more than a husky grumble. He scraped his fingers over stubble covering his jaw and cleared his throat. "You okay?"

He heard her breath rush out of her chest, and then she was hurrying across the hallway, unsnapping his jacket. "I'm sorry. You'll want this back."

"That's all right." He captured her arms and the jacket beneath his hands before she could shrug it off her shoulders. Jane froze at his grasp and the front gaped open, allowing him a glimpse of pert nipples clearly outlined beneath the pink T-shirt she wore. His hungry gaze danced over the pebbled tips and inevitably dropped to that strip of naked skin peeking between the hem of her top and the waistband of cotton plaid. His blood roared in his ears and zinged straight to his groin. He was in dangerous territory here, reacting to her taut body and subtle vulnerability like a man half his age. Maybe he should cover her before something perked up that even the shadows couldn't hide. He tugged his jacket back over her shoulders and pulled away. "Do you need me to turn on the heat?"

Her eyes widened. Her lips parted. Desire throbbed down south before he realized the double entendre of what he'd said. "The furnace. I mean the furnace. Do you want me to turn it on?"

Turn it on? Hell, it was a good thing the lights were

dim and they were the only two sleeping upstairs. Well, the dog didn't count. His face heated, and he imagined his cheeks were a deep brick red.

Either sensing his discomfort or relieved to know she wasn't the only awkward participant in this conversation, Jane smiled. She tucked her loose hair behind her ears and actually chuckled. "No. I'm fine. It'd be silly to run the air during the day and turn on the heater at night. Did I wake you?"

The amusement that softened her features reminded him how rare her smiles were and triggered an answering grin. A pleased feeling that he'd relieved the stress she seemed to live with 24/7 tamped down the heat coursing through him. "I was doing some reading. I heard footsteps."

The humor left her expression and that frown dimpled between her eyebrows. "I'm sorry. I couldn't sleep. I didn't want to wake anyone downstairs by going to the kitchen for a snack or a glass of milk."

"Dad snores like a diesel engine. He won't hear you. And Millie sleeps in her suite with one of those white noise machines going—so she doesn't hear Dad across the hall." Her lips curved into a soft pink arc again. Happier to see that shy smile than a boss ought to be, he pointed to the stairs. "Go on down to the kitchen. I think you can turn on all the lights down there and even run the blender without waking Dad or Millie."

"Thanks." She retreated a step toward the stairs. "Could I bring you anything?"

"Are you worried about what happened tonight at the restaurant?" He took a step toward her and she stopped. The smile disappeared, too. "In some ways, the incident reminds me of the shooting at my daughter's wedding back in February."

"You said that. That the guy in the van wanted to scare you, send a message."

"I think he inadvertently scared you, too. Thanks to the work of my sons, Dad's shooter was identified. He turned up dead when Duff found him. But my boys and KCPD aren't resting until we find out who hired him and why. There was a special belt buckle he wore that Duff believes the man who hired him cut off him so the body would be harder to identify. If we find out who has that belt buckle... Sorry." Thomas was going into too much detail about a gruesome crime. Not the images he wanted to leave with a woman who was already having trouble sleeping. "If tonight's drive-by is related to that, they'll figure it out. They don't know how to quit."

"You don't quit, either." She hugged her arms in front of her and drifted a step closer. "You're working on the case, too, aren't you?" She inclined her head toward the doorway behind him. "I saw your light on. I thought you must have fallen asleep and forgotten to turn it off. But you were in there working, weren't you?"

He didn't correct her by admitting the mystery surrounding her was the case he'd been working on. But it wasn't a lie to say he'd spent countless hours looking for answers to explain why someone wanted to hurt his family.

"I'll do whatever is necessary to protect my family." Funny how she could talk about bullets flying at him, Millie and Seamus in her detached, businesslike tone. But if he tried to steer the conversation to the reason why she thought she might have been the intended target, she changed the subject, locked down or walked away. Maybe a little reassurance that she was in a safe place, and that he was a safe person to confide in, would help her relax and open up. "Because you're living with us, because you're so important to Dad and his recovery, you're part of this family, too, and that protection extends to you."

"Part of your family?"

The frown reappeared between her eyes. She seemed not to understand the concept.

"Look, I know you and I don't always see eye to eye on things. I guess it's inevitable. We're both used to being in charge—my house, your patient." He wanted to smooth away that frown dimple from her forehead with the pad of his thumb. Instead, he opted for the more practical, less personal option of straightening the folded collar of the jacket. But he still had to curl his fingers away from the urge to trace her delicate collarbone over to...the scars? How had he missed seeing those little puckers of white skin at the base of her throat? Probably because she usually kept her body pretty covered up. He took a deep breath to keep the suspicious anger from boiling over. Surgery marks? Or evidence of something more sinister that she'd endured? "That doesn't mean you're not an important part of the team. If the guy who put the hit on Seamus threatens my family again, I will protect you. I'll protect you from anyone who tries to harm you."

The promise hung in the charged, silent space between them. Her hazel eyes searched his. Her shoulders lifted with a thoughtful breath. And then she changed the subject. "Your bandage is wet." She grasped him by the wrist and turned his forearm to the light shining from his bedroom. "That won't do the healing process any good and could damage the surrounding skin. And the wound is too fresh to leave it uncovered."

"I'm fine."

Ignoring his words, she shifted her grip to his hand and tugged. "Come with me."

She led him to the upstairs bathroom at the end of the hall. Using only the glow of the night-light beside the sink, she urged him to sit on the lid of the toilet while she opened the medicine cabinet and pulled out the supplies she needed. In every aspect of her life, save the one he wanted to talk about, Jane was a confident, efficient woman, just as she was now, gently peeling off the gauze and tape that were still wet from his shower, moving around his knees to toss it in the trash and back again to inspect the wound before covering it with a fresh bandage. For a few minutes while she worked, Thomas simply watched the grace and gentle certainty of a mature woman who knew what she was doing. He'd forgotten how good a woman could smell, especially one who bathed and shampooed in something citrusy and fresh.

He suspected that taking care of others came more naturally to Jane than taking care of herself. With every brush of her fingers across his skin, every bump of her knee against his, he wanted to pull her into his lap and hold her close, convincing her with his body the promise she refused to believe. He would keep her safe if she'd let him. He'd protect her from those ghosts haunting her eyes.

A boss probably shouldn't be thinking thoughts like that about his employee. But a man would have those thoughts about a woman he cared for, a woman who was coming to mean more to him than any woman had for a long time. He'd dated a few times over the years since Mary's death. And he certainly had friends who were female. But Olivia had been right at the wedding. He'd shut off his heart for a long time after Mary's murder. He'd always love Mary, always miss her, but the grief and pain had been dealt with, boxed up and put in the past. There was something about this woman peeling the gauze off the scraped-up skin of his elbow that woke things inside him that had been dormant for far too long. Sure, his hormones buzzed close to the surface any time he inhaled Jane's scent or glimpsed her lean, womanly shape or saw her pink lips soften into a sensuous smile.

But there was something more going on here. She wasn't afraid to argue with him, and he liked a woman who sparked off him like that. She made him feel alive. Young. Virile. More than that, she needed him. Well, she needed someone to have her back and help her with whatever secrets were nipping at her heels. And he wanted it to be him. He knew she didn't have many people in her life. But he was here. Right here in front of her. He'd been a son, a dad, a cop and a widower for a lot of years. Jane made him feel like a man. Thomas hadn't been needed in a long time. He hadn't been a man a woman needed for a very long time.

Thomas was lost in his thoughts, lost in the way her silky hair brushed across his skin when she leaned over his arm, when she asked, "Why did you kiss me? At the restaurant before I left with Conor?"

When she straightened to look down at him, her fingers were cupped against the cheek he'd kissed, as if remembering the touch of his lips there. He remembered it. His lips instantly warmed with the memory of her skin heating beneath his touch. When she saw him focusing on the same spot, she curled her fingers into her palm, drawing them away from her cheek.

"Did I overstep the bounds of our professional relationship?"

"Forget about that. I'm not a naive girl who isn't aware that there's some chemistry between us. You've never crossed a line that made me uncomfortable."

"Until tonight?"

"You didn't answer the question."

So she could push for answers, but he wasn't allowed to? The argument was poised on the tip of his tongue, but he thought better of antagonizing her when she was already too unsettled to relax. "I wanted Wildman to know you had somebody looking out for you. In case..."

Thomas stood, taking up more room in the small space than he realized. Retreating a step to keep some distance between them, Jane's feet hit the edge of the tub, but her body kept moving. She let out a tiny yelp and windmilled her arms to stop herself from falling. But before she could regain her balance, Thomas grabbed her by the waist to catch her, his fingers sliding beneath her top, singeing against her cool skin. With her hands clutching his biceps and her arched back throwing her hips into his, they froze. For several seconds, the only sounds in the room were the stuttered whooshes of their startled breathing trying to return to its normal rhythm. He was hyperaware of her strong thighs squeezed to either side of his bum leg and her hip pressed against a part of him that was much more sensitive to touch. Her eyes had darkened to the green side of hazel and looked up at him through long golden lashes. His mouth hovered close enough above hers to feel her warm breath dance across his lips. He wasn't sure how to finish this without kissing her until he got this crazy, inappropriate lust out of his system, and revealed his mixed up feelings for her.

"In case what?" she prompted on a whisper.

His expertise when it came to dealing with affairs of the heart might be a little rusty, but his skill set was razor sharp when it came to recognizing when someone was in trouble. His gaze zeroed in on the scars on her neck. "In case he's the one hurting you."

"Hurting? Conor hasn't hurt me. He's…" Her eyes shuttered and she pushed him away, snapping the jacket together at her neck and twisting from his grasp. "I can't talk about it." And there was the lockdown on her features again. She flipped on the light switch beside the door, forcing him to lower his eyes and turn away from the harsh light while she cleaned up the mess and put away the first-aid supplies. "Thank you, Thomas. I *was* scared earlier tonight. Scared for you and Millie and Seamus. But knowing you were there for me grounded me. You shared a little bit of that quiet strength of yours and I could deal with what I needed to handle." She tossed the last of the soiled gauze into the trash behind him before glancing up at him. "So thank you. I would regret if something happened to any of you because of me."

And now she was walking away. Thomas pursued her into the hallway.

"Because of you?" He snatched her by the arm and turned her to face him. He couldn't keep the frustration and concern from filtering into his voice. "Who wants to hurt you? What do you need to handle? I'm trying to help you here."

She braced her hands against his chest when he refused to let go, and he felt a pinch as the tips of her fingers curled into the muscle there as she considered her answer. He was getting a dangerous sense that she was feeling that pull of desire between them, too. But she was strong enough to push him away and turn to the stairs. "I think I will go down and get a little bowl of cereal. Maybe that'll help me sleep. Good night, Thomas."

"Good night, Jane."

Maybe a mutual attraction was wishful thinking on his part. But he was certain in his bones that Jane was in trouble.

After she'd gone down and he saw the kitchen light shining through the hallway at the foot of the stairs, he looked through the open door into her bedroom. He saw her phone lying on her bed. It would be a gross invasion of her privacy, and he certainly didn't have any legal justification to do so, but he wanted to have a look at it. He wanted to find out exactly what or who it was that kept her up at night and put that worried look into her eyes.

The cop in him would have waited. The man in him couldn't.

The man won.

He checked the stairs one last time to hear her working in the kitchen, and then strode into her room.

Chapter Five

Jane survived the weekend without any more accidental late-night run-ins with Thomas. Maybe it was fear and fatigue, or maybe the hushed intimacy of a shadowed hallway and a quiet house that had screwed with her common sense.

Even if the older generation was sound asleep a floor below, she and Thomas weren't kids sneaking out of their bedrooms to talk and touch and almost kiss. Yeah, for a few minutes there, she'd been certain he was going to kiss her again. And the foolish thing was she'd been completely ready to kiss him back, ready to taste those firm lips moving over hers, ready to wind her arms around his neck and pull herself into the heat and strength of his body. She'd felt his arousal pressing against her hip. She'd felt the brand of his fingers against her skin. He hadn't been shy about putting his hands on her—to comfort her, to catch her, to keep her from bolting—and a man's touch had felt so good. So warm. So tempting. So normal.

But she'd seen his eyes land on the scars on her neck, and felt the rage at the injuries she'd suffered subtly change his hold on her. It had been the reminder she needed that she wasn't normal. She didn't get to give in to her body's desires. She wasn't the kind of woman who could surrender to a man who stirred things inside her. Not when her life depended on her keeping her secrets. Not when those secrets could endanger the loving, character-filled family she'd grown to care about these past few months.

So she'd kept her conversations short. She'd avoided him as much as possible at the house. And she'd bundled Seamus into her car and scooted him out of the house Monday morning for an occupational therapy session even before Thomas had left for work.

All the tension from Friday night—from the drive-by shooting to Conor's warning to that hallway rendezvous with Thomas—had thankfully shifted to a back burner in her mind while she focused on driving Seamus around Kansas City on some errands to give him real-world practice dealing with maneuvering his walker through shop doors and checkout lines, and giving him someplace different to walk besides at home and the park. He'd handled asking for directions at the pharmacy, reading Millie's shopping list and picking up items of different shapes and weights off the grocery shelves and putting them into their basket.

Now, as he pushed their shopping cart out to her mini SUV, she kept hold of the side of the basket more as a precautionary measure rather than an effort to help him with any of the muscle work. She unlocked the car and opened the back gate, gesturing to the empty space. "You're up, Seamus. You can use your walker for stability if you want, but remember, the car is also stationary so you can use it to brace yourself. I want to see you negotiate the twisting action of unloading the cart and putting the groceries in the back."

"Tack-matter," he whined. But since he smiled, she didn't mind being called a taskmaster.

Taking Conor's advice to heart, while Seamus went through the exercise, Jane scanned the parking lot and the front of the store, looking for anyone who seemed extra interested in her and her car. The place was bustling, with people hurrying in and out the store, driving perilously close to pedestrians as they impatiently waited to find a parking space near the doors. Mothers warned small children to stay close. Infants cried. Friends waved, and drivers in various cars, trucks and vans zipped into parking spots or exited out onto the street. All in all, her surroundings looked perfectly normal for a busy morning in the city.

"Done." Seamus had unloaded the cart and was even reaching up to pull down the tailgate. Although the pulling motion taxed the strength in his good arm, he didn't hesitate to raise his weaker hand to catch the door so it didn't spring up on him. He'd come so far from the bedridden patient she'd first been hired to take care of all those months ago.

Jane waited until the door was shut before smiling and giving him a thumbs-up. "Nicely done."

She told him to wait for her to help him climb into the SUV and hurried the cart across the driveway to return it to the front of the store. She waited for a white car and van to pull past her before she could cross back to the car. A little ripple of unease shivered down her spine at the sight of the van. But unlike the shooting at the restaurant, this one was driving by at a normal pace. There were no gunshots, and the driver didn't seem interested in anything except following the traffic out of the parking lot.

She exhaled the breath she'd been holding, resumed normal breathing and hurried back to her car. Seamus was standing in the same place at the rear of the SUV, grinning. "Gonna let me drive dis time?"

He must be feeling good this morning to tease her. He knew the doctor hadn't cleared him yet for operating a vehicle. She teased him right back and tossed him her keys. "Think fast."

He fumbled them from one hand to the other, but caught them against his chest. Every time he used those muscles for something new, he was retraining the pathways in his brain and speeding his recovery.

Jane closed the distance between them and tilted her face up to kiss his weathered cheek. "Not this time. But your reflexes are improving." How many times had her grandfather played that same game with her as a little girl? Spending this time with Seamus reminded her of Cyrus Ward and the happy little girl she'd been growing up. "One day soon you'll be behind the wheel. Then you can take Millie out on a date all by yourself."

"Why would I want to…?" His pale skin colored with a mighty blush as she turned him toward the passenger door. "I know dat woman for tenty years and we never one-t gone out on date."

"Twenty years, hmm?" She buckled herself in behind the wheel and started the engine. "You Watson men do move slowly, don't you?"

Seamus pointed a bony finger at her as she backed out and pulled into the line of cars to exit onto Highway 40. "I S-peedy Gonzalez compared to you. Don't tink I haven't noticed you giving my t-son those looks at the dinner table. He look at you, too. But anyting happen? No."

Only while you're sleeping. Her cheeks heated with embarrassment. Even though he'd been joking with her—at least she hoped he was joking—he hadn't really caught her sneaking looks at Thomas, had he? Any reference to that fruitless attraction ruined her cheery mood and reopened the door to those thoughts and feelings she'd been trying to ignore. Flexing her grip around the steering wheel, Jane stepped on the gas and turned the spotlight away from her. "I was merely pointing out that when those gunshots were fired Friday night, your first instinct was to protect Millie." She slowed at the Lee's Summit Road traffic light and turned. "You can't tell me you don't feel something for her."

"One-t a cop, always a cop. My job to protect." Was that all that Thomas's questions and late-night touches and hushed conversation had been about? He was a cop, and protecting those around him was second nature to him? Or was there something more personal to his prying into her problems? It certainly felt personal. If she were living a different life, she wouldn't be averse to Thomas feeling a *personal* interest in her. But relationships were off the table for her right now. They had to be.

She'd crossed I-70 and had nearly reached the Thirty-Ninth Street turnoff when Seamus spoke again. "I not much a man right now. Want to be whole before I ack Millie out."

Jane put on her turn signal and switched lanes to make the left as the conversation turned serious. Seamus's admission tugged at her heart. "That doesn't matter to her and you know it. She sees the handsome man you are, the man who makes her laugh when you're not biting someone's head off, the strong man you will be again."

"I already old." He seemed distracted by something in his side mirror. She hoped he wasn't embarrassed to be honest with her. She was responsible for his mental state as well as his physical recovery.

She tried to encourage him with the first example that came to mind. "Do you think Thomas sees himself as half a man because of the injury to his leg? He's never going to lose that limp. But trust me, women are looking at those broad shoulders and that rugged jaw and those handsome green eyes, and they are not noticing his uneven gait. He walks and talks with an air of authority that commands a room without having to say much. He doesn't even have to work at it. It's just who he is. That's sexy."

When she stopped talking and glanced across the front seat, she realized Seamus was staring at her, with a sleek white brow arched above one eye. She'd given away far too much, and she forced her eyes back to the road. "You tink my boy is texy?"

She was probably blushing all the way down to her toes this time, judging by the way her temperature had spiked. She turned on the car's air conditioner to cool herself off. "The point I was making is that it runs in the family. Millie sees the determined man who's charming and gallant. She sees those blue eyes and that kind heart, not the walker or the weak hand." Jane buzzed a breath out between her lips. "Besides, she is one of the strongest women I've ever met. She has corralled five Watson men and Olivia for twenty-plus years. From the sound of things, she's never taken any guff off any of you. She's fed you and loved you all. If there's any woman who could put up with you besides me, it's Millie."

She'd expected him to react to that big speech, which she made certain was all about someone besides herself. But he'd drifted away from the conversation again.

"Seamus?" Was he tiring? She'd been pushing him for three hours now. Or maybe she'd flat-out embarrassed him by butting into his love life. "This talking is excellent therapy to build your stamina and improve your communication skills. We can change the topic if you want to, but I don't think we should stop."

And then she realized his posture had changed. He might have been retired for more than fifteen years, but she recognized his shoulders coming back, that wary look. "White van from gro-cey tore turned last tuh-ree corners with us."

"What?" White van? She'd seen that very same van a few minutes ago, had talked herself out of that uneasy feeling and dismissed it as coincidence. But now that suspicion surged through her again. Jane checked her rearview mirror. She spotted the van three vehicles back. Her pulse rate kicked up a notch. It *did* look like the same one. She was already taking a roundabout route through the suburbs, avoiding the more direct route to the Watson home on the interstate. She couldn't see the driver or read any markings on the front. "You think he's following us?"

"We find out." He pointed to the next traffic light. "Get into turn lane. Go touth."

"But that will take us right back where we were." Conor's warning played in her head about mixing up routes and not making it easy for anyone to track her. "Okay. I'll turn left instead of going straight."

The van pulled into the turn lane and followed. If he wasn't stopping to make deliveries or pickups, why would the driver be following her in a circle? Was this the man who wanted to harm the Watsons? Was it...? She shook her head. Badge Man was in Indiana. The FBI widow he wanted to kill no longer existed, thanks to the US Marshals Service, and he had no idea she was now Jane Boyle, private nurse. How could he? Wouldn't he need to have some kind of inside information to learn her new identity and location? The possibility of someone leaking her information to a serial killer made her sick to her stomach. *Focus!*

Jane stepped on the gas. But when she sped up, the van zipped through traffic to stay with her. "I can't shake him. Can you read the license plate?"

Seamus was clutching the armrest and center console now, but his eyes were glued to the mirror. "No. Too many cars."

"Hold on." She made a sharp, squealing turn as she hit the entrance ramp to the interstate and merged into the fast-moving traffic. The cars honking at her weren't any louder than her own heartbeat pounding in her ears. The white van barreled down the entrance ramp behind them. "Um..."

"Phone?" Seamus asked.

"In my purse." On the floor of the back seat. No way could Seamus turn around and reach it. And she couldn't afford to take her hands off the wheel.

The van passed the car behind her and pulled into the narrow space between them. The vehicle picked up speed, looming up in the back window and mirrors as if it was going to swallow them. "Can you see the driver's face?"

All she saw was the glare of the sun off the van's windows. She needed to concentrate on her driving. Seamus leaned toward the side-view mirror. "Tocking mask."

"Look out!" She felt the slightest tap on her car and Jane screamed. The wheel jerked in her hand, but she gripped it tighter and held on.

Seamus swore. "He going to cause accident."

One way or another, the driver of that van seemed intent on killing someone.

Badge Man had worn a stocking mask that night in DC. So had the man who'd shot at them Friday night. "He won't hurt you," she promised. "I won't let him hurt you."

He tapped the bumper again. The car swerved and she fought against the skid, praying there were no other vehicles coming up in the lane beside her. She regained control and jerked into the next lane, but the white van followed. Thank God it wasn't rush hour with backed-up traffic to plow into. But still, at this speed, if he tapped the corner of her bumper just right...

Badge Man toyed with his victims. Followed them. Terrorized them before he struck. Except for that state trooper in Indiana. That had been an impulse kill, a reaction to being stopped by the officer. If Badge Man was changing his MO, changing his location, did that mean he was spiraling out of control? Would there be more bodies? Was he here in Kansas City? Was he twenty feet behind her going ninety miles an hour right now? Were she and Seamus about to become his next victims?

She should call Conor and shout "ANDROMEDA" from the rooftops and get the hell out of Kansas City.

But she couldn't even reach her phone. Plus, she had an eighty-year-old friend and patient in the seat beside her she had to protect. She had to get out of this. She needed to be safe. Seamus was telling her to change lanes, to get off the highway. But if that was Badge Man, and he caught them, Seamus wouldn't be able to protect her. Maybe no one could.

One image flashed in her mind. One person. "How do I get to KCPD headquarters?"

"Downtown?"

Her head jerked with a nod. It was old-school self-defense. If a woman was being followed, she should drive straight to the nearest police station. But not any police station would do. Not this time.

Seamus seemed to understand. He reached over to squeeze her shoulder and gave her the exit number.

The van slowed to a legal speed when they entered the downtown area, but he was still there, crowding her bumper, racing through at least one red light to stay with her. Jane's heart was still pounding. She couldn't think. She could barely see. She was experiencing some kind of panic attack, and her blood pressure was going through the roof. As her vision narrowed to tunnel-like circles, Seamus's voice telling her where to turn, where to stop, was probably the only thing that kept her from passing out and wrecking the mini SUV herself.

Jane screeched into the KCPD parking garage. The van drove past the entrance as they climbed out and hurried as fast as an eighty-year-old with a walker could across the street to the handicapped entrance of the remodeled limestone-and-granite monolith that served as KCPD headquarters.

The van circled the block again, and the faceless

driver slowed and pointed straight at her through the open window. "Go." She hooked her arm through Seamus's and practically lifted him through the thick glass doors leading into the marble-tiled lobby. "Go!"

No gun this time, thank God. But she still recoiled from the pointing finger as if a bullet had struck her. The van drove away at a perfectly normal speed, and the adrenaline crashing through her system nearly blinded her.

Seamus tugged on the sleeve of Jane's scrub jacket and pulled her to the elevator with him. He pushed the button and as they rode up, images of Freddie's mutilated body assailed her. After she woke up, she'd dialed 911, but she had no voice to cry out for help. Jane tried to fight off the memories, tried to stay in the moment. But when she closed her eyes, she relived the electric shock that had knocked her off her feet and sent the living room spinning around her. She opened her eyes but could still feel the long blue cord looping around her throat, choking the very air from her lungs. Her fingers went to her throat. She could feel her pulse throbbing beneath the scars there. She could feel the man on top of her, crushing her chest as she clawed for survival.

Two different eyes. An inspirational message, skewed into something hateful, inked onto a killer's neck. *Don't take no for an answer. Never submit to failure.*

Her head was pounding. Was this post-traumatic stress kicking in again? Surely she was past that. She'd done all the counseling. Why couldn't she focus right now? She wasn't physically hurt. Was she going into shock? She was a nurse, for heaven's sake. Why couldn't she diagnose what was wrong with her?

"We're here."

She startled at Seamus's touch, could barely see the worry in his blue eyes as she helped him off the elevator. They walked to the tall, dark-stained counter that marked the desk sergeant's station. She was vaguely aware of the sergeant and another uniformed officer coming over to strike up a friendly, good-to-see-an-old-friend conversation with Seamus.

Jane interrupted. "I need to see Thomas Watson. Lieutenant Watson."

"And you are...?"

Seamus answered for her. "This is Jane Boyle, my nurse and a good fam-ly fwiend."

"The lieutenant's in a seminar right now. He's teaching interrogation techniques."

She was having trouble seeing the desk sergeant's face. "It's personal. Please."

"If you'd like to wait or leave a message—"

"I can't wait." Jane spun around and bumped into a young detective in a charcoal-gray suit.

"Grandpa? Jane?" She jerked away from the hands on her arms before she recognized Thomas's son Keir. "Is everything all right?"

She pleaded with him. "I need to see your dad."

Seamus looked at his grandson and inclined his head toward her, sending some kind of silent message that Keir apparently understood.

Keir turned to the desk sergeant. "It's okay. They're with me."

He grabbed a pair of visitor badges and escorted them through the maze of desks and cubicle walls, which were surprisingly unoccupied. Keir guided Seamus to his own desk and pulled out the rolling chair for him.

"Hey, old man." A short detective with longish hair and blue jeans stood from his spot at the adjoining desk to shake Seamus's hand. Jane's thoughts skipped from panicked to lucid to blank. But somewhere in there she recognized Hudson Kramer, Keir's partner, a frequent guest at the Watson house whenever a big meal was served. "What's up?"

"Keep an eye on Grandpa?" Keir asked.

"Sure. Somethin' wrong?" He sounded concerned.

"I explain," Seamus said. He nudged Keir. "Go wit her."

Jane was either going to burst into tears or faint if she couldn't shake this miasma that had settled over her. "Where's your dad?"

"Right through here." She clung to the sleeve of Keir's suit jacket, wondering where she'd left her real self. Back on the highway, perhaps? Further back on that bloody bedroom carpet in DC? A rational little corner of her brain knew she should pull it together. She should apologize to Keir and Hud and Seamus and drive her patient home. She should remember that Conor Wildman and the US Marshals office had sworn to protect her. Keir opened a door between two glass panels and ushered her into the back of a large conference room. She looked over rows of narrow tables that spanned almost the width of the room, over dozens of police officers taking notes on laptops and notepads while they listened to the man at the front of the room gesturing to a flowchart on the screen behind him. "There he is."

Even though Keir had whispered, and the speaker's booming voice didn't need to be miked to fill the room, Detective Lieutenant Thomas Watson seemed to sense the intrusion. When he turned around and saw her, he stopped.

Maybe this was a bad idea. One by one, the men and women in the room turned their heads to look at her. As the fog in her brain started to clear, the temperature in the room dropped and suddenly Jane was freezing. Someone mentioned early lunch and she turned to the door.

But before she got there, her path was blocked by a wall of neatly pressed broadcloth and a suit jacket of rich brown tweed. "Jane?"

The room was a buzz of white noise behind her. She shook her head. "I'm sorry. I shouldn't have come. I wasn't thinking straight."

"Is Dad all right?" Thomas asked. When she nodded, his hand was already at her elbow, guiding her out the door. "Come with me."

"I'll find out what I can from Grandpa." Jane was vaguely aware of Thomas's youngest son excusing himself.

As the squad of detectives filed out of the conference room behind them and headed toward the cubicle desks, Thomas led her in the opposite direction, down an empty hallway and through an office door. He closed the door behind him and pulled the blinds for privacy.

"What's happened?" When he turned around to face her, Jane walked right into that big chest, sliding her arms beneath his jacket and pressing her ear to the sure, steady beat of his heart. "Hey. You're shaking." He wrapped his arms around her and pressed his lips to the crown of her head. One hand settled at the nape of her neck. "You're like ice. It's not that cold outside. Are you hurt?" Jane linked her fingers behind his back and burrowed beneath his chin, letting his enveloping strength and heat surround her, seep into her pores, jump-start her brain. "I need details, honey. You need to talk to me."

Inhaling a ragged breath at the gentle command, Jane shook her head and the words spewed out. "How did he find me? Killed a state trooper. White van following us. Same one? Some crackpot having fun at our expense. Seamus noticed him. He was worried. I could see it. And I drove. So fast. Hit the car. I couldn't think straight. I...I wanted to come here."

Thomas cupped the back of her neck and tipped her head back. Then his big hands were framing her face. His firm mouth folded over hers, shocked her out of her rambling. A light turned on inside her, a beacon to chase away the darkness and the chill. When he lifted his head, Jane pushed up onto her toes and reconnected the kiss. She pulled her hands to the front of his jacket and curled her fingers into the lapels, chasing the light. She touched her tongue to the seam of his lips and they opened over hers. His tongue stroked against hers before he sucked the curve of her lower lip, stirring tendrils of long-absent heat inside her. For a few sweet, sensual moments she clung to him and they explored each other's mouths.

And then he was pulling away with a heavy groan. With her jaw still captured between his hands, his fingers caressing the back of her neck, he touched his forehead to hers. She looked up into green eyes that were narrowed and dark like rich, lush grass, and he smiled. "There you are."

She *was* back. In her right mind. In the moment. With Thomas.

Sliding her arms around his waist again, she nestled into his warmth and that simple spicy smell that was only his while he massaged her neck at the base of her ponytail. He'd kissed her for real this time, and everything in her had centered. And yet something had changed irrevocably at the same time. She was still afraid. She knew she and Seamus had had a dangerously close call. But she could think. She could move past the fear and the flashbacks. She could deal.

"Are you hurt?" he asked.

"No."

"Is Dad?"

"No." She smiled against the nubby tweed. "He was wonderful."

Thomas's fingers stilled their soothing massage. He backed away, but caught her hand and pulled her down to sit on the brown leather sofa beside him. His knee butted against hers and she didn't pull away. "I'm all for inflating my dad's ego, but I need a little more to go on."

"Sorry about the freak-out," she apologized, studying how pale and small her hand looked in his. She tilted her face to eyes that were analyzing every nuance of her expression. "I haven't done that in years. I'm pretty sure it was a PTSD episode."

Instead of asking what traumatic stress event she'd flashed back to, he stroked a fingertip across her forehead, catching a lock of hair that had come loose from her ponytail and tucking it behind her ear. "Wouldn't surprise me. Do you want a glass of water?" Jane shook her head. He squeezed his hand around hers, pulling it atop his thigh and holding it there. "Take a deep breath and talk to me."

She hesitated for a moment, simply because she'd been trained for so long to keep her past a secret. But scary things were happening around her and she needed to confide in someone she trusted. "We were coming home from our occupational therapy session—basically running Millie's errands—when Seamus spotted this van following us. Like the one at the restaurant Friday night. I tried to lose him, but then we were out on I-70, going so fast, and he clipped my bumper. More than once. I know he was trying to..." Her brain sidetracked and she pushed to her feet. "I left my purse and my phone in the car. I didn't even lock it. There's probably damage to the rear end. I need to get my phone and report this to Conor."

Thomas tightened his grip, keeping her from moving to the door. "Conor Wildman? The guy with the gun strapped to his leg Friday night?"

"You saw that?" Of course. A veteran detective with Thomas's experience probably didn't miss much. She sank back onto the sofa beside him. She could read the truth in his eyes. "You know, don't you?"

"Not about the car chase. I'll have Keir look into that and retrieving your purse. But I know some. I've got a lot of blanks that need filling in, though." He released her hand and she curled her fingers inside the cuffs on her jacket, missing his warmth. "Duff works with a multiagency task force. I've had him checking his connections to get some intel on Wildman." He stood, propping his fingers at the belt of his khaki slacks that held his badge and gun. "Slap my face if you want. But I took a look at your phone. I could tell something was wrong. I thought he'd been harassing you. Stalking you, maybe." He leaned his hip over the corner of the desk and sat, facing her. "Duff's connections are good. I know Wildman is a US marshal."

"I knew you were too good a detective not to figure it out eventually." Drawn to his heat or his honesty or both, Jane got up and crossed the space between them. "I'm a witness in an ongoing federal investigation. My husband was murdered. Fred Davis. My real name is Emily Ward Davis—but forget you even heard that. I have to be Jane Boyle for the rest of my life. Freddie was an FBI agent. His killer got away, but I can ID him. Once someone catches him. I'm the only surviving witness from his attacks."

Thomas gently tugged at the neckline of her scrubs and touched a fingertip to the scars on her neck. "The man who murdered your husband—he did that to you?"

She nodded, pulling back the material to hide the marks Badge Man left on her. "He crushed my larynx when he strangled me. There was swelling. The paramedics had to do a tracheotomy so I could breathe. Then I had surgery to repair the damage. I never got to go back to the house to get any of my things. I didn't even get to go to Freddie's funeral. I don't have any immediate family, but I wish I could have said goodbye to my in-laws. They were always nice to me. By the time I got out of the hospital, the Bureau was taking me away to a safe house in DC. And then I met the marshals and they moved me to Kansas City."

Somewhere during that explanation, his hands had settled at either side of her waist to pull her into the vee of his legs. "And Wildman is your handler here in KC?"

"I should tell him that you know. I'll probably get in trouble for it. I wasn't ever supposed to tell anybody. Secrecy means security. What happened this morning might not even be related to that night. It could be related to whoever wants to hurt your family. I'm so sorry if I put Seamus or any of you in danger because of me."

"Don't apologize. You hurt one of us, you hurt all of us." They were standing close enough that she felt the muscle spasm in his damaged thigh against her hip. Although he clenched his jaw against the pain, he didn't complain. "So you got spooked, maybe by this guy who killed your husband and attacked you. And instead of calling Wildman, you came to me?"

A healer at heart, Jane dropped her hand to his thigh and dug her fingers into the knotted muscle there. She heard an audible grunt at his initial jolt of pain and he jerked from her touch. But Jane refused to stop when he was so clearly hurting, and gradually his breathing eased as the spasms eased and the cord of muscle relaxed. This was the kind of thing a woman would do for her man—it was a private help, an intimate connection two people who understood each other's secrets shared. And she realized that was the bond she shared with Thomas. Workplace propriety and WITSEC rules couldn't change that. "I couldn't reach my phone to call him. I couldn't even think. I was just reacting. I needed to feel safe."

"I make you feel safe?" He put his hand over hers, stopping the massage, waiting for her answer.

That's why her instincts had driven her here. To Thomas. She tilted her gaze to his and nodded.

Thomas wound his arms around her, pulling her onto her toes as he hugged her tightly against him. "I'll go with you to talk to Wildman. I'll tell him we've expanded your protection detail." She felt him nuzzling the crown of her head before he pressed a kiss there. "I told you I protect my family. I don't ever want you to feel like you're not safe again."

Chapter Six

"Yes. I understand."

Listening in on this end of the phone call while he drove Jane across town to the house she still maintained as a meeting site with her WITSEC handler, Thomas gathered that whatever Marshal Wildman was telling her wasn't making her happy. Although that blank look in her eyes and the pallor of her skin had improved since she'd walked into the back of the conference room that morning, the tone of her voice sounded tired, resigned even. She'd picked at the chef's salad Millie had prepared for their lunch after taking Seamus home to rest. Maybe he should have insisted she stay home and nap, too, while he handled this conversation with Conor Wildman and his supervisor alone.

"No, I don't want to put it off."

But whether she slept or ate or flashed back to a nightmare that had sent her straight into the arms of a man who was closer to sixty than she probably realized, the woman was stubborn. And strong. And determined to take an active part in tracking down Badge Man, even if it put her own life at risk.

"Of course I remember him. I didn't realize he was working on the investigation."

Two thoughts were eating away at Thomas's insides as he checked his mirrors and the road ahead of him once again, looking for a white van or signs of anyone else who might be following them. One, he couldn't believe Badge Man was the killer she'd identified as her late husband's murderer. The man had been preying on law enforcement officials for eight years now, yet had gone to ground after each kill and eluded capture. There were few wanted men in the whole country more dangerous than the calculating killer who carved a message in every victim's chest.

And two, what was he supposed to make of Jane's confession that *he* was the man who made her feel safe? He was almost twenty years older than her. Maybe it was a paternal thing—she said she didn't have any family. A father figure was probably reassuring to her. Only, that woman did not make him feel like her daddy one bit. Not when she put her hands on him and clung to him and kissed him like that. Not when he could get stiff just by accidentally rubbing against her curves and smelling her sweet, fresh scent. He knew he had that whole life experience thing going for him—he knew a lot about a lot of things, he knew how to pull rank and take charge of a situation. And he was in good shape for a man his age—he had to be to wear the badge. But he also needed reading glasses to go over a crime report and had a leg that could cramp up and fail him if he pushed its endurance too far.

Testosterone and good old-fashioned male pride had pumped through his system when he realized she'd come to him before any other man on the planet to help her through that PTSD episode and ease her fears. She'd needed him. And hell, he hadn't had a woman need him for anything other than his badge or an escort to some boring charity banquet for a long, long time. Thomas wanted to protect Jane more than anything. He wanted to be the man she needed. But that kind of need scared the crap out of him, too.

What if his eyes or his leg failed him? What if he was too slow? What if he found out she wanted a daddy or a Dutch uncle, when he wanted her to call him darling?

Well, one thing wisdom and experience had taught him was that it was smart to think five or six steps ahead in any situation—but it was also vitally important to stay in the moment, to deal with the task at hand. All that planning for possible scenarios, good or bad, wouldn't do him a damn bit of good if he didn't survive the present.

"We'll be there in about five minutes." Jane was ending her phone call from Wildman. "Thanks for the heads-up."

She dropped her phone back into her purse on the front seat of the truck. Even with a dent from a bullet in the tailgate and a new set of tires on the back, he trusted the horsepower and solid steel construction of his pickup more than any rental or borrowed vehicle. The fact was, his truck *had* stopped those bullets, and from here on out, Thomas planned to do whatever was necessary to ensure Jane's safety.

Her sigh was audible as she leaned back against the headrest. "It won't just be Conor's supervisor there with him. Apparently, that state trooper's murder has galvanized the Bureau's investigation. There's an FBI agent there from Washington, DC, too, to interview me."

"Can you tell him anything new?"

"No. I didn't get a look at the shooter on Friday or

the driver this morning. All I saw was a gun or a finger pointed at me. I certainly didn't get close enough to tell if he had two different-colored eyes or a tattoo on his neck."

"KCPD has a BOLO out for the van. Thanks to the partial Dad gave us Friday night, we could trace it back to a delivery company that went out of business last year. The owner claims a lot of his assets were stolen before he declared bankruptcy."

"Sounds like an insurance scam."

"Or his lax security was the reason he went out of business. Hud and Keir will follow up on it."

She'd changed into blue jeans and a cotton turtleneck, and Thomas idly realized that this was the first time they'd ever spent any time together when she wasn't dressed in one of her nursing uniforms...or her pajamas. He liked the way these clothes gently hugged her curves. Probably liked it a little too much. "I should probably tell you that I know the agent who'll be there. He and Freddie worked together in the violent crimes unit. They were friends."

"Maybe he volunteered to come to KC to conduct the interview so he could check on you, make sure you're in one piece. I used to check on my partner Al's wives— one at a time, I promise—and he'd look after my Mary any time one of us pulled stakeout duty or an undercover assignment." He and Mary had shared a lot of good times and family events with Al and wives one and two before Mary had died. Wife three had come after Mary's death, and the marriage had barely lasted a year. But Thomas had still looked in on Brenda Junkert for those thirteen months of marriage if Al had asked him to. In fact, even though Al was more businessman than cop these days, it would be worth a phone call to him, as well as his sons and daughter whom he'd already alerted to Jane's situation, to get his help keeping an eye on her until Badge Man was apprehended or Jane was moved into a safe house. "When you work together in a dangerous job, you get close. Not just with your partner or team, but with their families. But you probably already know that. I'm guessing he wants to see with his own eyes that you're okay."

"I guess. But I thought that Levi—Agent Hunt—and the people Freddie used to work with didn't know where I'd been relocated. I haven't seen him in three years. I was surprised to hear from him."

"You still want to do this?"

"Will you be with me?" Her fingers inched across the seat.

Thomas reached out to meet her halfway and squeezed her hand. "Every step of the way."

Her grip was strong when she squeezed back. "Then yes. I want to do whatever I can to help catch this guy."

A few minutes later, he pulled up behind a big black government-issue SUV and a sporty Cadillac with rental plates in front of the unassuming brick ranch house that Jane called home. When she reached for her door handle, Thomas patted her arm. "Hold on a sec."

He climbed out of the truck and scanned the surrounding houses, making sure there was nobody hanging around who didn't fit the suburban atmosphere or who seemed extra curious about the parade of vehicles parked on their block in the middle of the afternoon. Then he went to both vehicles. The Cadillac was locked and empty, and he showed his badge to the driver sitting in the FBI car, asking him to identify himself with his FBI badge in return. Once he was certain the area was secure, he went back to the truck and escorted Jane into the house.

Conor Wildman greeted them with handshakes and an apology to Jane. "Sorry to gang up on you like this," he whispered before bolting the door behind them and walking them into the living room.

A dark-haired man about Thomas's height, but with the build of a distance runner beneath his black suit and tie, rose from the sofa where he'd been chatting with another man and strode across the room to swallow Jane up in a big hug. "Hey, pretty lady. Aren't you a sight for sore eyes. The marshals office isn't exactly keen on giving up where they stash their witnesses. But I made a pretty good case to see you again." He pulled back to sweep his gaze over her from head to toe. "You're not a blonde anymore. And you've lost weight. But you're looking great. How are you?"

Thomas might have bristled at the way the agent kept his hands on Jane's shoulders, but she was smiling. "The blond wasn't natural, so this is a lot easier to take care of. How are you, Levi?"

"I'm good. Miss your stuffed jalapeño bites at our backyard barbecues, but I'm good."

"And Dorie?"

He rolled his dark eyes. "Pregnant again."

"What is that, your fourth?"

"Fifth." At last he lowered his hands. "You missed one since you've been gone. Another boy. Dorie's still hoping for a girl."

"Tell her I wish her luck."

The other man from the couch got up, buttoning his gray suit jacket as he joined them. "You won't be telling her anything. Emily Davis is dead, remember?" He thrust a hand at Jane. "Oscar Broz, area supervisor, US Marshals Office. Ms. Boyle."

Thomas's hand was at the small of Jane's back the moment she jumped at Broz's abrupt interruption. She shook the black-haired man's hand. "Marshal Broz."

Thomas thrust his hand into the mix, too, reminding them all that Jane wasn't alone here. "Detective Lieutenant Thomas Watson, KCPD."

Marshal Broz's skin was unnaturally sallow for a man with such black curly hair. Thomas imagined his unhealthy pallor had a lot to do with job stress or smoking the cigars whose scent clung to his clothes, or both. Although he shook Thomas's hand, he was quickly dismissed as the senior marshal chided Jane. "You do remember the WITSEC agreement, don't you? I wasn't pleased to hear that you told a civilian about being a protected witness. One small leak and the whole dam can break."

Jane's chin came up and she defended him before Thomas could say a word. "Lieutenant Watson is hardly a civilian. He's a decorated police officer and air force veteran with more years of defending people than you've had. I trust him."

Broz's nostrils flared and he turned away to call someone on his cell phone, muttering something about spoiled women not following the rules. Thomas was about to point out to Broz that if his office had done a better job following the rules, then Jane wouldn't have been in the middle of two possible attempts on her life.

But Jane slipped her arm behind his waist and pulled him forward to meet her friend. "Levi, this is Thomas Watson. Agent Levi Hunt."

"Glad to know you, Lieutenant."

"Agent Hunt."

"Levi. Please." He glanced over his shoulder to make sure Oscar Broz was intent on the man he was chewing out on his phone before he leaned in and whispered. "Frankly, I'm glad to know Emily's got backup of her own."

"You mean Jane," Thomas corrected, reminding him to protect her identity.

"Right. If she was in DC, all of us who worked with Freddie would be stepping up to help. I mean, the marshals program is solid, but this Badge Man is clever. He doesn't leave prints or DNA. He's functional enough to go for months at a time without anyone being suspicious of him. And he knows police procedure. Identify a target. Learn his routine. Know when the target is going to be vulnerable to attack. Alone. Asleep."

"Freddie was asleep in the house by himself that night. I was supposed to be at work until seven a.m., but I got sick." Jane's fingers fisted at the small of his back. The details weren't new to her, but reliving the timeline of her husband's last hours had to be difficult. A quick glance down showed her hazel eyes were clear, even glittering with a bit of angry gold. Good. She wasn't going into another flashback. Still, unless she protested, he was sliding his arm around her shoulders. She didn't, and Thomas pulled her to his side.

"Doesn't sound like the kind of guy to try to run somebody off the road on a busy highway," Thomas pointed out.

Levi stuffed his hands into the pockets of his slacks and shrugged. "True. But our guess is that he's spiraling out of control. Killing that state trooper was already a deviation from his routine—impromptu isn't this guy's way." He frowned when he looked down at Jane again. "And if he's heading west to find the one person who can identify him…"

"Then he's already broken his pattern." Thomas understood profiling, too. "All his victims have been men in law enforcement. Coming after Jane is new territory for him, so his methodology could be changing."

"That's why the Bureau wants to move on this. The odds of him making a mistake are a hundred percent more likely when he doesn't stick to what he knows. Our chances of catching him now are stronger than ever."

Jane might be reliving some bad memories, but she tamped them down to be a part of the conversation. He was proud to see that resilient strength in her. "Has your investigation into Freddie's murder, and the other murders, stalled out?"

The dark-haired agent shrugged. "Let's just say they've cooled. Sad to say, but we're hoping that him killing that trooper in Indiana will give us some new intel."

"And you want to interview me again to compare my testimony to anything you might find there?"

"Exactly. We could use the help. If you're up to it."

Jane took a deep breath and nodded. "Anything to help catch this guy. Freddie would want me to."

Conor stuck his head around the corner from the kitchen. "I made coffee. I had a feeling this could take a while."

After they all poured some coffee and doctored it to their tastes, Agent Hunt took Jane into the back bedroom to conduct his interview while Thomas got to hang out with Marshals Broz and Wildman in the living room.

Although these men were professionals, trained to watch what they said and revealed to others, Thomas had conducted enough interrogations and observed enough suspects to pick up on subtle behavior cues.

Levi Hunt might be buddy-buddy with Jane, but there was something eating at him. Maybe it was the guilt and frustration of not being able to solve his friend's murder.

Conor Wildman seemed to be a laid-back guy at first glance. In a way, although their physical looks were different, he reminded Thomas of his youngest son, Keir. He could be charming and friendly on the surface, but underneath, he was serious about his job, determined to do right by the witness entrusted to his care. Maybe the only reason he hadn't voiced the objections he was clearly stewing about was because he was deferring to his supervisor's authority.

As for Oscar Broz, if that guy interrupted another conversation to make or take a call with someone named Jackson, he was going to smack that phone out of his hand. A couple of the calls he'd overheard had been about stocking and prepping a new safe house in the KC area. Others had been about transferring funds to take care of whatever Jackson kept pressing him on. What the man lacked in manners he made up for in condescending rudeness. He only hoped Broz was better at the job of managing his projects and backing up his marshals on the front line than he was at public relations.

"I'm aware of the profile." Thomas didn't ruffle when Broz pointed out that his being a cop made him a potential target if Badge Man decided to come to Kansas City. "Every man here is wearing a badge, and your guy doesn't discriminate between agencies. You're as much a target as I am, Marshal. That doesn't mean we stop doing our jobs."

A snickering expression from Wildman earned a snort from Broz and another call to the mysterious Jackson.

When the boss left the room, Conor set his cold mug on the coffee table and leaned forward on the sofa to rest his elbows on his knees and finally talk some useful business with Thomas. "I've read everything I can find on this guy, and the FBI doesn't have much more than a profile to go on. How are we supposed to protect Jane when we don't know who we're watching out for?"

The young man definitely reminded him of Keir. Conor Wildman wanted to learn, and he wanted to be good. Thomas sat in the chair to Conor's right and matched his posture. "I think there are tells we can look for." He'd been giving this some thought since listening to Jane's story and reading up on the case himself. "I'm sure the FBI has looked into Badge Man's motives. He's either been the victim of police—the child of a cop or agent who abused him, a criminal who got roughed up more than he liked or set up by a crooked cop—or he's a cop wannabe who washed out of academy training or was relieved of duty somewhere. He's showing us he's better than we are."

"I thought maybe he'd lost someone he loved to a shooting and this was payback."

Another possibility. "The point is he knows a lot about cops and how they behave. He may even have a uniform. But he's not going to be interacting with other law enforcement unless he's ready to strike. We look for that kind of activity around Jane—a stranger who's armed and alert, probably hanging back and observing, maybe following in a car at a distance. He may be wearing sunglasses or a hat of some kind to mask his face." An inkling of something flashed through his brain, but it was such a ghost of a memory that the notion disappeared as quickly as it had tried to show itself. Not unlike the serial killer they were discussing. "If there are crowds, he'll blend in. If you're alone, check the shadows. This guy knows how to run a stakeout. If he comes to Kansas City, that's what he'll be doing."

The young man straightened. "I already advised Jane to vary her schedule and location so that if he is watching, it'll be hard to pin down an opportunity to get close to her."

"With his last kill only a few days out, he's not going to know the area." Levi Hunt strolled out of the hallway, his jacket slung over his shoulder and his sleeves rolled up. How intense had that interrogation gotten? "Since all his other victims were localized in the DC area, I doubt he's native to this part of the country." When he saw Thomas's questioning glance, he shrugged. "Emily, uh, Jane is taking a minute to freshen up."

Thomas balled his hands into fists. This meeting wasn't about old friends reconnecting and going over an eyewitness account. And Oscar Broz's foul mood had nothing to do with his health or administrative concerns, but with that hands-tied frustration that he wasn't being allowed to do his job the way he wanted. Thomas's knee twinged as he pushed to his feet a shade too quickly. "You're using her as bait, aren't you? You want him to come to KC."

"There haven't been indications that Badge Man knows she's still alive. Emily Davis's gravestone is right next to her husband's." The concerned agent looking out for a friend's widow disappeared as he rolled down his sleeves and buttoned his cuffs. This guy was all about getting the collar. "We're here because he's surfaced again. That pushes our investigation to the top of the list. And the fact that he's moving west probably means he's hunting for someone in particular." He glanced back down the hallway. "I can't think of who else it would be. The possibility that he's tracking her is too important to ignore."

Funny how Hunt didn't claim they were getting so close to catching Badge Man in DC that he'd fled his comfort zone to get away from the heat of the Bureau closing in on him. This guy had no shot at catching this killer without Jane's help. "And the attempts against her life?"

Marshal Broz pocketed his phone and rejoined the conversation. "We've done our research, Lieutenant. We know about your father's shooting and the dustup at your daughter's wedding last February. You or your father could very well have been the target, not Ms. Boyle. We feel that moving her now would only draw attention to her. A woman suddenly disappears, and people start asking questions."

"And this has nothing to do with conserving your resources?" Thomas challenged. Several of Broz's many phone calls to the mysterious Jackson had to do with allocating funds for various projects. "You're saving money by not putting more protection on Jane?"

"Secrecy protects as much as manpower." The older marshal defended his decision. "We don't want to spotlight her and bring this guy to Kansas City."

"What if he's already here?"

Conor stood, siding with Thomas on the stupidity of this plan. "For what it's worth, I recommended moving her." He glared at Broz and Hunt. "But I got outranked and outvoted."

A toilet flushed down the hallway, and water ran in a sink. Thomas felt a weight squeezing around his heart at what Agent Hunt was suggesting. Did Jane fully understand what the FBI was asking of her? "You're herding him straight to her—the one person who could look a killer in his face and put him away for good."

Agent Hunt didn't miss a beat. "I can't put him away if I can't catch him. I don't want any more blue blood on my hands."

If everyone's decision was made here, so was Thomas's. "Just so you know, I'm stepping up her protection level. I don't know how you run things in the marshals office, but at KCPD, we put the victim's well-being first."

Levi slipped his jacket on over his shoulders. "We appreciate the assistance from another agency in safeguarding our witness." Reasoning with this guy wouldn't make any difference. "But don't get in the way of my investigation. If I can arrest the man who murdered Fred Davis, I will. If I can save the lives of other cops, including you, Lieutenant, that's my goal. Giving Badge Man a name and putting him in prison on death row is the best thing I can do to ensure Emily's, er, Jane's safety. My partner and I will be actively pursuing the investigation in Indiana, but if we get any indication that our killer is headed to Kansas City—"

"Or is already here," Thomas repeated what his gut was telling him. "It wouldn't surprise me if you leaked her location."

"—we'll give you a heads-up, ASAP."

At least Oscar Broz was an equal opportunity sharer of his bad mood. "You'll call us first, Hunt. We're better equipped to move Ms. Boyle out of harm's way on short notice."

Levi nodded. "Obviously. Our star witness's safety is our top priority."

Jane reentered the living room before Thomas could give his doubtful opinion of Agent Hunt's plan. "I'll be fine here, with Conor and Thomas watching over me."

"You agreed to this?" Thomas prodded.

He knew Jane wasn't a stupid woman, so either she was so worn down by fear and flashbacks that she was willing to do this crazy stunt, in an attempt to make the nightmare stop—or she was a lot braver than even he'd given her credit for. The reproachful look she gave her late husband's friend as she moved past him to Thomas's side told him it was the latter. "Just do your job, Levi, and find him before he kills again."

"Or finds you," Conor pointed out.

Thomas slipped his hand around Jane's. "He won't."

Chapter Seven

"We have company." The sun was setting as Thomas drove past the car with rental plates parked in front of the house and pulled into the driveway. There were a lot of homes in this neighborhood, but he knew most of his neighbors and what they drove. Strange cars made him uneasy.

"Who is it? Another one of your offspring stopping by to babysit me?" Jane asked.

"I don't recognize the vehicle." He nodded to the black pickup parked in front of the second garage door. "That's Duff's truck. If he thought there was any kind of threat, he would have called. Still…" He'd called in favors from his sons and daughter and his former partner, Al, to keep another set of eyes on the place 24/7. He'd call in every damn favor anyone owed him if it meant keeping his family and Jane safe. With Badge Man's taste for killing men with badges, he wouldn't hesitate to take out any one of them to get to her. That's why he didn't intend to let anyone get close enough to Jane to even try. Thomas pulled his truck into the garage and closed the door behind them. "I want you to stay behind me when we walk into the house."

Laughter and the smells of Millie's home-cooked tomato sauce and garlic bread greeted them when Thomas pushed open the back door. But the kitchen was empty. Ruby's claws clicked on the hardwood floor as she charged down the front hallway to greet them. "Hey, girl." The big dog propped her paws on Thomas's chest and pushed her head into his hand for a welcome-home scratch around her muzzle and ears. "Glad someone's keeping an eye on things."

Ruby dropped to all fours and switched her attention to Jane for another round of petting. "Where is everyone?"

The laughter abruptly stopped and Duff strode into the kitchen from the front hallway. "Dad. I saw you drive up. I'll put Ruby out in the backyard and do a walk-around while you enjoy this blast from the past."

Thomas frowned at the cryptic teaser. "What?"

"Hey, Jane." Duff squeezed her arm before heading out into the garage. "Watch out. Grandpa's right in the middle of this party. You'll have a hard time getting him to do his physical therapy now."

"Party?" She seemed as bamboozled as Thomas was.

"Don't worry. We're taking the threat to you seriously. Watsons have each other's backs." Duff unhooked the strap over his Glock on his shoulder holster and palmed the weapon before scooting the dog out and closing the door behind him.

Thomas heard a trample of footsteps coming down the hall into the kitchen and instinctively moved between Jane and the approaching guests. "What the...?"

Whistles and catcalls led the way as two men, a tall one with blond hair silvering at the temples and a shorter one still wearing his brown hair military-short like their first day together at Whiteman Air Force Base, came in with their arms outstretched.

"There's the man we came to see," the short one cheered, crossing the kitchen to pull Thomas into a back-slapping hug. Murray "Mutt" Larkin stepped back for the taller man to trade hugs.

"What are you two yahoos doing here?" Thomas asked, pulling away from Jeff Fraser and letting the wary tension ease out of him. He pulled Jane forward to introduce her and let her know his old friends posed no threat. "Jane Boyle, I'd like you to meet some faces from my past. Jeff Fraser and Mutt Larkin. We served together in the air force over in England a few years back."

Jane shook each of their hands. "Mr. Larkin."

"Mutt," he corrected, flashing her the same goofy smile he'd always had. "On account of this handsome bulldog face." He thumbed over his shoulder to the taller man. "And because I always hung out with this guy."

"Mutt and Jeff?" Jane smiled and shook her head at the joke that was still pretty lame after all these years. "Nice to meet you both."

"Ma'am." Jeff took her hand as if he intended to kiss it, but nodded his head instead. He pointed to Thomas and then back to her. "Are you and Thomas an item?"

The yes on the tip of Thomas's tongue was drowned out by Jane's, "I work for him. I mean, we're friends, but I take care of Seamus."

Inside, Thomas's ego took a small hit. Yeah, it had to be the paternal thing that made her feel safe with him. They really needed to talk about that kiss that had happened at precinct headquarters if she intended to keep things at friend status between them. *He* really needed to put a tourniquet on his desire and those far-too-personal emotions that had been flowing through him from the first moment she'd turned into his arms, seeking his comfort and strength.

"Friends?" Jeff's follow-up comment seemed to confirm that there was no relationship happening here, despite the dangerous circumstances that had forced the two of them together. "I wondered if you'd ever be able to love anyone else after Mary. I remember the day I first saw her in the office at Lakenheath. That was the RAF base where we were stationed in England," he explained to Jane.

Thomas remembered the first day he'd met Mary Kilcannon, too. He wasn't sure if he believed in love at first sight, but he certainly believed in love at first conversation, because it had happened that fast for him and Mary over her secretarial desk that day. He'd been drawn to her Irish lilt and had stayed for her clever wit and kindness. Jeff went on, "When I saw that sable hair and heard that accent, I was lost." He clapped Thomas on the shoulder. "It's the quiet ones you have to watch out for. I didn't realize how fast a worker you were, Watson. You stole Mary right out from under my nose."

Mutt laughed and butted shoulders with Jeff. "You can't lose what you never had, my friend. You and I were in that office a whole month before Thomas transferred in. We all had a crush on Mary. But you went out with her one time. So did I. You had your chance."

Jeff held up one hand, conceding the point before he grinned. "I remember Mary's big brother, Ian, wasn't too happy his sister was dating any of us Americans."

Marrying her within a month and taking her away to the US hadn't been popular with the Kilcannons, either. The last time Thomas had seen Ian Kilcannon had been at Mary's funeral. Ian and Mary's parents still exchanged Christmas cards during the holidays, and sent birthday mementos to Duff, Niall, Keir and Olivia. But Thomas knew there would probably always be some blame on him for taking their daughter away, never to return.

Remembering that his promise to Jane was more important than his hormones, disappointments or a trip down memory lane, Thomas ushered his buddies back toward the living room and the front door. "It's not the best time for a surprise visit right now. I'm working a case."

"I can see you're still being the tough guy." Jeff nodded toward the gauze bandage on Thomas's forearm, exposed by the edge of his rolled-up sleeve. "That hurt much?"

The bullet graze from the drive-by shooting was healing to the point that it was more itchy than achy. But he really didn't want to get into what the injury was and how it had happened. He, Mutt and Jeff had once solved a lot of cases together in the OSI. He had a feeling if they heard he was working on a more personal investigation that they'd want to jump in and help for old times' sake. And didn't he already have plenty of people he needed to look out for right now? "Are you two in town early for the reunion?"

"I flew in today from Seattle. Jeff picked me up at the airport. I thought maybe we could go get some drinks," Mutt suggested. "The three of us, like we did back at Whiteman and Lakenheath."

Millie and Seamus had joined them at the kitchen island by the time they reached it. "I asked them to stay for dinner instead," Millie announced. "Now that you and Jane are home, I'll dish it up." She pulled her apron off one of the stools at the island and tied it around her waist. She stopped beside Thomas and whispered, "I thought that'd be safer than you or Jane going out in public someplace?"

It seemed everyone was in on Jane's protection detail. Thomas leaned over to press a kiss to her round cheek. "Thanks, Millie."

The older woman raised her voice to quiet the rowdies in the room. "Everybody get cleaned up and find a spot at the table."

After the delicious meal with almost constant talking as Mutt and Jeff caught Thomas up on their families and jobs, Jane pushed her chair away from the table. She offered Seamus a wry smile. "It's late. It's been a long day. And I know an exhausted patient when I see one. Let's get you to bed."

Seamus had grown quiet over the course of the meal. Not any quieter than Jane had been throughout the whole course of lasagna, ice-cream sundaes and coffee. At least she hadn't spent the meal reading texts that stamped a look of anxiety on her face. Of course, now that he was in the loop on what she was dealing with as a witness in the US Marshals program, Thomas was a lot less put off by the alerts and updates she received from Conor Wildman. Now he'd worry if she got a text, although Wildman had promised to copy him on any developments in Levi Hunt's investigation or any sightings of a man fitting Badge Man's description.

Still, his father was a social animal by nature, and being reminded that his stamina wasn't what it had been before the stroke made him sit up straight and joke. "I gwown man. I only go to bed when pwetty lady involved."

Mutt, Jeff and Duff laughed. Millie blushed and bustled away to get the coffeepot to refill their cups. Jane propped her hands on her hips. "I'm not pretty enough for you? I'm taking you to bed now, old man, so move it."

Her teasing threat was met with a chorus of oohs and whistles. Seamus grinned, happy to have the last word. "Now doesn't dat tound interesting."

"Need any help?" Thomas offered as Jane fetched Seamus's walker and braced a hand under his elbow to help him stand.

Jane's gaze snapped to the head of the table where Thomas sat. "I've got this."

She'd had it since day one when she'd moved into the house and taken point on Seamus's recovery. She'd made it clear that she was the boss of Seamus's care, and that she was perfectly capable of handling whatever needed to be done—physically, mentally or emotionally. She looked as surprised to hear the words come out of Thomas's mouth as he'd been to say them. So why had he made the offer? Buying himself a few seconds to think, he reached down to scratch the soft fur on Ruby's warm head as the dog sat beside his chair, patiently hoping for an ice-cream dish to lick. Probably because, as much as he enjoyed Mutt and Jeff's company, and enjoyed catching up with his air force buddies, he'd rather be spending time alone with Jane. He'd rather be coming up with a plan for her protection detail that would allow her to lead as normal a life as possible without risking her safety, or anyone else's, more than necessary.

Or maybe he wanted that time alone with her so he could clarify this relationship that was happening between them. If he had an option, he wasn't voting for father figure when too many of his thoughts lately had dealt with kissing Jane again. Kissing a lot of different places on her body, learning her curves and sensitive places as well as he knew his own randy urges to possess her in every way a man could. But if that authority figure was what she needed from him, then he'd rein in his inner young man's desire to bury himself inside her and be that paternal safety net she craved. But if she didn't—if there was a chance she could look at him and see a man, a mate, a regular, eligible guy who was falling in love with her—then he wanted to give that relationship a chance.

Once Badge Man was captured and Jane was safe.

Thomas was a patient man. He'd be whatever Jane *needed* him to be. He just prayed that he could keep her alive long enough for him to be what she wanted.

"G'night, boys. Good to tee you again. Jane is right, as usual. De old man *is* tired." Seamus leaned heavily on Jane's arm until he felt secure with his balance on the walker and took a step on his own. When Millie returned with the coffee, Seamus pulled his shoulders back and shook off Jane's guiding hand. "G'night, Millie."

"Good night, Seamus." Millie set the carafe down beside Thomas without pouring anyone a cup. "Scrambled eggs with ham and cheese tomorrow for breakfast?"

"Tounds good."

Well, hell's bells. What was that little interchange all about? Had his dad just puffed up like a young stud to hide his pain and fatigue in front of Millie? And had she stopped to put on a fresh coat of lipstick while she'd been in the kitchen? Thomas picked up the coffee to pour his own refill. Maybe he wasn't in control of anything going on around this house anymore.

Leaving Duff and the dog to help Millie clear the table and clean up the kitchen while Jane followed Seamus to his room and closed the door, Thomas walked Mutt and Jeff to the front door.

"You'll be at the big party this weekend, right?" While Jeff thanked Millie for the dinner, Mutt took Thomas aside and whispered, "I thought stopping by here tonight would throw him off the trail of the surprise birthday party at the reunion. I need you there to back me up when Jeff gets a snootful and tries to deck me for puttin' one over on him."

"I'll do my best to get there." Thomas shook Mutt's hand.

"Bring your girlfriend. There'll be dancing, you know. She's sweet. Well, sweet-looking, anyway. A little on the bossy side, if you ask me. Your dad puts up with that?"

"He respects it." Thomas was certain of that, at least. "We all do."

Jeff clapped him on the shoulder as he rejoined them. "You take care of this family, Thomas. You're a lucky man."

"I know it. Good night." Thomas waited out on the front porch until his air force buddies got into Jeff's car and drove away.

Once the space had cleared, he looked across the street to see Al Junkert sitting behind the wheel of his sporty black Jeep. Illuminated by a halo of light from the streetlamp in front of the car, Al saluted him. Through thick and thin, that man had always had his back. He owed Al a lot more than a chilly night sitting out in his car like their old stakeout days before his partner had gone to graduate school to get his MBA, and Thomas had kicked himself upstairs into training and investigative consultations with the department.

He pushed open the front door and yelled back to the kitchen. "Hey, Millie? We got any coffee left?" A few minutes later, Thomas was carrying a travel mug of coffee out to Al along with a wrapped slice of garlic bread.

"Hey, Tommy boy."

Thomas scanned up and down the street, seeing nothing and no one out of place as he strolled across and presented the snack to his friend. "It's not a doughnut, but I thought you might appreciate a little home cooking."

"Millie's homemade bread?" Al slipped the mug into the cup holder beside him and took a big bite of the garlic cheese bread. "Yum. I swear to God if that woman was twenty years younger, I'd marry her. Just for her cookin'."

"I think you might have some competition there." He turned to lean against the door frame beside Al's open window.

"How so? Millie got herself a beau after all these years?"

"I think my dad was hittin' on her tonight."

Al laughed. "Well, the two of them have been living together ever since Mary's death. I remember you had to build that extension on the back of the house when they moved in—you, four kids, Millie and Grandpa all squished into four bedrooms upstairs was pure chaos. And now they're downstairs together. Unchaperoned. You don't suppose they've ever sneaked across the hall to visit each other at night, do you?"

Only he did that with Jane. But Thomas came up

with a more appropriate response for his friend. "Eww. That's my dad you're talking about."

Al laughed. "You can fall in love at any age."

Thomas reached in and thumped him on the shoulder. "You've had plenty of practice doing that, haven't you?"

"I loved every one of my wives when I married them. Minus the alimony, in some way or another, I still do." Al took a couple of swallows of coffee before looking up at Thomas again.

Al stuffed the last of the bread into his mouth and brushed off his hands before patting Thomas's arm where it rested on the edge of the open window. "It's been twenty years you've been alone. Don't you ever think about taking the plunge and falling in love again?"

Thomas nodded to his neighbor, who rolled his trash can out to the curb for tomorrow morning's pickup. The rest of the block seemed pretty quiet, with cars parked along the sidewalks and in driveways on either side of the street as the suburban neighborhood turned in for the night. "Yeah. I haven't always been ready to let someone else into my heart. But now, if the right woman comes along…"

"I've seen you with Jane. She's not the right woman?"

Thomas straightened, patting Al's shoulder as he pulled away from the car. His feelings for Jane were too new, too complicated, to share, even with his former partner. "It's got to be mutual, my friend, for anything to happen. Hey, if Duff doesn't come relieve you at midnight, text me and I'll give him a call and wake him up."

"But you do care for her." Al wasn't fooled by Thomas's nonchalant dismissal of his feelings for Jane. "I mean, isn't that why you've got one of us sittin' here around the clock, helping you keep an eye on things?"

Chapter Eight

Thomas's thigh protested every step as he and Ruby climbed the stairs after one last outing in the backyard.

His knee joined the complaining muscles and frayed nerve endings as he slowed his pace near the second-floor landing. Just when his thoughts strayed to the memory of Jane's strong fingers digging the knots out of his injured leg the way she had that morning, the dog squealed with excitement and darted up the last few steps before disappearing around the corner. As if Ruby might actually go after an intruder, Thomas touched the gun at his hip, although he was 99.9 percent sure of Ruby's target.

When he rounded the railing at the top, he was smacked by a wagging tail and greeted with an, "I wuv you, too." Jane was in those sweet pink pajamas again, kneeling down to pet Ruby while the eager dog licked her chin.

Crossing his arms over his chest, Thomas leaned against the wall beside the bedroom that Niall and Keir had shared as boys. "She'll get down if you tell her to. You don't have to let her lick your face."

Jane put up a hand to stave off the marauding tongue and urged Ruby down to the floor for a tummy rub. "It's nice to have someone around who's always happy to see you. Even if it's only been a couple of hours since we were separated."

The light seeping in from the streetlamp outside emphasized the shadows beneath Jane's eyes. He already knew the answer, but he asked, anyway. "I don't suppose it'd be easy for you to have a pet in WITSEC."

"No." She encouraged Ruby's spoiled-rottenness with some nonsense chatter that made the dog's tail wag. "I can't imagine having to leave someone I loved behind if I had an emergency evac situation. The marshals office wouldn't be as concerned about my pet as I would be."

He still wasn't convinced that Marshal Wildman and his boss, Oscar Broz, were properly concerned with Jane's safety and well-being, either. "Did you manage to get any sleep over these last two hours? Or have you been pacing the hallway again?"

She confirmed his suspicion by not answering. "You're up late. Is everything secure?"

"Yes. The house is locked up tight. Duff is watching out front. Keir will relieve him in the morning. I've arranged for somebody to be out there around the clock, and I, or someone I trust, will be inside with you." He pointed to the big Lab with her paws in the air and her tummy exposed. "Along with the guard dog there. At least she'll make some noise if somebody tries to come into the house."

"Right before she rolls over on her back and asks the intruder to scratch her belly." Jane patted Ruby's tummy one last time before pushing to her feet. She tugged down her little pink T-shirt, but it instantly sprang back to reveal that tiny quarter inch of creamy skin that made things leap with interest behind the zipper of Thomas's jeans. "Your friends Mutt and Jeff were a pair of characters, like little boys stuck in grown men's bodies. I'll bet you were the Three Musketeers back when you went into the air force together."

"We were close. Dead serious when it came to getting our work done, but I suppose we did have a few adventures after hours. After training at Whiteman and shipping over to Lakenheath, our unit was pretty tight."

"Jeff said you were all OSI. What's that?"

When she hugged her arms around her middle and rubbed her hand above the scab that had formed on her elbow to warm herself, Thomas got busy shooing Ruby into his bedroom and distracting the dog with a chew toy before he acted on the urge to take Jane into his arms again. "Office of Special Investigations. It's like NCIS for the air force. We were moving around a lot of nukes back then, training the Brits in laser-guided technology. So security was pretty tight. We checked out a lot of suspicious or criminal activity—both civilians messing with our people, and our people getting into trouble off base. Our job was to keep the people on the base and in the air safe."

Jane was huddled in his doorway when he turned back to the hallway. "Is that where you first got into law enforcement?"

"Trained as an MP over at Whiteman. I guess I don't know how to do anything else." He tapped his torn-up thigh. "Even after this. I thought that wreck would end my career. Hell, I suppose it could have ended my life. But then I found other ways to be a cop—to mentor younger detectives, teach them skills I've learned over the years."

"You're very good at what you do. I can see it in the way everyone at the precinct respects you and listens to what you have to say. And the way so many of your friends and family are willing to step up and help you now." That frown mark between her eyebrows appeared. "I don't know what happened to me this morning—a panic attack, I guess. Levi seemed to think that van had more to do with you and Seamus than with me and my past. Logically, I know that Badge Man's MO isn't anything like a high-speed car chase. And he didn't have a gun that night he attacked Freddie and me. Didn't stop me from freaking out. Usually, I can keep it together. I'm stronger than that."

"I know you are." Thomas crossed the room, stopping close enough to her that he could smell the lingering scent of citrus shampoo in her damp hair. He cupped her cheek, and though she initially tensed at his touch, she breathed out a sigh and turned her face into the palm of his hand. He gently pressed the pad of his thumb to that dimple before smoothing it away. "You were scared, exhausted. We'll get ahead of this thing."

"I've never been kissed out of an episode before," she confessed. "Once I remembered where I was—who I was with—I didn't want to stop kissing you. Kind of overstepped the boundaries of our professional relationship, didn't I?"

"I was overstepping right along with you."

"I won't let it happen again."

The kiss or the PTSD episode? The possibility that she could deny either of them worried him. Did she regret that kiss? He didn't. Maybe for propriety's sake, he should. But he couldn't bring himself to regret getting closer to this brave, beautiful woman. As for any kind of flashback or panic attack—she shouldn't apologize for that, not with what she'd been through with the serial killer who'd murdered her husband.

"If it does, we'll deal with it."

What was it about quiet conversations in the shadows of a quiet house that felt so private and intimate? As if they were sharing their darkest secrets? Making solemn vows? But then, he must be the only one feeling the charged energy simmering between them, because Jane pulled away to walk back to her bedroom door. "I know you're upset with me after my meeting with Agent Hunt. All that Levi asked was that I not go to a safe house. Give him a chance to capture Badge Man."

"I think Hunt's a better salesman than he is an agent. He's more interested in his case than he is you." Thomas followed her to her door. "You said no one in your husband's DC office knew you'd been relocated to Kansas City. Did Hunt tell you how he found out?"

"He has a contact within the US Marshals Office. Once Badge Man killed that officer in Indiana, he said it was a courtesy to alert them to the potential threat to one of their projects." Jane rolled her neck as if the muscles were cramping there. "Trading information like that isn't supposed to happen, is it?"

"Not typically. Unless it's a joint operation. Did he say that it was?" Jane shook her head, stirring her damp hair off her shoulders. The possibilities were grim. If it wasn't out-and-out incompetence that had let her info slip into Hunt's hands, then there was a conspiracy going on—either on Hunt's team or within the marshals office. And both possibilities were too close to Jane for his liking. "Did he say who his contact was?"

"No. I assumed it was Oscar Broz. He seemed to

be making all the arrangements for Levi to interview me." He saw the goose bumps prickle along her arms before she faced him. He wished he had his jacket to put around her shoulders again. No, he wished he had the right to put his arms around her and hold her until she could chase away all those *"see Jane die"* scenarios running through her head. "Do you think anyone else could find me? Like if they were tailing Levi or Broz? I haven't seen anyone with heterochromia, so Badge Man can't be that close to me. Unless he's wearing tinted contacts to mask the condition." She was smart enough to think of the possibilities. But that meant she also knew all the other reasons to be scared for her future. "I'll never see this guy coming, will I? He's probably already insinuated himself into my life somewhere, and I don't know it. He works at the hospital or one of the businesses I frequent. Maybe I should go back to my house and have Conor stay with me."

"Conor is one man. I've got an army lined up to protect you here."

"But that army is your family, your friends—the people you love." She tilted her chin up at a determined angle, but that worried frown had returned. "I care about your family, too. It was wrong of me to involve you, to put your and their lives at risk."

He balled his hands into fists at his sides to keep from reaching for her. "Once I figured out the kind of trouble you were in, nothing could have stopped me from becoming involved."

"You're a good man, Thomas. And a better friend than I deserve. You have your own issues to deal with without dumping mine on top of them. 'Thank you' seems a little inadequate. But thank you." It might have been a trick of the dim light and shadows, but he thought he saw her uncurl her fingers to reach for him, but she circled her arms around her waist and hugged herself instead. "Good night."

"Good night, Jane."

Her eyes glimmered like pale gold as she held his gaze for several moments. But then she blinked and closed the door.

Thomas's breath squeezed in his chest as he looked at the oak barrier she'd isolated herself behind. In all his days, he'd never known anyone as good at being alone as Jane Boyle. He turned toward his own bedroom door. She shouldn't have to be strong enough to cope with all this mess on her own. While he admired that kind of strength, that stoic courage didn't sit well with him. That woman needed comfort, protection, love. And damn it, he wanted to be the one to… His chest squeezed even harder.

You know what you need to do, Watson.

Once the decision was made, he inhaled a deep, unfettered breath and marched into his room.

"Get up, dog." Ruby raised her head, then popped to her feet. "I need backup, and you're it." He grabbed the dog's bed and chew toy, clicked his tongue against his teeth for the mutt to follow, and Ruby eagerly trotted along behind him. Thomas knocked twice on Jane's door and pushed it open.

She was sitting up in bed, sketching something in a small notebook. "What are you—"

"Scoot over." He set the dog bed near the wall beside the door and tossed the toy into the middle of it, pointing to Ruby to take her place for the night. He plucked the notebook from Jane's hands and looked at the scribbling of stars in some kind of formation he didn't recognize, surrounded by words and phrases he did. She was trying to figure out the damn case—trying to figure out how to survive. On her own.

Brown/Ice Blue. Contact lenses? Glasses?

5'10" Strong. STRONG. Where does he carry cord? Didn't see.

Taser. Knife.

Don't take no for an answer. Never submit to failure.

See him before he sees you.

Andromeda?????

"Who's Andromeda?"

She climbed up onto her knees to snatch it back. While she closed the notebook, he toed off his shoes. "Not who. What," she answered. "It's my WITSEC code word, in case my security is compromised and I need Conor to take me to a safe house, or he's alerting me." She watched him pull off his belt and holster. "What are you doing?"

"And 'Never submit to failure'?" He rolled up his belt and set it and his Glock on the table beneath her lamp. "Words to live by?"

"More like words to die by." He drilled her with a glare, demanding an explanation for that glib riff of sarcasm. She pulled the covers up over her lap and hugged her knees to her chest. "It's part of the tattoo on Badge Man's neck. I want all the details to be fresh in my mind, so I at least have a chance to see him before he k…finds me."

Kills me. That's what she'd been thinking. *Before he kills me.* Did she believe that was the only way this was going to end? His chest was hurting again.

Thomas pried the notebook from her hands and

tucked it into the drawer of the bedside table. "That's the last thing you need to be reading before you go to sleep tonight."

"Who says I'm going to sleep?"

"Scoot over."

"Thomas, you shouldn't be here."

"And you shouldn't be playing bait for a serial killer. You shouldn't have to be afraid." Before she could slide out from under the covers on the opposite side, he was climbing onto her bed, lying on top of the quilt and gathering her into his arms. "How long will it take you to fall asleep tonight?"

The quilt tangled between them as she squirmed. "I don't know."

"Are you even planning on trying to sleep? Or will you be up roaming the halls again?"

She pushed at his chest and squiggled in his grasp. "I'm sorry if my insomnia disturbs—"

"Frankly, Ruby and I won't be sleeping at all, worrying if you're in here facing the nightmare of what happened three years ago. Reliving what happened Friday night and this morning. It's fresh for you all over again. You got scared. Rightly so. I've seen your scars. I've seen pictures of what Badge Man does to his victims, and I know you saw it firsthand. I'd have been seriously concerned if you hadn't reacted. Dad said you did some pretty crazy driving to stay ahead of that guy, and though you seem to think it's a weakness, you went and got help when you needed it. You handled it the smartest way you could under the circumstances. Nobody got hurt. That's always a good thing."

Jane stopped fighting him halfway through the lecture. He was more aware than he should be of her hands resting against his chest, of his thigh thrown over hers. Even with his beat-up nerves and a quilt between them, he could feel the sleek, warm curves of her body pinned against him. She wasn't fighting to get away anymore. Her fingers had curled into the cotton of his faded gray KCPD T-shirt, and her hips had gone still against his.

And that smile, on lips that didn't smile often enough to suit him, might well be the most beautiful thing he'd ever seen. "Ruby worries about me?"

Making her smile like that made him feel whole and powerful and potent.

Thomas brushed a satiny fall of hair off her cheek and tucked it behind her ear. "She loses a lot of sleep over you."

"Does she now."

"Yes."

Jane was stretching up to meet him as he lowered his mouth to claim hers. Her lips parted, welcoming his hungry foray over every soft, silky centimeter of that smile. She scraped her palm over the stubble of his jaw and slid her arm behind his neck, running her fingers through his short hair and kneading his scalp. The tips of her breasts rubbed against him and pearled, branding his chest. He turned his attention to her sculptured cheekbone, the soft hollow underneath. He nibbled his way along the line of her jaw to the warm beat of her pulse beneath her ear. While he buried his nose in the citrusy clean scent of her hair, her teeth gently closed over the point of his chin, igniting a raw heat inside him.

Her clever, confident hands roamed at will over his hair and face and neck and shoulders. And when one slipped beneath the cotton of his shirt to palm the flat of his stomach, his muscles jumped, each cell eagerly volunteering to meet her touch as she explored his chest and flank. Her hips twisted between his thighs, rubbing against his swelling heat, triggering a whole new kind of want inside him. Thomas tugged at the covers, needing to erase the barriers between them. He hooked his foot behind her knees and palmed her bottom, squeezing and pulling her into the helpless thrust of his hips. Reclaiming her mouth, he rolled her back onto the bed, partially covering her body with his weight. She kissed his neck, beneath his jaw, the corner of his mouth, before her fingers tangled in his hair and guided his mouth back to hers.

Thomas willingly accepted the command, drinking his fill of the passion erupting between them. He fought with the quilt and the sheet and the elastic waistband of her pajamas until he could get his hand inside to grab a handful of her smooth, round bottom and angle her hips into his stiff arousal. She dug her fingers into his back and mewled in her throat as if she was as frustrated by the layers of material between them as he was.

Drawn to the sexy purr, Thomas's lips skidded over the tip of her chin to capture the sound of mutual desire. He touched the small knot of puckered skin and a warning bell went off inside his head. By the time he reached the second scar and pressed the gentlest of kisses there, he knew his timing was off. He must be sorely out of practice to think ravishing Jane was the smartest way to keep her safe.

Exhaling a bone-deep sigh filled with the longing and regret that battered at his rusty emotions, he lifted his head and rolled back onto his side. He propped himself up on one elbow, willing the need stretching his shorts and jeans to defer to common sense. He pulled her pajamas back into place and tugged the covers over her.

"Thomas?" Her eyes were dark with desire, almost completely green as she looked up at him. "Did the scars bother you?"

"No." It irritated him for her to even consider that he didn't think she was beautiful. "Do mine bother you?"

"No."

Her hand cruised over his hip toward his mangled leg, as if to prove her point. Reminding himself that he was trying to do the right thing here, he grabbed the straying temptation and brought her fingers up to his lips to kiss each one before splaying them over his heart. "As much as I'd like to finish this right now, you need your sleep."

Jane shifted onto her side, mirroring his position. She searched his face before reaching up to smooth down the wayward spikes of his hair. "This scares me—you and me."

"Haven't you got enough to be scared about?"

"Thomas, I never thought I'd have feelings for another man after Freddie." She slid her fingers through his hair one last time before an earnest frown dimpled her smooth skin. "Given everything that's happening, I don't think I'm the best choice for you—for any man. Not until this is over. And it may never be over."

He leaned in to kiss the frown mark, gentling the spot until the tension eased beneath his lips. "Stop thinking and go to sleep."

She closed the few inches that separated them to rest her cheek against his shoulder. "Thank you for everything today. Will you stay with me?"

"I thought I made that decision clear."

"Maybe instead of barging in and telling me, I wanted to ask you."

"Why didn't you?"

"I wasn't sure you'd say yes." Thomas's pulse quieted as he listened to the hushed tone of her voice.

"Yes. My answer is yes."

"I didn't ask yet."

Thomas growled. Was she teasing him with this battle of he said-she said?

"I'm just talking about sleep," she explained. "You're right. I'd love to see where this chemistry between us leads, too. But the timing is off. We both need our rest so we can do our jobs and stay alert to our surroundings. But I seem to be cold a lot lately. I'd appreciate something warm to cuddle up against."

"Fine. I'll be your furnace." He rolled onto his back, slipping his arm behind her and snugging her to his side. "We'll lie here for a while until you get warmed up. I can even get Ruby up here if you're still cold."

"I think you can handle the job." He held himself still until she found a comfortable position to rest her arm across his stomach, and then she burrowed into him. "Did that hurt your feelings when I told Mutt and Jeff we were just friends?"

"Don't worry about it."

"So it did. I'm sorry. I could tell they thought we were a couple. I didn't want to embarrass you."

Thomas scoffed at the notion. "Why would that embarrass *me*? I'm the one who's twenty years older than you. If it was true, they'd think I was a lucky son of a gun, and that you were stuck with me."

She braced her hand against his chest and pushed herself up onto her elbow beside him. He'd seen that chiding look in her eyes before when his dad said or did something she didn't agree with. "No woman would ever be *stuck* with you. There's not that big an age gap between us. And if there was, it wouldn't matter. Not to me. You're a grown man and I'm a grown woman. We both know how relationships work. Whatever we feel for each other..." He held his breath, waiting for her to finish that sentence. She changed course instead, settling back down beside him. "You're already doing me this huge favor. I think things are too new between us to identify yet. I mean, this morning I was a crazy lady, and tonight you're in my bed. There's that whole boss-employee relationship I'm supposed to respect that's clearly gone out the window, and I don't even know if you still have feelings for your wife."

Why did tonight's conversations all seem to come back to his late wife? "Mary's been gone twenty years."

"There's no timeline for grief. I lost a husband—I know. Most days I'm okay. I treasure all the laughs we shared, and how thoughtful he was. I've closed that chapter of my life and moved on. I've had to. But sometimes, I miss the plans we made that never came to fruition. Every now and then something completely unexpected will trigger a memory of Freddie, and his loss will feel fresh all over again." She fell silent for a few moments, as if one of those memories had just hit her. But then she quietly added, "Mary's picture is over the mantel in the living room. And you still have a picture of you and Mary on your wedding day in your bedroom." Apparently, being still didn't come easily for Jane. She pushed herself up again to find his gaze in the lamplight. "I wasn't spying. Millie asks me to bring your laundry up with mine so she doesn't have to do the stairs."

Thomas sifted his fingers into the fall of dark honey hair that brushed his chest. "The pictures are for my children. I always want them to know how much Mary loved them, and that her spirit will always be with them. As for me…" How did he feel about Mary now? He'd been lucky to have her in his life for even a short time. "There's a part of me that will always love her. I think of her when I see her blue eyes in Keir, her love of books in Niall, in Duff's big stubborn heart. And Olivia's a dead ringer for her mama. I was shell-shocked when Mary died. I grieved for her. I was angry. Afraid about raising my kids on my own and being enough for them." He tucked her back to his side, guiding her cheek to the pillow of his shoulder. "I made sure the men who killed Mary were arrested, and they will stay in prison for the rest of their lives. But I've put her to rest. I'm not stuck in the past if that's what you're asking. I'm not looking to replace her. If love comes around again, with the right woman, I'd be ready for it."

"Is there a woman, Thomas? Maybe you shouldn't be in bed with me. Maybe I shouldn't even be in this house with you."

When she started to pull her arm from his waist, he caught her hand to hold it in place and keep her beside him. "Go to sleep, Janie. There's no other woman."

And hell. There wasn't. Jane was the first woman to jump-start his heart since he lost Mary. It wasn't all about the sexual attraction that hummed through his blood every time he saw her or touched her or talked to her. It wasn't just about her needing him—needing a cop, needing his badge and experience to allay her fears and have her back. He was more alive arguing with this woman, kissing this woman, loving this woman, than he'd been with anyone else in years. He'd been dead inside, his feelings dormant. Like some little girl's fairy tale, he'd been asleep until that first day at the hospital when Jane had challenged his authority over Seamus and she'd awakened his heart. No other woman besides Mary had ever possessed that kind of magic power over him.

Maybe he'd be smart to think this through before he admitted anything like that, though.

"Is there another man?" He should have asked that sooner. "Even with those baggy clothes and high collars you hide behind most of the time, you're a pretty woman and I know they're looking."

"Right." She snorted against his chest. "Have you ever seen me go out on a date? Men aren't comfortable around me. Most of the time I know what needs to be done so I take care of things. A lot of people interpret that take-charge personality as being, well, bitchy."

"Jane—"

"Don't think I haven't heard your sons refer to me as Battle-Ax Boyle." Before he could protest, he felt her mouth soften into a smile against him. "And don't go calling any of them to chew them out on my behalf, either. Once I established myself as a member of this household, Duff, Niall and Keir treated me with nothing but respect."

Thomas was glad to hear that. But he still wasn't happy to hear her describe herself as being some kind of witch who frightened men away. For all her strength, he was learning that there was an equal degree of vulnerability in her. Maybe that was why she insisted on being so stubbornly independent. "For the record, I'm not intimidated by you."

Her arm tightened around him in a hug. "Clearly. Or you wouldn't be here. Most men turn away when I put on my back-off-and-leave-me-alone armor. But not Thomas Watson. He doesn't scare easily. That's one of the things I...like...about you." She pulled her hand back between them, almost curling herself into a ball beside him, as though thinking she'd said the wrong thing or revealed too much. The teasing energy left her voice. "The only other man in my life is your father."

Like. Right. This was just a friendship clouded by fear and fatigue. She wasn't going to admit to anything like love, and he wasn't going to force her to turn a little bit of lust and gratitude into something more. "Dad doesn't count. I think he's sweet on Millie."

"He is. But he doesn't think he's the right man for her. With his injury and age, he doesn't feel like he could make a relationship work."

Yeah, there was a lot of that going around. A deep breath eased in and out of Thomas's tight chest.

"I doubt I'll get much sleep tonight," she went on. "It's already late and you've taken on the extra job of watching me, so you must be tired. If you want to go back to your room, I understand."

He tightened his arm behind her back, wishing he could squeeze the tension out of her body. "I'm not going anywhere."

But she was still trying to make light of the intimacy of their conversation—and of the deeper revelations that weren't being shared, but that hung in the shadows around them. "I can take care of myself, you know. Insomnia is a classic symptom of PTSD. If the nightmares come or I hear something outside and get scared, or my thoughts are going ninety miles an hour and I have to get up, I will deal with it. I'll try not to wake you. I'll go out in the hall to pace so you and Ruby can still get your rest."

"Will you stop talking and relax? Do an old man a favor and go to sleep. I'm not leaving you. You need me—I'm here. You're safe."

Jane nodded, perhaps finally believing him. "You're not an old man," she murmured, snuggling into his side. A big yawn turned her next words into a mumble that sounded a little like, "Too sexy for cats." Since Ruby wouldn't tolerate a feline in the house, he suspected she'd paid him a very nice compliment.

Thomas smiled and pressed a kiss to her citrus-scented hair.

She was asleep before he reached over to turn out the light.

THE UNHAPPY MAN smiled as he watched the light go out in the upstairs bedroom window.

Even from this distance, sitting in his dark car, blending in with all the other vehicles parked along the street, he had a pretty good idea of the scene playing out in Thomas Watson's house. He'd gotten a glimpse of the shadows moving through the hallway at the top of the stairs—Thomas's big frame and the woman's shorter, slighter silhouette. They'd been standing awfully close to each other.

Had they gone to bed together? Was Thomas defiling his wife's memory with that worthless substitute even now?

His blood burned in his veins. His knuckles turned

white on the steering wheel and he felt like he could break it in two beneath his hands.

Thomas didn't deserve to get laid. He didn't deserve to find happiness with another woman. Mary Kilcannon should have been his. He'd loved her in a way Thomas never had. Mary never would have died so senselessly on *his* watch. Not if she'd been his.

Thomas had to pay for taking Mary from his life.

He'd ruined the wedding of Thomas's daughter.

He'd put Thomas's father in the hospital, made sure Thomas and his sons and daughter would never rest easy because they didn't know where the threat to their family was coming from.

Now he wanted to break Thomas's heart the way his old friend had once broken his. There were only a few days more until the anniversary of Mary's death. And then Thomas's punishment would end.

Thomas Watson would end. Along with that little tramp he had the hots for.

He opened his grip on the steering wheel and flexed his fingers, taking in several deep breaths to cool his vengeful temper back to rational thought. He relived the fun he'd had earlier yesterday morning, playing dress-up and driving like he was on a NASCAR track. He'd enjoyed it so much more than hiring someone else to do the job for him. At first, he'd been concerned about someone recognizing him and spoiling his retribution. He'd been content to watch the Watsons' lives implode from a distance.

But now he realized he'd been cheating himself out of the rush of inflicting the pain himself. He'd really put the fear of death into that woman. Maybe the old man, too. They'd run straight to Thomas for help. Watson knew his family was under attack now, and the things he cared about could be taken from him. Good. The more Thomas suffered, the more elated he felt. Vindication for Mary's murder would soon be...

Wait. Something was happening. A light briefly flashed as a vehicle door opened and closed in the Watsons' driveway. Duff, Thomas's oldest son, was climbing out of his truck. Duff was keeping watch over the house through the wee hours of the morning, just like him. Only, he was content to sit and observe whereas Duff was taking action. Why? Was there a threat? For such a big, overbuilt version of his father, Duff moved with surprising stealth through the darkness. The Unhappy Man watched in his side-view mirror as the brawny detective crossed the street and jogged about half a block, pulling out his flashlight and the gun holstered beneath his arm.

What had caught the other man's attention?

The Unhappy Man adjusted his rearview mirror for a better look, peering through the disorienting light cast by a streetlamp between his position and Duff's. Now the detective was circling a small, dirty pickup truck. Once Duff seemed certain the vehicle was empty, he holstered his weapon and pulled out his phone, snapping a couple of photos of the pickup and plates before punching in a number.

He was calling in an unfamiliar vehicle, no doubt having someone run plates to identify the owner. The Unhappy Man eased back into his seat, expecting no less from a family of experienced law enforcement officers. Fortunately, his own vehicle wouldn't draw any undue attention.

A glimpse of movement off to the right captured his

attention. Something had shaken the neighbor's hedge across the street from Thomas's house. But there was barely enough breeze to stir the fading leaves, much less move an entire bush.

And then he saw the dark figure, moving from one shadow to the next, clinging to the next house as he moved in the direction opposite of Duff's location.

Well, now, wasn't that an interesting development? He wasn't the only one staking out the Watson house.

A motion-detector light came on over the next garage, and the man quickly ducked down behind a pair of garbage cans. But not before the Unhappy Man caught a glimpse of the lurker's face and smiled in recognition. That man had been at the restaurant the night of the drive-by shooting. Wearing sunglasses. Like tonight. The Unhappy Man chuckled. Nothing suspicious about that, right?

While Sunglasses Guy crawled along the base of a privacy fence, the Unhappy Man checked his rearview mirror again to see Duff Watson circling the truck. Although the big bruiser cop didn't seem aware of anyone else moving through the neighborhood, he'd inadvertently cut Sunglasses Guy off from his transportation and escape route.

With Duff occupied with the phone call he was making, the Unhappy Man peered through his windshield to see Sunglasses Guy pop out from behind a parked car several houses down. Flipping up the collar of his denim jacket, Sunglasses Guy skulked across the lawn to the next intersection, glancing in every direction but behind him. Poor fool seemed lost. On foot, he wouldn't get far before some identification was made on the truck and the department tracked him down. Unless it was stolen. In which case, Duff would be calling for backup, and a full-scale search through the neighborhood would ensue.

Inhaling a decisive breath, the Unhappy Man started the engine and pulled out of his parking space, passing a couple of houses before switching on his headlights. He turned the corner and caught up with the man in the sunglasses. He stepped on the brake and rolled down the passenger-side window. "Looks like you need a ride, my friend."

Sunglasses Guy stopped, his expression obviously unreadable. "You a cop?"

The driver saw the other man open his jacket and stroke his fingers over the Taser tucked into his belt. He held up both hands, showing the other man that he meant him no harm before he reached down to hit the unlock-door button.

"Get in. Let's talk."

Chapter Nine

Running was supposed to alleviate her stress.

"Come on, girl." Jane tightened her grip on Ruby's leash and urged the chocolate Lab to pick up the pace beside her. "You need to lose some weight, and I don't want to be out here any longer than I have to be."

With the dog loping along on her right, Jane swept her gaze across the asphalt path ahead of her, taking in the white rail fence and busy street to her left, and the creek and stand of trees that were starting to change from green to reds and golds beyond that on her right. Although her muscles relished the workout she'd skipped the past few days, and her lungs appreciated the deep influx of oxygen, the peace of mind she normally achieved on her morning run wasn't happening. The beauty of Mother Nature on this cool, misty morning couldn't pierce Jane's anxious mood.

"Giving the dog a pep talk, Boyle?" Conor teased her through the two-way radio clipped to her ear. "I told you I'd be happy to run with you instead of thirty yards back. Bet I'm a better conversationalist."

"Don't count on it." Jane dropped her chin toward the microphone hidden inside her jacket. "Besides, I feel better knowing you've got my back."

"Um, you do know I can barely see your back through this fog, right?"

Thomas's deep voice followed a crackle of static over her earbud. "Then move up so you have a clear line of sight, Wildman."

"Yes, sir—"

"Not too close." A third man's voice buzzed in her ear. Levi Hunt and his partner were parked somewhere in the area, close enough to monitor her actions without giving their presence away. "Doesn't do us any good to set up a sting if we scare the guy away," he cautioned.

Thomas's growly voice answered before she could. "Doesn't do us any good if something happens to Jane and you lose your one chance at catching this guy, either."

Bless his large-and-in-charge heart. Thomas's vehement defense of her, reminding Levi she was a human being, not just the bait on this fishing expedition, took the chill off the foggy autumn morning.

Jane smiled, knowing he was waiting in the parking lot across the road from the terminus of the running path that circled the woods. He'd dropped them off at the start of their run, driven his truck around the multi-acre park and bordering neighborhood where the path was located to scout for anyone or anything that seemed suspicious, and promised to be there to pick them up when they were done. She'd been connected to him, Conor and Levi over the radio this entire time. She knew that if he could have run the three miles, Thomas would have been right beside her. Instead, he'd suggested Ruby take his place.

"Guys. I'm okay," Jane reassured them. Well, mostly Thomas because he was starting to pick up some of her sleepless-night habits. And she already felt guilty enough about involving his family and putting their lives at risk. "Maybe he's not even in Kansas City."

"He's here." Levi's certainty had a fatalistic ring to it that erased her smile. "Come on, Watson. Even you have to agree. That truck abandoned near your house that your son ran the plates on was stolen. We got fingerprints off the steering wheel that match prints on that state trooper's car. That's Badge Man. Just because he's not in the system doesn't mean we can't put two and two together and know he's got Emily's scent. He's here. And I intend to apprehend him."

"Get her name right," Thomas ordered. "We should maintain radio silence in case one of us spots something suspicious. Or Jane needs assistance."

"Agreed. Wildman out."

Levi was slower to respond to the order. "Hunt out."

Jane patted Ruby's warm flank to encourage the dog and herself to keep moving forward, toward Thomas and the end of the path. "Boyle out."

All these layers of protection surrounding her should reassure her, right?

But it was the threat she couldn't see that worried her the most.

Jane checked her watch and saw that her pulse rate had increased, even though she hadn't pushed her speed in the second mile, the way she normally did. Her elevated pulse was purely an emotional reaction because she knew the killer could be watching her right now. That truck Duff had checked out meant Badge Man had already found her, and was simply biding his time for the perfect moment to strike.

She knew his profile by heart—how he liked to scout

out an area and learn his target's schedule. Now the plan was for her to ignore common-sense survival tactics and maintain her old routine. Morning run. Work with Seamus. Run a few errands and hang out at the Watson house. Argue the risk she was taking with Thomas and, if she was really lucky, wind up in his arms for a few hours of sleep each night.

She'd watched the news reports from Indiana and DC. The profile the FBI had given was pretty accurate, and the fact that Levi had mentioned having a witness who'd given them a lead during one of those press conferences had no doubt put the killer on her trail. Even though he hadn't mentioned her by name, since Emily Davis was the only surviving witness, the guy didn't need to be a brain surgeon to figure out Agent Hunt was talking about her. If Badge Man knew she'd changed her name to Jane Boyle, then tracking her down hadn't been as hard as she'd wanted it to be. And since Thomas was convinced that someone on Oscar Broz's team had leaked her new name to the FBI, it was reasonable to assume that the FBI, if not Levi himself, had leaked her name as well to lure Badge Man into their trap.

But she imagined the serial killer was completely aware of the Kansas City detective, US marshal and federal agent keeping her company this morning. With his gruesome obsession for killing and carving up law enforcement, he probably saw the protection surrounding her as some kind of dare. One he would cleverly and covertly plan to circumvent, bringing him some sick pleasure at not only eliminating her, but besting the very men he despised.

She scanned the trees to her right, seeing them as little more than distant shadows through the fog where a man could easily hide. The dangerous possibilities tightened her chest. Two days of not having anyone chasing her or shooting at her felt more nerve-racking than dealing with a direct threat. At least with an attack, she had someone to fight. The demons inside her head were a much trickier adversary to fend off, and she had a feeling her enemy knew that.

So what if she'd been drinking enough coffee to burn a hole in her stomach, and her appetite was practically nil? What did the man who wanted her dead care if the only deep sleep she'd had recently had been the last two nights she'd spent in Thomas's arms?

She knew Thomas wanted something more from her. And she wanted that, too. After all, it was hard to resist a handsome man with enough mileage on him to make him interesting and sure of himself, compassionate and sexy in ways a young buck with something to prove to the world could never understand. A sharp mind, sure hands, that broad chest and the ability to kiss her senseless only added to the attraction she felt toward the veteran cop who'd become more friend than boss. She imagined his patience and experience would make him an unforgettable lover. Not since Freddie's death had she even considered being with another man. And now she was thinking of Thomas nearly every waking moment—during some of the sleeping ones, too—and how good it would feel to really be with him. She'd be proud to claim him as her man and warn any other interested parties that the lieutenant detective was taken. She'd willingly give him her heart, and, in fact, knew that a subconscious part of her already had.

But the overwhelming sense of security Thomas provided was the thing she needed most right now—not a lover, not a relationship. Although she wrestled with the guilt of knowing Thomas deserved a partner, not a project, she was thankful that he was willing to give her that sense of calm she craved without pressuring her for something more.

Playing bait for Levi and the FBI was supposed to put a stop to the post-trauma fugues and the growing suspicion that every shadow was a threat and every face belonged to the man who wanted her dead. Agreeing to Levi's plan to capture Freddie's killer might be the only way to prevent Badge Man from eluding the FBI until he surfaced in a few months to claim another victim. And the thought of the marshals office packing her up and shipping her off to someplace far away from Thomas and Seamus and the city she'd grown to love made her heart seize up in her chest.

They all needed her to do this. *She* needed to do this. Putting Badge Man behind bars was the only way she'd ever find justice for her murdered husband and seven other law enforcement officers. It was the only way to get her life back again. The only way she could ever move on to another relationship with any man, the only way she could become the woman Thomas deserved.

Ignoring the emotions that such logic couldn't dissuade, Jane inhaled more deeply from the damp air and dropped down a small incline to run beside the shallow water's edge. Ruby barked and tugged at the leash, crossing in front of her to greet two cyclists who materialized out of the shroud of morning fog and pedaled toward them. "Ruby!"

Unable to stop her forward momentum, Jane bumped into the dog, almost sending her tumbling. She tugged on the leash, pulling Ruby with her into the grass. Ruby was up on her hind legs, offering a friendly woof as the two men waved and veered around them. "Sorry!" Ruby nearly pulled her off her feet, eager to give chase as the bicycles disappeared into the fog. "Crazy dog."

"Jane?" She thought she detected the sound of a vehicle door opening. Thomas was getting out of his truck. "Answer me."

"I'm fine. We're fine," she reassured him, making eye contact with the excited dog and silently reminding the mutt that *she* was the authority Ruby needed to answer to right now. Seeming eager to trot along beside her once more, Ruby resumed their run in the proper direction. "Two cyclists startled us. I didn't recognize them. But they had on helmets and sunglasses so I couldn't see much. Ruby wanted to greet them."

She heard Thomas close the door to his truck and exhale a heavy breath. He'd had eyes on her almost 24/7 since the night of the restaurant shooting. And now it was killing him that she'd been out of his sight for almost half an hour. She suspected he was on his way to meet her at the terminus of the circular running trail across the road from where he'd parked. She knew he'd appreciate a report on exactly what she'd seen.

"Do we know those guys?" she asked.

"They're not ours," Conor answered. They ran several more strides in silence before he added. "Hunt?"

"Negative," Levi answered. "Bartlett and I are the only ones who came in from DC. I don't have approval yet for an area-wide manhunt."

"The bikers are clear," Conor reported. "But look out coming up behind you, Boyle. Another runner just passed me. Black shorts, gray hoodie. I'm picking up the pace to keep him in my sights."

"I hear him." Jane grinned as Ruby's gait changed to a hopping jump rather than an even jog. "So does Ruby. I think two and a half miles is the limit of her interest in running with me."

Conor laughed over the radio. "Too bad it's a three-mile course."

"She's ready for snacks and playtime."

Thomas's voice growled in her ear. "Listen, you two…"

"We're almost there, boss," Jane teased, feeling the stress lifting with every step that took her closer to Thomas. "Make sure you've got treats and some water waiting. Come on, Ruby girl. Just a little farther."

Her footsteps turned hollow as she hit the narrow wooden bridge crossing over the creek. Even more startling than the changing resonance beneath her running shoes was the second set of footsteps hurrying onto the bridge behind her.

"On your left," a friendly voice that went with the footsteps announced.

She politely drifted as close to the railing as she could. But Ruby zigged when she zagged and Jane accidentally stepped on one of the dog's paws. Ruby squealed in pain and jerked to the side. Jane cringed with an instant slap of guilt and lost her grip on the leash. "Ruby!"

She'd barely made a lunge to recapture the dog when the man bumped her shoulder and sped on past. Jane stumbled into the railing. "Watch it."

"My bad." He waved with a gloved hand as he disappeared into the fog ahead of her.

"A little help? Hey!" Jane had missed her stab at

Ruby's collar and the dog raced off into the mist after the man. "Now you want to run? Ruby!"

"Damn it, Boyle, where are you going so fast?" Conor whined in her ear. "I don't have eyes on her."

"Report," Thomas shouted into the radio. "Somebody tell me what's going on."

Jane charged up the last hill after the man in the black shorts. She didn't want Ruby following him into the street. "Hey! Can you grab my dog? Thomas, Ruby's following that guy. I dropped her leash. They're running straight toward you and the street."

So much for stress relief. Anger and concern for Ruby fueled her steps. Screw Levi's plan to capture Badge Man. She'd run her three miles on the treadmill at the house from here on out and pretend she didn't feel completely trapped or that she was putting the entire Watson family in danger by being there with them. Now she'd even put poor Ruby in danger.

As Jane neared the end of the path, she spotted a broad, shadowy form at the top of the hill. She'd know that imposing silhouette anywhere. "Thomas! Catch her!"

A shrill whistle rang in her ear and she knew he was calling the dog to him. Thomas's familiar form took shape and color as she got closer. His dark jeans and cream-colored shirt. The gun and badge anchored on his belt. The piercing scowl that lined his handsome face. "Some guard dog you are," he chided, stepping on Ruby's leash, securing her before kneeling to curl the strap around his wrist.

Even after years of running, Jane's lungs burned with the uphill sprint. "Did you see him?" she gasped, bracing her hands against her knees beside them and sucking in several deep breaths. Gnawing on the latest treasure she'd found somewhere along her romp of freedom, Ruby stretched out on the grass beside Thomas. Jane glanced across the road. "Did Mr. Rude head for the parking lot?"

Thomas shook his head as he pushed to his feet and shoved her behind him. "I didn't meet anybody crossing the street." The tight grip on her arm eased when he recognized Conor racing up the hill. Thomas nodded toward the curve in the asphalt path that led back toward the trees. "He must have circled around that way before I got here."

Conor paused long enough to ask her a silent *You okay?* before trading Jane a thumbs-up and dashing off in the direction of the trees. "I'll see if I can catch him." He tapped the link to his microphone before disappearing into the fog. "Hey, Hunt. You want to put on your running shoes and help me track this guy?"

"I'm not giving away our presence here in KC until we have something concrete to follow," Levi answered. "I don't want Badge Man to know how close we are to catching him."

"Oh, so now you don't just want my help—you want me to do your job for you."

"Wildman, you wouldn't know—"

Thomas tugged at the collar of the black KCPD jacket she was wearing and reached inside to turn off the radio. "Why do I get the feeling I'm working with a couple of rookies?"

The chatter in her ear ended, and Jane tipped her nose to the sky and inhaled deeply as her breathing started to regulate. "That guy was wearing earbuds and listening to music, so maybe he didn't hear me call after him."

Thomas's green eyes narrowed as he met her gaze. "And maybe I don't like the idea of some random guy accosting you and wreaking havoc when we're in the middle of a sting operation. The whole idea of a setup is to have control of everything except the target." He swiped his palm over his square jaw to muffle a curse. "I don't feel we have control of anything." He softened the frustration in his tone by straightening the collar of the jacket and holding it together at her neck. "Are you okay?"

Jane wrapped her fingers around his wrists, holding on to the tenuous connection to him. "I'm fine. I'm just glad Ruby didn't follow that guy into the road. Traffic might not have seen her until it was too late." When he nodded, she pulled away and glanced down at the dog. No longer interested in running, the Lab mix held something long and skinny and muddy between her teeth. "What is she chewing on?"

Thomas knelt in front of the dog. "Hey, girl. What do you have there, Rubes?"

Ruby raised her head and the object dangled from the side of her muzzle.

Jane's breath locked up in her chest.

Ruby's souvenir was a length of blue nylon cord. Tied into a noose. Like the noose that had been cinched around Freddie's neck. Like… Jane's fingers flew to her throat as her blood ran cold.

She dropped her other hand to Thomas's shoulder. "Take that away from her." Jane was vaguely aware of the slam of a car door in the distance, and an engine gunning like the snarl of a waking tiger. But her head was filling with the remembered images of a nightmare. The man bumping into her and that rope were no coincidence. The man in the gray shorts had wanted Ruby to get away from her. He wanted the dog to have that creepy reminder of her husband's death, of the attempt on her own life. He wanted her to see it. Jane struggled to stay in the present. "Don't touch that. I mean, get it away from Ruby, but...it's evidence."

Thomas's muscles hardened beneath her touch. He didn't ask questions, didn't argue.

"Drop it," he ordered. Ruby did, in exchange for a scratch around the ears and her master's praise. "Good girl."

Pulling a bandanna from the back pocket of his jeans, Thomas wrapped the blue rope inside and tied it off in a makeshift pouch before standing and facing Jane. He slid his warm fingers against the side of her neck and cupped her jaw.

"I'd feel better if you had a little color in your face." He held the pouch up between them. "Tell me what this means."

Death. It means death.

Before she could form the words, she heard Conor's voice buzzing from Thomas's earbud. "Hey, Boyle. How fast was that guy running? I don't see him anywhere."

She didn't get the chance to answer either question. The noise of the waking tiger roared in her ears and she spun around. Suddenly, the square shape of a familiar white van filled up her vision like a wall closing in on her.

"Jane!" Thomas's arms snapped around her and they were airborne. Jane felt a wave of heat and wind as the speeding vehicle swerved toward them and took out the crosswalk sign. She saw a black-gloved hand come out the driver's-side window, heard the *pop, pop, pop* of gunshots. She and Thomas hit the ground hard and they were rolling, sliding, tumbling down the hill toward the creek. Ruby yelped and tumbled with them. Every impact jarred through Jane and she was dizzy, disoriented, terrified. When they slammed into the cold water, her body chilled and her senses sharpened.

Thomas twisted off her, raised his head, straightened his arm and returned fire. For several endless seconds, her world was nothing but loud noises, the smoky stench of gunpowder and the weight of Thomas's arm pinning her in the shallow water as he positioned himself between her and the bullets pinging off metal and thumping into the mud beside them.

She heard someone swearing beneath the screech of tires. Conor ran into her line of sight, diving for the ground and firing from the edge of the running path above them. The gunfire stopped with the spit of flying gravel as the tires spun for traction on the shoulder of the road. Thomas rolled over on top of her, hugging his arms around her until the stony rain ceased. The tires finally found solid asphalt, and the van lurched forward and sped away.

For a split second the world was eerily quiet. A moment later, Thomas exhaled a wheezing groan and Ruby whimpered beside them. A few choice words peppered the air as Conor ran to the edge of the road. He had his cell phone to his ear, giving someone a succinct description of the van. Jane still had Thomas's weight bearing down on her, making it difficult to breathe.

"Thomas?" she gasped, seeking out his familiar green eyes. So many bullets. And other than the terrain itself, he'd had no cover to protect him. Soaked to the skin and spattered with mud, Jane ignored her shivers and the aches in her bruised joints, and pushed at his shoulders. "Thomas!" Why wasn't he moving? She squiggled her hips from beneath his and tried to free herself. A fear as heart-wrenching as coming home to find Freddie's mutilated body fueled her actions. "Are you hurt?"

Instead of answering, he braced his arms on either side of her and pushed himself up, rolling off into the slick grass with a grunt. His fist was still clenched around his gun, and the skin beside his mouth was tight and pale as he sat up on the incline leading down to the creek. "Everybody okay?"

His question included Conor, who was sliding down the hill to check on them. She could hear now that he was talking to Oscar Broz. The younger man gave Thomas a thumbs-up as he reported the incident to his supervisor.

"Jane?" Thomas prompted.

"I'm fine." But he wasn't. She sized up the clarity of Thomas's green eyes and quickly ran her hands over his head, arms and torso. Thank God there were no bullet holes. But when she reached his rebuilt leg and unwound the dog's leash that had tangled around his ankle, he visibly flinched.

Conor disconnected the call. "I found footprints leaving the trail. Led back to the road about a quarter mile north of here. I would have followed, but I heard the gunfire. That van was waiting to pick him up, wasn't he?"

Thomas nodded. "Waiting to pick him up and then take us out. Or maybe just scare us again."

Conor speculated along with him. "Maybe they were buying time so we couldn't pursue them."

Jane handed the leash to Conor. "Take Ruby. Thomas is hurt."

"I'm fine." Thomas pushed her hands away as she probed his ankle and knee, but Jane pushed right back. She felt his narrowed eyes assessing her responses as deliberately as her fingers were evaluating the muscles spasming in his calf and thigh. "That runner was Badge Man." He was looking for answers she didn't want to admit to. But *relentless* was his middle name. Thomas leaned over to snatch up the bandanna he'd dropped on their muddy tumble and prodded her for the truth. "This was a message from him, wasn't it?"

Jane nodded, wishing her hands would stop shaking, wishing she had an ice pack for his swollen knee, wishing he'd sit still and let her do the one helpful thing she could besides bait a trap that had nearly gotten them all killed. "He used a rope like that to kill Freddie. Used it on me, too. The color of the rope wasn't released to the press or—"

Another speeding car lurched to a stop near the crosswalk and broken sign at the top of the hill. With a shrill warning, Jane tried to push Thomas to the ground to protect him, but he pulled her into his chest instead, twisting toward the road and raising his gun to do battle once more.

She recognized Levi Hunt's black SUV and exhaled her relief before realizing that both Conor and Thomas had positioned themselves between her and the big black vehicle. They lowered their weapons as Levi opened the passenger-side window. "Was that a getaway van? Did you lose him?"

"We never had him." Thomas waved the federal agents away. "White van. Headed south. I think I clipped the driver—"

"Go!" Levi instructed his partner to drive after the van. The SUV made a tight U-turn and raced off in pursuit.

Conor jumped up, swearing after the useless agent. "I thought he was supposed to be here to back us up. Do you think he'll catch the shooter?"

"Forget Hunt," Thomas commanded between tightly clenched teeth. "He's not going to catch that guy, and he doesn't want anyone helping him because he wants the collar." He must have realized how tightly he still held her plastered to his side because he eased his grip and let her slide down to the grass beside him. "You're sure neither one of you is hurt?"

"I'm fine." Jane resumed the task of determining the extent of his injury, wondering if he ever admitted to anyone how much pain he was in. Until she could get him home to his prescription meds and a hot shower or heating pad, she'd try to relieve some of the cramping by massaging the damaged muscles.

Conor holstered his weapon beneath his jacket. "I'm good."

Thomas stowed his gun, as well. "Let Hunt play the hero if he wants to. Priority one is to get Jane someplace safe."

"Your place?" Conor asked.

"My place."

Conor nodded. "Hand me your keys. I'll get the truck and drive it over here so you don't have to walk as far."

"I'm not an invalid," Thomas groused. But aching or not, the man was practical. He pulled his keys from his pocket and tossed them to Conor. "Take the dog, too. She's probably anxious to get inside someplace."

While the younger man jogged across the street with Ruby, Thomas covered her hands with his, stilling them against her thigh. "You're shivering."

"I'm soaked to the skin." She turned her hand to lace her fingers through his. "And I almost got you killed."

He squeezed her hand before releasing her and rolling over onto his good leg to stand. "Just a little beat up. I've walked off worse than this. Now help me up."

Jane was by his side in an instant, pulling his arm across her shoulders and sliding her arm around his waist to grab his belt and steady him as they climbed the hill. Although he moved without complaint, his limp was exaggerated, and when she looked up, a muscle ticked along the edge of his jaw from clenching it so tightly. Bracing her own legs, she took a little more of his weight until they reached the flat surface of the running path again. "Tell me what you're feeling."

"Like I'm a step behind this guy and two steps behind keeping you safe."

"I meant—"

"I know what you meant." He hugged her close to his side and kissed the crown of her head. "I'm fine, honey. But you were right out there in the open. He could have run you down or shot..." He tugged on the hand that held his at her shoulder and gently twisted her arm to inspect the blood seeping through the sleeve of the jacket she wore. It wasn't immediately noticeable through the black nylon, but Thomas Watson rarely missed a detail. "You're bleeding."

"I knocked the scab off my elbow when we fell.

Sorry I messed up your jacket. I owe you a new one. But I'll live."

"So will I." His hand was resting on the butt of his gun as they stopped beside the shattered signpost and churned-up gravel and mud where the white van had skidded onto the shoulder. He was in professional mode now, studying the ground for identifying marks or tire tracks, noting the number of shell casings scattered across the scene. "I'd better call in a crime scene team."

Jane watched him put in a call to Dispatch and verify that a uniformed officer was en route to secure the scene. She felt the lurch in his body as he stiffly went down on one knee to inspect a trail of red dots on the asphalt. Blood. Something she'd seen far too much of in her life. Blood that could have been Thomas's or her own if he hadn't reacted so quickly. She knelt with him, waiting for him to snap some photos with his cell phone before helping him stand again. She heard his gasp of pain, felt the jerky effort to maintain his balance.

She was a professional, too, a professional at knowing what *all right* looked like, and this wasn't it. With the siren of a KCPD squad car approaching in the distance, Jane tilted her gaze to Thomas's, demanding he look at her. "Look, you shoot guns and give orders. I take care of people. And I always count on you for a straight answer. How badly are you hurt?"

Thomas knew she wasn't going to back down on this. "I came down on my bad hip pretty hard. Jarred my knee, too. Every nerve ending in between is screaming at me."

Compassion, admiration and the deeper feelings this man stirred in her squeezed around her heart. Without questioning the impulse or pausing to debate whether she had the right, Jane cupped his jaw, angling his face to hers and lifting her mouth to kiss him. She pressed her lips against his, felt the firm line of his mouth soften beneath the caress. She caught his bottom lip between hers and gently pulled his lips apart before rising onto her toes to push her mouth against his, deepening the kiss, demanding his gentle response, eagerly surrendering to the answering claim of his lips on hers.

Jane's world righted itself in those few moments. Her heart beat strongly. Her body surged with life. She didn't feel quite so cold or afraid.

Dropping back on her heels, Jane ended the kiss. But the link between her hand on his jaw, and the heat of his handsome green gaze burning into hers, remained. The strength and the reassurance she felt did, too.

"I needed that," she admitted, before pulling away to slide her arm behind his waist again. "Come on. Let's get someplace safe where I can take a better look at that leg."

Hurting or not, Thomas knew how to plant his feet and stand his ground. Before she could take a step, his arm tightened around her. He caught her chin between his thumb and forefinger and bent his head to cover her mouth in a hard, quick kiss. "I don't want to lose you," he whispered in a deep, guttural tone that frightened her with its intensity as much as it exhilarated her. "I need you to know *that*."

Myriad possible responses bounced around inside her brain, but she didn't have the time she needed to choose what she wanted to say. Instead, she had to turn her eyes away from the bright lights of the black-and-white squad car that pulled up. Thomas eased some space between them, although he kept hold of her hand while he gave the uniformed officers some quick directions for securing the scene. There were *yes, sirs* and hurrying to do his bidding before Conor pulled up in Thomas's red truck.

They stepped around the drops of blood before opening the back door of the extended cab. "You think you winged the driver?"

"Yeah, but the blood pattern doesn't fit someone speeding away in a van. Those are something else."

As in, someone else had gotten hurt because of her? Instead of climbing in, Jane opened the front passenger door so she could help Thomas get in. She saw the grim look on Conor's face. "What about you, tough guy? You're not lying about being hurt, are you?"

"No." Conor nodded toward the back seat. "But we need to make a detour to the vet's office."

"Ruby?" Jane scurried around the open door. "Oh, no."

She was surprised to feel Thomas's hands at her waist, half lifting her into the truck as she climbed into the seat where Ruby lay. The dog had twisted herself into a circle so that she could lick at her back leg. "How is she?" Thomas's voice mirrored her own concern.

Jane let Ruby sniff her closed hand so she wouldn't startle the dog when she pushed her head away from the injury. "I'm not a vet." She palpated Ruby's right leg. The dog's muddy, dark brown coat had masked the blood initially, but it wasn't hard to find the small hole. Jane's heart sank when she felt a hard mass in the meat of the dog's hip. When she pressed on it, the dog whimpered and tried to curl around to lick at it again. "She's been shot."

Thomas closed the door behind her and pulled himself up into the front seat. "Drive," he ordered before closing the door and buckling up. Conor shifted the truck into gear and took off while Thomas looked back at her. "How bad?"

Jane kept one comforting hand on the dog and reached over the seat. "Get me the first-aid kit. I restocked it after that night at the restaurant."

Thomas rattled off directions while he dug the kit out of the glove compartment and handed it to her. "Jane?" He wanted a report.

"The bullet is still in her, lodged in her hip. It doesn't look like it hit the bone or anything vital. But she'll need X-rays and surgery." Like dog, like master, they were both going to be limping for a while. Scratching Ruby's flank with one hand, Jane used her teeth and the other hand to tear open a gauze packet to stanch the bleeding. Ruby licked her fingers, then tried to get at the wound again. "You poor baby."

"Here's a treat to distract her," Thomas offered.

Jane refused the food and asked for a chew toy instead. "I don't want anything in her stomach, in case she reacts to the anesthesia."

"Tennis ball." After handing it to her, Thomas straightened in his seat. Ruby gladly took the ball in her big jowls to chew on. But there was still an occasional whimper as Jane doctored the wound as best she could. She knew Thomas was hurting far worse than he let on, too. "We're about ten minutes from the vet."

She concentrated on stemming the bleeding and monitoring the dog's pulse so she didn't flash back to the noose and the bullets or that helpless sense of being a devious man's target. But it was impossible to completely block the bleak inevitability of how she could be hurt—how others could be hurt because of Badge Man and what she knew about him.

"There was only one person in the van when it chased Seamus and me down the highway," she speculated.

Thomas nodded. "Only one that night at the restaurant, too."

"This time there were two," Conor added, taking a turn toward the vet's office.

Jane remembered the blur of the image she'd seen in that split second before Thomas had knocked her to the ground. "A driver and a passenger."

"And one of them has a bullet wound." Thomas pulled his phone from his pocket and called Duff, giving him a bare-bones account of the incident and telling him to notify area hospitals and clinics in case a patient who's been shot checked in.

By the time he ended the call, Ruby seemed relatively comfortable, content to chew on her ball while Jane finally buckled herself in. "Badge Man was the only person there the night Freddie was killed. Badge Man works alone."

"Not anymore."

Conor spun around another corner. "If he's got a partner now, that changes the profile completely. Makes him unpredictable."

Jane sank against the seat, keeping a soothing hand on Ruby as the hope drained out of her. She remembered Freddie talking about profiling a suspect. Unpredictable meant dangerous. Things were going to get a lot worse before they got better—if they ever would.

Thomas unfolded the sun visor in front of him and found her gaze in the mirror there. "Hunt's plan to capture him won't work."

Chapter Ten

"We're doing this by the book," Thomas concluded. "*My* book. I train cops to handle this kind of fugitive scenario. It will work. But I need everyone's help here to make it happen. Thank you."

The noise level in the living room increased exponentially the moment Thomas stepped away from his imaginary lectern and the individual conversations started. The Watson house was as crowded and busy as any holiday gathering of family and friends. Thomas's four children and their spouse or significant others, the baby who would soon be Niall's adopted son, Millie, Seamus, Al, Conor Wildman and Oscar Broz, Levi Hunt and his partner were all here, along with Keir's partner at KCPD, Hud Kramer, and Olivia's partner, Jim Parker. They spread out around the living room, entryway, dining room and kitchen—taking notes, asking questions, nodding heads.

Millie had stepped up like the veteran aide-de-camp she was, and put together a giant pot of potato soup and sandwiches for everyone to eat. Mutt and Jeff had shown up with sodas and beers for anyone who wanted a drink. And Ruby wasn't letting her shaved backside, a handful of stitches or the cone of shame around her neck stop her from accepting bites of meat or a tummy rub from any of their guests.

Only there was little for Thomas to celebrate this evening.

This was a war room. And he was the general.

He'd taken half a dozen ibuprofen in lieu of his muscle relaxers so that he could keep a clear head and get this thing organized. He'd called in every favor anyone had ever owed him to help capture Badge Man, identify the serial killer's new partner and do whatever was necessary to protect Jane. While the house reverberated with arguments and suggestions, opinions and laughter, his gaze settled on the woman with the honey-brown ponytail who was far too quiet for his liking as she moved around the living room to collect dirty dishes and refill drinks. The moment he'd finished laying out his plan, Jane had pushed to her feet and gone to work at the mundane tasks.

She was locking down her emotional armor. Next thing, she'd be avoiding him completely. He couldn't allow that to happen. He was done being a victim of the unseen threat targeting his family. He was done seeing the people he cared about hurt by an unknown enemy. He wasn't about to lose the woman he loved to violence a second time.

He turned away from his friends and family and drifted toward the relative privacy of the foyer stairs. Scrubbing his palm over the stubble lining his jaw, he pondered that last mental vow. The admission that he loved Jane should have worried him more than it did. Falling in love again after all these years should take him aback, make him question the wisdom of his emotions. But all he could feel was a sense of rightness, of everything that was missing from his life finally falling into place.

Of course, there was that whole sucky-timing thing. But the nagging doubts about the difference in their ages or mistaking friendship or gratitude for something deeper had vanished. He loved Jane Boyle. She'd become part of his family long before she'd become part of his heart. He believed she cared about him, and he had every intention of making her presence in his life a permanent thing.

Whenever she was ready to commit to a new relationship.

And he could erase the terror that ruled her life.

And eliminate the threats that tainted his own world.

It probably wasn't fair to either of them to force a relationship this complicated to happen. But he was a patient man. And he was damn good at his job. If he could get rid of the external conflicts that dictated Jane's choices, then maybe those internal conflicts could heal and she'd give him a chance. She'd give *them* a chance.

Before she buried herself too far inside that armor of hers, he wanted to remind her she wasn't alone in this fight—remind her that this bond between them didn't only exist in the upstairs hallway in the middle of the night.

Thomas turned toward the kitchen to go to her, but Levi Hunt stepped into his path on his way to the front door. "Agent Hunt. Thank you for listening to my proposal."

A little making nice between federal and local agencies could never hurt.

Levi's efforts to be polite were less successful. "I admit that this morning was an epic fail. That whole attack was planned out. There was nothing random about Badge Man making contact with Freddie's wife." Why couldn't the man say Jane's name? Thomas bristled, but didn't let it show. If he could hide how badly his leg was hurting, he could hide his irritation with this glory-seeking pissant. "We found no sign of the van, the driver or the man who left that noose for her. But I'm not leaving Kansas City. I'll back off and let you take the lead on this. For now. Your people better find my unsub, Watson."

Thomas ignored the thinly veiled warning. "We know KC in a way your people never will. If he's still here, and I believe he is, we'll find him. As long as no one goes off script, my plan will work. I'm more than happy to let you make the arrest and take Badge Man out of my city."

"Keep me posted. You have my number."

Thomas gladly held the door for Agent Hunt to exit and rejoin his partner out in their black SUV. But when Thomas shut the door and made a second effort to reach Jane, he was met with a wall of his four grown children.

Niall adjusted his glasses on the bridge of his nose and spoke first. "The lab analyzed the bullet the vet took out of Ruby. It's a match for the forty-five mil I pulled out of your truck. So we know it's the same guy."

Keir nodded. "If we find that gun, we have our shooter."

Olivia had always been the voice of reason for her three older brothers. "But you won't have Badge Man. I think Jane's right—he doesn't shoot people. He likes the hands-on experience of strangling his victims. She told me one of the things he said the night of her attack, that he gets off on seeing the light go out in his victim's eyes." This time, he couldn't mask the way that knowing Jane had seen and heard such unspeakable violence up close and personal turned his stomach. No wonder she felt she needed to be so tough. Without that kind of strength, she wouldn't be able to deal with the memories, much less the ongoing threat. Olivia must have read his concern because she slid her arms around his waist and hugged him. "I love you, Dad. We're with you and Jane all the way on this."

When she stretched up on tiptoe to kiss his cheek, Thomas dipped his head to do the same before she pulled away. "Love you, too. You four mean the world to me."

"What she said. Only, I'm not kissing you." Duff squeezed Thomas's shoulder before pulling back to cross his arms over his big chest. "I've got calls out to every hospital and clinic in the metro area. No gunshot wounds have shown up yet."

Thomas had expected as much. As well-planned as each of the incidents had been, their perps would either have sufficient medical training or access to someone who could treat any injuries without reporting them to the authorities. "I'm thinking the impossible. But it's the only scenario that fits. The man who's been after us has teamed up with Badge Man. He's probably been stalking us right along, keeping tabs on the family ever since Olivia's wedding. He must have spotted Badge Man following Jane, recognized a fellow pervert and—"

"We'll get this guy, Dad." His youngest son, Keir, wasn't looking so young anymore. "I know Jane means a lot to you. She means a lot to Grandpa. She's already a part of this family as far as we're concerned."

Thomas needed this dose of family support right about now. "So no more Battle-Ax Boyle?"

"No, sir," they answered in unison.

"And if I wanted to get serious with her, you all would be on board with that?"

"It would be the logical next step since you're in love with her." Every head turned at Niall's matter-of-fact statement. "That's how Lucy explained it to me. When you're willing to do anything and everything for another person, when it hurts inside that you might lose her—that's love."

Were Thomas's feelings that obvious?

Duff thumped his middle brother on the shoulder. "Dude, since when did you become an expert on this kind of stuff? Usually we have to explain it to you."

Niall arched a dark brow above the rim of his glasses. "I'm an intelligent man. I pay attention to details and I learn." He tapped a finger into the middle of Duff's chest. "You should try it sometime."

"You don't have to give me any coaching with the ladies, Poindexter. You don't hear any complaints from Melanie, do you?" Duff's eyes narrowed. "*Do* you?"

Olivia linked arms with her two oldest brothers and turned them toward the living room, eyeing Keir to lead the way. "Don't worry, Dad. I'll make sure they stay out of trouble."

Thomas's gaze wandered to the family portrait over the mantel that had been taken when his brood were small children and Mary had been alive. He offered Mary a silent prayer, hoping she shared the pride and joy he felt at seeing Duff, Niall, Keir and Olivia happily matched to good, loving partners, and grown into successful adults. He also made a mental note to move the old picture to a less conspicuous spot, or maybe even the attic, so that Jane wouldn't feel threatened by the life he'd once shared with his late wife.

Al Junkert shoved his hands into the pockets of his jacket as he joined him in the foyer. Turning to stand by Thomas's side, his friend smiled at the family portrait and nudged his shoulder. "She'd have loved all this activity in her house. Not for the reason we're gathered here, of course, but she'd have been in all her Irish glory surrounded by family and friends like this." Al's hands stayed in his pockets as he faced him. "Tommy boy, I'm getting too old for this kind of thing. Now Millie's in the kitchen and instead of your kids running around the house, they're wearing guns and putting their lives on the line."

"They're not children anymore, Al. They're doing their jobs. And they're good at it. I couldn't be any prouder of the adults they've become."

Al nodded his agreement. "Mary would be proud of them, too. If this plan of yours works, I'll be right there beside you and the others to take this guy down." He pulled his hand from his pocket to shake Thomas's. "I'd better head out. I had to cancel dinner with Cheryl to be here, but I promised her a late drink."

"Cheryl? What happened to Renee?"

"Who?"

"The gal from the restaurant. The one you met… Never mind." Thomas opened the door and sent Al on his way with a grin.

Thomas suppressed the urge to groan in frustration when Mutt and Jeff stopped him before he could reach the kitchen and Jane. For his plan to work, he needed everybody to play their assigned role, so blowing off his air force buddies wasn't an option. "I appreciate you two stepping in to help. I know this isn't what you had planned for reunion week."

"It's like old times, huh?" Mutt's tone was a little

slurred with the alcohol. "The three of us saving the world again. You taking point. Us following your lead."

Jeff laughed at the trip down memory lane. "The hair's a little grayer. Or there's a little less of it. But it'll be nice to see some action again."

Thomas shrugged. "I hope it won't come to that. My goal is to control everything that happens Saturday night. That gives us plenty of time to coordinate with hotel security and set up the sting. Guide this guy right into our trap."

"Your fugitive will be the only variable."

"I hope."

"Too bad we don't get to wear our badges again," said Mutt.

"I want my badge to be the only one our perp sees on Saturday night," Thomas reminded him. "His focus should be on Jane and me. You two are strictly backup if this goes south."

"Right. You're the conquering hero and we're the second bananas. Like I said, like old times." Mutt swallowed another drink of beer before raising his bottle in a toast. "For Mary."

Thomas frowned, wondering how many beers his buddy had had. "You mean, for Jane."

"Well, sure. I just meant..." Mutt's dark eyes looked confused, as if he'd forgotten what he'd said. "Slip of the tongue, I guess."

"Give me that before you put your other foot in your mouth, too." Shaking his head, Jeff eased the bottle from Mutt's fingers. "Let's find you some black coffee."

Thomas mouthed a silent thanks to Jeff. But before he could connect with Jane, Oscar Broz called him back into the living room. The senior US marshal looked irritated with the whole evening, but then Thomas hadn't seen the man show any other expression in the two times they'd met.

Broz pulled the cell phone from his ear and hugged it to the lapel of his wrinkled suit jacket. "I've been running your scenario over with my colleagues, and I have to tell you I can't sign off on Jane's security because no one's following US marshal regulations anymore."

"You gave us some leeway when we were running things Agent Hunt's way—dangling Jane out in the open like bait," Thomas argued.

"Do you know what kind of money it costs to relocate a witness and guarantee her protection?"

"Do you want to tell me how Levi Hunt knew Emily Davis had become Jane Boyle and moved to Kansas City? How Badge Man found out?"

"If he had caught the guy, the Jane Boyle project would be moot. I'd save the service a ton of money."

Thomas boiled beneath his collar. Broz's inadvertent confession was evidence enough for him to know how Hunt had gotten Jane's location and information. Badge Man probably already had Hunt and his unit on his radar. Once the secret was out, he could even have trailed Hunt to KC, straight to Jane.

Thomas leaned in closer to the black-haired man and snagged his wrist to keep him from putting that blasted phone back to his ear. "People are not bottom lines, Broz. When this is over, I'm filing a complaint with your superior. I don't know what kind of bureaucrat you are, but you don't meet your budget constraints by risking a woman's life."

Broz pulled his arm from Thomas's grasp. "She was willing to take that risk."

"I'll tell you how you can save some money, Oscar," Conor Wildman intervened in a deceptively lighthearted voice. "I've been thinking about quitting WITSEC. Making KC my permanent home. You could deduct my salary from the payroll. Oh, and I've got a ton of vacation hours due me. I think I'll take them this weekend and go wait tables at an air force reunion."

Broz's eyes darkened like black marbles. "You and me, outside, Wildman. Now. We need to talk."

Thomas shook his head. He had to grin. Conor's smart-assery was just the thing he needed to cool his temper. Giving the young man a grateful salute as he followed his boss out the door, he finally made his way to the kitchen.

But the room was empty. And other than Jane's scent lingering faintly in the air, there was no sign of her.

He didn't think she'd do anything as foolhardy as wandering off the premises by herself, so he didn't panic. Didn't mean he wasn't anxious to see her and talk to her and hold her in his arms again. He pulled down a couple of mugs from the kitchen cabinet and poured them each some coffee, adding half-and-half from the fridge to Jane's the way she liked it. Maybe she'd holed up in her room upstairs or, more likely, had insisted on putting his father through his usual physical therapy, despite the stresses of the day.

He found her in the back hallway outside Seamus's room, chatting with Mutt and Jeff. Or rather, she was standing with her arms crossed, listening to his buddies run on while she had a blank expression on her face.

Her gaze shot over Jeff's shoulder to meet his as he approached. She forced a smile onto her pale lips and turned back to Mutt and Jeff. "If you'll excuse me, I really do need to see to my patient."

"Think about what I said," Jeff reminded her. What exactly had the three of them been talking about?

Seamus's door swung open and his aging father propped his walker in the middle of the hallway, forcing the two men back a step. "Jane is part of dis fam-ly. The Wat-ons protect our own."

What had him riled up?

Jane squeezed his arm. "My hero. But I'm okay. I'll get your shower ready."

After she disappeared inside Seamus's suite, Mutt realized Thomas was standing behind him and turned to apologize. "I didn't mean anything. If I hurt her feelings I'm sorry. My concern's with you, pal. We ain't the spring chickens we used to be. You're risking your life for her."

More curious than affronted by whatever his tipsy friend had said, Thomas nodded. "I appreciate it. I've always appreciated you guys. When we served together. When I lost Mary. Now."

Jeff pushed the shorter man down the hallway in front of him, pausing beside Thomas. "Same here." He reached out with a one-armed hug, carefully avoiding the two mugs of coffee. "C'mon, Mutt. I'm taking you home."

Once they'd gone, Thomas looked down to see his dad frowning. "What was that about?"

"One of dem was warning Jane dat dey didn't want to tee you get hurt 'cause of her. Don't know if dey meant you need to watch your back or your heart." Seamus lifted his pale blue eyes, reminding Thomas of the stern police sergeant who'd raised him. "I didn't like de tone of what I could hear troo de door."

Now he was more curious about the exact words, and

why they'd felt compelled to confront Jane. "Thanks for defending her. Mutt's had too much to drink. But that's no excuse."

"They're right, t-son. You could get hurt."

"My backside or my heart?"

Seamus didn't smile at the joke. "You've lost too much already."

"Anybody in this house could be hurt, Dad. Badge Man kills cops. Someone's had a grudge against us even before he came to town. We're all targets."

"Whose house is dis?"

"Mine."

"Whose family is dis? Whose fwiends?"

"Mine." Why had he ever thought he was in charge around here? "I know where you're going with this, Dad."

"You have most to lose." Seamus thumbed over his shoulder to the sound of water running in the en suite. "Whose woman?"

Jane wasn't his yet. She might never be. "Do you agree with Mutt and Jeff? That Jane's a danger to me? To us?"

"No." Seamus sounded pretty emphatic for a man with a speech impediment. "I like Jane. I want her to tay. Go get bad guys." He turned his walker and headed back into his room. "And den you go get her."

THE UNHAPPY MAN'S smile faded the instant he stepped out of Thomas Watson's house and left the reminiscences and loyal promises behind him. How could they still be talking about Niall and Lucy's wedding and celebrating Seamus's birthday and being happy when everything about that picture of familial bliss was completely wrong?

Thomas didn't know it yet, but he was planning a

suicide mission. He'd listened to his war-room scenario to rescue his Boyle tramp, and made sure he was a part of it. But the fact that Thomas hadn't been able to keep his eyes off Jane while he talked about controlling the situation, and getting Badge Man to focus on Jane and him rather than the setup closing in around him, only bolstered his need to make Thomas pay for taking Mary from him and letting her die. And to look at Jane that way in Mary's own house! With her beautiful blue eyes smiling from her portrait over the mantel, Mary had to watch her worthless husband making cow eyes at that skinny little nurse. Such a grand plan to save the wrong woman when he should have done half as much to save Mary.

And though Thomas still didn't suspect him after all these months, Thomas was certain he was dealing with two unsubs now, working in tandem. The Unhappy Man would make sure Thomas knew the truth before he killed him—and that wouldn't happen until he'd forced him to watch his new girlfriend die. The Unhappy Man pulled out into traffic and revved the engine a little too eagerly as that euphoric thought washed over him. Thomas would know what it felt like to have his heart ripped from his chest, just as his own heart had been when he'd lost Mary all those years ago.

The Unhappy Man eased up on the accelerator and merged with the traffic heading toward the interstate. Patience had never been his strong suit. But he wasn't about to blow a plan that had been twenty years in the making because of a speeding ticket. Nothing had been right in those twenty years. He'd lost the woman he loved with no hope of ever winning her back because of Thomas's carelessness.

But he was making things right now. And payback was a bitch.

He'd turned Thomas's life upside down. Turned his father into a stuttering invalid. Threatened his children. Made the Watsons afraid of their own shadows. Turned that prickly Jane Boyle into the target of a serial killer.

Saturday night, their lives would be destroyed.

He'd waited twenty years for this—he could wait a couple more nights.

He drove across town and pulled into the parking lot of a nondescript motel. Carefully ensuring that he hadn't been followed and that no one was overly curious about his arrival, he parked in front of room 17 and tapped three times on the door.

"Yeah?"

"It's me."

The door opened a crack for the occupant to identify him, then closed again to unhook the chain and let him in. Despite the nip of fall in the air, his new friend was dressed in nothing but his jeans. His new compatriot chained and bolted the door behind him before walking to the far side of the bed, where he scrubbed his fingers through his wet hair and paced.

The Unhappy Man's shirtless friend usually hid the writing tattooed around his neck, and the badge inked into the skin over his heart. The poor sap must be killing himself every time he carved that emblem into another victim's chest. The young man had told him his sob story about why he needed to kill—about his daddy the cop who'd been so well liked and respected, and how behind the closed doors at home, his hero abused him with a dangerously strict discipline that had warped both his mind and body. Instead of manning up and becoming a cop like Daddy, he'd murdered him instead.

The Unhappy Man had listened to the young man's hate and how it all came down to never measuring up to his vaunted father. He'd washed out of the police academy because he couldn't pass the psych evaluation. He couldn't even keep a job as a security guard because of his penchant for violence.

The Unhappy Man had listened. Not because he cared, but because he needed to know everything about this instrument for revenge he was using against the Watsons.

"Did you see her?" the tattooed man asked.

"Yes."

He finally stopped pacing. "Did she remember me?"

The Unhappy Man took note of the accoutrements arranged in precise rows on the faded bedspread. The blue rope, the Taser, the knife, his neatly folded clothes. "She didn't recognize you. Couldn't give much of a description to the police. But she remembered the noose. She has no doubt you're after her now."

The younger man swore and resumed his pacing. "I told you that was a bad idea. She's the only one who lived, you know. I should have gotten rid of her and moved on. I don't like playing games like this."

But he did. "She's frightened. Don't you get a rush from that? They're all afraid of you."

"That'll just put them all on guard against me." His restless friend finally picked up a black turtleneck off the bed and covered himself. "I watched her at the house. I saw her at the hospital. She's there twice a week with the old man. I even passed her in the hallway when I borrowed that custodian's outfit. It would be so easy to kidnap her there. I don't like taking chances like this. I should move on. You said she didn't recognize me when I bumped into her. She didn't see my face. I should leave."

The Unhappy Man raised his uninjured hand, urging the other man to calm down. He wasn't finished with him yet, and needed him to have as much of that fractured brain thinking about the job as possible. "But you're not alone this time. You have me. It's easier with a partner, isn't it? You don't have to take care of every detail yourself."

"I *like* taking care of those details."

And *he* liked being the one in control of this game. That boob he'd hired to shoot up Olivia Watson's wedding had gotten careless. He'd left a trail of clues that led the Watson boys to identify him as Gin Rickey, the code name for a hit man who worked for a gunrunning organization in the Ozarks. And now that Duff Watson and his girlfriend had broken up that hillbilly Mafia, the people who'd been running it might talk about his involvement in exchange for a lighter sentence. He doubted they could identify him by name, but they could identify him by the job he'd hired their man to do. Any intel they shared might lead back to him.

He wasn't about to rely on anyone else to bring his mission to punish Thomas Watson to the satisfying conclusion he wanted.

He picked up the tattooed man's mirrored sunglasses off the bed and put them on. When the younger man's territorial OCD kicked in and he started to protest, the Unhappy Man pulled out the gun strapped beneath his jacket and pointed it at him. The little tug of pain at the bandaged wound on his wrist didn't stop him. "It's not your decision to make. Now let me tell you how this is all going to play out."

Chapter Eleven

Thomas pulled his head from beneath the shower's spray and let the hot water beat down on his sore leg for a few minutes. Between ibuprofen and the heat, the electric shocks of pinched nerves and the ache of muscle cramps had subsided enough that he thought he could forgo the prescription painkiller he kept on hand. Other than past midnight, he had no idea what time it was. The house was finally quiet. Everyone had gone except for Keir, who was parked out front, keeping an eye on things through the night. Because of her injury, stairs were tricky for Ruby, so she was sleeping down in Millie's room. He was alone upstairs with Jane.

Correction. He was simply alone.

Jane had retired to her room long before the last of their guests had left. But he'd seen her light on beneath her door and knew she was still up, probably scribbling notes or drawing rudimentary blueprints of crime scenes—real or imagined—in that journal of hers. She'd let him read what she'd remembered from the night her husband had been murdered, trying to figure out how Badge Man had gotten into their house without breaking in, how he'd tracked her to the running path and how Saturday night's sting operation was going to play out without anyone else dying.

No wonder the woman couldn't sleep. Her nightmares were real. And she couldn't make them go away simply by waking up.

He wished she'd talk to him, though. After helping his father get ready for bed, she'd thanked him for the tepid coffee he'd brought her, set it on the kitchen island without taking a sip and excused herself to go to bed. He knew she was exhausted and frightened. He knew she was fighting an ongoing battle to keep the demons of PTSD at bay.

But he also knew she was smart and strong and determined to do whatever was asked of her to expose not one criminal mastermind, but two, and see them both put away. He only wished she'd let him share the burden she carried. That's what big shoulders and life experience and late-night conversations were for, weren't they?

He wasn't just a cop coordinating a makeshift joint task force—he was a man protecting what was his. Short of barging into her bedroom again, though, he wasn't going to get the chance to explain that to her. He grunted a humorless sound in his throat and shut off the water. If he did tell her what he felt, would she listen? Would she at least let him hold her again tonight, and allow herself those few precious hours when she could drop her guard and feel safe?

He was knotting a towel around his waist when he heard a soft knock on the bathroom door. Thomas released the tension that had strained across his chest and smiled.

"Are you decent?" Jane asked.

"No. But you can come in, anyway."

He saw a misty silhouette of pink and plaid and heard a soft laugh when the door opened. "That's an old joke."

"Well, it's not because I'm an old man."

Any evidence of a smile had vanished by the time the steam from the shower had cleared the room. For a split second, he thought something was wrong. But then he realized the cloud of steam had impeded her vision, too. Her gaze was wide and staring, scanning him from shoulder to shoulder, from chest to towel and farther down, her eyes darkening with a hungry look as she took in his state of undress.

The breathless parting of her lips triggered a heated response low in his belly. "Did you need something?" he asked, hearing the timbre of his voice drop a few pitches and grow husky.

"I, um, came in to check your leg before you turned in for the night." She cleared her throat, trying to erase the hoarseness that had sneaked into her voice, too. "And your arm."

Thomas dutifully stood still, curling his toes into the bath mat as she stepped into the room. His eyes invariably moved to that sexy strip of skin showing beneath her pajama top. Reining in the desire that instantly traveled south, he squeezed his eyes shut and inhaled a steadying breath, only to breathe in the citrusy scent of her hair. Cursing his own randy libido, he resolutely stared into the mirror over the sink, counting the gray wisps dappled through the darker hair curling across his chest.

For several seconds, Jane was all businesslike, taking his arm and turning it to inspect the new skin growing over the wound. "This is healing nicely. I think we'll let it air out tonight and wait until the morning to put on a new bandage."

Good grief. Was she sneaking peeks at his chest? Had her fingers lingered longer than was necessary against his skin? And was that a pert nipple straining against the pink cotton of her T-shirt reflecting in the mirror? Was she as aware of her actions and reactions as he was? Maybe he should have rethought this and excused himself to get dressed before she examined him further.

When she knelt in front of him and wrapped her hands around his ankle and calf, Thomas audibly groaned.

"Does that still hurt?" Running her fingers over his tensed muscles and the harder ridges of surgical scars and skin grafts was sparking a very different sort of ache in his body. And he couldn't say he was still feeling the heat from that shower. "On a scale of one to ten, what's your pain level?"

"Jane…" Her fingers were dancing perilously close to the promised land if she massaged much farther up beneath the towel.

"Your quad is still knotted like a rock." She dug her knuckles into the damaged muscle and he flinched. "If I could loosen it up."

Enough. There were limits even to *his* patience. Thomas grabbed her by the shoulders and pulled her to her feet. "I am not an invalid."

"I never said you were."

"I'm a man." Her hands braced against his chest as he lifted her onto her toes. "I don't want to be your boss, a father figure, your best buddy or even friends with benefits—and no, I'm not so old that I don't know what that means. I don't want a nursemaid. And I don't want security to be the only thing you need from me." He eased his grip on her arms and moved his hands up to her face. He slipped his fingers into her silky hair, tilting those green-gold eyes and beautiful mouth up to his. "But if I don't kiss you right now, if I don't hold you…"

For an endless moment, they were locked together like that, searching each other's eyes for understanding.

Then Jane slid her arms around his neck and kissed him boldly on the mouth. There were no more words, nothing to discuss, only a long-denied need rising to the surface.

Thomas took over the kiss, sliding his tongue into her mouth as his hands found their way to the skin at her waist and snapped her body to his. Her hands roamed over his shoulders and chest and up against his damp hair. She nipped at his chin when he came up for air. She tugged at his towel when he backed her against the sink and rubbed his thighs against hers. He slipped her pink shirt off and covered her small, perfect breasts with his hands while she pressed kisses to his chest and squeezed his bare bottom. Every place she touched him kindled a new fire that heated his blood. A flick of her tongue against his own taut nipple made him gasp for breath and sent a jolt of need straight to his groin.

He reclaimed her mouth, telling her with his tongue all the things he wanted to do with her body. Her eager responses made him feel male, powerful, whole. He tugged at the elastic of her pants, and they pooled around her ankles. He slipped his hands beneath her bottom and lifted her onto the edge of the counter. Her knees squeezed around his hips as he moved between her legs. This was what he needed, man to woman, skin to skin, need to need.

He peppered kisses down her neck and over the curve of one breast until he pulled a sweet, pearled nipple into his mouth. Jane jerked against the intimate touch, but she tunneled her fingers into his hair and held him there until he tasted her again. He grinned at the needy hum in her throat and turned his attentions to the other breast until that hum became a breathy groan.

He kissed her again, slipping one finger inside her hot, weepy center, testing her readiness for him. She bucked against his hand and he slipped a second finger inside, teasing the delicate vibrations of her response.

The soft claw of ten fingertips kneaded his shoulders as she gasped against his mouth. "Thomas... You better want this as badly as I do."

"I do."

Sparing one moment for reason, he opened the drawers on either side of her in a frantic search to find a box of condoms he hoped one of his boys left behind. They shared a laugh when they finally found a packet in the last drawer. Jane's hands were there with his to slide it on. And then he was inside her. Pausing a moment to catch his breath and savor the moment, he saw them reflected together in the mirror, and Thomas knew that nothing in his life had ever looked so sexy, ever felt so right.

The word *love* was right on the tip of his tongue, but Jane locked her feet around his backside and pulled him into her so deeply, he thought he'd lose it right there. Before the pleasure could overtake him, he leaned her back against his arm, slipped his thumb down to that sensitive spot where they were joined, claimed her mouth with his and swallowed up the joyous gasps of her release. And while the aftershocks of her climax danced around his hard length, he pumped into her again and again until it was all he could do to stay on his feet and ride the waves of his own release deep inside her.

When he knew himself again, when he felt warm hands gently stroking the length of his spine and soft lips pressed against the juncture of his shoulder and neck, Thomas hugged Jane close until their breathing synced into an even rhythm. He disposed of the condom, washed them both with his damp towel, scooped her off the counter and lifted her into his arms.

"Your leg."

"Not an old man. Remember?"

He kissed her answering smile, feeling his strength returning, his happiness, too, both growing more powerful than he'd felt in a long time. Jane looped her arms around his neck and he carried her through the hallway to his bedroom. He laid her against the pillows and she scurried beneath the covers, holding them up so he could crawl in beside her.

Thomas wrapped her in his arms and she snuggled up against him, sliding a creamy thigh between his legs, pillowing a breast against his bare skin, heedless of the scars and years and losses between them.

And when she drifted off to sleep the way she had each night he held her, Thomas pressed a kiss to the crown of her head and whispered, "I love you."

JANE AWOKE TO BLACKNESS. She was trapped. Her legs were bound. She couldn't breathe. "No!"

She sat up with a jolt, twisting against her bindings until she realized her legs were simply tangled up in the sheets. Had she screamed out loud? Or had that helpless terror been part of the nightmare?

The covers had gotten over her head somehow. She could see now, but the blocky objects around her were all in shadows. A thin beam of light swept across her face, blinding her for an instant. When her vision cleared, a broad figure towered over her in the darkness, and she scooted back against the pillows and headboard.

"Jane?" The tall figure backed away. The light flickered over her bare belly and she realized she was completely naked. She grasped the sheet and quilt and tugged them up to her chest. "It's okay, honey." She knew that voice. A deep-pitched rumble in the night. "You're okay. It was a bad dream."

It wasn't *him*.

"What happened? Why is it so dark?" Those frissons of panic were still coursing through her blood, making it difficult for her to concentrate. "Am I awake?"

"Yes." The shadowy figure was wearing a faded T-shirt that read USAF. United States Air Force.

The lingering vestiges of fear shook her fingers as she gripped the covers. "Thomas?"

The familiar figure nodded and held out both hands, showing her a small flashlight and a framed picture of a young couple in a wedding gown and dress uniform. "You're in my bedroom. Kansas City, Missouri. The sun hasn't come up yet. I didn't want to turn on a light and wake you." Thomas slipped the small picture frame into the top drawer of his dresser and pushed it shut. Then he sat on the edge of the bed near her feet, reaching out a hand to her. "Tell me you know where you are and who I am."

She pushed a tangled fall of hair off her face and

tucked it behind her ear. "I know who you are, Thomas." She trained her gaze on the concerned green eyes that were waiting for her to prove she was all right. "I guess I was having a nightmare. I thought…"

"I can imagine what you thought." He found her foot through the covers and gave her toes a reassuring squeeze before he moved closer to sit beside her. He set the flashlight on the bedside table and turned on the lamp there instead. As soon as his face came into focus, she reached out to cup his jaw and felt reassured by the brown-and-silver dots of stubble tickling her palm. He let her press her fingertips to the smooth line of his mouth and brush aside the spikes of hair that fell over his forehead before he spoke. "Are you with me now?"

Jane nodded, feeling his strength feed her own, letting his presence calm her. The memory of the needy, potent way he'd made love to her came flooding back, suffusing her with a heat that chased away the last of the dream. "Sorry for the little freak-out."

He pressed a kiss into her palm, then captured her hand against his thigh. "You scare me when I lose you like that."

"I don't mean to. I suppose the stress of everything manifested itself. I don't even remember the images. Just being afraid. But I'm okay now. I promise." The sweatpants he wore were soft with wear and warm from the heat of his body. She wished she could snuggle up inside them herself. Instead, she glanced over at the dresser. "You were looking at Mary's picture. Do you have any regrets about what happened between us?" She wasn't hurt by his actions, and she wasn't jealous of Mary. But she didn't want him to feel guilty about the changing nature of their relationship. She hadn't felt so thoroughly loved, so treasured and important to another person, in years. She hoped he'd found at least half that much satisfaction and a sense of being cherished from her. "I don't."

"Neither do I." A grin softened his rugged features. "But I feel kind of awkward having someone watch while I make love to you."

"Why? Are you thinking of doing it again?"

He scooted closer to her, bracing his hands on top of the quilt on either side of her and leaned in. "What kind of stamina do you think I have, woman?"

Not feeling one whit of a threat with him trapping her like that, she splayed her fingers over his heart. "A lot. More than me. As I recall, I'm the one who dozed off."

"You've got more sleep to catch up on than I do."

And there it was again. The danger in the room. Her fingers curled into the soft cotton of his shirt. "Do you think your plan will work? That Badge Man and his accomplice will show up at the reunion?"

"Unless he gets inside this house, he won't have access to you anyplace else between now and then. The wait will make him antsy, eager to make a move. And since he's watching us, he'll know I'll be there and you'll be with me." She believed him when he spoke, but the worry returned as he continued. "Plus, the guy who's targeting me likes a big stage with lots of people. It's a more public stab at me, the potential for more collateral damage to fill me with guilt. They'll be there."

Now she felt guilty. How could she ever allow this good man and the people he loved to be harmed? "Collateral damage? Maybe I should stick with the WITSEC program, ask Conor to relocate me. I think I'd break if anyone else got hurt because of me. Especially you. And your family."

When she tried to pull away, he simply moved closer, forcing her to clutch the sheet against her breasts to maintain any sort of barrier between them. Even from the dim light of the lamp, she could see how dead serious he was about this. "If you relocate and get a new identity, I won't be able to be with you—because of Dad and Millie, and my responsibilities to the department. The kids are making new lives for themselves, and I want to be a part of that."

"You should be. Thomas, I don't want to take anything away from you."

"You've already taken the most important thing." He pried her hand from the covers and placed it back over his heart. Jane almost cried at the silent message he was sending. "Hell, if you change your name and move someplace new, I might never be able to find you." His eyes narrowed and lines of strain deepened beside them. "He'd still be after you, and I wouldn't be there to protect you. I don't want to lose you. Not now, when I think there's a chance we could make something work."

She reached out to soothe the worry lines. "I want that chance, too. After Freddie, I never thought…I didn't think it was safe to care about anyone again. But I can't help it." She blinked a tear from her eye and swiped it off her cheek. She was still desperately afraid that someone would get hurt, but now she was determined to fight for the chance to live a normal life and find real love again. This wasn't just for Freddie anymore. It wasn't just for her. "I'll do whatever you tell me to make this sting you've planned a success. Let's take our lives back."

Thomas nodded. "Let's take our lives back."

This time, he initiated the lovemaking. Her skin quickly warmed beneath the crush of Thomas's chest as she hugged her arms around his neck and kissed him. He laid her back on the bed and stretched out beside her. Unlike that frantic, pent-up release earlier, this time was slow and deliberate, as if it was important to both of them to create a lasting memory that neither time nor danger nor death could ever take away.

Blissfully exhausted, her body still humming with satisfaction, Jane fell asleep in his arms again. If she'd known Thomas was the tonic to keep the nightmares at bay and find her way back to a normal life, she'd have let herself love him sooner.

SATURDAY NIGHT COULDN'T come soon enough, and now that it was here, Thomas wished he had another week to gather intel and prepare his team. He wished he had another lifetime to spend with Jane in his home and in his bed and in his family, to continue these last two idyllic days locked inside a guarded cage where the outside world couldn't reach them. They'd lived their lives as a couple, arguing a little, touching a lot, laughing and snuggling, reviewing escape scenarios, talking about anything and everything except for the fragile L-word that neither one of them wanted to risk sharing again, in case the unthinkable happened tonight.

Thomas straightened his tie and the lapels of his suit jacket in the foyer mirror before resuming his pacing at the foot of the stairs while he waited for Jane to finish getting ready.

"You wear hole in rug," Seamus chastised him. His father stood in the archway leading into the living room, leaning on the cane he was now using to move around the house. The blue blood running through his veins showed in the worry lines on his face. He understood the game plan for tonight. Part of him was as worried about the success of Thomas's plan as he was—and part of him probably wanted to be in on the action, defending their family against the threats that had plagued them for too many months. But he settled for simply keeping his son company. "Always worth it to wait on a woman."

"Jane's not late," Thomas automatically defended her. "I just want to get this night started and done with as soon as possible."

Millie toddled down the hallway with the sweater she'd fetched for Seamus and helped him slip into it. "You know not to worry about a thing here, right?" She brushed aside a mote of lint from the navy blue wool and patted his father's chest. "Seamus unlocked his service revolver and has it loaded. Gabe and Olivia have already checked the doors and locks. After they're done eating dinner, we've got a new deck of cards to play penny ante poker until everyone comes home safely. We'll be fine."

Thomas stopped pacing and pulled back the front of his jacket to prop his hands at his waist. He frowned at the two seniors. "Dad, your hand isn't strong enough to hold and fire that gun."

"If anybody comes here and t-treatens my fam-ly, I will."

Thomas raked his fingers through his hair and started toward the kitchen. "I'm telling Olivia to un-load that weapon and lock it back up in the closet."

He hadn't taken three steps when he heard the click of heels coming down the stairs. He froze when he saw

Jane, forgetting how to breathe. She wore a high-necked red sleeveless dress with a few sparkles dancing over the satiny finish.

And those high heels. Two black straps and a silver heel. His blood raced through his veins as she descended the stairs toward him. He'd never seen her in anything but her uniform clogs or running shoes or barefoot. The height of those heels and the dress that skimmed the top of her knees made her legs look longer than he remembered and, well, irresistibly hot.

"Do I look okay?" she asked when she reached the foyer. "Too much? Not enough? I borrowed the dress and shoes from Kenna. She thought they'd be appropriate for a cocktail party." Had he even blinked? She'd swept her hair up in some elegant loose knot thing that he desperately wanted to undo with his fingers. She looked amazing, and for a few seconds he felt a rush of pride and appreciation that made him wish that this was a real date. "I chose red because I thought it was patriotic. We're celebrating the air force tonight, right?"

His father, ever more eloquent than Thomas, limped up beside her. "Well, if he won't say it, I will. You a knockout."

"Thank you." Jane smiled and kissed his cheek.

Seamus turned and swatted Thomas on the arm. "Close your mouth, t-son."

Thomas snapped his lips together, feeling the embarrassment of adolescent lust warming his cheeks. He'd never get over how this woman transformed him into a man who felt twenty or thirty years younger. "It's perfect. You're perfect."

Millie pulled out her phone and nudged Thomas toward Jane. "Stand together by the stairs. I want to get a picture."

Although he obliged by sliding his arm behind Jane's waist, he felt duty-bound to remind all of them, including himself, that tonight wasn't a date. "It's not the prom, Millie."

Jane's hand settled at his back, brushing against the gun he'd holstered there. When she stiffened, he gave the pinch of her waist a reassuring squeeze. She didn't need the sobering reminder that tonight's celebration served an ulterior purpose.

"We'll be fine, dear," Millie assured him, snapping a couple of pictures despite the grim expression on Jane's face. "And I know you. Those men won't get away."

"Do you have your tracker on you?" Thomas asked. "In case we get separated. Not that I'm letting you out of my sight."

"Right here." Jane patted her chest, where the tiny electronic device was hooked to her bra. "Do you?"

He touched the pocket of his jacket, indicating he was plugged into the KCPD surveillance that would be tracking their movements tonight, too. "We'll double-check with Keir and Agent Hunt in the command van to make sure they've got us on radar when we get to the hotel." He held out his arm and she linked her hand through his elbow. "Let's do this."

Twenty minutes later they pulled up in front of the Muehlebach Hotel in downtown Kansas City. Thomas exchanged a nod with Hud Kramer, who was working as a valet, when they got out of the car.

"We're all hooked up by radio," Hud confirmed, indicating the police officers and volunteering friends stationed throughout the hotel and conference center.

"If anything goes down, we'll all know about it. You'll have backup before you know you need it."

Then he drove off to park the truck and Thomas escorted Jane inside the historic landmark hotel. They followed the trail of bright lights across the carpeted lobby to the escalator leading down to the reception areas. They passed Al Junkert sitting in the bar off the lobby. He acknowledged them with a slight raise of his glass before turning to resume a conversation with the woman beside him.

By the time they'd checked into the air force reunion, gotten their name badges and traded hugs with Mutt and Jeff, Jane's fingers were shaking against his arm. He covered her hand with his, stilling the nervous twitching, and leaned over to press a kiss to her temple. "Remember, we've got eyes all over the place here. All you have to do is enjoy the party."

"And look for a guy with heterochromatic eyes and a neck tattoo."

The evening progressed without incident. Mutt got up on the stage and surprised Jeff with the birthday announcement, and they all sang "Happy Birthday" and the air force hymn. A couple of the guys on the planning committee had come up with the idea of awarding prizes for the veterans who'd traveled the farthest, served the longest and had the most grandchildren. The commander at Whiteman Air Force Base gave a short speech and thanked them all for their service.

Then the band played and the dancing started. And as Thomas had asked them to, Mutt or Jeff kept Jane company whenever he couldn't be at her side.

Thomas was returning to their table with two glasses of ice water and two beers when he spotted Jeff's blond hair and tall frame guiding Jane across the parquet dance floor after a '70s-era line dance ended. He set one beer in front of Mutt at the table and emptied the rest of the tray, waiting for Jeff and Jane to join them.

"Is one of those for me?" Jane asked. A sheen of perspiration dotted her forehead. Making such a conspicuous show of herself out on the dance floor was probably giving her a better workout than her morning runs.

He handed her one of the waters, and the other beer to Jeff, who swallowed a long draft before reminding them of a pledge they'd made earlier. "Don't forget, at the end of the evening, we'll toast Mary."

Mutt stood and raised his bottle. "And all the friends and fellow airmen and women we've lost along the way." He held his hand out to Jane. "My turn again?"

When he saw that stress dimple appear on her forehead, Thomas set down their glasses and took her hand instead. "I appreciate your willingness to help, boys. But how about you let me dance at least once with my own date?" Jeff eyed his bum leg. And was that a snicker he heard from Mutt? "Yes, I can dance."

Jeff clapped him on the shoulder and nudged them out to the dance floor as a slow song started. "We'll see you at eleven."

Thomas turned Jane into his arms and settled into a swaying rhythm. "Thank you for the rescue. Between these high heels and Mutt's toe stomping, my feet are killing me." Her hand slid from his shoulder to the nape of his neck, teasing the sensitive skin there as she summoned a weary smile. "But they have been as attentive as good watchdogs. One or the other or both have been with me all evening, whenever you're not here."

"I trust those yahoos with my life. I trust them with yours, too."

A few more seconds of him enjoying her hips butting against his ended with the sobering question he knew she wanted to ask. "Have you seen anyone who looks suspicious?" He'd just come back from slyly checking with every undercover operative here. Conor serving drinks. Duff posing as one of the security guards at the front entrance. Keir in the van and Hud keeping watch for anything suspicious outside. Niall in the hotel's security office, watching live camera feeds from several monitors. "Do you think he's here? Watching me right now?"

He leaned in to kiss that frown on her forehead, willing the mark to relax. "Everybody's watching you. You're the most beautiful woman here, and they're all wondering how I got so lucky."

For a moment, her lips softened into a genuine smile. "Trust me, Thomas—I'm the lucky one. I'm sorry you're not getting to enjoy your reunion."

"I've had enough conversations with old cronies to catch up." He pulled her a few inches closer and surveyed the packed room, abuzz with laughter and music and conversation, for that one person who was more interested in them than in the reunion. "It was good to see my commanding officer from Lakenheath again. I can't believe he's ninety years old and still fits into his old uniform. I want to age like that."

She nodded her agreement, although her thoughts were already drifting. "Are you certain they'll be here?"

"My aching bones, and a little profiling, tell me yes." He stopped moving and caught her shoulders between his hands, gently rubbing away the chill he felt on her skin. She hadn't complained once, hadn't admitted her fear. And that kind of bravery in the face of waiting danger had to be wearing on her. "Do you need a break from the spotlight?"

"I could use a stop at the ladies' room."

"I'll walk you out."

After a quick stop at the table to retrieve her purse and let Mutt and Jeff know they were free to socialize with the other guests for a few minutes, they headed toward the exit doors and the quieter public area and restrooms beyond. They were waylaid by a table of former members of Thomas's training class who wanted to meet Jane and chat. By the time they reached the exit doors, the band was taking a break and the commander was back up onstage to honor more of their esteemed guests and the volunteers who'd help put the reunion together. Other guests were filing back in and turning their attention to the stage.

With a hand at the small of Jane's back, Thomas turned her away from the line of women waiting at the nearest restroom and they walked around the corner to search for another facility. But there they ran into the spill-out crowd from a function in a neighboring ballroom. Jane stopped for a second and groaned. "I just needed a few minutes of quiet and some fresh air."

"How are your feet holding up?"

"Well, I'd rather not go for a hike right now."

"Let's find an empty sofa and have a seat out here." But it was a busy night at the hotel, and locating a free spot where two people could sit together wasn't easy to come by.

By the time they'd walked the length of the carpeted hallway and turned back, the security guard stationed near the elevators asked if they were lost. "We're looking for a place to sit and relax for a few minutes."

The young man smiled and pushed the elevator call button for them. "Two floors up. There's a walkway over to the adjoining hotel across the street. It's less crowded there."

"Thank you." Jane smiled up at him and stepped onto the elevator when the doors opened.

The guard followed Thomas in behind her. "I'll ride up with you."

The doors were already closing when Jane's tired brain realized what she'd just seen.

One brown eye, and one blue.

"You!"

He fired the Taser in his hand at Thomas, hitting him in the chest and stunning him before he could reach the gun at his back.

"Thomas!" She caught him in her arms and collapsed to the floor with him as the guard slid a key card into the slot beside the door, overriding the second-floor command and taking them down to the basement garage.

Chapter Twelve

Thomas woke up with one hell of a headache battering against his skull. His chest felt as though he'd met the front grille of a speeding Mack truck. What time was it? Where was he?

But sitting up to take some deep breaths and get his bearings proved almost impossible because he couldn't get his hands to cooperate to push himself up.

"Thomas?" He heard the urgently hushed whisper of a woman's voice. Jane's voice. "Oh, thank God. Are you okay?"

Suddenly, there was enough adrenaline pumping through his system to clear his head and blink his surroundings into focus.

The first thing he saw was Jane's face. Brave, beautiful Jane, more worried about him than she was for herself. Her eyes were dark and unreadable in the rocking metal box they were in. A van. The back of a van. And the reason he couldn't push himself up was because his hands were tied together and secured over his head to the grate that separated the van's storage compartment from the driver in the cab.

Although there was little feeling left in his hands, he curled his fingers into the grate and pulled himself up to a more comfortable sitting position. His ankles were tied together and his leg was protesting however he'd been dragged and dumped in the back of the moving van. Jane was bound in a similar fashion with a familiar blue nylon rope, far enough away from him that they could do little to help each other escape. He felt the empty space at the back of his belt and knew his gun was gone. But his head was clear and they were both still alive. And he had more backup than their kidnapper could ever imagine.

He peered through the grate to see the silhouette of the driver in a black security guard's uniform, and the passing streetlights as they drove through the city. He looked around at the rusted empty interior. The cage between them and the cab was locked. There was some trash bouncing along with them in the back, as well as with a coil of the blue nylon rope with an ominous noose tied at the end. Two little dots of light flashed through the back door, and he realized he was looking through a pair of tiny holes that went clear through to the outside.

Bullet-sized holes.

"The white van?" He kept his voice as low as Jane's, so their conversation wouldn't be overheard.

"We're in it." They jolted over a bump that pulled at their wrist bindings and she winced. "He had me tie you in first."

"You tied me up?"

The burst of hope that there was an easy way out of this quickly dissipated. "Sorry. He checked my handiwork and tightened the knots. He Tasered you a second time when you started to come around."

That explained the rock on his chest. "Any idea where we are?"

"I can't be certain, but he always seems to be turning left, like we're going around in circles. I don't know if he's lost or he's trying to disorient us—"

"Or he's killing time until he meets his accomplice." He inclined his head toward the driver. "Is that...?"

Jane nodded. "I saw his eyes in the elevator before he tagged you. And I struggled when he tied me up. I pulled at his collar and saw the quote tattoo. It's him."

When she turned her head away to tamp down the memories and emotions, he saw that the front of her dress had been sliced open from one shoulder down to her cleavage. The rage that lit in his belly nearly blinded him. "What did he do to you?"

Jane glanced toward the cab as he raised his voice above a whisper. But the traffic noise and earbuds the driver was wearing must have been loud enough to mask it. Jane reminded him to whisper. "He didn't hurt me. He said he wasn't supposed to yet." What the hell did that mean? She was the witness he wanted dead. The fact that he was keeping her alive only confirmed to Thomas that Badge Man was now working with a partner, and that whoever that partner was had a very personal connection to Thomas. "He knew about our trackers. He took them." Jane leaned back against the metal wall of the van. "No one will know where we are. What are we going to do?"

He stretched his legs out to touch her bare foot with his shoe because that was the only comfort he could give her. He should be happier about being right. His experience had told him exactly where tonight would lead. Only, seeing Jane tied up like a lamb for slaughter kept him from feeling good about anything.

Be a cop. Assess the situation. Learn the facts. Know what you're up against before you act.

"How long was I out?"

"Ten, fifteen minutes."

Thank God he had a partner who could keep her head in a crisis. As long as he kept her focused, Jane would stay in the moment with him and be an asset. "Do you know how many times we've turned?"

She shrugged, thinking. "Maybe six times. And we haven't gone very fast, so I'm sure we're still in the city."

"Six turns, we're probably still in the same neighborhood." That meant help wouldn't be too far away. If it could find them. He turned to inspect the knots around his wrists. "The first thing we need to do is find a way to free ourselves."

"His knife and Taser are in the front seat with him. Along with your gun."

"Then we need to get him to bring those weapons back here to us."

Her eyes widened. "What?"

He curled his fingers into the grate again and jiggled it. A couple of the screws securing it to the ceiling were missing. He wasn't a superhero, but he did know how to make himself heard. He glanced over at Jane, silently telling her to grab hold of the grate, too. "Make some noise."

They rattled the loose grate and yelled at the driver, startling him enough to make him pull out those earbuds and warn them to be quiet. They rattled the grate again. Thomas warned him he was a cop and that his actions were being monitored. Jane got her feet beneath her and stood up, threatening Badge Man in a tone that made Thomas proud and a little wary about ever getting on her bad side. "You stop this van right now!"

"Shut up!" the driver ordered, swerving into a different lane. "Stop it!"

They yelled louder and banged and threatened and rattled until the driver skidded them into a sharp left turn and braked to a sudden stop that knocked Jane off her feet. They'd pulled into a warehouse or garage somewhere. Thomas heard the *rattle* and *bang* of a large door closing and hurried footsteps across pavement before the back door swung open. He smelled the fumes of gasoline and oil and caught a glimpse of old brick and a rack of tires before the man climbed in and shut the van door behind him.

Thomas knew crazy when he saw it. He'd studied enough criminals to recognize it. Reasoning with him wasn't going to work.

"I said to shut up, Officer," he warned, sliding along the far wall toward Jane. "Not one more peep out of you or I'll kill you first and carve you up. She missed the show the last time. I'll make sure she sees exactly how I choke the life out of you, Daddy."

"I'm not your father. I would never hurt you."

"I said shut up! I'm in control here."

Jane was visibly shaking by the time the younger man tucked the Taser into his pocket and pulled out his knife to cut her loose from the grate. Was that fear? Anger? One could paralyze her. He prayed it was the other, and that she was thinking ahead to the next step like he was.

"My feet, too," she argued boldly. "Unless you want to drag me everywhere."

With an annoyed huff, he sliced through the knots at her ankles, then dragged her to her feet. Jane swayed against him, knocking him into the side of the van. "Hey!"

He screamed a hateful epithet at her and yanked on

her bound wrists, pulling her up against him as he raised the knife. But Jane tangled her feet with his, tripping him as he lunged. They landed on top of Thomas's legs, sending a jolt of pain through him. But the pain told him he was alive and that he could put those legs to good use. When the attacker's hand hit the floor, he lost his grip on the knife. He rolled off Thomas, pinned Jane beneath him and closed his hands around her throat, stopping her scream. When he rose to crush her windpipe for a second time, Thomas kicked him in the side of the face with both feet, knocking him off Jane and stunning him.

"The knife! Get the knife!" Thomas yelled.

Jane pushed up to her hands and knees, searching for the weapon that could even out the odds in this fight. But the moment she spotted it and lunged for it, so did Badge Man. He shoved her aside and outreached her. Thomas kicked him again, this time drawing blood from the split skin on his cheek.

Badge Man instantly turned his rage on Thomas, backhanding him across the mouth, then punching him from the other side. He tasted the coppery tang of blood in his mouth. His vision blurred as the man with free hands hit him again and again.

"You. Can't. Hurt. Me…"

His attacker froze with his fist in the air. His eyes were wide, his pupils tiny pinpoints. Tremors shook his body. Thomas's senses cleared long enough to hear the distinct buzz of an ongoing electric shock. The young man was still convulsing when he fell onto his side on the floor. Thomas followed the two wires up to the Taser in Jane's hands, and on up to the ferocious anger stamped on her beautiful face.

"Jane. Jane!" He called to her a second time. Her gaze darted from her target to him, and he gently spoke again. "He's out, honey. You can stop."

She dropped the weapon, pushed their kidnapper aside and picked up the knife. She cut Thomas's wrists free, then his feet. By the time she'd handed him the knife so he could slice through the rope that still bound her hands, she was kneeling beside him, plucking the handkerchief from his pocket and dabbing it against his split lip. This was his Jane, practical and efficient, determined to do what needed to be done. "Oh, God, you're hurt. Now what?"

He cupped her cheek in a quick caress before picking up the same ropes they'd been bound with and tying up their incapacitated serial killer. "Communication. And my gun."

Heaving a steadying breath, she checked the unconscious man again. "We'll have to go around to the front to get them." Ignoring the twinge in his leg, he pushed to his feet. "Let's go."

Jane nodded and hurried to the back door. But it opened a second time and she jumped back.

The too-tanned skin of a receding hairline was a welcome sight.

"Al. Thank God. You must have followed us. I need you to call—" Thomas's blood ran cold when Al snagged Jane's wrist and pulled her in front of him, pinning his forearm around her neck and pressing the barrel of the gun he held against her temple. His actions didn't make any sense. And then suddenly, everything made sense. "You son of a bitch."

"You always have to have everything your way. Don't ya, Tommy boy?" When Thomas stepped over

Badge Man's inert body, Al shoved the gun hard enough to leave a mark on Jane's skin. "Don't come any closer. And you can lose the knife."

Thomas dropped the knife to the floor and put up his hands, freezing in place. He'd take the crazy boy over a betrayal like this any day. Why hadn't he noticed the contempt in those familiar eyes before? "Why? Why do you want to hurt me like this?"

"Because you hurt me."

The oddly critical comments. The failed marriages. Ah, hell. Al hadn't been his friend all these years. He'd been keeping tabs on him, waiting for his moment to strike. "Mary."

Al nodded. "Mary." He used his toe to pull the coiled blue rope toward him. Then he stooped down, lowering the gun just long enough to loop the noose around Jane's neck.

Her frightened gasp cut right through his heart. "Stay with me, honey."

She gave him as much of a nod as a woman with a gun to her head and a noose around her throat could manage. Good. If she flashed back into one of her fugue states, she'd be completely vulnerable. They didn't have much of a chance here, but they had one.

Al was someone he could reason with. "Let me guess, you blame me for Mary's death. You fancied yourself in love with my wife."

"I don't fancy anything. I loved her and she loved me." Al jerked on the noose and Jane's fingers flew to her throat. "She was there for me when my marriage broke up. She held me and listened. She was always there for me."

Thomas's whole body tensed with an unfamiliar rage.

It was a struggle to keep his voice calm. "You were part of the family, Al. She loved you like a brother. Like I did."

"You're wrong. The only reason she didn't leave you for me was because of the children. I had to admire her for that. I could live with her being that kind, noble beauty with a sense of duty to her family." He worked his mouth as if he was fighting back tears. "But then you let her die."

Thomas's eye was swelling shut from the pounding he'd taken, but he didn't let it stop him from surveying his surroundings, taking note of every option that wouldn't end up with Jane dead. "I loved my wife. You don't think her death gutted me? You don't think I would have taken those bullets for her? Do you know how many nights, how many years, I wished it had been me in that store that night instead of her?"

"Thomas..." Jane's gasp was full of concern for him. *For him.* How could one man be lucky enough to know that kind of love twice in one lifetime? How could he be cursed enough to have it taken from him twice?

"It's going to be okay, honey," he promised. One way or another, no one was ever going to hurt her again.

"No, it's not." Al rubbed his cheek against Jane's hair. "You take a good look at this face, Tommy boy. Remember what she looked like when she's dead."

Jane was still in this fight. "You tried to kill me before. Run me off the highway. Shoot me. You couldn't get the job done, could you?"

He tightened the noose another fraction. "You'll die when I'm ready for you to. I want him to understand first."

"Understand what?" Thomas prompted. Anything to keep Al talking instead of shooting or strangling Jane.

"The kind of pain I've been in, watching you live your life and be happy and fall in love and forget all about

Mary. Actually, I tried to kill you once before." His sick blue eyes glanced down at Thomas's mangled leg.

"You totaled the cruiser during that high-speed chase on purpose."

"But then I realized killing wasn't good enough. I enjoyed seeing you in pain. You needed to suffer. You needed to feel pain and helplessness and the fear of losing everything that I've felt all these years."

"So you hired a hit man to come after my family."

"It's been hell for you for seven months now, hasn't it?" Al laughed. "You didn't know who your enemy was. You didn't know who to trust. I turned your life upside down."

"Your attacks have made my family stronger, tighter than we ever were before."

"Liar. I'm going to kill the woman you love in front of you the same way you killed mine."

Thomas kept talking. He'd spotted the Taser on the floor, and knew the knife was still within reach if Al didn't shoot him first. "We're celebrating Niall's marriage this month. On Seamus's birthday. And thanks to Jane there, Dad's going to be okay."

Al shook his head, dragging Jane with him as he moved to one side to get a clear look at the unconscious man on the floor. "Don't try to act like you're happy. I know you better than that."

"You don't know me at all."

"Kick that knife over here. I know you're thinking up a dozen different scenarios inside your head on how this is going to play out."

Thomas kicked the knife across the floor and watched it land near Jane's feet. "They all end up with you dead," he promised.

"I don't think so." Al trained his gun on Badge Man's still form. "Now, what's going to happen is this. You two are going to die—at the hands of Badge Man. I came in and killed him, but couldn't save my best friend and his little tramp. When I'm done, and call 911 for backup, I'll be a hero. And my Mary will have been avenged."

"That's your plan?" Thomas challenged, praying that Jane would follow his lead.

"Better than yours."

Jane answered, "I don't think so."

Al turned the gun on Thomas and squeezed the trigger. Jane bit down hard on the arm around her neck and Thomas charged. The bullet that clipped his shoulder didn't stop him from hitting them both and shoving them against the wall. The van rocked. Jane twisted free and staggered away while the two men fought for the gun.

Al side-kicked Thomas's bum leg and the stupid limb gave way. But Thomas rolled. Jane shoved the man with the gun. Al smacked her across the face and she fell back. Thomas came up with the knife in his hand and plunged it deep into his former partner's heart.

WITH HIS BEST friend dead beside him, blood running down his arm and a serial killer moaning about his headache, it kind of made sense to Thomas that he was hearing sirens.

"Are you with me, Thomas?" Jane had laid him down on the floor of the van, peeled off his suit jacket and tie and was busy tying a tourniquet of sorts around his left arm. "Thomas Watson, don't you leave me."

He opened his eyes and smiled, then sat up even when she told him not to. He cupped the side of her face, hating the red marks bruising her skin. They were beat up. But they were alive. They were safe. "I love you."

There. He'd said what needed to be said.

Tears filled her pretty eyes and she smiled. "I love you, too."

The van doors swung open and a trio of dark-haired men trained guns on them. Thomas instinctively pulled Jane behind him. But she laughed.

"Dad?" The biggest of the three lowered his weapon first.

"Duff. Sons." Niall and Keir quickly holstered their guns, as well. He didn't even jump when the passenger door opened in the front of the van and a waiter barged in. The young man quickly lowered his gun. "Wildman." He turned back to Duff, Niall and Keir. "How did you find us?"

Jeff Fraser squeezed into the picture. "You didn't show up at eleven to toast our Mary."

Mutt, never to be left out of the action, was there, too. "We knew something was wrong, so we alerted Duff."

His oldest son climbed inside to help them to their feet. "When your trackers stopped moving, we knew something was wrong and had already started a search."

Keir caught Jane by the waist to help her down to the garage's concrete floor. "Hud found the discarded trackers down in the parking garage, so we knew we were looking for a vehicle."

Niall moved in to check Thomas's injuries as soon as he sat on the bumper and he let his boys throw blankets around them both. "Since the white van was the common denominator in each of the previous attacks, we put out a BOLO on it. Pinged your cell phones. Led us right to you. In other words, your plan worked."

"It was Al, huh?" Duff knelt beside their former family friend. "You're going to explain all this to us, right?"

Thomas nodded, wincing between the double dose of Jane's and Niall's first-aid ministrations. "Later."

"Come on, buddy." Duff helped a woozy Badge Man to his feet and handed him off to Conor.

"I've already notified Agent Hunt," Conor reported. "He's on his way to pick up his prize." He winked at Jane. "I guess you and me won't be seeing each other much anymore. Especially once this guy's trial is over."

She squeezed Conor's hand. "I don't know about that. You were my first and best friend here in Kansas City. I'd like to keep in touch."

"Me, too."

As soon as he'd taken Badge Man away, Duff jumped down from the van, reading a name off the driver's license he'd taken from their prisoner. "His ID says Emerson Grady Shrout. With a name like that, no wonder the guy was psycho." He walked over to Mutt and Jeff. "You boys need a ride back to the hotel?"

Keir pulled his phone from his ear. "I've got an ambulance en route. I'll call Grandpa and Olivia and tell them you're all right."

Niall looked down at him. "Will you be okay if I go check the dead body now?"

Jane linked her arm through Thomas's. "I'll keep an eye on him."

For a few peaceful seconds, he and Jane were alone. "It's over, honey. It's finally over."

Jane shook her head as she lifted his uninjured arm over her shoulder and snuggled in beside him. "No. It's starting. My life is finally starting again."

Epilogue

"I'm happy, Thomas."

He chased after Jane's lips when she broke away from his kiss and leaned back against the ornate paneling in the recessed nook off the narthex of the church. She allowed him one more nibble before pushing him back to straighten the boutonniere she'd just pinned to the lapel of his tuxedo. It was a sunny, brisk September afternoon, almost seven months to the day after the shooting at Olivia's wedding in this very church. They'd already had birthday cake for breakfast to celebrate Seamus's eighty-first birthday and made love in the shower before getting dressed for Niall and Lucy's wedding.

She let her hand linger against his heart. "I didn't think I would ever be this happy or feel this normal again."

"Normal? You think anything to do with my family is normal?"

He stopped her answering laugh with a kiss that made him long for the shower again. But he had something serious he wanted to say, now that their injuries were healing, Emerson Shrout was in a DC jail awaiting trial, and he knew who he could and couldn't trust in his life once more.

"What is it?" she asked, sensing his changing mood.

"I don't want to upstage any of my boys and their fiancées. And it is the second time around for both of us. Maybe you and I could take a trip to Vegas?" The dimple on her forehead appeared. Not good. "Or maybe a justice of the peace here in Kansas City?"

The frown disappeared. "I like that idea. Keep it simple. Just your family."

"*Our* family," he corrected.

She smiled, even as tears gathered in her eyes. "I haven't been a part of a family for so long. Do you think they'll accept me as more than the hired help?"

Thomas wiped away the tear that spilled onto her cheek. "They love you. You're already part of us. The most important part if you ask me."

She wound her arms around his neck and stretched up to give him a kiss. "I like your plans."

The kiss had barely gotten interesting when they were interrupted by a cough and a deep-pitched chuckle.

"Are you two done making out?" Duff tugged at the collar of his shirt, uncomfortable in the tuxedo and tie, but not so uncomfortable that he couldn't give his dad a hard time. "We've been looking for you."

Keir stood at his shoulder in a matching tuxedo, grinning. "The organist is ready to start the processional, and I have to escort Jane to her seat before the wedding party can go down the aisle."

Duff shook his head. "I'm going to escort Jane."

Keir swatted his big brother on the shoulder. "It's my job. I'm the usher. You're the best man."

"Exactly. I'm the *best* man. Besides, I'm the oldest. It's my prerogative to escort our future stepmother down the aisle if I want to."

Keir wasn't having any of that. "Oldest? I'm the cutest. I'm the one with style. She'll want to be seen with me. I'll do it."

Niall walked up behind them, nudging his siblings apart. "I'm the groom. My day. My decision." He turned and extended his elbow to Jane. "May I?"

Jane smiled up at all three sons. "I'd be honored if any of you did." She shrugged before taking Niall's arm. "But it is Niall's day."

Niall arched a dark brow at his brothers. Before he took his victorious walk into the church, he turned to Thomas. "Now go get my bride. I'm anxious to marry her. And, Dad, um…" He pointed to his mouth, indicating that Thomas check his.

"Oops." Jane pulled a tissue from her purse and wiped away the lipstick that had smeared across his mouth.

When they left, Duff crossed his arms over his chest and groused, "I hate that logic of his."

Keir agreed. "Yep."

Thomas remembered he was the dad in all this happy chaos and pushed them toward the sanctuary. "Boys, you'd better get to your places. I'll go get Lucy."

A few minutes later, Thomas stood at the back of the church. He paused in the archway with Lucy on his arm. There were a few roped-off pews and a boarded-up stained glass window that were still under repair. But the light was shining in through all the other windows, and the music from the organ loft above them played a regal, happy melody. This place that had once been the scene of so much destruction and fear was a place of peace and worship and celebration again.

He glanced up to the heavens and smiled. *We're all okay, sweetheart. This family is different without you.*

*But we know how to love because of you. For that, I
will always be grateful.*

When the processional started, Thomas escorted
Lucy down the aisle. He saw Duff and Niall at the
altar with his daughter Olivia, the matron of honor. He
looked over at his friends and family. Keir held Kenna's hand beside Seamus and Millie, who was holding
Lucy and Niall's son, Tommy. He saw the rich red hair
of Duff's fiancée, Melanie, and followed her gaze up
to Duff, where his oldest son had to be reminded to
pay attention to the ceremony and quit grinning at her.

His family was safe. His father was healing. He'd
raised three good men and a fine young woman. After
kissing Lucy's cheek and placing her hand in Niall's,
Thomas took his seat beside Jane. She laced her fingers
through his and leaned against his shoulder. "I saw you
at the back of the church. I'm sure Mary is watching
over all of you."

Thomas carried her fingers to his lips to kiss her
hand. "And I'm sure she's happy for us, too."

There was no longer an empty hole in his life where
his heart used to be. Jane had filled it.

* * * * *

Don't miss the previous three books in
THE PRECINCT: BACHELORS IN BLUE
series

APB: BABY
KANSAS CITY COUNTDOWN
NECESSARY ACTION

Available now from Mills & Boon Intrigue.

"So you think you're safe? Or do we need to run now?"

She gaped at him. "We?" She shook her head. "Even if I'm compromised, you didn't vouch for me. Whatever happens to me, I won't betray your cover. This is about me."

"No, it's not. We're a team now, you and me."

The idea flooded her with warmth, made her feel more secure and more afraid at the same time.

If this was just about her, she wouldn't hesitate. It was worth the risk.

But it was no longer just about her. "I don't think he's going to say anything, but I can't be positive."

Marcos nodded, stepping a little closer. "Nothing in life is a guarantee, especially in undercover work."

Her pulse picked up again at his nearness, her body wanting to lean into him. "What do you think we should do?"

"If you don't think you're compromised, we stay."

If she stayed here much longer, she was definitely going to be compromised, but in a completely different way.

SECRET AGENT SURRENDER

BY
ELIZABETH HEITER

First Published in Great Britain 2017
By Mills & Boon, an imprint of HarperCollins*Publishers*
1 London Bridge Street, London, SE1 9GF

© 2017 Elizabeth Heiter

ISBN: 978-0-263-92907-2

46-0817

Our policy is to use papers that are natural, renewable and recyclable products and made from wood grown in sustainable forests. The logging and manufacturing processes conform to the legal environmental regulations of the country of origin.

Printed and bound in Spain
by CPI, Barcelona

Elizabeth Heiter likes her suspense to feature strong heroines, chilling villains, psychological twists and a little romance. Her research has taken her into the minds of serial killers, through murder investigations and onto the FBI Academy's shooting range. Elizabeth graduated from the University of Michigan with a degree in English literature. She's a member of International Thriller Writers and Romance Writers of America. Visit Elizabeth at www.elizabethheiter.com.

For Andrew—I couldn't have imagined
a better real-life hero.

I love you!

Chapter One

"This is a bad idea," Marcos Costa muttered as he drove the flashy convertible the DEA had provided him into the middle of Nowhere, Maryland. Or rather, *up* into the middle of nowhere. He could actually feel the altitude change as he revved the convertible up this unpaved road into the Appalachian Mountains.

"It was your idea," his partner's voice returned over the open cell-phone line.

"Doesn't make it a good one," Marcos joked. The truth was, it was a brilliant idea. So long as he lived through it.

The DEA had been trying to get an in with Carlton Wayne White for years, but the man was paranoid and slippery. Until now, they hadn't even had an address for him.

That was, assuming the address Marcos was heading to now actually did turn out to be Carlton's mansion and not an old coal mine where a drug lord could bury the body of an undercover agent whose cover was blown. Namely, his.

"According to the GPS, I'm close," Marcos told his partner. "I'm going to hide the phone now. I'm only going to contact you on this again if I run into trouble."

"Be careful."

"Will do." Marcos cut the call, hoping he sounded confident. Usually, he loved the thrill of an undercover meet. But this wasn't their usual buy-bust situation, where he'd show up, flash a roll of money, then plan the meet to get the drugs and instead of doing a trade, pull his badge and his weapon. Today, he'd been invited into the home of a major heroin dealer. And if everything went like it was supposed to, he'd spend the entire weekend there, being wined and dined by Carlton.

Because right now, he wasn't Marcos Costa, a rising star in the DEA's ranks. He was Marco Costrales, major player in the drug world. Or, at least, aspiring major player in the drug world, with the kind of money that could buy a front-row seat in the game.

Pulling over, Marcos slid the car into Park and popped open a hidden compartment underneath the passenger seat. Ironically, the car had originally belonged to a dealer down in Florida, and the compartment had been used to hide drugs. Today, Marcos turned off his cell phone to save the battery and slipped it in there, hoping he wouldn't need it again until he was safely out of the Appalachians.

This was way outside normal DEA protocol, but Carlton Wayne White was a big catch, and Marcos's partner was a fifteen-year veteran with a reputation as a maverick who had some major pull. Somehow, he'd convinced their superiors to let them run the kind of op the agency hadn't approved in decades. And the truth was, this was the sort of case Marcos had dreamed about when he'd joined the DEA.

"Let's do this," Marcos muttered, then started the car again. The dense foliage cleared for a minute, giving him an unobstructed view over the edge of the mountain. His breath caught at its beauty. He could see for miles, over peaks and valleys, the setting sun casting a pink-and-orange glow over everything. Carlton Wayne White didn't deserve this kind of view.

Then it was gone again, and Marcos was surrounded by trees. The GPS told him to turn and he almost missed it, spotting a narrow dirt trail at the last second. He swung the wheel right, giving the convertible a little gas as the trail got steeper. It seemed to go on forever, until all of a sudden it leveled out, and there in front of him was an enormous modern home surrounded by an ugly, electrified fence.

Most of the people who lived up here were in that transitional spot between extreme poverty and being able to eke out a living to support themselves. They had a reputation for abhorring outsiders, but rumor had it that Carlton had spread a little cash around to earn loyalty. And from the way the DEA had been stonewalled at every attempt to get information on him, it seemed to have worked.

Marcos pulled up to the gate, rolled down his window and pressed the button on the intercom stationed there. He'd passed a major test to even be given this address, which told him that his instincts about the source he'd been cultivating for months had been worth every minute. "Hey, it's Marco. Here to see Carlton. He's expecting me."

He played it like the wealthy, aspiring drug dealer they expected him to be, entitled and a little arrogant. His cover story was that he came from major family money—old organized crime money—and he was looking to branch out on his own. It was the sort of connection they all hoped Carlton would jump on.

There was no response over the intercom, but almost instantly the gates slid open, and Marcos drove inside. He watched them close behind him and tried to shake off the foreboding that washed over him. The sudden feeling that he was never going to drive out again.

Given the size of his operation, the DEA knew far too little about how Carlton worked, but they did know one thing. The man was a killer. He'd been brought up on charges for it more than once, but each time, the witnesses mysteriously disappeared before he could go to trial.

"You've got this," Marcos told himself as he pulled to a stop and climbed out of the convertible.

He was met by his unwitting source, Jesse White. The man was Carlton's nephew. Jesse's parents had died when he was seventeen and Carlton had taken him in, provided him with a home and pulled him right into the family business. Unlike Carlton, Jesse had a conscience. But he was desperate to prove himself to the uncle who'd given him a home when no one else would. Marcos had spotted it when he'd been poring over documents on all the known players. He'd purposely run into Jesse at a pool bar and slowly built that friendship until he could make his approach.

"Hey, man," Jesse greeted him now. The twenty-four-year-old shifted his weight back and forth, his hands twitching. He was tall and thin, and usually composed. Today, he looked ready to jump at the slightest noise.

Please don't get cold feet, Marcos willed him. Jesse didn't know Marcos's true identity, but that didn't matter. If things went bad and his uncle found out Jesse had brought an undercover agent to his house, being a blood relative wouldn't save the kid.

Marcos tried not to feel guilty about the fact that when this was all over, if things went *his* way, Jesse would be going to jail, too. Because Marcos also saw something in Jesse that reminded him of himself. He knew what it was like to have no one in the world to rely on, and he knew exactly how powerful the loyalty could be when someone filled that void. In Jesse's case, the person who'd filled it happened to be a deadly criminal.

Marcos had gotten lucky. After spending his entire life in foster care, being shipped from one home to the next and never feeling like he belonged, he'd finally hit the jackpot. In one of those foster homes, he'd met two boys who'd become his chosen brothers. He wasn't sure where he would have wound up without them, but he knew his path could have ended up like Jesse's.

Shaking off the memory, Marcos replied, "How's it going?" He gave Jesse their standard greeting—clasped hands, chest bump.

"Good, good," Jesse said, his gaze darting everywhere. "Come on in and meet my uncle."

For a second, Marcos's instinct was to turn and run, but he ignored it and followed Jesse into the mansion. They walked through a long entryway filled with marble and crystal, where they were greeted by a pair of muscle-bound men wearing all-black cargo pants and T-shirts, with illegally modified AK-47s slung over their backs.

One of them frisked Marcos, holding up the pistol he'd tucked in his waistband with a raised eyebrow.

"Hey, man, I don't go anywhere without it," Marcos said. A real aspiring dealer with mob connections wouldn't come to this meet without a weapon.

The man nodded, like he'd expected it, and shoved the weapon into his own waistband. "You'll get it back when you leave."

Marcos scowled, acting like he was going to argue, then shrugged as if he'd decided to let it go. The reality was that so far, things were going as expected. Still, he felt tense and uneasy.

Then Jesse led him down a maze of hallways probably meant to confuse anyone who didn't know the place well. Finally, the hallway opened into a wide room with a soaring ceiling, filled with modern furniture, artwork and antiques, some of which Marcos could tell with a brief glance had been illegally obtained.

From the opposite hallway, a man Marcos recognized from his case files appeared. Carlton Wayne White was massive, at nearly six-and-a-half-feet tall, with the build of a wrestler. His style was flamboyant, and today he wore an all-white suit, his white-blond hair touching his shoulders. But Marcos knew not to let Carlton's quirks distract him from the fact that the drug dealer was savvy and had a bad temper.

"Marco Costrales," Carlton greeted him, appraising him for a drawn-out moment before he crossed the distance between them and shook Marcos's hand.

Marcos wasn't small—he was five-nine—and made regular use of his gym membership, because he needed to be able to throw armed criminals to the ground and hold them down while he cuffed them. But this guy's gigantic paw made Marcos feel like a child.

"Welcome," Carlton said, his voice a low baritone.

"My nephew tells me you're in the market for a business arrangement."

"That's right. I'm looking—"

"No business yet," Carlton cut him off. "This weekend, we get to know one another. Make sure we're on the same page. Things go well, and I'll set you up. Things go poorly?" He shrugged, dropping into a chair and draping his beefy arms over the edges. "You'll never do business again."

He gave a toothy smile, then gestured for Marcos to sit.

That same foreboding rushed over Marcos, stronger this time, like a tidal wave he could never fight. He could only pray the current wouldn't pull him under. He tried to keep his face impassive as he settled onto the couch.

Then Carlton snapped his fingers, and three things happened simultaneously. Jesse sat gingerly on the other side of the couch, a tuxedo-clad man appeared with a tray bearing flutes of champagne and a woman strode into the room from the same direction Marcos had come.

Marcos turned to look at the woman, and he stopped breathing. He actually had to remind himself to start again as he stared at her.

She was petite, probably five-four, with a stylish shoulder-length bob and a killer red dress. She had golden brown skin and dark brown eyes that seemed to stare right inside a man, to his deepest secrets. And this particular woman knew his deepest secret. Because even though it wasn't possible—it couldn't be—he knew her.

"Meet Brenna Hartwell," Carlton said, his voice bemused. "I can see you're already smitten, Marco, but don't get too attached. Brenna is off-limits."

It *was* her. Marcos flashed back eighteen years. He'd been twelve when Brenna Hartwell had come to the foster home where he'd lived for five years. The moment he'd seen her, he'd had a similar reaction: a sudden certainty that his life would never be the same. His very first crush. And it had been intense.

Too bad a few months later she'd set their house on fire, destroying it and separating him from the only brothers he'd ever known.

After all these years, he couldn't believe he'd recognized her so instantly. He prayed that she wouldn't recognize him, but as her eyes widened, he knew she had.

"Marcos?" she breathed.

And his worst nightmare came true. His cover was blown.

Chapter Two

Marcos Costa.

Brenna couldn't stop herself from staring. Fact was, she might have been drooling a little.

What were the chances? She hadn't seen him since she was eleven years old, a few short months after her whole world had been destroyed and she'd found herself dropped into a foster home. She'd still been reeling from her mother's death, still been physically recovering herself from the car crash that had taken her only family away from her. She'd walked into that foster home, terrified and broken and alone. And the first person she'd seen had been Marcos.

Back then, he'd been twelve, kind of scrawny, with dimples that dominated his face. Even through her devastation, she'd been drawn to him. To this day, she couldn't say quite what it was, except that she'd felt like her soul had recognized him. It sounded corny, even in her own head, but it was the best she'd ever been able to understand it.

Now, there was nothing scrawny about him. Next to Carlton, sure, anyone looked smaller, but this grown-up version of Marcos was probably average height. It was hard to tell with him sitting, but one thing she could see quite well was that he'd filled out. Arms that had once resembled twigs were now sculpted muscle, easily visible through his polo shirt.

And the dimples? They were still there, like the cherry on top of an ice-cream sundae. The man looked like a movie star, with his full, dark head of hair and blue-gray eyes that popped against his pale skin. And just like when she'd been eleven, she couldn't stop staring into those eyes, feeling like she could happily keep doing it for hours.

"You two know each other?"

Brenna snapped out of her daze, realizing Carlton was glancing between them suspiciously as Marcos told her, "Marc-OH. My name is Marco."

"Marco," she repeated dumbly, still wondering what in the world he was doing here. Of all the ways she'd imagined running into him again, in the middle of the mountains at a drug lord's lair certainly wasn't one of them.

And if she didn't get her act together fast, she was going to get both of them killed.

Brenna tried to clear the dazed expression from her face. "Sort of," she answered Carlton, wishing her voice had come out as breezy as she'd intended, instead of breathless.

She glanced back at Marcos, praying whatever he was doing here, he'd leave before he could ruin things for her. This was a once-in-a-lifetime opportunity, and she wasn't going to let it slip away, not even for the first boy who'd made her heart race and her palms sweat.

She strode through the enormous room, her too-high heels clicking against the marble floor, and then settled onto the chair next to Carlton. "I picked him up at a bar. When was it? A couple of years ago?" She shook her head, letting out a laugh, hoping Marcos would go along with her story.

She could have told them she'd known Marcos from the foster home. Carlton knew her history—at least the version of it she'd chosen to let him hear—and he definitely knew about her time at that foster home. But Marcos was using a fake name, and she didn't know what his game was, but she didn't want to contradict whatever story he'd given Carlton. Because no matter how much her heart hurt at the idea of the adult Marcos being a criminal, she held out hope that he was here for some other reason. And she definitely didn't want to cause his death.

"Sorry for telling you my name was Crystal," she said to Marcos.

Carlton guffawed and relaxed again. "Lucky man," he told Marcos.

Marcos's gaze lingered on her a moment longer before he looked back at Carlton. "Yeah, until she slipped out at dawn. But you never forget a face like that." His eyes darted back to her for a split second, and then he accepted the glass of champagne the butler held out.

Brenna relaxed a tiny bit. She shook her head at the butler when he stopped in front of her and simply watched as Carlton, Jesse and Marcos toasted to a potential friendship.

Disappointment slumped her shoulders. She knew what a "potential friendship" toast meant. Marcos Costa was a drug dealer.

She should have recognized it instantly. There weren't very many reasons someone would come out to Carlton Wayne White's secret mansion. To even earn an invite, Marcos had to have some serious connections.

But Brenna couldn't help herself. She looked at him now and she still saw the boy who had opened the door for her, taken her pathetic suitcase in one hand, and her hand in the other. That foster home hadn't been anything close to a real second home to her, but she'd realized after being sent away a few months later that she'd gotten very, very lucky at that first introduction to life in the system. She'd gotten very, very lucky meeting Marcos.

She'd spent most of the rest of her life dreaming of him whenever things got tough, creating a fiction where she'd see him again and he'd sweep her off her feet. She knew it was ridiculous, but that didn't matter. The dream of Marcos Costa had gotten her through the worst times in her life.

It made her sad to see that he'd grown up into someone who'd have a "potential friendship" with the likes of Carlton Wayne White. Of course, what must he think of her? She wondered suddenly if he'd ever suspected she'd set the fire eighteen years ago that had separated them.

Why would he? Brenna shook it off and tried to focus. She couldn't let Marcos Costa—whatever his agenda—distract her.

She'd worked hard to get this invite to Carlton's house. She'd spent weeks planning ways to catch his attention, then even more weeks testing those theories, until finally he'd taken the bait. But Carlton hadn't gotten to where he was by being careless, or being easily distracted by a woman who wanted to trade assets. She knew he didn't trust her yet. And there was only so far she was willing to go to earn that trust.

But she needed to get close to him, so she could dig up his secrets as thoroughly as she knew he'd tried to look into hers. Because the events of that day eighteen years ago, when the study had gone up in flames around her, still haunted her. And she suspected that Carlton Wayne White, whether he knew it or not, was connected to that day. And that meant he was connected to her. He just didn't know it yet.

If everything went as planned, he wouldn't know it until it was far too late.

THREE HOURS LATER, after a ridiculously heavy five-course meal filled with meaningless small talk, Brenna walked gingerly toward the room Carlton had put her in. Her feet were killing her. The shoes he'd bought her boasted a label she'd never be able to afford, but as good as they looked, they were far from comfortable. Give her tennis shoes over these heels any day of the week. But she'd never tell him that.

Carlton had bought her the dress, too, as well as a necklace that probably cost more than her car. So far, he seemed to be respecting her boundaries: she'd made it clear that she wasn't interested in being anyone's mistress. But she'd also dropped hints that she liked the sort of life her job with the state could never give her.

Slowly, over the course of a series of dinner meet-ups where she'd pretended to be naive enough to think he was interested in simple friendship, he'd dropped his own hints about what he could offer her. About what she might offer him in return.

And now here she was, at his mansion, far from help if he discovered her real intentions, being "interviewed" as clearly as Carlton was doing to Marcos.

Marcos. It had been hard to keep her eyes off him during dinner, a fact she was sure Carlton hadn't missed. Even if Marcos hadn't been her first childhood crush, he was exactly her type. Or at least, he would have been if he weren't a drug dealer.

Besides his good looks, the man was charming and

funny and interesting. Maybe a little more cocky and entitled than she'd have expected, but then again, never in a million years would she have pegged that he'd grow up and fall into crime.

He'd seemed so well-adjusted those few months she'd known him, doing well in his classes, having a clear bond with two older boys in the house, a brotherhood that went beyond blood. What had happened to him after that fire?

She knew he and his brothers had been torn apart. All six foster kids had been sent to different places. But that was all she knew; she'd thought about looking him up more than once over the years, but she'd never done it. Now, she almost wished she didn't know the path he'd chosen.

Was it her fault? If she hadn't walked into the study when she had, if that fire hadn't started, would he have traveled a different path?

"Brenna."

The soft voice behind her startled her, and Brenna stepped sideways on her stiletto. She would have fallen except a strong hand grabbed her waist. For a moment, her back was pressed against a ripped, masculine frame she didn't have to see to instinctively recognize.

She regained her balance, her pulse unsteady as she spun and found Marcos standing inches away from her. This close, she should have seen some imperfection, but the only thing marring those too-handsome features was the furrow between his eyebrows. It sure looked like disappointment.

Her spine stiffened, and she took a small step backward. "Marcos, uh, Marco." She glanced around, seeing no one, but that didn't mean much. Carlton was notoriously paranoid. For all she knew, he had cameras inside his house as well as around the perimeter.

Marcos must have had the same thought, because his words were careful as he told her, "I never expected to see you again after that night. And now you're with Carlton, huh?"

All through dinner, she could see Marcos trying to figure out her relationship with Carlton. The drug kingpin had seen it, too, because he'd made offhand comments that implied she was his, without being so obvious she'd be forced to correct him. But apparently, Marcos had bought it.

She flushed at the idea that he thought she was sleeping with a drug lord for jewelry and cars. But she also heated at the idea of keeping up the ruse that she'd spent a night in Marcos's bed.

What would that be like? Her thoughts wandered, to the two of them, sweaty, limbs tangled on the huge bed in her room. She shook it off, but it must not have been fast enough, because when she focused on Marcos again, the look he was giving her told her he'd imagined it, too.

"Uh, no. Carlton and I aren't dating, if that's what you're asking."

"I'm not sure that's what I'd call it," Marcos replied softly.

She scowled at him. "We have a business arrangement, and it's not what you think, so stop looking at me like that. The fact is, my arrangement with him is probably not all that different from yours."

Except it was. The ruse she was running with Carlton was about access, not drugs. If she really planned to go through with what she'd promised him, though, it was probably worse than dealing drugs.

His eyes narrowed on her, studying her with a too-keen gaze, and she tried not to squirm. He had the look of a lot of criminals who made it long enough to build an empire—or so she'd come to believe in her limited experience. Oddly, it was a similar probing look that cops used.

"So, Brenna, what do you do when you're not hanging out in Carlton's mansion, wearing spectacular dresses?" Marcos asked, shifting his weight like he was getting comfortable for a long chat.

The urge to fidget grew stronger. Lying didn't come naturally to her, as much as she'd tried to convince her superiors that she could do it—that she could do *this*, come into a drug lord's home and lie to him over an entire weekend, get him to give her insight and access. She'd actually felt pretty confident—well, a careful balance of confidence and determination—until Marcos had shown up. Now, she just felt off balance.

"I work for the foster care system." She kept up the story she'd given Carlton. "I grew up in the system," she added, even though he knew that. But it was more a reminder to herself: always act as though Carlton or one of his thugs was watching. "And I wanted to be on the other side of it, make some changes."

Marcos tipped his head, his eyes narrowing, like he suspected she was lying, but he wasn't sure about what.

She longed to tell him the whole truth, but that was beyond foolish, and one more sign that her boss was right. She wasn't ready for undercover work, wasn't ready for an assignment like this.

If she told Marcos the truth, she'd be dead by morning.

Still, she couldn't help wondering what he'd say. The words lodged in her throat, and she held them there.

I'm a cop.

Chapter Three

Brenna Hartwell was lying to him.

Marcos didn't know exactly what she was lying about, but he'd been in law enforcement long enough to see when someone was doing it. And not just to him, but to Carlton, too. He prayed the drug boss didn't realize it.

"What do you do for the foster care system?" he asked, wondering if even that much was true.

She fidgeted, drawing his attention to the red dress that fit her like a bandage, highlighting every curve. She was in great shape. Probably a runner. Or maybe a boxer, given the surprising muscle tone he'd felt when he'd grabbed her to keep her from stumbling in her shoes.

"Right now, placement," she said, but something about the way she said it felt rehearsed. "But I'm trying to get them to start a program to help kids transition out of the system."

It was a notoriously tricky time. Kids who spent their lives in foster care hit eighteen and that was it. They were on their own, and they had to learn to sink or swim without any help pretty fast.

Some—like Marcos's oldest brother Cole—did whatever it took. Cole had taken on two jobs, built up his bank account until he could afford an apartment big enough for three. Then when Marcos and his other older brother Andre had been kicked out of the system, they'd actually had a home waiting for them.

But Marcos was lucky. And he knew it. Most foster kids didn't have that. Most kids found themselves suddenly searching for shelter and a job. Tons ended up instantly homeless, and plenty took whatever work they could get, including something criminal.

Had that been what had really happened to Brenna? When she'd shown up on their foster home doorstep that day eighteen years ago, her chin up, blinking back tears, his heart had broken for her. A few months later, she'd been gone. He'd always wondered where she'd ended up, but he'd been too afraid to search for her.

Some kids got lucky, ended up in foster homes with fantastic parents who ultimately adopted them. Others, like him, bounced around from one foster home to the next, from birth until eighteen. He supposed he'd never searched for her because he'd always wanted to believe she'd been one of the lucky ones.

"What about you?" Brenna asked, and he was surprised to hear the wary disappointment in her tone.

She was in Carlton's house because she could offer him something. If it wasn't sex, like Carlton had been implying over dinner, then it was some kind of criminal connection. So, who was she to judge *his* motives?

Still, he felt a little embarrassed as he gave his cover story, the way a real dealer would. "Carlton and I share similar business interests. We're talking about a transaction, but I need to pass his test first." He gave her a lopsided grin. "How do you think I'm doing so far?"

She shrugged. "I wouldn't know. I think you and I are in similar positions."

Interesting. So her association with Carlton was relatively new. He wondered if he could get her out of here when he left, convince her to move her life onto a different track. Maybe all she needed was a little help.

It was a thought Marcos knew could get him killed. Doing anything to disrupt Carlton's life before he committed to the deal and Marcos could slap cuffs on him threatened the whole operation. But the idea hung on, refusing to let go.

For years, he'd had an image of Brenna Hartwell in his mind: a perfect, grown-up version of the little girl who'd made his heart beat faster. And even though she probably couldn't have lived up to that fantasy even if she weren't a criminal, he was still drawn to her in a way he couldn't really explain.

"I should go to bed," Brenna said, interrupting his thoughts. She stared a minute longer, like she wanted to say something, but finally turned and headed off to her room.

All the while, he longed to call after her, longed to ask her why she'd set that fire eighteen years ago. Instead, he watched her go until the door near the end of the hallway clicked quietly shut behind her.

Then Marcos headed to his own room, down a different hallway. He'd just turned the corner when Carlton pushed away from the wall, out of the shadows, nearly making Marcos jump.

The drug kingpin's eyes were narrowed, his lips tightened into a thin line. "Maybe I didn't make myself clear at dinner," Carlton said, his voice low and menacing, almost a snarl. "So, let me be plain. Stay away from Brenna. Or our business here is finished before we get started."

"SHE'S A ROOKIE!"

"Sir, she's determined. She dug all this up on Carlton Wayne White herself. She's found an angle we never even considered and I think it's going to work. She—"

"She's got no undercover experience."

"No, but we can give her a crash course. She's smart. We've never gotten this close to him before."

"I don't like it. And the DEA wants this guy for themselves. They won't be happy if we jump into their territory."

"So don't tell them. It doesn't have anything to do with drugs anyway. Not really."

"Hartwell could get herself killed."

Brenna had overheard the conversation last month, between the chief at her small police station and her immediate boss, the guy who'd convinced her to join the police force in the first place. Victor Raine was the closest thing she had to a friend on the force. She'd met him years ago, when she'd first gotten out of foster care and gone to a presentation on job opportunities. He'd been there, talking about police work, and she'd gone up and asked him a bunch of questions.

Ultimately, when she'd gotten a surprise college scholarship offer that covered not just her tuition, but also part of her lodging, she'd chosen that instead. But years later, after she'd graduated and bounced from job to job without feeling fulfilled, she'd looked Victor up. She'd visited him at the station, and somehow found herself applying to the police academy.

Before she knew it, she had graduated and was a real, sworn-in police officer. It was scarier—and better—than she'd ever expected. But typical rookie patrol assignments had lost their luster quickly, and she'd started digging for more.

Her plan to infiltrate Carlton's network had come to her by accident. She'd been on foot patrol with her partner, a newbie right out of the academy, barely out of his teens. Next to him, her six months of experience had seemed like a lifetime. They'd gotten a call about a disturbance, and when they'd arrived, they'd found a kid stabbed and left for dead on the street.

She'd cradled his head in her lap while she'd called for help, and tried to put pressure on his wounds. He'd stared up into her eyes, his baby blues filled with tears, silently begging her to help him. But he'd been too far gone. He'd died before the ambulance had gotten there, and she'd been left, bathed in his blood, to answer the detectives' questions.

She'd had nothing to tell them. He hadn't said a word, just looked at her, his gaze forever burned into her memory. So, as they'd dug into his murder, she'd followed the case's progress.

She'd learned the kid's name: Simon Mellor. And she'd discovered he was just eighteen years old, a few months out of the foster care system, probably killed running drugs for someone because he couldn't find any better options for himself.

The fury that had filled her then still heated her up whenever she thought about him. The investigation had stalled out and it looked destined to become a cold case, so Brenna had made it her mission to figure out who'd killed the kid. What she'd discovered had led her back to Victor, to the biggest favor she'd ever asked her mentor.

And he'd agreed, gone to their chief and begged for her chance to go undercover in Carlton's operation. Brenna had stood outside the door, just out of sight, but she'd heard her chief's "no way" coming long before he'd said it.

So when he'd announced, "Hartwell could get herself killed," Brenna had pushed open that door, slapped her hands on her hips and told him, "That's a chance I'm willing to take."

This morning, as she slipped into another slinky dress Carlton had bought her, she realized that was a strong possibility. She was way out of her league here. The quick training she'd received on undercover work— how to remember a cover story, how to befriend a criminal and keep the disgust she really felt hidden—could only take her so far. And now, with Marcos here, she felt unfocused when she needed every advantage she could get.

Carlton Wayne White was behind Simon Mellor's death. He hadn't held the knife—he was too far up the chain for something like that. But he'd ordered it. And Brenna was determined to make him pay.

But if that was all there was to it, her chief never would have approved this assignment. What Brenna had uncovered went way deeper than one boy's murder. Because he wasn't the only kid who'd wound up dead shortly after getting out of foster care, with rumors of a drug connection surrounding his murder. She didn't know how he was doing it yet, but Carlton was using the foster care system to find pawns for his crimes.

If she was right, he'd been doing it for years, building his empire on the backs of foster care kids.

Most of what she remembered from that horrible night eighteen years ago was the fire. The smell of the smoke, the feel of it in her lungs. The heat of the blaze, reaching for her, swallowing up everything in its path. But one of the things in its path had been papers, and years later, when she'd seen similar papers at the foster system headquarters, she'd known.

Carlton Wayne White was using someone in the system to get names of kids who were turning eighteen. Kids who'd have nothing: no family, no money, no help. He'd swoop in and offer them a chance to put a roof over their head and food in their bellies. And then they'd die for him.

It all ends soon, she promised herself, yanking open her door and striding into the hallway—and smack into Marcos.

What was he doing outside her room?

She didn't actually have to speak the words, because as he steadied her—yet again—he answered. "Carlton told me to come and get you for breakfast."

She couldn't help herself. Her gaze wandered over him, still hungry for another look after so many years. Today, he was dressed in dark-wash jeans and a crewneck sweater that just seemed to emphasize the breadth of his chest.

"Brenna," he said, humor and hunger in his tone.

She looked up, realizing she'd been blatantly ogling him. "Sorry." She flushed.

The hunger didn't fade from his eyes, but his expression grew serious. "Brenna, I want—"

She wanted, too. Maybe it was just the chance to finally do something about her very first crush, or the fact that she'd never expected—but always hoped—to see Marcos again.

It was foolish and wrong for so many reasons, but she couldn't seem to help herself. She leaned up on her tiptoes in another pair of ridiculous shoes and practically fell toward him, looping her arms around his neck.

His hands locked on her waist, and then her lips were on his, just the briefest touch before he set her back on her feet.

"Brenna," he groaned. "We can't do that. Carlton—"

"He's not here right now," she cut him off, not wanting to think about Carlton and the dangerous mission she'd begged to get assigned to. Because all she could think about was Marcos. The boy she'd never been able to forget, morphed into a man she couldn't stop thinking about. She leaned back into him, and she could tell she'd caught him off guard.

Before he could protest again, she fused her lips to his. Just one real taste, she promised herself, and then she'd back away, leave him alone and go back to her mission.

He kissed the way she'd imagined he would in all those childhood fantasies she'd had, where she grew up and got out of those foster homes she'd been sent to after the fire. Like a fairy-tale ending come to life.

Except this wasn't a fairy tale. And Marcos was a drug dealer.

She pulled away, feeling dazed and unsteady. He didn't look much better; he actually seemed shocked he'd kissed her back at all. But as she stared up at him, breathing hard and trying to pull herself together, she could see it on his face. He was thinking about kissing her again.

And, Lord help her, she wanted him to.

"I warned you to stay away from her!"

Carlton's voice boomed down the hallway, making her jump. She almost fell, but braced herself on the wall as Carlton strode toward them, fury in his expression and ownership in his voice that made a chill run through her.

Then he snapped his fingers and his thugs pounded down the hallway, too.

Marcos put his hands up, trying to placate him, but it didn't matter. One of the guards slung his semiautomatic rifle over his shoulder and punched Marcos in the stomach, making him double over.

As Brenna gasped and yelled for Carlton to stop them, the thugs each took Marcos by an arm and dragged him down the corridor.

And she knew what was going to happen next. They were going to kill him.

Chapter Four

Marcos tensed his muscles, but it didn't stop the pain when one of Carlton's guards slammed an oversize fist into his stomach. The punch doubled him over, his eyes watering. They'd been hitting him for five minutes, and he could feel it all over his body. Gasping for air, he staggered backward, giving himself a few precious seconds to gauge his options.

Fight or flight?

His car was a few feet behind him, his DEA phone secreted in the hidden compartment, his keys always in his pocket. But there was no way he'd make it. Both bodyguards had semiautomatic weapons slung over their backs. He couldn't run faster than they could swing the weapons around and fire.

Fighting was a problem, too. These two might have looked like more brawn than brain, but they weren't stupid. They were staying on either side of him, one at a time stepping forward for a hit, the other keeping enough distance that he couldn't take on one without the other being able to fire.

Besides, Brenna was still inside. He could hear her, screaming at Carlton to stop them. And it didn't matter what deal she had with the drug kingpin. If Carlton was this angry at Marcos for a simple kiss, what would he do to Brenna for choosing Marcos over him? Marcos couldn't leave her.

Not that he was going to have much of a choice, the way things were going. The guy came at him again, before Marcos could fully recover, and swept his feet out from underneath him.

He hit the concrete hard, pain ricocheting through his skull. Black spots formed in front of his eyes and bile burned his throat. His biggest undercover assignment, and he was going to die all alone in the middle of the Appalachians. Would they even find his body? Would his brothers know what had happened to him?

The thought gave him strength, and as he made out a size thirteen crashing toward him through his wavering vision, Marcos rolled right. His stomach and his head rebelled, but he held it together, shoving himself to his feet. He was unsteady, but standing.

And then he spotted her. Brenna stood in the doorway to the house. She was screaming, he realized—it wasn't just his ears ringing. Carlton had his arms wrapped around her, lifting her off the ground, but not moving as she swung her feet frantically, trying to escape.

Fury lit Marcos, and it seemed to intensify the pain in his head. He must have swayed on his feet, because the guards both moved toward him at once, smiling, and Marcos recognized his chance.

The first guard swung a fist. Instinctively, Marcos ducked, then stepped forward fast, getting close enough to slam an uppercut into his chin.

The guard's head snapped backward, but Marcos didn't waste time with a follow-up punch. He twisted right, bringing his palm up this time, right into the second guard's nose. Blood spurted, spraying Marcos as the guy howled and staggered backward, his hands pressed to his face.

In his peripheral vision, he could see Carlton's surprise as he let Brenna go. She stumbled, losing one of her shoes as she came running toward him. Behind her, Marcos could see Carlton's hand reach behind his back—surely where he had his own weapon.

He opened his mouth to warn Brenna to duck when the first guy he'd hit shoved himself to his feet. Marcos barreled into him, taking him to the ground hard, his only hope to grab the guy's weapon and shoot first.

It was a desperate move, and unlikely to work, but he didn't even have a chance to try, because the second guy pulled a pistol that had been hidden under his T-shirt. He was swinging it toward Marcos when Brenna slammed into him, taking the guy down despite the fact that he must have outweighed her by a hundred pounds. They fell to the ground together, but Marcos didn't have time to do more than say a silent prayer neither of them had been shot as the guy underneath him suddenly rolled, bucking Marcos off.

He shoved to his knees, ready to slam into the guy again, but he'd somehow managed to yank his AK-47 up toward Marcos.

Marcos's breath caught and then a gunshot rang out.

Shock slammed through him, and it took several seconds before he could process it. He hadn't been hit. The guy in front of him was down, though, eyes staring blankly at the sky, gun lying uselessly at his side.

Marcos glanced over at Carlton, but the man looked as surprised as Marcos felt. Carlton's weapon dangled in his hand, like he'd been getting ready to use it but hadn't been fast enough.

Swiveling to stare at Brenna, Marcos watched as she slowly lowered the weapon she'd somehow gotten away from Carlton's other bodyguard. He lay half underneath her, moaning in pain.

She was breathing hard, blinking rapidly, and he knew instantly that she'd never killed anyone before.

Marcos saw movement from the corner of his eye, and he knew before he looked up that Carlton was raising his gun hand. Marcos gauged the distance to the nearest AK-47, but it was too far, and he knew it even before Carlton barked, "Don't even think about it."

His gaze lifted, and he readied himself for a second time to be shot, but Carlton wasn't pointing the pistol at him.

He was pointing it at Brenna.

"DO YOU HAVE some kind of death wish?"

Carlton's voice, usually loud and boisterous, was scarily quiet. But the menace came through as clearly as if he'd screamed at her as he pointed the gun at her head.

Brenna realized her mistake instantly. She shouldn't have lowered her weapon. She should have swung it toward Carlton.

But she'd never shot anyone before. Sure, she'd fired a weapon hundreds of times. In practice. She'd even held a weapon on resisting suspects before. But she'd never had to use it to protect herself or someone else.

Until now.

There was no question Carlton's bodyguards were going to kill Marcos. Nothing she'd said had swayed the drug lord. And when he'd released her, she'd acted on instinct. Instinct and fury, and something fiercely protective that scared her.

And afterward, when the man had dropped to the ground, no dying scream, no time for surprise to register on his face, her hand had just gone slack on her. She hadn't even consciously decided to kill him and now it was over.

She'd just *killed* someone. Regret hit with the force of a tidal wave, but there hadn't been any other way. She couldn't just stand by and watch Marcos die.

Pushing the emotions down, Brenna tried to focus, telling herself she could deal with her regrets later—assuming she lived through the next few minutes.

"Carlton," Brenna said, her voice shaky. "I was just trying to—"

"You'd die for this man?" Carlton boomed, making her flinch. "After just a one-night stand?" His eyes narrowed, and he glanced from her to Marcos and back again, but too fast for her to lift her own weapon.

He suspected she and Marcos had a deeper connection than the lie she'd given about picking him up at a bar. And Carlton was right. But she and Marcos had only known each other for a few months. A few months of the worst pain in her life. A pain that had brought her here.

Resolution overtook her fear. She'd come this far. She wasn't going to die without a fight.

And with Carlton, she knew her best weapon wasn't her fists or the gun clutched in her hand. Tossing the pistol away from her, she lifted her hands in the air and got slowly to her feet, stepping slightly away from the bodyguard moaning on the ground.

Her hair was a disaster; pieces of it stuck to her lipstick, more of it was in her eyes. Her knees were skinned and bloody, her dress hiked up way too high. She ignored all of it, locking her gaze on Carlton and tipping her chin up. "You read my file, right? You know about the fire?"

She sensed Marcos tense, but she couldn't dare glance at him as Carlton gave a brief nod.

"Then you must know the rest of it, too." Her voice hitched, remembering the things that had come after that fire, when she'd been sent to other foster homes. Places without smiling boys with dimples to greet her and hold her hand, but older boys with a scary gleam in their eyes.

Carlton's eyes narrowed even more, but she could tell he was listening. Maybe he even cared.

"If you really looked, then you know this isn't about Marcos. Marco," she corrected herself. "It's about me. I'm here because I want a different life from the one I grew up with. I want security. I want to feel safe." She let the truth of those words ring through in her voice. "So, I'll work with you, but you don't own me. If that's what you want, I'm not interested."

A smirk twisted his lips, then faded, and she wasn't sure if she'd just signed her death warrant or gotten through to him.

Beside her, the bodyguard she'd knocked to the ground pulled himself to his knees, snarling at her. For a second, she thought he was going to jump up and tackle her, when Carlton fired his gun, making her jump.

His bodyguard slumped back down, dead.

She stared at Carlton, speechless, and he shrugged. "He failed me. Kind of like you, Brenna."

She hadn't gotten through to him. Brenna took a breath and closed her eyes.

"This is supposed to be a business arrangement, right?" Marcos spoke up.

Brenna opened her eyes again, glancing at him, wondering if it was smart of him to remind Carlton of his presence.

"Because I've got to tell you," Marcos continued, getting to his feet, too, and leaving behind the bodyguard's weapon, which had been at arm's length away, "this is how my family did business. All these feuds. It's derailing their business. Why do you think I want to branch out on my own?"

His family? Brenna frowned, wondering what game he was playing. Some of the kids in the foster homes she'd been to had family out there, either people they'd been taken from because of neglect or abuse, or people who'd given them up. But not Marcos. She knew he'd grown up in the system from the time he was an infant, that they'd never been able to find any extended family. Had that changed? Had he found blood relatives after the fire?

"Let me ask you something, Marco," Carlton replied. "Or is it Marcos?" His gaze snuck to Brenna, then returned. "You've met Brenna once? She was that unforgettable?"

Marcos frowned, and a sick feeling formed in her stomach at the way the drug lord's eyes wandered over her, way more blatantly than he'd ever done before. As if she was his, whether she liked it or not.

Carlton Wayne White was a killer. A man who'd use kids with no one to help them as disposable pawns in his business. Why should it surprise her if he was also a rapist?

She'd been clear with him that she didn't want to sleep with him. She'd thought he actually respected that; she'd believed he saw her as a better business partner because of it. But maybe she'd been fooling herself. Maybe he'd never cared because he hadn't planned to ask.

Before Marcos could answer Carlton's question, he continued, "Or you just have a problem with loyalty? Is that why you're dealing with me instead of sticking with family? I looked into you, Costrales. You're the black sheep, aren't you?"

Marcos shrugged, spitting blood onto the ground. "You say black sheep. I say visionary."

Carlton snorted. "You're awfully confident for a man I still might kill."

"My family and I may not always see eye to eye, but they're pretty good at blood feuds."

Carlton nodded slowly and lowered his weapon. "So they are." He gave a slight smile. "I suppose I don't want to have to deal with your entire family coming after me. Too messy for me to clean up." He nodded at Brenna. "I guess this means you're vouching for her?"

Marcos paused a long moment and Brenna held her breath, not sure what to hope for. Whoever Marcos's family was—if his story was even true—they had sway. But if Marcos vouched for her too quickly, would Carlton really buy that they didn't know one another well? Or would he think the two of them were playing some kind of scam on him, maybe trying to steal away his business?

"I don't really know her," Marcos said, not even

glancing her way. "And I don't know what kind of business arrangement you two have. So I'm not sure I can do that. But I'll tell you this much. I betray you? Fine, kill me. I'd do the same. But playing some sort of ownership game with a woman who's not interested and shooting anyone who gets in your way? That's not how I work. So, I tell you what. You leave her alone and so will I."

Carlton tucked his gun back into his waistband and Brenna let out a breath, tugging down her dress and yanking the hair out of her face.

"Well, hasn't the mob gotten progressive?" Carlton asked. "All right. We've got a deal." He glanced at Brenna. "I guess this means our time together is over."

He turned and walked inside, and Brenna stood rooted in place. That was it? All the months of work and she'd let a foolish attraction to a man she hadn't seen in almost two decades ruin everything?

She blinked back tears as Marcos sent her a brief, unreadable glance and followed Carlton, leaving her all alone in the drug lord's driveway.

Chapter Five

When she'd joined the police department, Brenna had known the day might come where she'd have to shoot someone in the line of duty. It was a responsibility she'd accepted, the idea that she might have to take one life to save another.

But nothing could have prepared her for the roll of emotions making her chest feel tight and her stomach churn right now. She pressed a hand to her stomach and tried to calm her breathing as she stood just inside Carlton's mansion.

His two remaining guards had been called up and were dealing with the bodies outside, and then they were supposed to escort her to her car and send her home. But after all the work she'd put in to get here, she couldn't leave. Not like this. Not with Carlton still planning business deals, and Simon Mellor with no one else willing to take up his cause.

The truth was, there were a lot of Simon Mellors out there. Other kids just like him who were getting ready to leave the foster system and had no idea the challenges that awaited them. Kids who Carlton might target by offering them things they couldn't resist, like a way not to be homeless and hungry.

Brenna straightened and strode to her room. She yanked off the dress, heels and diamonds Carlton had been trying to woo her with, and she'd been pretending to be infatuated with, and traded them for her normal clothes. Then she headed to the living room, where Carlton had settled alone after killing one of his own guards. She might have thought he felt some regret, too, but she didn't think the man knew what that meant.

Throwing the clothes and jewelry at him, she planted her hands on her hips and exclaimed, "I thought you were a businessman!"

He shoved the items off him onto the floor and raised an eyebrow. "And I didn't realize that you were a drama queen."

"I came here because of all the things we talked about over the past few months. I came here to start a business deal with you, and this is what you do to me?"

"Careful now," he said, the amusement dropping off his face. "I gave you a second chance today. Don't make me regret it."

"How is this a second chance? Sending me home with nothing?"

"I'm letting you live, aren't I?"

His words stalled her angry tirade, but she shouldn't have been surprised. She hadn't had enough of a plan when she'd come out here.

Taking a deep breath, Brenna started over. "Look, we each have something the other one wants. You plan to find someone else in the foster care system who can do this for you? Fine, give it your best shot. Most of them are overworked and underpaid and are either there because it's what they can get, or because they want to make a difference. You approach the first type and yeah, you might get a bite, but they won't be as aggressive about this as I will. You approach the second type, and you'll get turned in to the police so fast your head will spin."

"The police," Carlton mocked. "They're not smart enough to prove anything."

But she could see on his face that her words were getting through to him, that he wanted her connections more than he was showing, so she pressed on. "I started working in the system because I thought maybe I could make things better for kids like me. But the truth is, that will never happen. Someone like *you* is their best chance. And you're mine, too, because I might not have had control over my life since I was thrown into the system, but I do now. And I plan to make the most of it."

A slow smile spread over Carlton's face. "I may have acted too hastily, Brenna. Consider your invitation to stay here extended, and our business deal back on." He looked her over, from her well-used tennis shoes to her inexpensive T-shirt. "But before I hand over any more benefits like diamonds and clothes, you're going to have to prove yourself."

She nodded, elation and disgust with herself at the tactics she was using fighting for control. In the end, determination won out. Before this weekend was over, she was going to have Carlton on the hook with a plan he couldn't resist.

And that would be the beginning of his downfall.

"What are you doing here?" Marcos had been sitting on a bench outside, but he lurched to his feet, nearly groaning aloud at the pain that spiked all over his body.

He almost thought the hits he'd taken to the head were giving him hallucinations.

But there was no way even his mind could conjure up Brenna like this. She looked antsy in a pair of jeans and a loose aqua T-shirt that made her brown skin seem to glow and brought out the caramel highlights in her hair. Instead of the stilettos she'd been wearing all weekend, she wore a pair of hot pink gym shoes. The outfit looked way more natural on her than the skintight dresses and ridiculous heels.

She was also teary-eyed as she looked him over, her gaze lingering on his myriad of bruises that had turned a dark purple since this morning. But she didn't say a word about them, just took a deep breath.

He'd expected her to be long gone by now. And he'd been equal parts relieved and depressed over it all morning.

"I convinced Carlton that we should still be working together."

A million dark thoughts ran through Marcos's mind as he lowered himself carefully back onto the bench. "How?"

"Carlton might have a bad temper—and apparently a possessive streak—but at heart, he's a businessman."

Marcos felt himself scowl and tried to hide it. A real drug dealer would think of himself as a businessman, not a criminal.

By the expression on her face, she'd seen it, but she didn't say anything, just continued, "I have access that he wants. And he's better off with someone who will do the job without a personal distraction."

He held in the slew of swear words that wanted to

escape and instead asked calmly, "You sure it's a good idea after what happened today?"

"No." She let out a humorless laugh and sank onto the bench across from him. "But I've come too far to give up now."

What did that mean? He suddenly realized he'd been so distracted by seeing her again that he'd failed to dig into why she was here. He knew what Carlton could offer Brenna: money. But what could she offer him, especially now that she'd made it clear sex was off the table? She said she worked in the foster care system, not exactly the sort of connection Carlton would need.

"What exactly is your arrangement with Carlton?" Marcos asked.

She fidgeted, as though she'd been hoping to avoid this question. "I can get him information he needs."

The answer was purposely vague and Marcos raised an eyebrow.

"How about you, Marc-O?" she pressed. "What can you give him?"

"A new network," Marcos answered simply, wishing he didn't have to lie to her. Wishing it didn't come so easily. But that was good—it meant all his training had worked if he could even lie to Brenna.

"For drugs? How?"

It was time to get off this topic and convince Brenna to rethink her decision to stay here. "Carlton is dangerous," Marcos said softly.

"Yeah, no kidding," she replied, looking him over again.

Her voice cracked as she asked, "How badly are you hurt?"

"Could have been worse. Thank you for that. Where'd you learn to fight?"

Her legs jiggled a little, a clear sign he was about to get less than the full truth. "Foster care." She glanced around, then lowered her voice. "Not all of us can find long-lost family."

"Yeah, well…" Now it was his turn to feel antsy, but he'd had a lot of practice being undercover. So why did lying to her feel so wrong? "Carlton doesn't know about my years in foster care, and I'd like to keep it that way."

She tipped her head, like she was waiting for more details, but he stayed silent. Better if she just kept her mouth shut about his past altogether. Because the story Carlton knew didn't match up with Marcos *ever* having been in foster care.

As far as Carlton knew, he'd grown up in the massive Costrales family, where joining organized crime was in the blood. The DEA had backstopped a story for him that involved being a bit estranged from his family, but still on the payroll. As far as they could tell, Carlton's empire didn't yet stretch to the area the Costrales family ran, but there was no way to prepare for all possible overlap.

On paper, Marco Costrales was the youngest son of Bennie Costrales, born of a mistress. He hadn't grown up with the Costrales name, but he'd been given it—and a large sum of money to build his own empire—when he'd hit eighteen. On paper, Marco had gone to jail a few times, but never for anything major. Just enough to show he was in deep to something the Feds couldn't prove.

It was their best way in, because years of trying to infiltrate Carlton's organization had proved he wasn't willing to work with anyone he didn't know. This was the DEA's way of upping the ante, because they knew Carlton had always wanted to expand his connections. The problem was, if Carlton had a personal connection to the Costrales family they didn't know about and he asked about Marco, he'd quickly find there was no such person.

And then today's beating would look like a party in comparison to what would happen to Marcos.

"How are Cole and Andre?" Brenna asked, bringing him back to the present. "The three of you are still family, too, I assume? Even after your biological family came into the picture?"

Was that wistfulness in her voice? Had she never found anyone to call family in all her years in the system?

He knew it happened. He'd bounced around from one foster home to the next from birth until he was seven. Then he'd landed in the foster home with Cole Walker and Andre Diaz, and for the first time in his life, he'd realized how little blood mattered. These were the brothers of his heart. Five years later, when their house had burned down, they'd been split up until each of them had turned eighteen. And now they lived within an hour of one another and saw each other all the time. The way real brothers would.

"They're doing good. Both are getting married in the next year." He didn't mention their profession, because how could he explain being a drug dealer if he told her Cole was a police detective and Andre an FBI agent?

"Did they ever put you back together?" She twisted her hands together, like she knew she was getting into dangerous territory.

"You mean after you set the house on fire?"

She flushed. "I didn't know you realized...I was young. It was stupid."

"Why was our foster father in the back of the house with you when that fire started?" It was something he'd been wondering—and dreading finding the answer to—for months. He'd never expected to be able to ask Brenna herself.

"What?"

Brenna's eyes widened, and she had to be wondering how he'd known that when he shouldn't have even known she'd set the fire in the first place. At the time, all the reports on the fire had called it an accident. Only recently had he seen an unsealed juvenile record showing that Brenna had set the fire. But it had been his brother who'd remembered that neither Brenna nor their foster father had been where they should have been when the fire started.

The rest of the family had been upstairs in bed, asleep. So why had Brenna and their foster father been downstairs, in the back of the house, in his study?

"How did you know that?"

"Was he hurting you?" Marcos's chest actually hurt as he waited for the answer.

She shook her head. "No. It was...look, he found me in his office. I'd lit the candle, and he came in and I tossed it."

Why was he positive she was lying? "I don't believe you."

She looked ready to run away on those more sensible shoes. "Why not? You said you knew I'd set the fire."

Marcos leaned back, studying her, wondering why she'd lie about the reasons for setting the fire, the reasons for his foster father being nearby, when she so easily admitted to setting it. His agent instincts were going crazy, but he wasn't sure about what. "I meant, I didn't believe you about why he was there." There was way more here than he'd ever realized. "I think you owe me the truth."

"You, Cole and Andre were reunited, right? What does it matter now? I was upset about my mom's death. I—"

"I almost didn't make it out of that house." The fact was, it was amazing none of them had died in there that day.

She sucked in an audible gasp.

Those moments after he'd dived through the living-room window came back to him, Cole slamming into him, knocking him to the ground and patting out the fire that had caught the back of his pajamas. He remembered Brenna running around the side of the house a minute later, just as the ambulance doors had closed. He didn't think she'd seen him, but it was the last memory he had of that day.

Brenna's terrified face, their house burning to the ground behind her.

"STAY HERE!"

Her foster father's voice rang in her ears now as clearly as if he was sitting right beside her, as clearly as if it was eighteen years ago. But back then, she couldn't have moved if she'd tried.

She'd been dry heaving into the grass, her lungs burning from all the smoke, her eyes swollen almost shut. The fire had caught fast. She wouldn't have made it out of there at all if he hadn't screamed at her, then yanked her right off her feet and ran for the back door.

He'd practically flung her on the grass, then turned back, surely to return for his wife and the other foster kids in the house. But the door they'd come through had been engulfed by then. She'd watched through watery eyes as he'd tried to break a window, searched for another way in. She didn't know how long he'd contemplated, before he took off running for the front of the house.

She'd picked herself off the ground and limped after him and relief had overtaken her. Their foster mother was clutching two of the foster kids close. Three more were huddled together closer to the house. Only—

No, it wasn't three. It was two, with a paramedic tending to one of them.

Panic had started anew because Marcos had been missing. Then she'd seen the ambulance as it flew away from the house. She'd started screaming then, and hadn't stopped until someone had told her over and over again that Marcos was okay.

Within hours, she'd been at the hospital herself, getting checked out, then hustled off to a new foster home. She'd never seen anyone from that house again. The truth was, she'd never expected to.

"I saw the ambulance," she told Marcos now. "But they told me you were okay, that it was just a precaution."

She must have looked panicked, because he got up and sat beside her, taking her hand in his. And it should have felt very, very wrong so close to Carlton's house, after what had just happened, but instead it felt right. Her fingers curled into his.

"I'm okay. But I spent years wondering what bad

luck it was that I'd finally found my family, only to have them torn away from me."

Tears pricked the backs of her eyes. She knew exactly how that felt, only in a different order. All her life, it had just been her and her mom. They'd been more than family; they'd been best friends, the two of them against the world. And then one drunk driver, one slippery patch of road, had taken her whole life away.

"At least you got them back," she whispered, even though she knew it was an unfair thing to say. It wasn't his fault her mom had died. And it wasn't his fault he believed she was to blame for splitting up him and his brothers. She'd told him as much.

"I did, eventually," he said softly. "What about you? You never found anyone to call family after you left that house? I'd always hoped you would."

Her hand tightened instinctively in his. She didn't like to think about those days. They were long gone now. "No."

"And what you were telling Carlton, about why you wouldn't sleep with him? About your file? You want to tell me about that?"

His voice was softer, wary, like he was afraid what she might say, and she hesitated. It was in her file in the foster system, because back then, she'd been stupid enough to think that if she could just get out of that house, the next one would be okay. Maybe it would be like the one with Marcos. Maybe they'd even move her wherever they'd sent Marcos. But they hadn't. And she'd learned to take care of herself.

She was going to shake her head, but when she glanced at him, she realized if she didn't tell him, he'd think the worst. And somehow, even after believing she'd purposely set fire to their house and almost killed him, he still cared what had happened to her.

"The place I was sent to next, there were two older boys who lived there. One was in foster care, like me. The other was the foster parents' son. The first night I was there, they came into my room, and they told me they owned me now."

Marcos didn't say anything, but his jaw tightened. "You were eleven."

"Yeah. Not all foster homes were like the one we were in." As she said it, she realized the irony. In his mind, she'd been the one to destroy that.

But all he said was, "I know."

"It was bad." She glossed through the rest of it. "They came after me, and I got lucky. And after that, I learned how to fight. That's what you saw today."

A shiver went through her at the memory. Those boys had been fifteen and sixteen, and much bigger than her. They'd come toward her, and she'd screamed her head off. One of them had tried to smother her with a pillow while the other yanked at her clothes. She'd expected her new foster parents to come running into the room, because she knew they were home, but they hadn't. Luck had been on her side, though, because police officers happened to be on a traffic stop down the street and heard her screaming.

She'd told the cops what had happened, she'd told the foster care workers what had happened, and instead of looking as horrified as she'd felt, they'd looked resigned. They'd moved her to a new foster home, and the first thing she'd done was to steal a steak knife and hide it under her pillow. That year, she'd stolen money from those foster parents to pay off some older kids at school to teach her to fight.

"And now?" he asked. "You didn't find family growing up, but what about afterward? You must have a circle of friends, a boyfriend?"

She shrugged. "Sure. Not a boyfriend," she added quickly, though it would probably be better for both of them if he thought she did. "But friends, sure." Sort of. She only let them get so close, though. Foster care had taught her how quickly people came and went, and it was usually easier to keep them at a distance.

"Are you sure this is the direction you want to go? Working with Carlton? There's still time to back out."

She shook her head. "No, there's not. He and I have a deal. And I might not be totally convinced he won't turn on me anyway, but I know one thing for sure. If I back out now, he *will* kill me."

Chapter Six

Brenna looked around the garden. It was late November, and what had apparently been a flower garden was now bare vines and plants. Around them, fir trees rose a hundred feet in the air, mixed with trees in various stages of losing their leaves. Everything was orange and red, and it reminded her of fire.

It reminded her of *the* fire. She wanted desperately to tell Marcos the truth, but that would blow her cover. And even though she couldn't reconcile the sweet boy with the huge dimples with the mob-connected man jumping into the drug business, she needed to remember he was a criminal. But *how* had he ended up with a mafia family?

"I thought you were Greek," she blurted.

"Yeah, well, apparently I got renamed when I entered the system," Marcos said as he pulled his hand free and stood. "My biological family tracked me down later. I went to live with my mom, and then my dad came into the picture, got me connected."

It made sense, and she knew it happened—people who'd lost their kids to the system reconnecting years later. So why did she feel like he was making up this story on the fly? Surely Carlton would know if he wasn't part of a Mafia family.

But he was backing away from her slowly, and she knew whatever his story, asking about it was driving him away. And he might be her best bet for information right now.

"Have you met any of Carlton's other business partners?" It wasn't her best segue, but he stopped moving.

"Not really. Just his nephew. That's how I got invited."

"His nephew." Brenna nodded, disappointed. She knew Jesse, too, and she felt sorry for the kid. Fact was, she felt a bit of a kinship with him. His family died, and he got thrown in with Carlton. What choice had the kid really had? Probably fall in line with Carlton or get tossed into the cold—or worse.

Anger heated her, the reminder of why she was here. It wasn't about Marcos Costa. It was about Simon Mellor, the eighteen-year-old boy who'd died in her arms.

"So you haven't seen Carlton with kids?"

"Kids?" Marcos frowned. "What do you mean?"

"Eighteen, nineteen. Kids who work for him?" The words poured out, even though she knew she was stepping in dangerous territory. If she wasn't careful, she was going to sound like a cop interrogating a suspect. Her heart rate picked up as he continued to stare at her, those gorgeous blue-gray eyes narrowed.

"I've never met Carlton before yesterday," Marcos said slowly.

She held in a curse. She should have realized this was a first meeting. She'd just assumed they'd had others and that this weekend was a final test.

"Why do you want to know about kids who work

for Carlton? And what exactly do you think they do for him?"

She tried to look nonchalant, even though her blood pressure had to be going crazy right now. "I'm just trying to figure out how his business works, what I'm getting into here."

He wasn't buying it. He didn't have to say a word for her to know she'd made him suspicious.

"What are you getting into, Brenna? You never did tell me exactly what kind of access you could offer Carlton."

In this moment, all the years they hadn't seen each other didn't matter. The fact that he was an aspiring drug lord with mob connections didn't matter. Because she knew without a doubt that if he figured out what she was pretending to do, he'd hate her. And he'd do whatever he could to stop her from working with Carlton.

He'd been in the system since he was an infant. And even at twelve years old, he'd talked to her about the plans he and his brothers had—plans to look out for one another when they left the system. He'd known there was no net for foster care kids. And the fact that she was pretending to take advantage of that would be a worse sin than anything he was doing.

"You work in the foster care system," he said before she could come up with a believable lie. "You said you wanted to start a program to help kids make the transition to the real world." He shook his head, looking disgusted. "What does that mean, really? Carlton sets up front businesses and you populate them with foster kids to do his dirty work?"

"I…" She faltered, trying to figure out how to smooth this over without risking him hearing the truth from Carlton anyway.

Then his eyes narrowed, and he took a step closer until she was forced to lean back to look at him. "What aren't you telling me, Brenna? Why are you really here?"

"You're a cop, aren't you?"

It made total sense, Marcos realized, instantly relieved. Except if a police department was running an operation on Carlton, the DEA would know about it. Anything to do with drug operations by any organization went into a system the DEA could access. And they'd made very sure before he came here. There was nothing.

She stared at him, her lips parted like she wanted to say something but couldn't figure out what, silently shaking her head. There was panic in her eyes.

But was it because he'd uncovered the truth? Or because she was afraid he'd peg her as a cop when she wasn't and Carlton would kill her for it?

As much as he wanted to believe she was here with noble intentions, the truth was that his judgment was compromised when it came to Brenna. His feelings for her were all tangled up in the past, in the first girl who'd ever made his heart beat faster. In the fantasies he'd had growing up, of one day seeing her again. The fact was, he'd never really given up on those dreams.

"No." She'd finally found her voice. "Why would you think that? Anyway, you really think a police department would hire someone who'd set a house on fire?"

"Probably depends on the department and the circumstances of that fire," he replied evenly, still studying her. She was flushed, nervous. If she was a cop, she had limited experience undercover—and what police department would send a rookie into an operation like Carlton Wayne White's? Still, his instincts were buzzing, telling him something here wasn't as it seemed. "That record just got unsealed. Why?"

"You saw it."

It wasn't a question, but it probably should have been, because there weren't a lot of reasons a criminal would have been able to access that record. He silently cursed himself. If he wasn't careful, Brenna's mere presence was going to make him blow his own cover.

"Yeah, I saw it." And it hadn't occurred to him before—why was it unsealed all of a sudden? "It was a trap," he realized. "A way to backstop you as a foster care worker with the right motivations to work with him, but that easily fit into your actual identity. Someone who had criminal actions in her past. And you must be new, if there's no easy way to track you as a cop. So, what department do you work for?"

"Stop saying that!" She jumped up, jammed her hands on her hips and got in his face, despite being a solid five inches shorter than he was. "If I'm a cop, then you're—" She went pale and swayed, then whispered, "No way. You're...what? DEA?"

He smirked at her, though inside his brain was screaming at him. "Don't try to turn this around on me."

Brenna took a few steps backward, still staring at him contemplatively. What she was trying to decide was written all over her face: could she trust him?

And that told him everything he needed to know.

He swore, harshly enough that she flinched in surprise. "You're going to get yourself killed," he snapped at her. "How many undercover operations have you run? You shouldn't even play poker!"

"Hey!" she snapped back. "Don't be a jerk! I'm not a cop, and I don't know what you're trying to—"

"You're right," he told her, breaking every rule in undercover work. "The mob story was backstopping, okay? I'm DEA."

Her lips parted and relief flashed in her eyes, followed by uncertainty. "Is this some kind of—"

"I'm not trying to trick you. You think I'd risk my life for that?"

"And it's perfectly safe to tell a criminal that you're an undercover agent?"

Marcos smiled. "It is when the criminal I'm telling is really a cop. Let's work together. We're after Carlton for pretty obvious reasons—he's got control of a big chunk of the heroin supply. What about you? Because if it was drugs, it should have been put in the system so exactly this didn't happen."

He held his breath as she stayed silent, clearly torn. He was pretty sure he was right, but if not...

"Yes, I'm a police officer. Out of West Virginia. And you're right, it's not in your system because this isn't about drugs. I'm after him for murder."

There was a long silence as they stared at each other. She looked as relieved as he felt, but he couldn't say exactly why. Probably because she had some form of backup now. His relief should have been the same, but the truth was, he was used to going into meets with drug dealers by himself. Maybe not for so long or this far from help, but it was a normal part of the job. And besides, it was clear she was a rookie, at least when it came to undercover work. No, his relief was all about Brenna the woman.

The fact that she wasn't using the foster care sys-

tem to lure newly released kids to Carlton meant he
didn't need to feel guilty that the attraction he'd felt
for her as a kid wasn't gone. Not even close. Because
even when he'd believed she was here for no good, he'd
been drawn to her.

But maybe that guilt was a good thing, because now
keeping his distance was going to be a real challenge.

"Just remember Carlton will kill you."

"What?" Brenna squeaked.

"Sorry." He couldn't believe he'd said that out loud.
He'd meant it as an internal warning to himself. Maybe
the hits to his head really had impacted his judgment.
"Just be careful," he amended.

She sank back to the bench. "So what now?"

"Well, you know pretty much all there is to know
about why the DEA is after Carlton—we have been for
years, and it's straightforward. He's a drug dealer, and
we want him gone. I want your story."

She glanced around, reminding him that despite
being several hundred feet from the house, with no good
way to sneak up without being seen, they were still on
Carlton's property.

"You're right about me being a rookie, and you're
right that it's the reason I'm using my real name. They
scrubbed me from the police records anyway, but there
wasn't much, and my department isn't big on putting
our faces on a website, thank goodness. So it worked
out when I brought them this plan to come in and play
to Carlton's weakness."

"What's that? Beautiful women?"

Her cheeks went deep red. "Thanks, but no." She
locked her hands together. "Six months ago, I was on
foot patrol when a kid died in my arms. He was eigh-

teen, barely out of foster care. And he was running drugs for Carlton."

Marcos nodded slowly. He understood that sort of motivation for pushing an undercover op, but her superiors were doing her a disservice by letting her follow through, with what had to be minimal training and experience. "So, you're here trying to prove Carlton ordered the hit? Because he's careful. I don't think—"

"Not exactly. What you guessed about what I was offering him is right. But I'm not the first one to do it."

Marcos leaned forward, grimacing as his entire left side protested. "Who?"

"I don't know. But I think Carlton has been using foster care kids just out of the system for a long time."

"We haven't seen evidence of that," Marcos said slowly. And yet, it made sense. The DEA's method when grabbing a low-level dealer was usually to try to flip the person to go higher. But with Carlton, that hadn't worked because no one had ever flipped on him, so they couldn't identify who his dealers were. Foster kids with no one in the world except a man who'd given them a roof and a job wouldn't turn on him. And if they'd tried, Marcos was pretty sure Carlton had gotten to them before they could get to the police.

He swore. "How did you get wind of this? The kid talked to you before he died?"

"No. And his case went cold. But I followed the progress. I looked into his life, saw some evidence that he'd approached the station a few times, indicating he might have some information on a dealer. But he never gave it up, so no file was opened. Eventually I tracked down an address he shared with a couple other kids, also out of the system. They wouldn't talk to me. But as I was leaving, I saw him. Carlton. And I knew. I mean, what better drug runners than kids coming out of foster care with no home, no money, no family? And who's going to push for answers if they get killed?"

Marcos nodded slowly. It was flimsy, so flimsy most departments wouldn't have even let her pursue it as a case, let alone an undercover operation. But he'd been doing this a long time, and he could feel it. She was right.

"There's more," Brenna said, taking his hand in both of hers.

He squeezed back, momentarily distracted by the softness of her skin. It was deceiving, because he'd seen her take down a man almost twice her size.

"The fire—"

"I know. The juvenile file was faked, right? You didn't set the fire." He prayed she was going to confirm it, but from the look on her face, he wasn't going to like her answer.

"No, I didn't set it. My department faked the file. We wanted to blend my real past with something that would make me seem as though I could be paid off. But I saw our foster father set the fire."

Marcos tried to line that up with what he remembered. "Why? He burned down his own house, risked all of our lives, his wife's life?"

"It wasn't on purpose. I don't think he expected me to be awake. I startled him when I came into his office— I was confused. I hadn't been in the house long, and I was practically sleepwalking, used to the layout of my mom's house." She let out a breath. "I'd been headed to the kitchen for a drink. But then he spotted me and jumped up. He knocked over a candle on his desk. He had so many papers, spread out all over it. The fire caught really fast. At first, he tried to put it out, but it jumped, and then he grabbed me and ran."

"It was an accident." All those years, the original accounts had been right—sort of. They'd assumed everyone had gone to sleep and someone had left a candle burning. But it was still an accident. A simple mistake that had cost him the presence of his brothers for six years. And Brenna.

"Yes, but the papers, Marcos. I saw them as we were trying to get out. I didn't put it together for years, but then I had to go to the foster system headquarters when I was trying to track down Simon—the kid who died—any family he might have had. I saw similar papers."

"Our foster dad was just fostering kids. He didn't work for them," Marcos said, confused. "Are you sure—"

"Yeah, I'm sure. That night is burned in my mind. He shouldn't have had those papers, and I don't know how he got them, but they weren't on us. There were other names on them. I couldn't tell you the names, but I know this much—"

"You think he was Carlton's connection, eighteen years ago?"

"Yes. I looked into it and from what I can tell, Carlton was just getting started then."

"And he built an empire on the backs of foster kids," Marcos said darkly.

He'd wanted to bring down Carlton before, but now that desire intensified until it became a smoldering hate in his gut. If this man held the truth to why he'd spent six years being tossed from home to home, always hoping to see Cole and Andre again, Marcos was going to get it. No matter what it took.

Chapter Seven

Dinner was uncomfortable.

Brenna kept her attention on her plate as she picked at her food. Across from her, Carlton's nephew Jesse did the same, clearly sensing the tension even though he'd managed to miss the beating and screaming and gunshots that afternoon. Apparently, he'd been in the basement, in Carlton's personal soundproofed gun range. Beside her, she felt Carlton's presence like a tornado on the horizon.

She'd been avoiding looking at Marcos all night. He sat on her other side, and he almost made her more nervous than Carlton, though for a completely different reason. DEA. Two days ago, if she'd been asked to guess what Marcos Costa was doing these days, neither mob-connected drug dealer nor DEA agent would have made the list. But it fit.

Now that she thought about it, it wouldn't surprise her if both of his brothers had gone into law enforcement, too. They'd been so different in the foster home: Cole, the oldest, reliable and even-tempered, the one everyone turned to if they needed something. Andre, the middle of the three, easygoing, but with intensity in his gaze, quick to stand by his brothers. And Marcos, the youngest, who could be quietly watchful or funny and gregarious, depending on his mood. But they'd had a core goodness to them that had her sticking close when she'd found herself all alone. And they hadn't let her down back then. They'd stood up for her, too, when she needed them.

She could imagine them all still living by that motto: helping people, defending people. Joining the police force was something that had ultimately pulled her back in, partly because she'd thought if she could return to her eleven-year-old self and tell Marcos, Cole and Andre she wanted to be a cop, they would have been proud.

"Don't be so glum," Carlton boomed, making Brenna jump in her seat. "Just because I tried to have you killed isn't a reason not to enjoy your filet."

He grinned, and Brenna was struck again by how much of a caricature he seemed, in his standard all-white suit with that white-blond hair brushing his shoulders. He probably had to have the suits specially made, given his size. He might have been in his midforties, but he looked a decade younger, probably from all the hours he spent in a gym. But it wasn't his size that made Brenna nervous. It was the contrast between his usually jolly nature and his quick temper.

Even without his two primary bodyguards, Carlton was still surrounded by protection. His chef—whom Carlton had apparently lured away from a five-star restaurant—was also a mixed martial artist who carried a Glock on his hip and constantly had a sharp knife in his hand. Another pair of guards had quickly taken the place of the first two, though she had no idea if they'd driven in or had been here the whole time. And then there was Jesse, who looked as nervous as she felt, but still reached instinctively for his gun whenever there was a loud noise.

"Don't worry about that," Marcos replied evenly, sounding like a seasoned dealer—or a really practiced undercover agent. "I won't take it personally unless you try it again."

Carlton guffawed. "Don't cross me and it won't be a problem. I'll make you rich."

Brenna glanced at Marcos as he smiled and took a bite of steak. "That's why I'm here."

Carlton tapped her hand, and Brenna resisted the urge to yank it away. "I'd planned to take you down to my gun range and teach you to shoot tonight, but since it appears you already know your way around a gun, perhaps we can talk business."

Her pulse picked up and she nodded.

Carlton slowly rubbed his fingers over her hand. "Who taught you to shoot, by the way?"

She pulled her hand free. "I taught myself. A couple hundred hours at a gun range, and you eventually pick it up."

"But today was the first time you killed anyone, wasn't it?" he pressed.

She looked him in the eyes. "Yes."

"And how did it feel?"

"What?"

Carlton leaned closer, a smile playing on one side of his mouth. "There's nothing like the power of choosing life and death, is there?"

She held back the shiver, but she didn't think it mattered—he'd seen it in her gaze. "That's not really my idea of fun," she said, her voice shaky. "I'd prefer to stick to paperwork."

Carlton leaned back, and she could see on his face that he'd gotten what he'd wanted from her. But what exactly that was, she couldn't tell.

"Do enough paperwork and the diamonds I let you wear earlier can be yours to keep."

She nodded, setting down her fork. "That's why I'm here. But as much as I love jewelry, I'd like to know how to turn it into cash without anyone being the wiser."

Carlton snorted. "You're looking for a tutorial from me on how to hide money?"

She shrugged. "You're going to pay me for a job. Obviously you don't want anyone to notice my new funds. And neither do I. What I want is a nest egg, so that I never have to rely on anyone ever again."

"I knew there was a reason I'd picked you," Carlton said, and Brenna could practically feel Marcos hiding a smile beside her.

Marcos had been right about her minimal training for undercover work. The fact was, this was her first undercover assignment. But the reason they'd gone with her real name was so she could stick as close to the truth as possible. Her trainer had told her to take her real emotions and channel them a different way—if she hadn't chosen law enforcement, if morals weren't an issue, what would matter to her most?

This kind of fiction was easy to remember, but it sure played havoc on her mental state. Because safety and security really *were* two of her life goals. She lived minimally, socking away her savings so that she'd always have a safety net. She relied only on herself, because that way she wouldn't be let down.

How different was she from the character she was pretending to be? And if Carlton found out the truth—

or turned on her again at random—and she died out here, what would she be leaving behind?

It terrified her that the answer might be nothing.

THE MEETING WITH Carlton had been a bust.

Sure, he'd given her a rundown on a million different ways to hide money from authorities—some she'd never seen before, even on the other side of the law. But whenever she tried to broach details on next steps with the foster system, he'd pushed her off, telling her they'd get to that later.

This had always been a long-term plan. No one at her police station who knew about the operation—which were very few, to avoid potential leaks—thought they'd get enough on Carlton over just one weekend. Talk had been of her keeping up her cover at the foster care system for months, maybe even years.

But she just had one more day to go at Carlton's hidden mansion, and already she was itching to return to her normal life, to take a dozen showers and wash off the filth she felt being surrounded by this much evil. And she wasn't sure she could wait a year to nail him for Simon's death. How many more boys and girls would die in that year?

Which was why, once Carlton had given her a lingering kiss on the cheek, shooed her out the door of his office and called Marcos in, she hadn't headed to her room to sleep. Instead, she was walking down the long hallway toward where she suspected Carlton slept and trying to look natural. Because though he might have been down two guards, he had two more who seemed anxious to prove themselves. And they eyed her with suspicion and distrust.

Besides, she knew it wouldn't take much to push Carlton back over the edge.

She shot one more glance at the ceiling, on careful watch for any cameras, and then slipped into the room she'd seen Carlton enter last night after he thought she was asleep. Blinking in the darkness, she let her eyes adjust and then gasped. This wasn't Carlton's bedroom. She'd just hit the jackpot. This was a second office.

Rushing over to the massive desk dominating the center of the room, Brenna almost tripped on a bear rug that looked real. She tried not to think about the poor creature who'd given his life to be walked on and went for the top drawer of the desk, heart pounding. It was locked.

She tried the rest of them, but they were all locked. There was no key in any of the obvious hiding spots and no papers lying on his desk. She swore under her breath, then hurried to the filing cabinet, with the same luck. It figured he'd be careful—if rumors were right, he'd been in the drug business for twenty years, and he'd never done hard time.

She might be able to pick the locks, but it would take her a while, and every second she spent in here could be the difference between making it back to her room safely or being dragged outside and shot. Still, she couldn't leave with nothing.

Then, she spotted it. The pad of paper on his desk was blank, but maybe… She ran back over there, happy to be in her regular gym shoes instead of those embarrassingly unsteady heels. She ran her fingers over the top sheet, and her pulse picked up for a new reason. Indentations.

Rather than trying to figure them out, she just ripped

the page off and shoved it in her pocket. She was reaching for the door handle when the door opened, almost slamming into her. Brenna jerked backward, out of the way, but there was no time to hide.

She braced herself for Carlton's wrath.

CARLTON WAYNE WHITE'S office was dressed in all white, just like him. It was an odd room, with a huge white desk that actually made Carlton look normal-size, and all white cabinets behind him. There was a framed blueprint of his mansion on the wall, the design signed by Carlton himself. Apparently the man had other hobbies besides watching his thugs beat up disobedient would-be business partners.

Marcos sat on the other side of the desk, feeling like he'd wandered into the twilight zone. This didn't feel like a drug lord's office. Then again, most of his meetings were with dealers out on the streets. They did business out of the back of a car, a hotel room or a fast-food joint. On the rare but wonderful occasions he got to arrest a big player, it still didn't tend to be in an office like this.

He'd done deals on luxury yachts, in luxury homes and in opulent clubs. But never in an office that looked like it could belong to an obsessive-compulsive architect.

"I thought we said no business this weekend," Carlton reminded him as Marcos pressed for the third time about details.

So far, the meeting in Carlton's office had been nothing but a test, Carlton asking questions about Marcos to make sure his story was consistent. Given the stakes—his life—Marcos should have been nervous.

But he trusted his training, and so far, he hadn't stumbled once. And he was getting tired of the third degree.

"And I thought I'd come here for a deal, not a beating and the runaround," Marcos replied, staying casual with his legs crossed in front of him while he slouched in the chair. The attitude of a man who'd grown up with a crime family guaranteeing power and money, but where danger was common, too. The real Costrales family had been known to take out their own for any kind of betrayal.

Carlton practically snarled as he leaned toward Marcos across the enormous desk. "I'd advise you to watch your tone."

"Look," Marcos said, straightening in his chair, "if you want to play games, fine, but I'm giving up a weekend for this. And I don't give up a weekend for anyone. Time is money, my friend, and if it's not going to be yours, it'll be someone else's. Now, I think you and I can build a great partnership here, but considering that you set your goons loose on me and I didn't walk, I'd like a little good faith in return."

Carlton stared at him a long minute and then nodded. "Fair enough. You've got balls, Costrales, and you'll need them in this business. But this vetting process isn't over, so I tell you what. You get one question."

One question. Marcos knew he should ask about distribution or sources, something they could use to find a leak in the organization if this operation didn't go as planned. But instead, he found himself asking, "If you and I go into business together, what guarantees do I have that nothing will come back to me?"

Not giving Carlton a chance to answer, he continued, "Because from what I can tell, what usually does people in with this sort of *business*," he said, grinning, "are the low-level dealers. It's why I've avoided getting involved before, despite the obvious cash flow. But your business intrigued me, because you don't seem to have that problem. So tell me this—how do you keep them from turning on you?"

Carlton gave a smug grin. "That's why Brenna is here."

Marcos's pulse picked up. This was exactly where he'd hoped Carlton would go with his answer. He feigned confusion. "Brenna? What does she have to do with anything? I mean, she said you two had business, but honestly, I figured it was minor. Doesn't she work for foster care? What can she offer you?" Carlton lifted an eyebrow, and Marcos let realization slowly show on his features. "You're using foster care kids? That's brilliant," he said, forcing admiration instead of disgust and anger into his voice. "But I thought Brenna grew up in the system? Now she's turning on it, handing over kids?"

How had his foster father gotten involved all those years ago? In retrospect, Marcos realized that the home office where the fire had started was a little strange for a factory worker to need—unless he was involved in some other business, too. But it was hardly a smoking gun. Had their foster father been an indirect connection—had he somehow gotten files on kids by pretending to be interested in helping them after they got out of the system? If so, maybe the system had started to get suspicious. Maybe Carlton hoped Brenna would be a more direct route.

"Not yet," Carlton said. "But the source we've always used is getting ready to retire." He laughed. "And she doesn't even know she's a source! And this time,

I'm going to be in charge of the source directly. Brenna still needs testing, but I've dug into her. She's got an angry streak, and we just need to pull it out, use it to our advantage."

Marcos nodded slowly, pretending to consider, when inside he was marveling at how wrong Carlton had it. Brenna didn't have an angry streak; she had a compassionate streak. And that was going to be Carlton's undoing.

"Happy now?" Carlton asked, standing. "You got your question. And I got some answers. Now head to bed. We have an early morning."

"Wait," Marcos pressed. "I said the idea was brilliant, not that it was a guarantee. How can—"

"These kids have no one," Carlton said. "I fill that void, but of course, not directly. They can't identify me even if they wanted to, and they're not about to turn on the one person who's offered them help."

"None of them can identify you? You use a middleman?"

"Something like that," Carlton said.

The brief hesitation told Marcos *some* of those kids could identify him, which matched Brenna's story that she'd first identified Carlton leaving Simon Mellor's place.

"Besides," Carlton said, "what you got this morning was a second chance. You're one of the few. I don't offer those to dealers who screw up."

"You kill them?"

Carlton smiled. "I've never killed anyone."

Right, Marcos thought.

Carlton held out a hand, gesturing to the door. As Marcos was walking through it, Carlton reminded him,

"Early tomorrow. You've got one last test, and then the real fun begins."

Marcos said goodnight and hurried to his room, feeling the same foreboding as when he'd first arrived. Did Carlton suspect something? He'd seemed satisfied enough to give Marcos details, and Marcos knew he hadn't misspoken on any of his backstory. But he didn't like the sound of Carlton's morning "test."

Stripping down to his boxer briefs, he yanked back the covers on his bed. And then he swore loudly enough that he worried for a moment he'd bring Carlton from across the house.

Because curled up under his covers was Brenna.

Chapter Eight

"Are you crazy?" Marcos demanded.

Brenna blinked up at him, too distracted by the wide, bare expanse of his chest to really comprehend his words. He wore nothing but a pair of snug boxer briefs, and even in the dim light of the one lamp lit in the room, she could see he took good care of himself. The man was covered in muscles that seemed to tense as her gaze shifted over them. Even the big bruise snaking up the right side of his stomach and the matching bruises on his arms didn't detract from how attractive he was.

"Brenna," Marcos snapped, grabbing his jeans off the floor and yanking them back on. Instead of buttoning them, he took her arm and pulled her out of his bed.

She hadn't intended to fall asleep. Really, she'd had no intention of going anywhere near Marcos's bed, with or without him in it. And from the way he was glaring at her now, he didn't want that, either.

She flushed, because with his obvious anger, she should have been less attracted to him. Instead, standing this close to him, she felt like she couldn't get enough air into her lungs.

And when she finally lifted her gaze to his eyes, she realized beneath the anger at her being in his room was something else. Something he was clearly trying to hide. Maybe it was the undercover training that made him so good at concealing his emotions, but even that didn't eliminate the desire in his eyes as he stared back at her.

A smile trembled on the corners of her lips.

"This isn't funny," he whispered. "If Carlton catches you in here, he's going to lose it. And I'm still healing from the first beating."

Any amusement instantly fled. Her free hand lifted, pressing flat against his abdomen, where that nasty purple bruise marred the perfection of his body.

He hissed in a breath.

"Did I hurt you?"

"No," he groaned, pulling her hand away. "Brenna, what are you doing in here?"

"Sorry." She stepped back, trying to regain her equilibrium, and bumped the bed. She swallowed, sidestepping it and crossing her arms over her chest. "Look, I—I messed up."

"Yeah, well, slip back to your room now, and it should be fine. Just don't get caught."

"It's too late."

"Someone saw you come in here?" he demanded.

"No. But while you were meeting with Carlton, I thought I'd take a peek in his bedroom."

Marcos sighed. "Why? What did you expect to find in there?"

"Something," Brenna replied, frustrated that he was angry with her for doing her job. "Anything. I can't take years of this, tiptoeing around Carlton's interest in me, pretending to leak him information so we can catch him. What happens in the meantime? I want to bring him down *now*."

"Yeah, I get that."

"I don't think you do. You got a family out of foster care. Even with the fire, even being split up, you and Cole and Andre found each other again. Me, I got ripped out of there and—"

Emotions overwhelmed her, the memory of standing in that hospital, watching them take Cole into a room beside her, his hands blistering and red, with Andre running after him. Begging the nurse to tell her where Marcos was, and hearing only that he was okay. Being shuttled into a car with some woman from Child and Family Services she'd never met. She'd watched out the window of that sedan until the hospital disappeared. She'd never seen any of them again. Not Marcos, Cole or Andre. Not the other two foster boys who'd lived at that house, or their foster parents, the Pikes. From that moment on, she'd really, truly been alone.

It had been nothing compared to the complete devastation of losing her mom a few months before that, of waking up in the wrecked car off the side of the road, bleeding and cold. Rescue workers telling her she'd be okay. But she'd seen her mom in the front seat, her head slumped sideways, no one helping her because it was already too late.

A few months later, she'd just started to come out of the numbness that had filled her. She'd just begun to feel like maybe one day she'd smile again. It had been Marcos who'd made her feel that way, and then he'd been ripped away, too.

"Brenna," Marcos whispered, his tone softer now, his hand palming her cheek.

She stepped quickly out of his reach, sucking in a calming breath, and spoke the other part of what had brought her here. "A kid died in my arms, Marcos. Eighteen. He was too far gone to even tell me his name." Sitting on the cold pavement, cradling his head in her lap as his blood soaked through her clothes, had taken her instantly back to those moments in the car with her mom, helpless to do anything.

She was going to lose it. *Don't cry*, Brenna pleaded with herself, shoving the memories into the back of her mind, where they were least likely to ambush her.

Marcos had stepped closer again, and Brenna held out her hand, flat-palmed against the center of his bare chest. "Don't. I'm fine. Look, I just—"

"This is personal," Marcos finished for her.

"Yes."

"For me, too," Marcos said, reaching up and taking the hand she was holding him away with and twining his fingers with hers. "You say this is connected to our past, and I want to know how. Because Carlton told me the reason he needs you is that his connection in foster care is retiring. That she doesn't even know she's his source."

"She," Brenna repeated.

"Yeah, *she*. Which means it can't be our foster father."

"THAT CAN'T BE RIGHT," Brenna insisted. "I know what I saw."

"It was a long time ago," Marcos reminded her, still way too distracted by her nearness. She had such soft, tiny hands, and there'd been so much vulnerability in her eyes when she'd talked about her past. And yet, she was here, in the den of a sociopath drug lord, risking her life. She was way stronger than she looked.

"Yeah, well, that day is pretty stamped in my memory."

"Mine, too," Marcos replied. "But maybe the papers aren't what you thought they were." When she tried to interrupt, he said over her, "Or maybe they weren't his."

"You think they were our foster mother's? That he found them, and that's why he was looking at them late at night?"

"Maybe."

"But she didn't work for the foster system, either."

"No," Marcos agreed. "Not that we know of. But she did work out of the house, part-time. Maybe her work was somehow connected."

Brenna shook her head. "No, I double-checked all of that. I can't find any connection between either of them to the system. Not to their biological son, either—he owns his own business, nothing to do with foster care."

Marcos frowned at her. "Then why are you so convinced our foster father is connected? That was a long time ago, and Carlton's operation was just getting off the ground back then. And I have to tell you, the way Carlton talked about the whole thing, I'm not even sure he's the one who found the source. Sounds like it was someone else in his organization, and that this time, he's happy because you're going to be *his* in directly." The thought gave Marcos pause—the way Carlton had said it, it had sounded almost like there was someone else who had as much, or more, power than him and he wanted to steal it. But that didn't make any sense, and he shook it off as Brenna jumped in.

"I know what I saw back then," Brenna insisted.

"And I don't know how our foster father is connected, but I know he is."

Marcos nodded slowly. Logically, it seemed like a stretch, but he could see how strongly Brenna believed it. Sometimes memories could betray you—gaining conviction over time, twisting and becoming unreliable. But he'd been an agent for a long time, and he also knew the power of a cop's gut. "Okay, I believe you."

She seemed surprised. "You do?"

"Yeah." He grinned at her, less stressed now that the initial surprise of finding her in his bed had worn off, and more intrigued. He was still holding her hand, and he turned it palm up and stroked the sensitive skin with his fingers. "Now, why don't you tell me what you were doing in my bed?"

Her fingers twitched, then curled inward. Her gaze dipped, lingering on his bare chest before meeting his again. "Uh—"

He took a step closer, suddenly uncaring that they were in Carlton's house. The drug lord had gone to bed. The guards he had left—hopefully—had gone to bed, too. No one had to know Brenna wasn't in her own room.

And it didn't matter how many years had passed, how much he still didn't know about her. He recalled the power of that first crush eighteen years ago. It had been sudden, like a sucker punch to the gut, only instead of leaving him in pain, it had made the world seem wonderful. Seeing her again, even under these circumstances, and he had that very same feeling.

"Marcos," she whispered, her eyes dilating as she tipped her head back.

He kept hold of her hand, sliding his other one around

her waist and pulling her close. She gasped at the full-body contact, and he swallowed it, pressing his lips to hers as her free hand wound around his neck.

She fit. The words rattled in his desire-fogged brain, and he knew it was more than the way her body molded so perfectly to his.

Eighteen years should have been more than enough time to move on. They'd both changed so much since those brief months they'd spent together, just trying to understand their place in the world, to find a real connection. Somehow, they'd both ended up in law enforcement, and when she'd said she didn't have a boyfriend, he'd known instantly that it was the same reason he'd never stuck around in a serious relationship. If he was being honest with himself, it was fear. Fear of a real connection that would disappear the way everything seemed to in his childhood.

But he wasn't a child anymore, and neither was she. He tilted his head, trying to get better access as her mouth glided over his again and again. The instant he slipped his tongue past the seam of her lips, she moaned and arched up, freeing their linked hands and grasping his back for better leverage.

He reached for her hand, hoping to redirect it around his neck, but it was too late. She froze and pulled her head away, her eyes wide.

"Marcos," she whispered, stepping out of his embrace and trying to turn him.

He planted his feet and refused to let himself be moved. "It was a long time ago."

Tears welled up in her eyes and one of them slipped free, running down her cheek and getting caught in the Cupid's bow above her mouth.

He reached out and swiped it free, taking her hands in his and trying to pull them up around his neck. "Come here."

She resisted. "Show me."

"It's not pretty," he warned her, nervous even though he knew physical scars wouldn't scare her off. People had seen the scars before, and he'd given the quick, easy truth: "Burns from a fire, a long time ago."

But it was different when he was showing someone who had been in that fire with him. Someone who—whether she admitted it or not—already felt guilty about the way the fire had started.

This time, he let her turn him slowly. She gasped when she saw his back, but he'd expected as much. What he didn't expect was to feel her fingertips glide over the mass of scar tissue that covered his back and then her lips to follow.

He drew in a breath. The pajama pants he'd worn to bed the night of the fire had been cotton—they'd caught fire, but not badly. But his top had been synthetic. The fire had sucked that material right into his skin.

The doctors had done their best, and the scars on other parts of his body—the ones the fire had left on the backs of his legs, the ones the glass had left on his face and hands when he'd dived through the window to escape—were almost entirely gone now. But his back?

He recalled the moment he'd tripped on those stairs, running down from the bedroom he'd shared with Cole and Andre. One minute they'd been in front of him. When he'd pushed back to his feet, they'd been gone, through a doorway he couldn't follow because flames leaped in their place. He'd gone the other way, the fire chasing him, and done the only thing he could do as it finally caught up to him: dived through the living room window.

When he'd landed on the grass in front of the house, he'd thought he was dying. He'd sensed Andre talking to him through his own tears, felt the weight of Cole's hands as they patted out the fire. Then he'd been loaded into an ambulance and passed out.

He'd woken in the hospital, a pain more intense than he'd ever known that seemed to heat every part of his body. But it was centered on his back. After a few months, he'd actually felt less on his back, from the nerve damage. But right now, despite how thick the scar tissue was, each light touch of Brenna's lips made his nerves wake up, sent desire spiraling through his body.

Marcos closed his eyes and let himself feel, then spun back around and captured her lips with his again. They tasted salty now, and he realized she'd been crying.

Instead of the frantic kisses from earlier, this time was slower, sweeter. When her arms went back around him, settling around his waist, it didn't bother him. In fact, it felt right. He pressed his mouth to hers, ready to stay there for a long, long time, when she pulled free.

"Marcos, I need to tell you something."

His fingers slipped under the hem of her T-shirt, discovering the skin there was somehow even softer than her palm. "Mmm. Can you tell me later?"

"No." She slipped out of his arms, stepping back and bumping the bed. Her voice was throaty, her lips swollen from his kisses. "Marcos, I just got tired waiting for you. I didn't mean to fall asleep. I didn't intend for you to find me in your bed."

"Okay," he replied slowly. Was she trying to tell him

she didn't want to jump into bed? "That's all right. We don't have to rush into anything." He moved toward her. "I just want to kiss you for a few hours."

She let out a noise that could have been anticipation, could have been surprise. But she put her hand up on his chest again. "No, I mean, I was waiting here to tell you something."

"Okay." He took her hand the way he had before, smiling at her, hoping it would work a second time as he drew circles on her palm. He was about to lower his head and trace them with his tongue when her words stopped him.

"Carlton's nephew caught me in the office."

Chapter Nine

"What happened?" Marcos demanded.

Brenna tried to focus, but her lips still tingled from his mouth and her fingertips still felt the uneven surface of his back. If only she hadn't gone downstairs for a drink of water in the middle of the night all those years ago. Things might have been so different.

Marcos wouldn't have the scars. It made her want to cry all over again, thinking of the pain he must have gone through. Maybe, if the fire had never happened, they all would have stayed together.

What had Marcos looked like as a teenager? What had he done when he hit eighteen and been kicked out of the system? What had made him decide to go into law enforcement? She wished she'd been there for all of those things.

But she couldn't go back and change any of it. All she could hope to do was make some kind of restitution now, by ensuring whatever her foster father had been doing that night ended.

"Brenna," Marcos prompted, and she forced her mind back on the present. "I thought you said you looked in Carlton's bedroom?"

"I thought that's what it was. But he has a second

office." She could see Marcos's instant interest and she nodded. "Lots of desk drawers and file cabinets, but they were all locked. I didn't have time to pick them. I'm not sure I got anything useful." She was about to tell him about the paper she'd grabbed when he spoke.

"What did you tell Jesse?"

"I said I got confused, that the house is like a maze. I wasn't in there very long, and I know he wasn't following me. He looked really surprised to see me when he flipped the light on."

"Well, that's believable. The house *is* like a maze, I think on purpose. But what was *Jesse* doing in there? Carlton doesn't seem like the type of guy who'd let people hang out in his personal office."

"I don't know." After her immediate relief that it wasn't Carlton, she'd wondered the same thing. "He didn't say."

"Did he buy your explanation?"

"I think so. I asked him not to tell Carlton—played it like I was nervous about what happened earlier, that it was an accident, but I didn't want him mad at me. Jesse seemed to understand that concept really well. Honestly, I got the impression he didn't want Carlton to know he'd been in there, either."

"So, you think you're safe? Or do we need to run now?"

She gaped at him. "We?" She shook her head. "Even if I'm compromised, you didn't vouch for me. Whatever happens to me, I won't betray your cover. This is about me."

"No, it's not." She realized he'd never let go of her hand as his fingers tightened around hers. "We're a team now, you and me."

The idea flooded her with warmth, made her feel

more secure and more afraid at the same time. She'd never let herself lean on someone, and the idea of leaning on Marcos now was way too tempting, for too many reasons. But the opposite was also true. If she didn't rely on anyone but herself and messed up, then no one else would get hurt.

If this were just about her, she wouldn't have hesitated. It was worth the risk.

But it was no longer just about her. "I don't think he's going to say anything, but I can't be positive."

Marcos nodded, stepping a little closer. "Nothing in life is a guarantee, especially in undercover work."

Her pulse picked up again at his nearness, her body wanting to lean into him. She stiffened, trying to let her mind rule. "What do you think we should do?"

"If you don't think you're compromised, we stay."

If she stayed here much longer, she was definitely going to be compromised, but in a completely different way.

As if Marcos could read her thoughts, a little smile tipped the corners of his lips, and then he was lowering his head to hers again. He tasted like the Bordeaux they'd drunk with dinner, intoxicating and rich. He tasted like every dream she'd had as an eleven-year-old girl, discovering her very first taste of love.

Love. The idea had her stumbling backward.

"What's wrong?" Marcos asked.

The concern on his face made her want to touch him even more. She folded her hands behind her back. "I should go." She sounded breathy and nervous, and silently she cursed herself. "I want to get back to my room before Carlton's other bodyguards start their nightly rounds."

"They have nightly rounds?" Marcos asked, but he

seemed way more interested in letting his eyes roam over her than the answer.

"Yes." Or if they didn't, someone had a serious sleep-walking problem, because she'd heard footsteps pass her room regularly last night. She glanced down at her watch, realizing that she really did need to slip back to her room soon.

On impulse, she leaned forward and pressed a brief, last kiss to his lips, then ran to the door. Peeking through it, her heart thundered in her chest, but not because she was afraid of getting caught so much as she was afraid to stay.

Puppy love was completely different from real love, she reminded herself. And that's what she had with Marcos—a lingering infatuation she'd never really been able to get out of her system. It was made worse because he'd been the thing that kept her going all those years in foster care. The idea of one day emerging on the other side of the system, to find him waiting for her.

But that's all it had been—a perfect, impossible idea. That's all Marcos was right now, too. She didn't really know the man, just the pedestal she'd put him on all her life.

She glanced back at him one last time, then darted into the empty hallway. All the way back to her room, she wondered if going undercover in the lair of a crazy drug lord wasn't the most dangerous thing she'd done this weekend. It was being in close proximity to Marcos that could really be her undoing.

"WE HAVE A traitor in our midst," Carlton announced calmly at breakfast.

Marcos paused, a bite of Parisian omelet halfway to

his mouth. He let his gaze move slowly over to Carlton, not to dart around the room and linger on Brenna the way instinct would have him do. Which one of them had Carlton discovered? Marcos prayed it was him.

All last night, after Brenna had left his room, he'd tossed and turned, unable to sleep. He couldn't keep his mind from wandering to the sweetness of her mouth, the softness of her skin under his hands. He couldn't keep from thinking about what an amazing woman she'd become, from wondering about all the years in between now and when he'd last seen her.

"What are you talking about?" Brenna asked when the silence dragged out.

She sounded nervous, a little defiant, but those should have been believable reactions even if she was completely innocent. Because the reality was, *completely innocent* was a stretch for the person she was pretending to be.

"Why don't you tell her, Marco?" Carlton asked, his cold blue gaze locking on Marcos.

He should have felt terrified. Out in the Appalachians without a weapon and surrounded by Carlton and all the guards he had left—which, from what Marcos could tell, were the two regular guards standing against the wall, plus the knife-wielding chef in the kitchen, and Jesse.

Instead, he was relieved. As long as Brenna's cover wasn't blown, maybe he could talk his way out of this. It wouldn't be the first time a drug lord had suspected he was in law enforcement. Actually, any drug lord with any sense at all would suspect everyone he did business with could be an undercover agent. Besides, Carlton hadn't used Marcos's real name, which meant whatever he thought he knew, he didn't have the full truth.

Marcos calmly set down his fork. He didn't have to look around the table to sense the tension increase. Jesse was a ball of nerves at all times, and Brenna was new to undercover. She wouldn't be used to this kind of constant testing.

Marcos prayed that's all it was, that Carlton hadn't discovered his real identity. But Carlton had promised him one last test this morning, and Marcos hoped this was it.

"I'm not sure I can," Marcos replied.

Carlton smiled, but there was nothing happy about it. He looked like a snake ready to pounce. "No?"

His attention shifted to Brenna, across the table from Marcos. "How about you?"

Marcos let his gaze shift to her, watched her narrowing eyes as she folded her arms across her chest. She was dressed in jeans and a long-sleeved red shirt today, and it looked so much more natural on her than the skintight dresses. Although he couldn't say he minded the dresses, this felt like the real Brenna. And the real Brenna was a lot harder to resist than the person she was pretending to be.

"This isn't what I signed up for," Brenna said, her tone a mix of fear and defiance. "This was supposed to be simple business, not beatings and accusations and..." Her voice trailed off, then she finished, "I had to shoot someone, Carlton, and whether it was your intention or not, I felt like I didn't have a choice. I'm looking for security. I'm not some kind of crazy adrenaline junkie."

"Don't forget that was my man you shot," Carlton said.

She set her napkin over her half-eaten omelet and stood. "I don't think I'm cut out for this."

"Sit down," Carlton snapped.

When she didn't immediately comply, one of his guards stepped forward from the corner and put his hands on her shoulders, shoving her back down.

Marcos felt his entire body tense, wanting to lay the man out for touching her, but he tried to keep the fury off his face. If this *was* a test, Brenna was playing it exactly right.

She glared up at the guard but kept quiet.

"It's too late to back out now, my dear. You're going to be *my* ticket," Carlton told her.

Marcos frowned, wondering once again if Carlton had someone else in the organization they didn't know about, perhaps a second in command who ran the current foster care connection. Maybe Carlton wanted to handle it himself. It would mean more possibilities for leaks to law enforcement, but also more power.

"And anyway, you're not the one I'm worried about," Carlton said. "I've got security cameras at my front door. I've got your little shooting on tape. Some creative editing, darling, and unless you want to try to explain murder to the police, I *own* you."

She stiffened, her fingers curling around the tabletop until they turned white, but she still didn't say a word.

This time, Carlton's smile was more genuine. "Don't worry. You'll still have your *security*. I just like some extra insurance, and your little display yesterday made it simple. It wasn't exactly what I had planned, but—" he shrugged "—you showed me I need to be more careful who I hire to keep me safe."

The guards behind Brenna stood straighter, their

muscles tensing at the implication they might be on the chopping block, too.

"So, you think *I'm* a traitor?" Marcos spoke up, wanting to get Carlton's attention off Brenna. "Why, exactly? Because all I've done is try to talk about getting some of your product to my networks. Is this your idea of one last test? Call me a traitor and see if I lose it? My family has done worse than that."

Carlton sneered. "Your family can't protect you here. And I see I haven't underestimated your intelligence, Marco. This *is* one last test. Because I'm not accusing you, either."

"Then who, exactly?" Marcos asked, but he suddenly dreaded the answer, because he knew what Carlton was going to say before he spoke.

Carlton's gaze moved to the last person seated at the table. "I never thought I'd have to eliminate yet another person of my own flesh and blood."

Jesse stood, shaking his head. His face flushed a deep, angry red—but from fear or anger, Marcos wasn't sure.

What did Carlton mean by *another* person? The DEA knew Carlton was a killer, but they had no intel on the man taking out anyone in his own family.

Marcos glanced from Carlton back to Jesse and realization made the omelet flip in his stomach. The car accident that had killed Jesse's parents and left the kid in Carlton's care. It had been deemed an accident. Lots of snow, slippery roads, combined with a blown tire had been fatal. But maybe that blown tire hadn't been an accident. What had Jesse discovered?

He held in a string of curses as Jesse insisted, "Uncle Carlton, I swear, I didn't betray you. Please—"

"You think I don't know you've been in my office?" Carlton boomed.

Both Jesse and Brenna jerked, and Marcos hoped Carlton hadn't also realized Brenna had been in his office.

"I doubt—" Marcos started.

"Did I ask your opinion?" Carlton yelled.

"Uncle—" Jesse begged.

"Stop! You can't explain this away," Carlton said, suddenly calm.

"He brought me here to you, to do business," Marcos said. "Why would he do that if he was betraying you?" He knew he was stepping into dangerous territory, opening the door to the idea that he was also a traitor, but Marcos couldn't stand by and watch Carlton kill his nephew.

Carlton's shrewd gaze shifted to Marcos, and he pressed his luck. "He's practically still a kid. There's no need to hurt him."

"Oh, I'm not going to hurt him," Carlton replied evenly. "This is your test. You're going to do it for me."

Chapter Ten

"I'm not the only one who was in—" Jesse started.

Marcos cut him off fast, before he finished that sentence and told his uncle that Brenna had also been in his office. "This is crazy," Marcos said. "Just because the kid was in your office isn't a sign of betrayal. I did the same thing to my dad—I wanted to know more about his business than he was willing to tell me."

The "kid" was twenty-four—only six years younger than Marcos. But for some reason, every time Marcos looked at him, he saw a scared boy pretending to be a badass.

Carlton's eyes narrowed on him, and Marcos couldn't tell if he was pissing the drug lord off or getting through to him, so he rushed on. "It wasn't betrayal for me, either. I just wanted to be part of it. I wanted to be like him."

Marcos nodded at Jesse and watched Carlton's gaze follow.

Jesse was sweating, his entire body shaking. He had a deer-in-the-headlights look, but at least the fear was keeping him quiet, giving Marcos a chance to talk.

"Your nephew and I met up and played pool about a million times before I got the invite up here," Marcos continued. "And all he did was brag about you. No details, of course, but he didn't need to do that. I already knew who you were. Just hero worship."

It wasn't exactly true, but it was close. Jesse adored the uncle who had taken him in after his parents died. But the adoration had felt a little forced, as though Jesse knew he shouldn't put his lot in with a criminal.

"Is that right?" Carlton asked, crossing his beefy arms over his chest and leaning back in his chair.

Was he pushing too much? Marcos wondered. Was Carlton about to turn on both of them? Only one way to know for sure.

"Yes. And look, I know you wanted me to vouch for Brenna here." He glanced at her, shrugged in feigned apology. "But I couldn't—don't know her well enough. But your nephew? I'd vouch for him. No way would he turn on you."

"That seems awfully foolish," Carlton said, as Jesse glanced between them hopefully. "For all you know, I have absolute proof of his betrayal and you've just signed your own death warrant alongside him."

Jesse went so pale Marcos thought he was going to pass out. One of the guards must have expected Jesse to run, because the guard stepped in front of the doorway, blocking the exit.

"I don't think you do," Marcos said, keeping his tone casual, almost cocky.

"No? And why exactly would the son of an organized crime boss vouch for an orphan?"

Jesse jerked, then pulled himself straighter, like he'd been insulted by his uncle's categorization of him, then gotten defiant. But thank goodness, he was keeping his mouth shut about one thing he'd seen in his uncle's office: Brenna.

Marcos shrugged. "I don't know how you get your kicks, but I don't kill kids. If you're looking for leverage on me, you'll have to find it some other way."

Carlton's expression got so dark so fast that Marcos knew he'd just pushed the drug lord too far.

"I don't think so," Carlton said, standing and snapping his fingers.

His guards' weapons came out, pointed at Marcos.

Carlton reached behind his back and revealed his own pistol. He emptied all the bullets on the table, except the one in the chamber, then handed it to Marcos. "Either you kill him, or they kill you."

BRENNA'S HAND CURLED around the butter knife she'd palmed almost as soon as she'd sat down for breakfast. It was instinct—had been for years, ever since that third foster home. She couldn't help herself.

The urge had faded as she'd gotten older. Instead of stealing dull knives everywhere she went, she'd started carrying a tactical knife on her at all times. Then, she'd joined the police force, and when she was on duty, she had her service pistol.

But up here in the mountains, with Carlton Wayne White, unarmed for her cover, she'd fallen right back into her old habits. She had a collection of Carlton's butter knives in her room. She was sure he—or his chef—had noticed by now, but no one had said anything. They probably figured it was irrelevant, that she either had a theft problem or that it wasn't going to make much difference against a pack of guns.

They were right about that. But as her gaze swiveled

from Carlton, smirking from the head of the table, to Marcos, way calmer than he should have been, to Jesse, terrified in the corner as one of Carlton's guards disarmed him, her grip tightened. She'd never live through attacking a pair of guards with a butter knife. And even if she did, she knew for a fact that Carlton was concealing more than just the gun he'd handed to Marcos.

Her heartbeat pounded in her ears as she prepared herself for a last stand. After all these years, she'd finally found Marcos Costa, only to die with him. She blinked back tears, wishing she'd stayed with him last night. Wishing she had at least that memory now.

"This is crazy," she said, needing to give reason one last try. "Why does anyone have to die? I thought this was a professional business operation." Her voice came out too high-pitched and panicky, and she didn't even need to force it.

"You want to play in the big leagues, you'd better get used to it," Carlton told her.

Ever since she'd turned down sleeping with him, he'd been far less interested in keeping her happy. Carlton's temper—and his unpredictability—were legendary. She'd known that before she'd pressed her boss to let her come up here. But she'd never seen him like this. It almost made her wonder if he was using his own product.

But no, the truth was much scarier. The truth was that he was really willing to watch his own nephew—and anyone else in his way—die to protect his business.

She stared at Marcos, praying that his years at the DEA, which involved a lot of undercover work, had given him practice in situations like this. That maybe he had a way out.

But he seemed as shocked as she felt. He glanced

down at the pistol in his hand, then back up at Carlton. The cocky, drug-dealer expression he wore around Carlton was gone, replaced by a seriousness she'd only seen when they were alone.

"Uncle Carlton," Jesse pleaded, his voice barely more than a whisper. "I was just looking for—"

"I know what you were looking for," Carlton replied. "And I'm sorry, kid. I really was hoping to groom you to work with me at a higher level." He shrugged. "But if I can't trust you, there's no way I can let you disrupt everything I've worked for all these years."

Jesse glanced at Marcos, then at her, like he was hoping one of them would come to his rescue, but all Brenna could do was stare back at him, helpless.

His gaze swung quickly back to his uncle, and Brenna thought he was going to blurt out that he'd seen her in Carlton's office, too. Instead, he asked softly, "Did you really kill my parents?"

"Nah, I didn't kill them," Carlton said, but there was nothing truthful in his voice.

He turned to Marcos. "Let's do this outside. I don't need a mess in here."

Carlton nodded at a guard, who grabbed Jesse and forced him to the door. He nodded for Marcos to follow, and when Brenna didn't move, he told her, "Let's go."

"I'm not watching this." Her feet felt glued to the floor. She couldn't just watch Jesse die, no matter what he did for a living. But how could she prevent it? If she went after a guard again, she'd be shot by the second one or by Carlton. This time, no one was going to underestimate her.

"Yes, you are," Carlton said, gripping the top of her arm so hard she knew it would leave a bruise.

She kept the knife flat against the inside of her arm, letting him drag her outside, because the truth was, she couldn't hide from this, either. Panic set in as they all stepped into the wilderness surrounding Carlton's home.

No one would hear the shot. And Marcos would become a killer.

"I HAVE A better idea," Marcos announced, taking in the gorgeous wilderness that surrounded Carlton's home.

The trees were really changing color now, fiery reds and oranges, with greens mixed in from the fir trees. He could hear birds in the distance, and the crisp air seemed to clear his mind.

"I'm getting tired of your stalling," Carlton said. He had a tight grip on Brenna, keeping her close, as though she might run and take out another of his guards.

The two guards had positioned themselves on opposite sides of Marcos, and the one who'd been holding on to Jesse shoved him, sending him sprawling to the ground.

Jesse skidded through a pile of dead leaves, but didn't bother trying to get up. He was crying now, silent sobs that sent tears and snot running down his face. But he'd stopped begging, probably knowing his uncle too well.

"Hear me out," Marcos insisted, the plan forming in his head as he spoke. It was a long shot, but he'd spent months reading up on everything the DEA knew about Carlton Wayne White before he'd even approached Jesse.

No one could identify how exactly Carlton had gotten started, but he was a perfect fit as a drug lord. Not only did he look the part—like someone no one would want to mess with—but even before he hit the DEA's radar, he'd had a reputation. As a kid, he'd been to juvie a few times, but he'd learned fast how to hide what he was doing.

In his early twenties, he'd become a boxer, and he'd been the guy who went for the KO right away and then immediately wanted a new opponent. His trainers had spent a long time convincing him to draw out the fight, to make it a show. But when he'd finally agreed to do it, he'd clearly gotten joy out of taunting the poor sucker scheduled to fight him.

Marcos knew Carlton liked the lead-up as much as the knockout, maybe even more so. "Even though I still think this is unnecessary, what's the fun of shooting someone in the head?"

Carlton smirked. "If you have to ask, you're not doing it right."

Beside him, Brenna was unnaturally still, her arm up at a weird angle as Carlton kept a grip on it. But that wasn't entirely why, Marcos realized. She was holding her arm awkwardly because she was hiding something.

No way had she gotten a gun into Carlton's mansion without it being taken away from her immediately, so what? He tried to figure it out, but gave up after a few seconds. He had more important things to worry about right now.

Jesse had picked himself off the ground, wiped his face on his sleeve and was now standing defiantly, his chin up as he stared at his uncle.

"Come on," Marcos said, moving in a slow circle, gesturing to the nature around them. "You have all *this* and you want to use a gun?"

Carlton's eyes narrowed. He was either intrigued

or starting to get suspicious about why Marcos wasn't pulling the trigger.

Marcos spoke quickly. "Let me work him over, then send him off. No one's going to help him, right? Not if he shows up with a shiner. They'd never mess with you by taking him in. And it took me forever to get up here, find this place. He's not making it back to civilization. It'll be starvation or hypothermia or some animal attracted to the blood."

Brenna's mouth dropped open, and she shook her head, like she couldn't believe what he was saying.

He avoided her gaze, not wanting her to think less of him. If Carlton went for his plan, it wouldn't be pretty. But at least it would keep the kid alive for the immediate future, give him a chance, unlike a bullet to the head—inevitable even if Marcos refused. Then it would be up to Jesse.

Carlton's gaze dropped to Brenna, then back up to Marcos, a slow smile spreading. "You're a lot crueler than I'd figured, Marco."

He shrugged, hoping he looked blasé with his heart racing, a pistol with one bullet clutched in a death grip in his hand. "Yeah, well, I come by it naturally. You know who my family is." It was a subtle reminder not to push him too far.

The drug lord nodded slowly, and Marcos held his breath, hoping he'd agree. It wasn't an ideal solution, but it was better than a shoot-out with one bullet on his side and whatever Brenna had clutched in her hand.

"Okay," Carlton agreed, and Marcos let out the breath he'd been holding. "Do it, but hand over that gun first."

Hoping Carlton hadn't just decided to shoot *him* in the head instead, Marcos held out the pistol.

Carlton had to step forward to grab it, and he let go of Brenna's arm. She tucked that arm close to her, confirming Marcos's suspicion that she had some kind of weapon.

"Now do it," Carlton said, holding the gun on him.

Marcos turned toward Jesse, who'd stiffened his spine and his jaw. He wanted to mouth an apology to the kid, but although Carlton was at his back, the guards would see it.

So, instead he pulled back his fist and swung. It landed with a solid crack, and Jesse flew backward into one of the guards.

The guard shoved him away, and Jesse fell face-first onto the ground as Brenna gasped.

It couldn't have gone better if Marcos had planned it that way. He got down next to Jesse, yanking him back to his feet with one hand, and slipping his car keys into the kid's hoodie pocket with the other. Then, he hit the kid again, pain knotting his stomach as if he were taking the punch instead of giving it.

Jesse went down again without a fight, just another grunt of pain. This time, he pushed himself to his feet, blood dripping from one corner of his mouth.

"Again," Carlton ordered.

"Carlton," Brenna protested.

"Again!"

"Stop!" Brenna yelled.

Marcos swung again. He tried to aim for places that would split skin and cause bleeding, but wouldn't do too much other damage, but he had to be careful. Carlton had been a boxer—he knew his punches.

This time, when Jesse went down, he pushed himself to his knees, then flopped to the ground again. He tried to get up again and stumbled into Marcos, who shoved him away, making sure to push the keys into the kid's stomach through his hoodie.

Please get the message, Marcos willed. Carlton's guards had moved Marcos's car into an outbuilding, then returned the keys to him with a warning not to go anywhere without Carlton's say-so. It was far enough away that Jesse could circle back and take it, hopefully after dark when there was less of a chance of one of Carlton's guards spotting him.

Once the car made it to civilization and Marcos didn't check in, a pack of DEA agents would surround it, since the phone tucked into the car's hidey-hole was tagged with a GPS tracker. When they found Jesse inside instead of him, they'd protect him. They'd also send a bunch of armed agents to retrieve Marcos.

Which meant time was running out if he wanted to gather evidence on Carlton. This was about to be the end of his undercover operation.

"Now, go," Carlton told his nephew.

Jesse gave his uncle one last lingering glance, full of betrayal and pain and hatred, then turned and walked into the wilderness.

Chapter Eleven

"Congratulations," Carlton told Marcos. "You passed my last test. You're in."

Marcos grinned as he walked by Brenna and headed back toward the house, but she could see the discomfort in his eyes, what it had cost him to beat up Jesse and send him to his death.

Bile gathered in Brenna's throat. Was this what it took to succeed undercover? In order to take down men like Carlton Wayne White, you had to become like them?

She couldn't do it.

How many times had Marcos faced similar situations undercover? How many decisions just like this one had he made over the years? And what had it done to him, having to make the choice between saving himself and saving a kid? Because it didn't matter that Jesse certainly belonged in jail himself for the things he'd done under his uncle's orders. At the end of the day, he was still young enough, probably hadn't yet crossed a line he couldn't come back from, that he had a chance to turn his life around. Or he might have, if he hadn't been sent out into the Appalachians to die.

"Brenna," Carlton snapped, bringing her attention back to him.

He was smirking at her, clearly amused by her reaction. But he didn't seem surprised; after all, she was pretending to be a foster care worker. She might have been willing to make a deal with the devil in exchange for her own security, but a woman like that still wouldn't be immune to violence.

Taking a deep breath of the bitterly cold air, Brenna tried to calm her racing heart. She couldn't stop herself from glancing back in the direction Jesse had gone, deeper into the mountains instead of toward civilization. Not that it would have mattered. It was a several-hour drive just to get out of the mountains, and even then, there was nothing around for miles, unless you could hot-wire a car someone had left before taking a wilderness hike.

And the threats were everywhere. Hypothermia was probably the biggest one, but the threat of other humans might not be far behind. Up here, people didn't ask questions first; trespassers were simply shot.

Marcos had been right when he'd listed Jesse's chances; the kid would never make it.

The desire to run after him, to try to help him, rose up hard, but Carlton was staring at her, one eyebrow raised and that pistol still clutched in his hand. She had no doubt he'd use it on her if she tried. And what could she really do, with no way to communicate with her fellow officers and no supplies other than a butter knife?

Failure and pain mixed together, reminding her of the day she'd knelt on the cold ground next to Simon Mellor and rested the kid's head in her lap. She'd ignored protocol and tried to stem his bleeding with her bare hands, even though she knew it was too late to save him.

With one last glance into the wilderness, Brenna walked back toward the house. Before she made it, Carlton grabbed her arm again.

Instinctively, she tried to jerk away, but his size wasn't for show. The guy was incredibly strong.

"I've been pretty understanding about your eccentricities, but that's an expensive set of flatware and I'm running out of knives."

She flushed and flipped her hand over, revealing the knife tucked against her arm. "It's—"

"Self-preservation," he finished for her. "Believe me, I understand the concept." He stared at her a minute longer, and she wasn't sure what he saw—probably fear and sadness and self-disgust—and then he told her, "Never mind. You keep it if it makes you feel better."

Then, he actually patted her on the back with his enormous paw, and she saw a flash of matching sadness in his eyes. Some part of him hadn't wanted to kill Jesse, she realized. But that brief hint of humanity didn't matter.

She nodded her thanks and turned away from him, striding into his house before he saw any other emotion on her face. Because her determination to bring him down had just doubled. And now she needed to do it fast, find a way to get out of here and get help before Jesse died in the Appalachian Mountains all alone.

"I DIDN'T MAKE the decision about Jesse lightly," Carlton told them, settling into the big chair in his living room and draping his arms over the edges. "But I want you to understand what happens to traitors. You're committed now, so I expect one hundred percent loyalty from here on out."

Marcos nodded solemnly as he sat across from Carlton, then glanced at Brenna. She stood frozen in the doorway. The expression on her face was unreadable, but her eyes were blazing with anger, fear and determination. He prayed that Carlton misunderstood which emotion was winning.

Her gaze met his only briefly before she ducked her head and took the remaining chair. She didn't have to say a word for him to know what had happened in those moments outside the house: she'd lost all respect for him.

The idea hurt more than it should have, and he wanted to explain his reasoning, but all he could do was continue his ruse with Carlton. At least it was working, because if Jesse was smart—if he waited until the cover of darkness and then took Marcos's car and booked it for civilization, then Marcos had until evening to make this happen.

The plan had always been to head home tonight. Although he'd hoped to be able to wrap up the weekend with enough for an arrest that would send Carlton away for the rest of his life, the truth was, it was unlikely. A smart drug lord would start out with a small transaction, give him just enough product to prove himself before moving to a bigger shipment. And Marcos needed serious quantity to put Carlton away for good.

He had no real hope of sticking with that plan now. Even if the DEA didn't swarm after Jesse showed up, if the kid had gotten the message, then Marcos had no vehicle. And while he was sure Brenna would give him a ride, it wasn't likely to go unnoticed that his car was missing from Carlton's outbuilding. If he left too early, it would be Carlton and his guards searching for Jesse instead of the DEA.

So, he needed to time this exactly right. Set up a deal with Carlton and get out of there in time to stop the DEA from blowing his cover, but still give Jesse a chance to escape.

He settled into his chair and crossed his legs at the ankles. He pasted a semi-bored expression on his face, as if beating up people and sending them to certain death was well within his comfort zone. Inside, though, he felt physically ill.

"What now?" Brenna asked, speaking up before he could.

Carlton smiled. "Now we make your boy toy over here happy. We talk business."

"Boy toy?" Marcos replied, trying to stay in character, trying not to imagine Jesse's eyes as he'd taken that final hit. Resolute to his fate, but determined to go out standing. "Sounds fun, but I'm no one's toy."

"We'll see," Carlton said.

Marcos could guess what he was thinking. To Carlton, Marcos was nothing but a chess piece on a much bigger board. Little did Carlton know, Marcos felt the same way about him.

Some of his colleagues at the DEA had questioned the intelligence of an operation that sent him alone into the home of a man as unpredictable as Carlton Wayne White. Carlton was flat-out crazy. If the DEA came in to rescue him and things went south, Marcos didn't doubt he'd go out in a blaze of glory if it meant taking out cops with him.

Marcos needed something substantial, and soon. He

didn't want to risk having to bring Carlton in without enough. Flipping him to get to his suppliers wasn't an option as far as Marcos was concerned. If Carlton was making money on the backs of foster kids, then Marcos wanted him to rot in prison for the rest of his life now more than ever. Not making a deal with the DEA and skating by in a cushy minimum-security federal penitentiary.

So, right now, Marcos let the insult go and leaned forward. "All right, Carlton. Let's get down to it. I passed your test, and I know why we did it in front of your house. It had nothing to do with bloodying up your marble floors."

Carlton grinned and shrugged. "Hope you smiled for the cameras."

"You've got your leverage and that's fine," Marcos said. "It wouldn't exactly be the first time—my family plays similar games. Now let's skip over some BS small-level deal. You've got this area locked up, but I can move you into New York, get you hooked up with my existing networks. We work together and in a few years, we'll both be tripling our income."

Carlton grinned, and Marcos could practically see the dollar signs flashing in his eyes. Carlton glanced over at Brenna. "What do you think, my dear? You ready for the big leagues?"

Brenna's eyes sparked at the endearment, and Marcos was pretty sure that was why the drug lord did it. He knew it pissed her off, and he liked seeing just how far he could push people.

"I set you up, and you do the same for me," she said flatly. But there was a dark undercurrent to her voice that made Marcos nervous.

What she'd seen with Jesse had tapped into that compassionate streak she had, and he knew it had just made her drive to bring the drug lord down even stronger. But she didn't know his plan, couldn't know they needed to stretch out the timeline.

Even before she spoke, he knew she was going to go the other way—try to rush Carlton into a deal and get out of there, and go looking for help for Jesse. And that would destroy any chance Marcos had of getting Jesse to safety while still keeping his cover intact with Carlton.

"What do you say you work out the smaller details with Brenna later?" Marcos jumped in. "To start, I'm looking for twenty-five kilograms. I'll bring the cash at the same time, but we do the trade on neutral territory."

"What?" Carlton mocked, not even blinking at the size of the deal. "You afraid I'll rip you off?"

"Nah," Marcos replied, refusing to be baited. "If you're smart—and I know you are—you're looking for a long-term relationship, not a one-off deal. But that doesn't mean I'm letting your goons take a piece of me again."

Carlton's guards tensed from where they'd taken up position near the doorway, and Carlton scowled.

"Glad you reminded me of that, Marco. Because you're going to add the cost of two new *goons* to the price of the shipment." Carlton glanced from him to Brenna. "Unless you think Brenna here should split the cost with you."

Not liking the implication Carlton put behind the word *cost*, Marcos shook his head. "It's fine. What's another fifty grand? But we do that, and the initial shipment goes up, too. Thirty kilos."

Carlton smiled slowly. "You really live up to the Costrales name, Marco." He leaned forward, held out a beefy hand. When Marcos took it, he said, "You've got yourself a deal."

BRENNA TOOK A sip of the champagne Carlton's chef handed her. The bottle cost a couple hundred dollars, but the liquid felt caustic on her tongue.

Across from her, Marcos and Carlton clinked glasses, both smiling. Carlton was surely dreaming of the windfall he expected to come his way, Marcos silently gloating over being able to bring Carlton down soon. And even though Carlton had finished discussing business with Marcos and then made her an offer that she could try to build a case on, she didn't feel any cause for celebration. All she felt was slightly ill.

Morning had rapidly passed, and no matter how many hints she'd dropped about needing to head out, Carlton wasn't letting her go anywhere. It had been six hours since Jesse had stumbled into the wilderness, bleeding and alone. Was he already dead? Even if he wasn't, did she have any chance of finding him? The fact was, simply following her own tracks back to civilization was going to take all of her concentration. Carlton's mansion was purposely well off the beaten trail. And by the time she made the long drive back to the station for help, chances were the temperatures would be down below twenty. How long could Jesse hold out, even if they could locate him?

"Don't you like the bubbly?" Carlton asked. "This is from my private collection."

She forced a smile. "It's very good. But I really

should leave soon. I don't want to be navigating the Appalachian roads in the dark."

Carlton gave her a slimy smile. "You could always wait until morning."

"No." She took a breath, tried to modulate her tone. "I've got work tomorrow. And I want to propose this new plan of ours, for helping kids make the transition out of foster care. I want to be at my best."

Carlton nodded soberly, and Brenna kicked herself for not using this excuse hours ago. She'd been so distracted by her fear for Jesse, by trying to hide her disgust for Carlton—even for Marcos—that she hadn't been thinking straight. Of course the best way to get Carlton to agree was to appeal to his own interests.

"That's a good point," Carlton said. "Finish your champagne, and I'll have my guards bring your car."

"We can get them," Marcos jumped in, so quickly Brenna frowned.

He'd been so determined to hang around Carlton's place, dragging out their discussion for hours, that it was strange he suddenly wanted to go, too.

Carlton shrugged. "Suit yourself. My guards will take you out there, then. I'm not sharing the lock code with anyone."

Marcos seemed to pale a little and Brenna studied him, trying to figure out what was going on with him. But she shook it off; it didn't matter. All that mattered was getting back to the station and sending resources to find the kid wandering around the Appalachian Mountains before it was too late.

She tipped back the glass and drank her champagne in several long gulps. When she set it down, empty, Carlton laughed.

"Okay," he said. "Guess that means you're ready to pack your bags. I have to say—" he looked her up and down "—I'm a little disappointed. But you remember the lesson you learned today about betrayal, and everything will go just fine. I'll give you your security and you give me what I really need."

Brenna kept her jaw tightly locked and simply nodded. What he really thought he needed were more impressionable kids to do his bidding. Kids he figured were expendable. Kids he wouldn't hesitate to kill if they interfered with his plans. Just like Jesse.

"Don't be so sensitive," Carlton said, clearly not fooled by her attempt to hide her true feelings. "Just ask Marco here. Over time, you'll get used to it. And believe me, the money you'll get in return is more than worth it."

Tears pricked her eyes. Was that how Marcos felt about what he did? That trading the life of a kid who'd already made the wrong choices was a small price to pay to bring down someone like Carlton? Was that what she'd have to accept to do the same?

She didn't think she could. And she didn't want to become someone who was okay with that sort of trade. But where did that leave her?

Pull it together, Brenna told herself. She could figure out the rest of her life once she made it out of here.

"I'll be in touch tomorrow," she told Carlton, amazed that her voice actually sounded normal. "Expect good news about the program."

He grinned. "I knew I chose you for a reason."

She nodded, anxious to get out of there. She didn't look back as she hurried to her room to shove her belongings into the small bag she'd brought with her. She was practically running as she returned to the living room, ready to go to her car and get out of this soul-stealing place.

But she skidded to a halt when she reached the living room, because instead of finding Carlton and Marcos happily sipping champagne like she'd left them, Carlton was fuming. And his guards were both pointing guns at Marcos.

She looked over at Carlton, her desperation turning into dread. "What's going on?"

"You tell me, *Officer* Hartwell."

Chapter Twelve

"What are you talking about?" Brenna demanded, a beat too late.

Not that it would have mattered if she'd denied it instantly. A minute after she'd left the room, Marcos had watched Carlton take a phone call. He'd glanced at the readout and then picked it up so quickly Marcos had known it was important. As the person on the other end spoke, Carlton's expression had gotten darker and darker, then his gaze had flicked to Marcos and he'd known the game was up.

Carlton knew the truth.

"You're a rookie," Carlton said now, sauntering over to Brenna, where she stood clutching a duffel bag and looking dangerously pale. "And your station let you come here?" He tilted his head, frowning. "You *are* a natural, I'll give you that."

Without warning, before Marcos could do anything to stop it—not that he could with a guard locked on each arm—Carlton's fist shot out, catching Brenna under the chin.

Marcos yelled and tried to yank himself free, but the guards had a tight grip on him, and all he managed to do was wrench his shoulders in their sockets. On the other side of the room, Brenna's head snapped back and she went flying. She slammed into the wall and then slumped to the ground.

Fury and panic mingled as she lay there unmoving.

Carlton sidestepped the duffel bag she'd dropped and started to walk toward her again, an angry purpose in his stride.

Marcos ignored the throbbing in his shoulders, tensed his muscles and dropped to the ground. The action caught the guards by surprise and they jolted toward him, falling with him in a tumbled mass of arms and legs and guns.

Sweeping his legs out wildly, Marcos lurched toward the guard to his right, trying to grab his weapon. Before he could get free of the second guard, who'd wrapped his arms around Marcos's shoulders, trying to pin him in place, Carlton ran over and lifted his own pistol.

He shoved the barrel against Marcos's head and snarled, "Try it again."

Marcos froze, and he could actually see the struggle in Carlton's eyes. The man wanted to kill him right now but knew it wasn't smart.

Time seemed to move in slow motion. It felt like hours, but surely had been less than a minute until Carlton slowly backed away and his guards stood.

"Get up," Carlton demanded.

Marcos did as he was told, his gaze going to Brenna, who was still out cold on the ground. He couldn't tell how badly she was hurt, but he knew one thing: Brenna couldn't weigh more than 120 pounds, and Carlton had once been a semiprofessional boxer.

He kept his hands up, submissive, willing Carlton to control his temper, praying Jesse had already gotten away. That the DEA would burst through the doors any second. That Brenna would open her eyes and tell him she was fine.

But it was all wishful thinking, and he knew it. He had no idea how Carlton had discovered the truth, but the drug lord had shown him the images someone had texted him: Brenna in police blues, out on the street, and him in a DEA jacket at a crime scene. Whoever Carlton's contact was, he had inside access. *Too* inside, because although Brenna had been using her own name, Marcos wasn't. And yet, Carlton had gotten off that call, looked him in the eyes and said, "Well, *Special Agent* Marcos Costa, after I kill you, I'm going to find your *actual* family and take care of them, too."

Marcos wanted to believe it was a bluff meant to scare him more than his own impending death. He wanted to believe that the fact that Cole and Andre didn't share his last name, weren't genetically related, would keep them safe. But Carlton had proved his source was way too good. And Marcos already knew he was a killer.

In that instant, he wished he could take back every decision he'd made in the past few months. He'd come here with noble intentions: to get a dangerous drug lord off the street. He'd known—and accepted—the dangers to himself. But *never* would he have done it if he'd thought he'd be putting his brothers—or Brenna—in danger.

Now they were all in the crosshairs of a killer. And it was entirely his fault.

IT FELT LIKE fireworks were going off inside her brain, each one bouncing off her skull before exploding.

Brenna squeezed her eyes shut tighter, fighting the pain, when her whole body seemed to slam into something metal, then slide into a warm body.

A warm, *familiar* body.

She struggled for consciousness. Ignoring the new pain it caused, she forced her eyes open, but that didn't change the darkness. Panic threatened, and then Marcos—the warm body pressed against her—whispered, "Brenna? Are you okay?"

He sounded both relieved and worried, and she resisted the urge to press closer to him and give in to the blackness threatening again.

Instead, she tried to get her bearings and figure out what had happened. She remembered Carlton striding toward her. She'd felt rooted in place with shock, and then it was too late. She'd barely even seen his fist coming and then it had landed. The pain had been instantaneous and intense. After that…nothing but blackness.

"Where are we?" She thought she was whispering, but her head protested like she'd screamed the words. She tasted blood and realized she'd bitten hard on her tongue when she'd taken the hit.

"We're in a covered truck bed. It belongs to one of Carlton's guards," Marcos whispered.

Now that he said it, Brenna realized they were moving—it wasn't just her own nausea. The ground underneath them was bumpy, and whoever was driving wasn't trying to avoid a rough ride. She also realized why she was pressed between Marcos and the cold metal of the side of the truck bed. He was trying to keep her from further injury.

She tried to move around and discovered her hands

were tied behind her back. Panic threatened anew, and Marcos shifted even closer to her, probably sensing it.

How he could control his movements at all, she wasn't sure. As much as she tried to hold herself in place, whenever the truck took a turn, she slid forward or backward. Without her hands free to brace herself, all she could do was hope she didn't hit too hard. Or that the impact wouldn't roll her over entirely. Because she wasn't sure she could take another bump to her face, no matter how small.

"Where are they taking us?" It was a stupid question; it was obvious Carlton wanted them dead. Knowing how or where wasn't going to change anything.

She struggled against the rope around her wrists, but her frantic movements just gave her rope burn and made her shoulders ache. Her breathing came faster, and she knew she was on the verge of hyperventilating.

"Try to breathe slowly. Relax," Marcos said in the same calm tone, and she wanted to scream at him.

How was she supposed to relax when a drug lord's thugs were about to kill them? But she closed her eyes and tried, breathing in frigid air through her nose until her pulse calmed. When she felt marginally in control again, she asked, "How long have we been driving? And how long was I out?"

"You were probably only unconscious for five minutes before they moved us to the truck. At first, Carlton was going to use my own idea against me and send us out into the Appalachians like Jesse."

Before he could say more, Brenna blurted what she'd been thinking ever since he'd suggested it that morning, "Wasn't there some other way? You sent the kid off to die."

"I gave him my car keys, Brenna," Marcos told her. "And when the guards took us to the outbuilding, my car was gone. He got the message. Hopefully, he's made it out of the mountains by now. If we're really lucky, the DEA has already found him and they're on their way up here. But Carlton and his chef took another car and headed down the mountain to try to intercept him. Carlton sent us with his guards instead of just leaving us to wander the wilderness."

Brenna let the information about Jesse sink in, and relief followed. She tried not to dwell on the part about where they were going.

"You really thought I'd just let Jesse die?"

"I thought it was the only option you saw," Brenna replied, but she felt guilty, because even though her words were true, she *had* thought it. That, given the impossible option of him or Jesse, Marcos had chosen himself.

"It's not ideal, I admit it. And I don't think Carlton realizes I gave him the keys. He seemed to think Jesse had hot-wired it on his own, but that's why we're here. He'd figured Jesse had no shot, and he wasn't about to take that chance with us."

"No," Brenna whispered. Of course he wouldn't. He'd discovered their true identities—she still didn't know how—so the only option was for them to disappear, with no way to tie it back to him. Which meant wherever the guards were taking them, Carlton figured no one would ever find their bodies.

That depressing thought had barely taken shape when the truck pulled to a stop and doors slammed from the front cab.

Brenna renewed her efforts to loosen the ties on her

wrists, rubbing them frantically against a rough spot in the truck bed, but it was far too little and far too late.

The cover over the truck bed was pulled back and the guards stared down at them, wearing furious expressions and pointing semiautomatic weapons at their heads.

"Get out," one of the guards said, and the other grabbed her by the elbow and pulled her to a sitting position.

The world around her tilted and spun, and when it finally settled, she glanced around. Nothing but trees as far as she could see to her right. And when she looked left…terror lodged in her throat.

A sharp drop off the side of the mountain.

Chapter Thirteen

They were out of time.

Marcos locked his hands together behind his back as he climbed awkwardly out of the truck. Somehow, it was even colder here than inside that truck bed, lying on the cold metal. Wind whipped around him, raising goose bumps all over his body. Or maybe that was due to their current predicament.

He'd managed to saw the ropes against a rusted-out spot in the truck bed, fraying them enough while they'd driven that he thought a hard yank might break them the rest of the way. Not that it mattered with two guards, each holding semiautomatic weapons.

Behind him, Brenna was trying—and failing—to climb out of the truck bed by herself. She was hunched over the edge, one leg dangling down, her face pressed to the metal like she was trying not to throw up.

One of the guards swore and went to yank her the rest of the way when the second one warned, "Don't. You want her puking on you? Wait a second unless you want to burn your clothes when we get out of here. Carlton said not to bring any DNA back with us."

Stay calm, Marcos reminded himself, standing beside the truck, pasting a dazed expression on his own face and hoping they'd think he was disoriented from the rough ride. He was closer to the tree line; Brenna was closer to the edge of the cliff. He wanted to step toward her, terrified one of those guards was going to just give her a hard shove and send her over.

But he didn't move, because he knew any fast movement on his part might cause them to do the same thing. Instead, he spoke. "You drive us out of here instead, and the DEA will pay a hefty reward."

The guards looked at each other and laughed, but Marcos had already known it was a losing play. He just wanted their attention off Brenna long enough for her to move on her own—preferably closer to him.

And finally, she did. She took a deep breath and hauled herself the rest of the way out of the truck bed, stumbling over and then slumping to the ground beside him.

"Shouldn't have messed with Carlton," one of the guards mocked her, striding over and putting his face near hers.

Marcos's pulse picked up. The guards were just like Carlton. And they were high on their new roles as his first line of defense since Carlton and Brenna had taken out the others.

He purposely didn't look at the second guard, just addressed the one leaning over Brenna. "Come on, man. He outweighs her by at least double. That wasn't exactly a fair fight."

Get closer, he silently willed the second guard, even as he tried to fight with his bonds behind his back. He kept his movements small, not wanting to alert them to what he was doing. But if Carlton wanted no DNA, that meant he probably didn't want them shot. No chance of blood splatter if they just jumped off the cliff on their own. Marcos was pretty sure that was the choice they'd be offered very soon: either jump or be filled with lead.

He needed to distract them long enough to give him a fighting chance. But even if he got his hands free, it was a long shot. Brenna was clearly out of the fight, hurt worse than he'd realized. And he was unarmed against two trained guards with weapons.

"No?" the guard continued to mock. "I guess all that police training is pretty useless, huh?" He nudged her side with the toe of his boot.

The second guard rolled his eyes and took a step closer. "Come on, let's get this over with."

The first guard smiled, a slimy grin that sent a different kind of fear through Marcos. "Don't you want to play a little before the kill?" He got down on his knees next to Brenna and took some of her hair between his fingers, sniffing it.

She turned her head a little, her lips trembling with a suppressed snarl as she pushed herself to her feet.

"Hey," the second guy said, grabbing his friend.

The first guard turned to shove him, and Marcos knew it was his moment. There was no time even for a quick prayer as he yanked his arms as hard as he could away from each other. There was a loud *rip* and then his hands were free.

"Watch out!" the first guard screamed, jumping backward and raising his weapon again.

Marcos leaped toward him, praying the second guard would spin to help and leave Brenna alone. He fell on top of the first guard, slapping the gun away from him.

It went off, a *boom* that sent the gun in an upward arc

as the guard tried to control the kick and fight Marcos off at the same time.

Using the gun's momentum, Marcos shoved it upward, slamming the weapon into the guard's face. He went down and Marcos hesitated, glancing backward. Continue fighting this one or go for the other?

Behind him, Brenna suddenly spun away from the second guard, as though she was going to make a run for it. The guard grinned, starting to lift his gun as Marcos screamed a warning and tried to leap on him.

Before he could, Brenna slammed her tied hands toward the guard and ran backward instead of forward, straight into him. Marcos saw a flash of metal—was that a *butter* knife?—then the guard screamed, and Marcos landed on top of him.

The guard had dropped the butt of his weapon in favor of clutching his bleeding leg, trying to pull out the butter knife Brenna had somehow lodged pretty far into his thigh. Marcos went for the gun dangling from the strap over his shoulder, but he knew he wouldn't get control of it fast enough.

The guard he'd dropped was getting up, lifting his own weapon, his finger sliding beneath the trigger.

Abandoning his plan to fight, Marcos spun away from them both and grabbed Brenna around the waist, redirecting her. Then he ran straight ahead, shoving her toward the downward sloping tree line.

Marcos picked up his pace. This was going to hurt, but hopefully not as much as a bullet.

The blast of one gun quickly became two as bullets whistled past, close enough for him to feel the displaced air. He increased his pace, his strides dangerously long in the slippery, dead leaves. Then his right foot lifted off the ground and didn't come back down onto anything solid again, and he was hurtling through the air, Brenna beside him.

ONE SECOND, SHE'D been running. The next second, there was nothing underneath her but air.

Brenna's stomach leaped into her throat, leaving no room for her to get a breath as she pinwheeled her legs uselessly. She yanked at the bonds holding her arms together, needing to get them free if she had any chance of bracing herself for the inevitable fall, but it was no use.

The ground came up at her hard and Brenna squeezed her eyes shut, curling into a ball at the last second. She slammed into the partially frozen ground, bounced off a tree and continued sliding down the steep hill.

It was better than the complete drop off the cliff in the other direction, but pain exploded behind Brenna's eyes at every jolt, reawakening the pain from Carlton's hit. Although she'd been playing up how badly she was hurt with the guards, it hadn't been far from the truth. It had been sheer will to survive—to make sure Marcos survived—that had given her the strength to jam the butter knife she'd hidden in her sock into the guard's leg.

She felt as if she bounced against every tree on that hill, like she was in a pinball machine, before she finally rolled to a stop at the bottom. Her vision still rolled along with the pain in her head.

"We have to move," Marcos said, and she tried, but when she attempted to get to her feet, she stumbled back to the ground.

Up felt like down and down, up. The attempt to stand sent everything spinning again.

In the distance, the shooting resumed, and bark kicked off a tree ten feet away. "Go," she managed to tell Marcos.

Instead, he picked her up, tossing her over his shoulder in a move that had her clenching her teeth to stop from throwing up. Then they were moving again, zigzagging through the forest, and all she could do was pray he held on to her.

It felt like hours, but Brenna was sure it was much less when Marcos finally stopped, lowering her carefully off his shoulder. Her whole body ached: her head, from Carlton's punch; her stomach, from bouncing on Marcos's muscled shoulder; the rest of her, from bumping every tree on the hill. She couldn't keep from groaning at the bliss of lying still for a minute on the cold forest floor, dead leaves scratching her face.

Brenna focused on breathing without throwing up while Marcos went to work on the ropes around her wrists. A minute later, her hands tingled at the sudden rush of blood flow, and her hands were free. Her shoulders ached as she shifted awkwardly on her side, getting them in a more comfortable position. Her eyes were still closed, but she could see her pulse pounding underneath her eyelids.

"How are you doing?" Marcos asked, his voice soft with concern as he brushed hair out of her eyes.

"I'm alive," she groaned, then cracked her eyes open, testing how badly it hurt. Realizing the trees actually blocked out a lot of the sun and that the world was settling around her, she opened them the rest of the way. "Did we lose them?"

"For the moment," Marcos answered. "But we'd better keep moving."

Brenna wanted to nod and climb to her feet, but everything hurt. She'd used the last of her reserves trying to take down the guard, and when she told her body to move, nothing happened.

"I think we can pause for a minute," Marcos finally said.

She closed her eyes again, wanting to just rest, and then he was lifting her carefully into his lap, tucking her head against his chest. His warmth seeped through her shirt, and she suddenly realized how cold she was.

Marcos's warmth seemed to replenish her strength, and Brenna sucked in a deep breath of the bitterly cold air. "You're right. We'd better go. If we get stuck out here overnight…"

He didn't finish her sentence, but he didn't have to. He had to know that if they were still here when the sun went down, their chances of surviving dropped even lower than the temperatures would.

Chapter Fourteen

Marcos glanced over at Brenna, trying to be subtle about it. He'd already asked her three times how she was doing since they'd started moving again, even offered to carry her again once. Each time, she'd responded in brief monosyllabic replies that made it clear she was doing this on her own.

But it wasn't her annoyance that concerned him. He knew she hadn't been short with him because she was mad; it was taking everything she had just to keep putting one foot in front of the other. He could see it in the tense way she gritted her jaw, in the careful steps, the glazed-over stare focused straight ahead.

She'd been unconscious for too many minutes after Carlton had punched her. Add the tumble down the hill, and he was worried her injuries were more dangerous than they appeared. He'd watched a friend in the DEA take a blow to the head and seemingly bounce back, only to die from it hours later. The idea of losing Brenna that way terrified him.

After all the years apart, he'd accepted that she was part of his past. That she was never going to be more than his first crush, and any imagining who she'd turned out to be was simple fantasy.

But now that she was in front of him again? The truth was, even though he barely knew her still, the fantasy couldn't even begin to compare with the reality. And he had a pretty vivid imagination.

Now, he was determined to do whatever it took to get them both out of this, so that he'd get a chance to really know her. To see if maybe they'd always been meant to have more than just a shared past.

Still, he respected her determination to survive this, to make it on her own. And the truth was, between bouncing down that hill and the beating he'd taken from Carlton's guards just yesterday, running with her for the few miles earlier had taken a lot out of him. He could probably carry her again for a while, but he wasn't sure how long. All he knew was, it wouldn't be long enough to make it back to civilization.

He glanced up at the setting sun. It had to be closing in on 5:00 p.m. now, and the sky was streaked in pinks and purples. Over the fiery shades of orange and red in the trees, it was gorgeous, but the sight made fear ball up in his gut. They weren't going to make it out of here before nightfall.

And as dangerous as the Appalachians were in the day, they were a thousand times worse in the dark. Especially with no flashlights to lead their way.

"We'd better look for a place to hunker down for the night soon." He finally spoke what he'd been thinking for the past hour.

Brenna slowed to a stop, turning to face him. "Shouldn't we push on? Those guards are still out there, still hunting us."

"Yeah, well, one of them is limping now." He stared at her, leaning close until a shaky smile stretched her lips.

"What are you doing?"

"Checking your pupils." Thank goodness, they looked normal. He reached out and stroked his fingers carefully over her cheeks to the back of her head, searching for another bump from when she'd slammed into the wall.

She went completely still as he probed the back of her head, discovering a small goose egg. "Does that hurt?" he asked.

"No," she whispered, staring up at him, her lips slightly parted.

He pulled back quickly. "Good. And your vision is okay?"

She threaded her hand in his, and his pulse picked up at how right it felt. It was ridiculous, given their situation, but he couldn't help it.

"Yes, I'm okay. I have a killer headache, but my vision is back to normal. I haven't thrown up or lost consciousness again. I'm okay."

He nodded, recognizing that she was listing the possible signs of a concussion. "Yeah, well, you were out for a while in the truck." He squeezed her hand and admitted, "You scared me."

She grinned. "None of this is a ball of laughs."

"True."

She looked skyward and bit her lip. "You're right. Wandering around in the dark probably isn't a good idea." Then her gaze swept the trees surrounding them, and he knew she had to be thinking about the animals that lived in these woods. "But are we any safer stopping? The guards might call it a night when it gets dark, but Carlton will probably have reinforcements by morning."

"We're at least a couple of miles east of Carlton's place now," Marcos told her.

"Really?" She let out a long breath. "I'm glad you know that, because I feel like we could be wandering in circles for all I can tell. Any idea how far we are from getting out of here?"

"Too far," he replied, and she didn't look surprised.

"Let's see if we can put a little more distance between us and them," she suggested.

He nodded, letting go of her hand as they started up an incline. He stayed slightly behind her, in case she slid backward.

He knew there were houses out here, but he hadn't seen a single one since they'd run from the guards a few hours ago. Which was probably good—Carlton's money had purchased plenty of loyalty. If someone in a house *had* spotted them, chances were that they'd tell Carlton—or simply shoot on sight—rather than offer help.

It had been nothing but dense woods. Mostly they'd been traveling slowly downhill, but every once in a while, they'd have to climb up to go back down again. He'd seen a trail at one point, but avoided it. No sense walking a path where they'd be easier to spot.

So far, they'd been keeping a brisk enough pace to help warm them slightly, but Marcos knew it would be a whole different story once they found a spot to settle in for the night. He wondered if Brenna was right about them keeping moving.

"Hey," she asked, turning to face him, walking backward now. "Do you hear that? I think—"

Her words ended on a shriek, and she suddenly dropped out of his sight.

"Brenna!" He ran forward, and as he emerged at

the top of the incline, he realized two things simultaneously: Brenna had heard the guards, whom he suddenly spotted in the distance off to the left, and they'd reached a summit.

Brenna had just dropped off the side of a cliff.

THE WIND SWALLOWED Brenna's scream as the ground disappeared beneath her, and then she was falling fast. Frantically, she grabbed for something, anything, and snagged a tree root.

The impact of holding it nearly yanked her shoulder out of its socket, but she squeezed tighter, her body swinging as she reached up with her other hand and held on with both. She took a few panicked breaths as her hands slipped a little…and then held.

Slowly, she looked down, and the vertigo she'd fought earlier struck again. This time, though, it wasn't because of the blow to her head. It was because solid ground seemed *miles* below her.

Holding tighter to the root and praying it wouldn't break, Brenna looked up. She'd fallen at least a foot off the edge of the cliff before she'd grabbed on to something. Above her, Marcos's terrified face came into view.

When he spotted her, instant relief rushed over his features, but new panic assailed her. Because off in the distance, she heard shooting. The guards had found them.

"Go," she told Marcos. "Run!" Maybe she could hang here until they passed, then find something else above this root to yank herself up with. But in the meantime, Marcos was right in the line of fire, an obvious target at the edge of a cliff.

She pushed off her disbelief, because it didn't matter now. What were the chances she'd turn just as the ground dropped away? Yeah, it was stupid, she realized now. She'd been cresting what she'd assumed was another hill. Not the top of a cliff. But the Appalachians were deceiving.

Instead of running, Marcos dropped flat on his stomach, and then he was dangling over the edge of the cliff, holding his hand out to her. "Give me your hand."

Brenna hesitated. Did he have hold of something with his other hand? Was he hanging too far off the edge to hold both their weight?

"Brenna!" Marcos insisted, his fingertips brushing hers.

The gunfire in the distance got closer, and now she could hear the guards yelling at each other, sounding triumphant.

Tightening her grip with her left hand, she hauled herself higher, reaching up with her right. And then she was soaring upward as Marcos hauled her over the edge like she weighed nothing.

As she crested the top, he hooked a hand in the waistband of her jeans and pulled her the rest of the way. She realized he *was* bracing himself with his other hand, using a tree he was lucky hadn't snapped with their combined weight. But there was no time to celebrate, because she could see the guards getting closer.

She started to get up, and Marcos pushed her back down, shoving her back the way they'd come, so she slid down the incline on her belly, making her body less of a target. She could hear him right behind her, and the guards coming from off to their left. Once the guards got to the edge of the cliff where she and Marcos had just been standing, they'd have a clear line of sight down below.

"Go," Marcos said as soon as she hit the bottom of the slope they'd just trekked up.

She lurched to her feet and ran, dodging trees and slipping in the dead leaves, only to regain her footing again. She had no goal, other than to run *away* from the bullets, but in the back of her mind, she realized she was probably heading straight back toward Carlton's mansion.

Changing direction, Brenna ran downhill instead of across. Her feet slid even more until she lost her balance. She caught herself on a tree, slowing, then took off again, trusting that Marcos was right behind her. She risked a glance backward and discovered that he was—in fact, he was *directly* behind her. As if he was trying to block her body from a bullet with his own.

How had she thought for a second that he'd let Jesse walk into the mountains to his death, without at least trying to do something? If she'd learned anything about this grown-up version of Marcos Costa, it was that he wasn't just brave. He was also smart. Every time they'd faced possible danger, instead of jumping to the gut reaction of fight or flight, he'd stayed in character and tried to reason his way out of it. Only when he'd absolutely had to had he fought.

And right now, if a bullet managed to find them through the trees, it would hit Marcos instead of her.

Brenna picked up her pace. Her feet barely seemed to touch ground and then they were up again, until she knew she was out of control, half falling down the incline and praying there wouldn't be another sudden drop-off ahead.

But it was working. She could still hear Marcos, staying on her heels. But the sounds of the gunshots were fading, and the guards' voices were distant now.

"Zag," Marcos instructed.

"What?" She glanced back at him and would have run smack into a tree if he hadn't grabbed her arm, re-directing her.

She ran the way he indicated, panting. Now that the threat was less immediate, her adrenaline started to fade. She realized her legs were burning from running, and she could feel every bruise covering her body. It was getting harder and harder to see, and Brenna slowed a little.

Then, Marcos's hand was on her arm again, and he pulled her to a stop. "I think we lost them."

He sounded out of breath, too, and he rested his arms on his thighs, just breathing heavily for a moment.

She leaned against the tree and did the same, watching him. He hadn't left her. Not that she'd expected him to, even when she was telling him to go. But she'd needed to at least try.

"You could have left me."

He swore and straightened. "Not a chance. We're a team, remember?"

"Yeah." She palmed his cheek, running her fingers over the scruff starting to come in. It was so dark against his pale skin, and the contrast fascinated her for some reason. Or maybe it was just the man who fasci-nated her. The truth was, he always had.

He pulled away. "We should keep moving, try to get a bit more distance from the guards."

"You still hear them?" She strained to listen.

"No, but I don't want to take any chances. I doubt we

have more than twenty minutes before we're completely out of light. So, let's get as far as we can and then find a spot to hunker down for the night."

Brenna glanced around her. As far as she could see, everything was the same. Towering trees with bare branches that cast ominous shadows in the semidarkness. Slippery leaves underfoot. In the distance—the opposite direction she knew the guards were—a big branch snapped, making her jump.

What animals were out here in the mountains? Bears, for sure. Maybe wolves?

Brenna shivered and moved forward, a little more cautiously, Marcos right behind her, as the night grew blacker and blacker around them.

Chapter Fifteen

Under any other circumstances, huddled in the dark with Brenna Hartwell sitting between his legs, her back against his chest and her head tucked under his chin, would be heaven.

Marcos had done the best he could, imitating what he'd seen his brother Andre do in practice before: camouflage them with their natural surroundings. Andre worked for the FBI as a sniper, but he'd trained with the military's best Special Operations groups, and he could make a hide pretty much anywhere.

Without Andre's training, Marcos knew his hidey-hole wasn't perfect. But ten minutes before the light would be completely gone, he'd pulled Brenna to a stop beside a huge, fallen fir tree. After checking carefully to verify that no animal had already claimed it, he went to work creating a space underneath it for them to wait out the night. He'd layered fir branches as a pseudo-carpet, to keep them off the cold ground. Then, he'd piled more tree branches around it, hoping to keep in as much warmth as possible, knowing the temperatures were supposed to drop well below freezing overnight.

Neither of them was dressed for it. He was slightly better off than she was, in jeans and a crew-neck wool sweater. Brenna had topped her jeans off with a lightweight T-shirt. Huddling close together and sharing their body heat was the smart move, but the feel of her body against his was distracting. Being in the dark, not being able to see her, seemed to make him hyperaware to every tiny movement she made.

"How are you feeling?" he whispered.

They'd been silent for the past twenty minutes, listening to a pair of owls that had claimed a spot somewhere in the trees above them. They hadn't heard the guards, but Marcos figured they'd returned to the mansion and would regroup in the morning. Which meant he and Brenna needed to start out again at first light.

"I'm fine," she whispered back, sounding like she was trying to be patient with his new favorite question.

Chances were slim that the guards were still searching, but they were keeping their voices low just in case. Especially since there was the possibility the guards would be afraid to return to face Carlton's wrath without having taken care of them for good.

"We should try to get some sleep," he told her, but ruined his own plan when a minute later, he couldn't help but ask, "What's your life like now, Brenna?"

He'd been wondering ever since he'd realized her true identity. Most of what he knew about her came from those few months when she was eleven years old. Although he'd tried to get close to her then, it had been in the innocent ways of a boy with a crush, and he'd mostly tried to support her in her grief.

During the five years he'd lived in that foster home with Cole and Andre, other kids had come and gone. The two boys who'd also lived there during the time of the fire he'd barely known more than the Pikes' biological son, Trent—grown and long gone before he'd moved in. But Brenna had always been different, and he didn't think a year had gone by since then that he hadn't wondered what she was doing.

It was hard to imagine the little Brenna Hartwell he'd known growing up to become a cop, and yet, somehow it seemed perfectly natural. The picture Carlton had flashed on his phone of Brenna wearing her police blues, looking so serious and focused, was such a contrast to the woman who'd attacked a guard to save his life, to the woman who'd melted in his arms that first night. He wanted to know all the different sides to her, and he was certain he'd only scratched the surface.

She shifted a little, the outsides of her thighs rubbing the inside of his. He looped his arms around her waist, holding her still, pretending he was just trying to keep her warm.

"What do you mean?" She sounded tentative, like maybe she didn't want to discuss real life with him.

But there was no need for cover stories anymore, and although he'd seen plenty of glimpses of the real Brenna, he wanted to know more. A lot more.

"What's your life like when you're not out here in a drug lord's house, playing a role?"

"I don't know."

She squirmed a little more until he laughed and told her, "You've got to stop doing that."

"Oh." He didn't need to be able to see her to sense her flush. "Sorry."

"Okay, I'll start," he said. "I work out of the DEA's district office in West Virginia. I've been there about five years, joined pretty soon after I finished school."

He paused, remembering the guilt he'd felt when

he'd first started college. He'd wanted to go so badly, had been willing to work to put himself through, but his oldest brother Cole had insisted he focus on school. So while Marcos had worked part-time, Cole had taken on two jobs. Both Marcos and Andre had gone to college, while Cole had worked to make sure they had the life they might have gotten if they'd grown up under normal circumstances, instead of foster care.

"Where'd you go just now?" Brenna asked.

"Just thinking about how lucky I got. The day I turned eighteen, Cole had a home waiting for me."

Her fingers twined with his in her lap. They were icy cold, and he held tight, trying to warm them.

"Most kids in foster care just suddenly end up on the street. Even though they've known it's been coming, they don't have a plan," she said. "But it doesn't surprise me what Cole did for you and Andre. Cole was always looking after everyone. And I might have only known you a few months, Marcos, but I know that even without him and Andre, you would have ended up somewhere like the DEA."

"Maybe. But what about you?"

"No one was waiting for me."

He'd expected as much, from some of the things she'd said in Carlton's mansion, but the thought physically pained him. He wished he could rewind eleven years and be standing on her porch the way Cole had been standing on his the day she'd turned eighteen. Except he hadn't known where she'd ended up. And the truth was, he'd been afraid to look, afraid where she might have gone after that fire, how she might have turned out. It was easier to imagine her happy than risk finding her not.

"You're sitting there feeling guilty about that, aren't you?" she asked incredulously. "I didn't come looking for you either, Marcos. We only knew each other for a few months."

"Yeah, but I never forgot you."

His words hung in the air a long moment before she replied softly, "I never forgot you, either."

BRENNA JOLTED AWAKE, freezing and disoriented.

Slowly, awareness returned: the scent of pine and old leaves surrounding her; the heat of Marcos's body against her back; blackness so complete she wasn't completely sure her eyes were open. Then, she realized what had woken her: branches cracking.

She twitched as the sound came again, and Marcos's breath whispered across her neck, then his arms closed tighter around her. "Deer," he said softly.

"Are you sure?" Her voice was so low it could barely be called a whisper, but somehow he heard her.

"Yeah. I peeked through the branches a minute ago. There's a little family of them."

She relaxed against him. "How can you see anything?"

"It's darker in here than when you look out. There are some stars."

"Enough to see a trail by? Maybe we should start moving again." She knew if the guards weren't still out there searching, they'd be looking again by morning light. And she was pretty sure that she'd actually run closer to Carlton's mansion when they were trying to escape the gunfire last night.

Realizing she'd lost all sense of time, she asked, "Is it still night?"

"Yeah, you slept about four hours."

"Did you sleep?"

"Some."

She had a feeling that meant only enough to rest his eyes for a few minutes and keep watch the remainder of the time. "We can take turns, you know."

"I'm not worried about Carlton's guards. I may not make the world's best hide, but it's good enough to fool those two. If they're still out there, they're not close by. But I think we should stay where we are for now. If you're cold in here, it's a good ten degrees colder outside."

We are *outside*, she wanted to say. But the truth was, the canopy of branches did give the illusion of being indoors. If indoors had a broken heater. She couldn't stop the shiver that worked through her, and Marcos pressed his arms and legs closer to her.

"Aren't you cold?" she asked.

"Yeah."

"You don't seem cold." In fact, compared to her, he felt downright toasty.

"I'm keeping warm imagining the two of us being back at my house, with the heat blasting on high."

His house. "What's that like?" Even as she asked it, she realized it was unfair to probe into his life when she hadn't been willing to tell him about hers.

Not giving him time to answer, she said, "Never mind. None of my business."

"It is if you want it to be," Marcos said softly, making her intensely aware of the hardness of his chest against her back, the muscled thighs pressed tightly to hers.

Brenna couldn't stop herself from tensing, and there was no way he wouldn't feel it, the way they were pressed so closely together. Did she want Marcos Costa to be her business? Probably more than she'd wanted almost anything else in her life.

But the Marcos of her fantasies wasn't the real thing. The man behind her was way more complicated, way more terrifying to her heart than she could have imagined. Because a fantasy she could hold on to all her life, a stabilizing force in a world she couldn't control, was one thing. Taking a chance on the real man and risking failure? She wasn't sure she could handle that.

Especially not now, when—even if they made it out of the mountains alive—her future seemed murky once again. Did she really belong in police work? Even though Marcos had made the choice that gave Jesse the best chance of survival, the question remained about her. Would undercover work—would any kind of work that involved regularly dealing with someone like Carlton Wayne White—change her in ways she didn't want to be changed?

She felt lost, not unlike the way she'd felt when that foster home had burned down all those years ago, or when the woman from Child and Family Services had showed up at the hospital a few months before that, right after her mother had died, telling Brenna she was going into the system. Over the years, she'd learned how to be alone. It was isolating, yes, but it was safe, too.

In some of those foster homes, it was the only way to survive unharmed. In others, she'd sensed a chance to make real friends, maybe even another person to consider family the way Marcos had found with Cole and Andre. But she'd never reached out, never taken that step, because it was too risky. And, if she was being honest with herself, even the idea had felt somehow like a betrayal to the mom who had done her best for Brenna, whose only failure was dying in that car without her.

The thought jolted her. Did she really think, all these years later, she should have died beside her mom in that car? Tears pricked the backs of her eyes, because she honestly wasn't sure. She missed her mom every day, but it hit now with a strength similar to the days after it had happened.

Was she willing to let anyone into her life? Willing to risk losing them? Even if that someone was the man she'd dreamed of since she was eleven years old?

"You're awfully quiet," Marcos said, making Brenna realize she let his statement go unanswered far too long.

Before she could figure out what to say, he continued. "We don't need to figure anything out here. How about this? You tell me about your place, and I'll tell you about mine. That's not too hard, right?"

"It's not about the house," she said, and cursed the crack in her voice.

"I know," he said softly. "You probably think that because I found Cole and Andre, my experience was really different than yours. And you're right."

She started to speak, but he kept going. "For five years, Cole and Andre and I were inseparable. And even after that house burned down and we were split up, in my heart I knew I was just biding time until each of us hit eighteen and we were back together. But I came to that house when I was seven. I was in foster care since I was born. They always say that babies have a better chance of being adopted, but when I was little, I had some issues with my heart. Gone now, but by the time they realized it wasn't a major issue, I was getting older. No one wanted me."

She tightened her hold on his hands, hurting for the little boy who probably hadn't understood why he didn't have a real family.

He was right about their experiences being different. She might have spent her life since her mom died feeling totally alone in the world, but that's how he'd entered it.

They'd chosen different paths. He'd let Andre and Cole in, made his own family when he'd had none. And she'd pushed everyone away, because she was too afraid of losing them to give anyone a chance. Maybe it was time to finally change that.

"I want you," she whispered.

Chapter Sixteen

I want you.

Brenna's words from a few hours earlier rattled around in Marcos's brain as he held her hand tightly in his, grabbing tree trunks for stability with his other hand as they picked their way down a steep incline. Snow had started falling sometime after she'd said those words, and now the ground was slick and he could see his breath.

She'd gone silent after that, and he hadn't pushed her, because he'd sensed in the tone of her voice that something important had just changed. Instead, he'd just held her, and eventually she'd drifted back off to sleep. He'd woken her a few hours later, battling his fears of venturing back out into the cold or waiting until it warmed up a little more and risking Carlton sending reinforcements on the mountain.

They'd been up now for a few hours, moving at a brisk jog most of the time. But this incline was slippery enough with the light snowfall that they were moving more carefully. The sun was starting to come up, and he'd been hoping it would bring warmth, but instead, the sky was hazy, threatening more snow. He prayed they were going the right way; his internal sense of direction was usually good, but they'd definitely veered off course running from the guards last night.

"We have to be getting close," Brenna said, every word puffing clouds of white into the air. Her cheeks and nose were bright red, and her fingers felt like icicles in his.

He'd stopped feeling his toes an hour ago, which made him worry how she was faring in her much lighter top. But whenever he'd asked, she'd given him a patient-looking smile and told him she was a skier and used to the cold.

"Yeah, I hope we're close," Marcos replied. The truth was, if they didn't emerge from the forest and onto flat ground soon, he was going to worry that this off-the-trail route he'd picked out for them wasn't as straight a shot as staying on the road. Of course, they couldn't stay on the road or they'd risk running right into Carlton. And while he hoped the DEA was also on that road by now, he didn't want to take the chance.

"You're a worrier," Brenna said.

"This seems like a good time to worry." He kept the rest of it to himself. He was mostly worried about *her*, that she was warm enough, that her head was okay after the hit she'd taken yesterday.

"Well, sure. But I feel a lot safer right now with you than I did in that mansion with Carlton." He must have still looked concerned, because she squeezed his hand and added, "We have to be close. Once we make it to civilization, then we worry about bringing down Carlton."

"I'm hoping the DEA is already there, and he's in handcuffs. Because if they didn't get the message and Carlton hasn't found us…"

"He's going to run."

"It's his best bet. He assaulted a police officer and a DEA agent—and killed one of his own guards in front of us. Besides, I heard him order his guards to kill us, so he can claim all he likes that they acted alone, but his testimony isn't going to sound better than mine."

Brenna picked up the pace. "Then let's make sure we beat him."

Her feet started to slide out from underneath her and he gripped the tree trunk, pulling her back toward him before she fell in the snow. She grabbed his shoulder with her free hand to brace herself, and then they were pressed tightly together, reminding him of the first night he'd seen her.

He must have telegraphed what he was thinking with his eyes, because her eyes dilated. All of a sudden, he felt like he was the one whose world was sliding out from underneath him as she leaned up and pressed her lips to his.

Her lips were cold, and so was the tip of her nose as it pressed against his cheek, but his must have been the same, because she leaned back for a second and whispered, "You're cold."

Then her tongue was in his mouth, and he didn't feel cold at all. He let go of the tree trunk and wrapped his free hand around her waist, bringing her closer still. And somehow, even in the frigid mountains with a drug lord out to kill him, he knew he was exactly where he was supposed to be.

For a few blissful moments, he let himself forget everything else and just *feel*. The way her fingers curled into his shoulder. The way she arched toward him whenever his tongue stroked the inside of her lip. The strength of her body underneath his hand as he palmed her lower back. For a few moments, there was nothing but Brenna.

In some ways, he knew nothing about her. He had no idea how she drank her coffee, what she liked to read, where she saw herself in five years. In others, he knew her better than most of the people he saw every day: the pain she'd survived; her determination in her job; her compassion for those she tried to help.

And yet, it wasn't anywhere near enough. Not the little bit she'd let him into her world and not this amazing kiss with both of them in too many clothes and with too many secrets still between them. Because what did she really know about him, either? Once they got back to real life, would they have anything in common?

If the answer was no, he half wanted to stay exactly where they were, no matter the consequences.

As if she could read his mind, Brenna pulled back and echoed his words from the other night. "I tell you what, when we get out of here, you show me your place and I'll show you mine."

She spoke fast, as though if she didn't get it out quickly, she wouldn't say it at all, and Marcos nodded just as fast. "It's a deal."

Then he grabbed the tree in front of him, keeping a tight hold on Brenna with his other hand, and started moving again.

CIVILIZATION HAD TO be close.

Brenna had been thinking it for more than an hour and, as big snowflakes started to plop on her head, she finally gave in to the worry that something had gone wrong. That getting out of the mountains would take longer than they'd estimated. Because although she'd been telling Marcos otherwise for hours, the cold was starting to affect her.

Now, when she grabbed the trees they passed for stability, she had to squeeze a little tighter in order to feel the bark. Her fingers were getting clumsy and numb, and her shivering had become erratic and violent. It hadn't warmed up, though, and her mind was still sharp enough to know her body was beginning to shut down.

Glancing up at the sky as another fat snowflake landed on her face and then slid down her neck, Brenna frowned and gave voice to her fears. "I think a storm is coming."

"I know." Marcos sounded as worried as she felt. "We either need to find shelter now and wait it out, or press on and get to help."

She looked over at him, noticing that his lips were tinged just slightly blue. "We might not make it to help if it gets much colder."

"A hide isn't going to keep us much warmer," Marcos said. "I did my best last night, but I'm not sure we can risk stopping. If we stop moving, we're going to lose body heat."

"If this snow keeps up, we've got the same problem. It's going to soak us."

"Let's try—" Abruptly, Marcos cut off, then pulled her another few steps forward, peering into the distance. "Is that—"

"A parking lot," Brenna realized. "And cars. Maybe someone will be there. Or there will be an emergency phone."

She moved faster, half speed-walking, half-sliding down the hill, Marcos's hand somehow still holding tight to hers. The descent felt only partly in her control, partly a dangerous slide she'd never come out of—much like her feelings for the man next to her.

Finally, they reached the bottom of the incline and Brenna might have cried tears of joy—except she was pretty sure they would have frozen the instant they touched her skin. The trees thinned out here, and then the end was finally in sight.

She glanced at Marcos, who was staring at the parking lot at the end of the expanse of woods with similar disbelief. He grinned at her, a full, dimpled smile that sent warmth back into her, and then they took off running.

Brenna had an instant flashback to being eleven years old. She'd been watching as Marcos, Cole, Andre and the other two kids in the foster home had played a game of touch football. They'd invited her, but she'd declined. Even after she'd healed from her injuries in the car crash, she'd felt like her world was in slow motion. Later, she'd recognized that she'd been in a deep depression, but at the time, she'd just felt dazed, unable to really connect with anyone around her.

Only Marcos had made her feel like she would ever come out of that daze. That day, in the middle of the game, he'd run over to the sidelines and handed her the football he'd just caught. Then he'd grabbed her hand and raced with her across the goal line. For a few brief moments, Brenna had felt her childhood return. She'd felt free, even happy.

The same feeling rose up now, and Brenna let out a joyful laugh. They were so close. She could see that the cars were empty, but there *was* an emergency phone, and it was in a little glass enclosure that would keep the wet snow off their faces and the wind off their backs. Then it would be a matter of half an hour—tops—and they'd be in a warm car and heading home.

And then what? she wondered, feeling her feet slow just a little. Would she and Marcos simply go their own ways? She'd invited him into her home—into her life—but soon, they'd have cases to finish, real life to resume. Even if he still wanted to take her up on her offer, would he like what he discovered?

Up in Carlton's mansion, she'd been playing a role. Although parts of the person she'd been pretending to be—someone who would take advantage of kids, who would work with a drug dealer—were despicable, other parts were who she *wished* she could be. Someone confident, the kind of woman who'd walk up to a man she hadn't seen in eighteen years and kiss him as if the next logical step was to yank him into her bed.

The real Brenna was different. More measured, careful about everything she did. Part of what appealed to her about police work were the rules and boundaries. And she sensed Marcos loved undercover work at the DEA for the exact opposite reasons. Would she measure up to whatever he expected her to be?

There was only one way to find out. As Marcos glanced at her questioningly, Brenna picked up her pace again, holding even tighter to his hand.

"Stop right there!"

The voice came out of nowhere and seemed to echo off the mountain behind them.

Brenna jumped and would have fallen if Marcos didn't have such a tight grip on her. Together, they spun, and disbelief and dread slumped her shoulders.

Carlton's guards had caught up to them.

Chapter Seventeen

No way were they going to die this close to freedom.

Marcos stared at the furious guards as they moved in, keeping their rifles leveled on him and Brenna. The anger on their faces was personal this time, and Marcos instantly knew why. Both of them were sporting shiners that matched the nasty bruise underneath Brenna's chin. Apparently, Carlton hadn't been happy when they'd returned last night and had to explain his and Brenna's escape. Not to mention the man Brenna had stabbed was limping, a little blood seeping through his camo pants.

"Very soon, you're going to wish we'd dropped you off that mountain last night," the guard who'd taunted Brenna after taking them out of the truck said darkly.

"That'll seem like a peaceful way to go compared to what Carlton will do to you," the other guard added, then gestured back up the mountain with his weapon. "Let's go."

"I don't think so," Marcos said, keeping hold of Brenna's hand and taking a step away from them, slightly closer to the parking lot.

"Don't move!" the second guard yelled as the first one moved quickly around to the other side, so they were bracketing him and Brenna.

"You try anything, and we'll shoot you right here," the guard near Brenna warned.

"Really?" Marcos asked, keeping his tone confident as he turned to face the guard closer to him—the one in charge, the one less focused on Brenna. "On camera? You think that's a good idea?"

"What camera?" the second guard demanded, even as the first one swore.

"In the parking lot," Marcos said. "Right above that emergency phone. It's meant to prevent car theft, but believe me, the cops who monitor it will be really interested in automatic gunfire."

"So, move," the first guard demanded.

Marcos took a step backward, and Brenna did the same. He felt her back press against his, and he didn't have to turn to know—she'd lifted her fists, just like him.

"Are you kidding?" the second guard mocked. "You don't stand a chance. We're the ones with weapons."

"Sure," Marcos agreed. "And you use them here, and you're going straight to jail. I'm not following you anywhere. You want to take us back to Carlton, you're going to have to drag us. And incidentally, I don't think Carlton will be happy if you take us out." He grinned, back in character. "I'm pretty sure he wants to do it himself now. Am I right?"

It was a desperate play, and he knew it. But it was probably his only play. Following the guards meant waiting for a time to attack and hope to overpower them a second time, and it was unlikely. They wouldn't be so easily surprised a second time, and the cold had sapped most of his strength. The fact was, he wasn't sure he and Brenna would even live through a trek back up the mountain.

The first guard snarled, glancing from him and Brenna back to his friend. "Guess we have no choice." He shrugged, but there was glee underneath it as he centered his weapon on Brenna's head. "The cops want to arrest me for this? They'll have to find me first."

"Let's do this," the second guard agreed, lifting his weapon on Marcos.

"Wait!" Brenna yelled, but they ignored her, nodding to one another.

Just before the guards' fingers depressed on the triggers, Marcos shoved Brenna to the ground.

BRENNA SHRIEKED AS she hit the wet ground and Marcos landed on top of her, knocking all the air from her lungs. It was only a temporary reprieve, and she knew it. Marcos had gambled—it had been their only option—but they'd both lost.

She'd never get the chance to figure out where this new connection with him was going. Never get to see his house, reconnect with his brothers, all grown up. Never get to see Marcos in real life, when he didn't have to spend half their time together playing a role. Never get to find out if the way she felt about him now was a leftover childhood crush or the real thing.

She braced herself for the feel of bullets, but instead, she heard cars screeching to a halt, and then voices shouting over each other. "DEA! Drop your weapons!"

Then the gunfire came, and dirt and snow smacked her in the face as some of those bullets struck too close to her. All she could do was curl up smaller, pray Marcos was unharmed on top of her, and wait.

As suddenly as it had started, it was over. Marcos was standing, pulling her to her feet and away from the guards, who were down for good. Red sprayed across the white snow, and Brenna fixated on it instead of looking at the guards as agents ran toward them.

A pair of agents confirmed the guards were dead, and then more agents were leading her and Marcos down to the parking lot, as if they were incapable of making it there themselves.

"You okay, man?" an older agent, wearing a DEA jacket, his hair more salt than pepper, asked Marcos.

"Now I am." Marcos pulled Brenna closer, and she realized she was wedged in the crook of his shoulder.

Odder still, she couldn't imagine being anywhere else right now.

The agent glanced from Marcos to her, then stripped off his jacket and wrapped it around her. "Let's get you in the car. Heat's still on," he told her, gesturing for Marcos to follow.

She glanced back at him, and he smiled at her. "Meet my partner, Jim Holohan. Jim, this is Brenna Hartwell. She's undercover with..." He frowned. "Which department, exactly?"

"Harrisburg, West Virginia."

"Long way from home," Jim commented, opening the door and ushering her into the back of a sedan.

A contented sigh escaped the second she sat down. Although she suspected it would take hours for her to defrost, it was warm in here. Now that she wasn't standing, she realized just how exhausted she was. Hopefully, in a few minutes, she'd start to feel her fingers and toes again.

She started to scoot over for Marcos to join her, but Jim slammed the door behind her. "Hey." She rolled down the window.

"She's okay," Marcos told his partner.

Jim seemed a little skeptical, but he nodded at Marcos and the two of them hopped into the front seat.

"Did you find Jesse?" Marcos asked.

"Yeah. Gave us a good scare when we spotted him racing out of the mountains in your car. We got him some medical treatment, and he's under arrest. Technically, we're holding him because he was driving a DEA car without authorization, but as soon as we have something more to make it stick, we'll be adding charges related to the drug-running operations. Me and a few of the other agents went straight up to Carlton's mansion, but it was empty."

"He was gone?" Brenna asked, surprised. "But his guards said they were taking us back to him."

Jim shrugged. "Our guess is he hasn't gone far. We're watching the airports, but a guy like that has resources."

"Are agents still there?" Marcos asked. "He's got a *lot* of filing cabinets."

Jim grimaced. "He *had* a lot of filing cabinets. Well, I guess he still does, but they've been totally emptied out. Security footage and computers are gone, too. Everything else, he left."

"You're kidding me," Marcos said. "How'd he do that so fast?"

Jim shrugged, then gripped Marcos's arm. "We're glad you're okay."

Brenna could tell the two of them were close. But she supposed that was to be expected; who wouldn't get along with Marcos?

"We had a couple of close calls." Marcos told him about being driven out into the wilderness and escaping.

"About this *we*," Jim said, glancing at her. "You

want to tell me exactly what you were doing in Carlton Wayne White's mansion without giving us a heads-up?"

"We can get into all of that later," Marcos said softly.

"He's a known dealer. Anything to do with him should have gone into our system," Jim insisted. "Her very presence could have gotten you killed!"

"Go easy," Marcos started, but Brenna spoke over him.

"My investigation wasn't about drugs. It was about murder. And it's not over."

SHE WAS HOME.

Brenna looked around her little bungalow. She'd lived here for almost a year, and it had always felt comfortable. A place to get away from the world and recharge, just her. It was the first place she'd actually owned, and she'd taken joy in painting the walls cheery colors, in picking out furniture she'd get to keep. She'd figured if she was really going to put down roots, it was time to stop living like she was still a part of the system, being hustled from one place to the next with her single duffel bag.

Back then, the only things she'd cared about were the belongings she'd managed to bring along from her real home. Pictures of her and her mom, her mom's locket, a cherished stuffed animal her dad had bought her when she was a baby, back before he'd taken off for good.

She'd always thought that the day she'd turned eighteen, she'd start collecting things that were really *hers*. Instead, she'd clung to that old life, something in her unable or unwilling to create anything that might be taken away from her.

But when she'd started this job, she'd decided to make a change. Real job. Real life.

Except now, looking around her, it felt empty. And she realized what was missing was Marcos.

She let out a burst of laughter to calm her raging emotions. That was ridiculous. In her entire life, she'd *spent a few months with him*. And only three and a half days of that time was as an adult.

It wasn't him she needed, she told herself as she sank into a big, cushy chair she'd bought because it was something her mom would have chosen. But maybe this was a wake-up call. It was time to stop living such an isolated life.

Even now, after almost being killed by a crazy drug lord, she was here, alone. The chief had offered her protection, but they'd both agreed it was probably unnecessary. Carlton was crazy, but crazy enough to seek revenge against an armed cop on her own turf when the whole force was looking for him and getting caught surely meant a life in jail? She felt safe enough, but for once, the isolation itself bothered her.

Sure, her chief had called to make sure she was okay—and to find out what they had on Carlton. And her mentor at the station had called, too. Victor's call was a lot more genuine, and she knew if she hadn't insisted she wanted to be alone, he would have already been at her house with his wife and their four kids. The same was probably true of some of the other officers she worked with, but it had been second nature to insist she was fine by herself.

She'd always been a loner. She had friends at work, but not the kind of friends she spent a lot of time with outside the job. And away from work? She had a few friends, but it was hard to maintain friendships when you didn't stay long in one place.

She should shower and change, maybe even go into the station and come up with a plan to get Carlton before he disappeared for good. But as the sun had started to set on the day, she'd discovered she had no energy left.

Marcos's partner had driven both of them to the hospital to get checked out. No surprise, they'd both been close to hypothermia. Even now, her fingers and toes throbbed. But at least she could feel them again. The doctor hadn't seen any sign of a concussion on her, and Marcos hadn't suffered any internal issues that they could tell from his beating. They were both going to be fine. Yet she was antsy, like her entire world had been upset and she'd never really be fine again.

Or maybe she hadn't really been fine since she'd been eleven years old.

"You're being a drama queen," Brenna muttered, forcing herself out of the chair. She was starving, but first she needed a shower and then, if she didn't fall asleep, food was next on the agenda.

She kicked off her shoes as she headed to her bedroom, and as she was shimmying out of her jeans, she realized there was something in the pocket. Pulling out the crumpled piece of paper, Brenna's heart rate picked up.

She'd forgotten all about the page she'd ripped out of the top of Carlton's pad in his office. Hurrying to the kitchen in her T-shirt and underwear, Brenna grabbed a pencil and shaded carefully across the page, hoping...

"Yes!" Indentations were on the page, and as Brenna squinted at it, she realized it was a phone number.

She probably should have called it in to her chief, have him run it, but she didn't want to wait. Carlton was out there somewhere, probably looking for a way out of the country if he wasn't already gone. And although her plan had been to get some sleep and go into the office as early as possible, when Jim and Marcos had dropped her off, she'd had no real leads.

She'd watched Marcos's curious gaze take in the outside of her little bungalow and bitten her tongue instead of asking him to come in with her. She'd half hoped he would ask—take her up on the promise she'd made on the mountain—but he'd just given her a quick hug goodbye. He and Jim had already been talking about the case as they'd backed out of her driveway.

Shaking off the disappointment that hit all over again, Brenna grabbed the cell phone she hadn't bothered to take with her to Carlton's mansion—not only would she not get service up there, she didn't want him looking through it. With fingers that felt oversize and clumsy, she dialed the number from the paper and held her breath.

It only took two rings and then a woman answered. "Hello?

Brenna drew in a sharp breath as the woman repeated her greeting twice more, then finally hung up. Then she sank into a kitchen chair in disbelief.

She knew that voice. She knew who Carlton's contact in the foster system had been all these years.

Chapter Eighteen

"Brenna Hartwell? From the foster home? Seriously?"

Marcos wrapped the blanket he'd grabbed as soon as he'd gotten home more tightly around himself. It didn't seem to matter how high he cranked the heat or how many hours it had been since he'd left the mountains. He couldn't seem to get warm.

His older brother Andre was still staring at him in disbelief. His oldest brother, Cole, frowned, watching him huddle more deeply into the blanket.

"Yes, that Brenna," Marcos said. "She's an undercover cop." His brothers had arrived an hour ago, after he'd spent several hours with Jim at the DEA office going over the weekend at Carlton's mansion.

His colleagues were busy trying to track Carlton and getting his picture out to anyplace he might try to travel. Eventually, once Marcos had given all the details he could, he'd known as well as they did that there was no reason for him to stay. Nothing besides his burning desire to be the one to slap handcuffs on Carlton.

But he wouldn't be any good to anyone if he couldn't function, and so he'd made Jim promise to call if they got a solid lead and had his partner drop him at home.

The entire drive, he'd been wishing Brenna was still beside him.

When they'd dropped her off at her cute little bungalow, he'd been shocked at how close they lived without realizing when he'd spent so many years wondering what had happened to her. He'd desperately wanted to tell Jim to forget the debrief and follow her inside. But time was essential if they wanted to find Carlton, and the truth was, if he'd followed Brenna inside, he'd be tempted to distract her from what she needed to be doing now too: resting and healing.

He hadn't expected to find his brothers waiting for him in his house, but he hadn't been surprised, either. When Jesse had shown up instead of him, the first thing Jim had done before racing up to the mansion was to call Cole and Andre, in case he'd contacted one of them. It wouldn't have been protocol, but Jim knew how close he was with his brothers. Besides, Cole was a detective and Andre was FBI, so they definitely had the resources to help him.

For the past hour, though, they'd both been in pure overprotective brother mode. Only now that he'd gone through the whole story with them—leaving out certain details between him and Brenna—was their concern shifting into something else.

Andre grinned at him. "You don't even have to say it. I see it all over your face. You're in love with this girl as much now as you were when you were twelve."

"I don't think…that's not…" Marcos stumbled, actually feeling the flush climb up his cheeks. Of all the times to suddenly get warm, this was just going to feed Andre's teasing. And that was usually Marcos's job.

He'd gotten used to teasing his older brothers, both of whom had dived headfirst into relationships over the past few months. He didn't like being on the other side of it. And Andre's word choice...

"I only spent a few days with her," he blurted. He couldn't be in love with her. He barely knew her. Except this overpowering mix of emotions he felt every time he so much as heard her name sure seemed like more than a simple crush.

Even Cole, who rarely resorted to teasing, was failing to hide his smile. "Well, at least now we know she didn't actually set that fire."

His words instantly changed the mood in the room, and his brothers got somber again.

"It sounds like it was just an accident, after all," Andre said.

"Yeah. It's still bugging me a little that Brenna was at Carlton's mansion because of what she thought she saw all those years ago, and now we know it wasn't our foster father."

"Well, are you sure?" Cole asked.

"Carlton talked about a woman as his contact."

"Maybe he was lying," Andre said.

Marcos slowly nodded. Carlton wasn't exactly a reliable source of information. There'd be no reason for him to lie about that and yet, the man was mercurial. Anyone who'd turn on a potential investor as fast as he had could easily lie about details of his operation just because he was paranoid. "Maybe."

"Maybe we should—" Cole started.

The ringing of Marcos's phone cut him off. He didn't recognize the number, but he picked up immediately, because he'd given Brenna his contact information before dropping her off. "Hello?"

"Marcos? It's Brenna."

"Brenna," he saw Andre mouth to Cole, and he realized he'd started grinning as soon as he'd heard her voice. He blanked his expression, but it was too late. His brothers were both hiding laughter.

"I thought you'd be asleep by now," he blurted.

There was a long pause, and then she said, "Marcos, do you remember how I told you I found something in Carlton's second office?"

Marcos sat straighter, dropping hold of the blanket. "No. What did you find?"

"Just a piece of paper. Turns out there was the indentation of a phone number on it. I called the number and I recognized the person who answered."

"Who?" Marcos glanced at his brothers, who both leaned forward as he asked, "Was it our foster father?"

"No. It's a woman who works in the Child and Family Services Division—not the location where I was pretending to work, but I've met her while setting up my undercover role."

"She knew you were a cop?" Marcos interrupted. Could that be how their covers were blown?

"No. She thought I was who I told Carlton I was. But it fits. She's set to retire in a few months. Carlton was recruiting me to replace her."

"Okay, I'll let my partner know. He can bring this woman in. What's her name?"

"I just wanted to give you the heads-up first," Brenna said, a stubborn undercurrent to her voice. "I'm going to get my department involved."

"Brenna, why don't you let the DEA handle this? We have more resources, and we've been working the Carlton Wayne White case for years."

Across from him, his brothers both cringed and

shook their heads at him, but he didn't need them to tell him Brenna wasn't going to like that suggestion. And he didn't care. When he'd seen her slam into that wall in Carlton's mansion and then slide to the floor unconscious, he'd never felt more powerless or afraid. He didn't want her anywhere near this.

"This is my case, too, Marcos," she said softly, angrily. "I'm not stepping aside."

He sighed, knowing it didn't matter what he said. She was going to stick to the case. And although he admired her for it, he also didn't want her doing it on her own.

"Tell you what. Why don't we join forces?" He pinched the bridge of his nose, wishing he could just keep her out of it, keep her safe. "Andre and Cole are at my house. Want to come over and figure out a plan?"

"I'll be there in twenty minutes."

"Brenna," he said quickly before she hung up.

"What?"

"What's this woman's name? The foster care connection?"

"Sara Lansky." Somehow, she must have heard his surprise in his silence, because she asked, "You know her?"

"I know the name," Marcos said grimly. "And you were right all along about our foster father. He is involved. Back when we lived in that foster home, he was having an affair with a Sara Lansky."

"Are you sure?"

"Yes. And it explains what Carlton said about his source not even knowing she was his source. It's because she wasn't. She was giving the information to our foster father. *He* was passing it on to Carlton."

His brothers both swore softly, and Brenna insisted, "Don't go anywhere without me. I'll be there soon."

Then she hung up and he stared back at his brothers, anger warming him faster than hours inside, almost faster than thinking about Brenna. He'd nearly died in that fire.

It didn't matter that the foster home had given him Cole and Andre. His foster father was going to pay for what he'd done.

SARA LANSKY. If the woman hadn't had such a distinctive voice, low and gravelly from years of smoking, Brenna wouldn't have recognized her so quickly. She barely knew the woman, after all. But Marcos's words rang in her head.

It made sense. Not just the way their foster father had gotten the records back then, but also the secretive way he'd slip down the stairs to his office in the middle of the night. Probably to call this woman.

Brenna had barely slept during those months at the foster home with Marcos and his brothers. A side effect of grief was that she startled to attention at every little noise. Twice, she'd crept down the stairs after their foster father, to see what he'd been doing. Once, she'd heard him open the back door and talk angrily to someone she'd later learned was his only nonfoster son, Trent, already grown and living elsewhere. The other time, he'd gotten on the phone and the conversation had quickly turned to things that at eleven years old, she hadn't understood. Now, she realized it must have been Sara on the line.

But how had their foster father gotten connected with Carlton in the first place to be passing information to him?

Brenna paused in lathering her hair, leaning against the wall of the shower. She'd spent so many years knowing that something had been wrong with what their foster father was doing that night, and determined to figure out what it was. Once she'd suspected the connection to Carlton, she'd been so focused on finding a way to bring Carlton down, she'd never stopped to wonder how they'd met.

Their foster father had to be at least twenty years older than Carlton, probably more. Eighteen years ago, he'd lived in a lower middle-class neighborhood, working a blue collar job. Apparently, he'd been cheating on his wife, but he'd come home to her every night. To her and their six foster kids, crammed into two of the four tiny bedrooms—plus her, as the only girl, stuck in a converted walk-in closet. They'd kept the third bedroom a shrine to Trent in case he ever wanted to come home. While she'd been there, he never had.

She'd never seen any evidence that their foster father was using drugs. And she couldn't imagine that he'd met Carlton—then a semiprofessional boxer—while at work at the factory. So, where?

Shivering, Brenna realized the water was starting to get cold, and she'd only planned to take a fast shower and change before heading to Marcos's place. She ran her hands through her hair, rinsing out the rest of the suds, then turned it off and stepped onto her rug as a soft noise sounded in the distance.

She froze, straining to listen. Was it her imagination?

After a minute of dripping onto her bathroom floor, attuned to any sound, Brenna let out a heavy breath and dried off. Grabbing a pair of jeans and a sweatshirt, she debated whether to waste time with makeup.

Just lipstick, she decided, swiping some bright red across her lips. As she was flipping the switch on her hair dryer, there was another sound, like something sliding softly across her kitchen floor.

Dropping the hair dryer, Brenna raced around her bed to the nightstand where she'd left her service pistol. From behind her, whoever was in her house must have realized she'd heard and no longer tried to be quiet. Footsteps pounded toward her, and the bedroom door was flung open.

Carlton stood in the doorway, looking larger than life in all black, his white-blond hair tied back, and fury in his eyes.

Brenna scrambled to open the drawer, then Carlton was on her. His massive hands closed around her shoulders, and he tossed her away from the table as if she weighed nothing.

She landed on the edge of the bed, then tumbled off the other side. Her body, already sore from running through the mountains, protested at the hard landing, but she pushed to her feet fast.

It didn't matter. He was already in front of her, blocking her exit.

He didn't have a weapon that she could see, but that didn't matter, either. Brenna knew what one hit from this man could do.

Holding up her hands in front of her, Brenna warned him, "If you're trying to silence me, it's too late. We've already found your real connection in foster care, and he's going to dismantle the whole thing."

Confusion passed over Carlton's face, then he shook it off. "It doesn't matter what you think you know. I'm not here to stop you from talking to your department." He cracked his knuckles. "We both know it's too late for that. I'm here to make you pay."

Chapter Nineteen

"How did you know about Sara Lansky?" Andre asked. "I don't remember her."

"Phone bills," Marcos replied, checking his watch again discreetly. It had been almost twenty minutes, and he was anxious to see Brenna again, even though his heart was telling him to keep her as far away from this case—and the danger—as possible. "Our foster mother was going through them one day. There were all these late-night calls to the same number. She'd circled it and written the name there."

"Did she confront him?" Cole asked.

Marcos shrugged. "I don't know. She saw me looking and covered them up, but by then, I'd realized what it meant."

"If you're right about this, then our foster father started giving Carlton information on foster kids eighteen years ago," Cole said.

"Yeah." Marcos considered what that meant. Eighteen years ago, Carlton had been just starting out, but he'd become a major player in the DC area pretty quickly. And that meant major money.

"They kept fostering after that house burned down," Andre spoke up. "I asked about them a few times over

the years. I guess early on, I was hoping that they'd
want us back. That the three of us would wind up back
together."

Cole nodded. "I think we all hoped that."

"Did he keep working?" Marcos asked. "Maybe they
just fostered so he'd have a connection to Sara."

Andre shrugged. "I always assumed so, but I don't
know."

"Let's find out," Marcos said, booting up his laptop
and doing a search. A minute later, he leaned back and
frowned. "Huh."

"What?" Cole asked.

"I can't find anything for at least a decade. It doesn't
look like he's at the factory anymore, and he hasn't
been for a while."

"Did he move somewhere else?" Andre wondered.

"I can't tell," Marcos replied. "I somehow doubt the
foster care system wouldn't get suspicious if he stopped
working all of a sudden, but I don't see anything."

"Well, what about the fostering?" Cole asked. "Is
he still doing it? Because I always got the feeling they
went into it because their own son was so distant, not
totally for the money."

"Yeah, me too, not that they really jumped into par-
enting," Marcos replied. His memories of that house
had been happy because of Cole and Andre. The foster
parents had just been there; not bad, not good. They'd
put a roof over his head and food in his belly and not a
lot else, though they'd been far better than some of the
other homes he'd lived in over the years.

But he remembered when he'd first arrived, his foster
mother talking about her son, Trent, who was grown and
had been out of their house for five years. According to

the stories, he'd been a genius, but a troublemaker who hung out with the wrong crowd. She'd spent so much energy trying to steer him in the right direction that once he was gone, she'd claimed she'd wanted a second chance. She'd also claimed she had nothing left to give.

Marcos had met Trent a handful of times over the years. He'd swing by for an hour or so, watch the foster kids with what looked like disdain, chat with his parents for a while, then head out again. With a son like that, it didn't surprise Marcos that they might want to try again, except they never really had.

"Maybe that was just an excuse," Marcos said. "Maybe she was in on it, too."

"I doubt it," Andre replied. "Not if the connection was through a woman he was having an affair with."

"Good point." Marcos glanced at his watch again and frowned.

Cole did the same. "Brenna should be here by now, shouldn't she?"

"I'm going to call her," Marcos said, already dialing. But it went straight to voice mail and a bad feeling came over him.

His brothers were already on their feet before Marcos realized he'd jumped up and grabbed his car keys.

Cole took them out of his hand. "I'll drive. You direct."

Marcos nodded his thanks, dread propelling him into a run. "Let's hurry."

ONE HIT AND it was all over. One hit and Carlton could knock her out and then kill her before she even had a chance to fight back.

Panic made Brenna breathe faster as Carlton took a

slow step toward her, a gleam in his eyes that told her he was going to enjoy hurting her. She had good reflexes— her years in foster care, some in houses with abuse— had taught her to dodge a blow instinctively. But he'd boxed semiprofessionally, and he'd already proved his fists could be faster than her reflexes.

But up in his mansion, she hadn't been expecting the hit. Right now, she was.

"You shouldn't have let Marcos drop you off and drive away," Carlton mocked her. "Maybe then you would have stood a chance. But I appreciate you sticking around while I learned where he lives."

Brenna's lungs tensed up, panic making it hard to breathe. After he killed her, he was going after Marcos. She forced the distraction to the back of her mind, knowing it was why he'd told her. Not just to torture her even more, but to keep her unfocused, unbalanced.

He proved it when he darted toward her, fist-first. Instead of an uppercut to her chin like last time, he went for her chest. Apparently this time, he didn't want her out of the fight right away—he wanted her to suffer.

She jerked sideways quickly and his fist soared past her, surprise in his gaze. Brenna changed direction just as fast, punching wildly, one fist after the other, both aimed at his throat. The first one bounced off, but the second one scored a solid hit.

He made a choking sound and stumbled back a step, but he regrouped quickly, and she hadn't expected anything less. With a past as a boxer, he knew how to take a hit and keep coming. Surprise would only get her so far. She needed a plan, or a weapon. Something. Because eventually, she wouldn't dodge fast enough and he'd take her down—or he'd decide to use brute strength and barrel into her.

Now, he gazed at her with a mixture of surprise, anger and a hint of respect. He smiled, and it was like a cat that knew it had a mouse cornered, but wanted to play with it awhile before making the kill.

"Not bad," he told her, and the way his voice came out broken told her she'd scored a better hit than she'd thought. "But not good enough," he added and swung his fist again.

This time his hand glanced off her side, but she knew if she lived through this there'd be a sizable bruise. She leaped right, and like a bizarre dance, he shuffled to face her.

Frantic, she worked through her options. Her gun was too far away. The hair dryer was discarded on the floor, running on low heat. Maybe she could yank the cord up and around him? There was a snow globe on her dresser that might do some damage if she could smash it against the side of his head.

Carlton was swinging again before she could decide, and she jerked right, almost stumbling over the hair dryer cord. She caught herself on the dresser at the last second, and then he was swinging again, and she knew she wasn't going to avoid this one.

Brenna ducked anyway, praying to minimize the damage, but before his fist landed, a crash sounded from behind them, startling him into pausing midswing and glancing back.

Not wasting any time, Brenna yanked the snow globe off the dresser and slammed it into the side of his head. The glass broke, cutting her hand and slicing into his scalp, making him yelp, but he was already swinging back toward her, fury in his gaze.

Then Marcos was racing through her bedroom door, and he jumped onto Carlton's back, sending the drug lord to the ground. Two men were right behind Marcos, and despite the passing of eighteen years, Brenna recognized them. Cole and Andre.

Before Brenna could fully wrap her mind around the fact that Marcos was here, he, Cole and Andre had Carlton pinned to the ground. Andre slapped a pair of handcuffs onto the drug lord, and then Cole was on the phone, calling for backup.

Andre and Cole literally sat on Carlton to keep him from racing out the door, handcuffs and all, and Marcos gripped her by the upper arm, looking her over carefully. "Are you okay?"

"I'm fine." She stared back at him, still in disbelief that he was here, in her house. "How did you know?"

"You took too long to get to my house." He pulled her to him, wrapping her in a hug tight enough that it made her side—where Carlton had gotten in a glancing blow—twinge.

But she ignored it, because the pain was worth it to be in Marcos's arms. She rested her head against his chest and closed her eyes, feeling safe despite Carlton still thrashing around on her floor. Feeling content for the first time in years.

Behind them, Andre loudly cleared his throat. "Not to interrupt the reunion, but do you want to give us a little help here?"

Brenna pulled free of Marcos's embrace to discover even with Cole and Andre both shoving him to the ground, Carlton was thrashing around, trying to pull himself free.

Marcos rolled his eyes and went to join them, but Brenna scooted past him, jammed a knee between his brothers on Carlton's back and yanked his cuffed hands straight up behind him.

Carlton roared and went still, and Marcos grinned. "Guess you don't need my help after all."

Then sirens sounded, and DEA agents were piling into her house and dragging Carlton off to their vehicle.

Brenna turned and stared at Marcos and his two brothers, all grown up. Cole and Andre weren't quite what she would have pictured, and yet, she'd recognized them instantly.

"It's good to see you, Brenna," Cole said.

"We've been hearing a lot about you tonight," Andre added, and then they were both hugging her.

It wasn't the sort of brief, polite hug you'd give someone after reconnecting, but a genuine hug, the kind you offered to family. Tears welled up in Brenna's eyes, and she blinked the moisture away before they stepped back.

"At least this is almost over," Marcos said. "With Carlton in custody and only his chef still in the wind from the mansion, now we just need to bring in his foster care connection. Then it will take some time, but the rest of his organization will begin to fall like dominoes."

"That's not all," Brenna said grimly.

"Why not?" Cole asked.

Brenna looked from Marcos to his brothers and back again. "When I told Carlton we were about to bring down his real foster care connection, he looked confused, like he didn't know who I meant."

"Maybe he just thought you meant someone working with Sara," Andre suggested.

Brenna shook her head. "No, I'm pretty sure he genuinely didn't know what I was talking about."

"He said that the foster care connection didn't even know she was his connection," Marcos reminded her. "Maybe he couldn't believe you'd really gotten on to our foster father." He looked pensive. "Although he obviously looked into your past. He knew you'd been in that house, since you specifically mentioned the fire as part of your cover. I'm surprised he wasn't suspicious from the beginning because of that."

"Maybe it's because he didn't know," Brenna replied.

"How could he not know?" Cole asked.

"I think he's the front man," Brenna answered, as the things that had been bothering her since she'd brought it up to Carlton suddenly fell into place. "I think someone else is the real mastermind."

Chapter Twenty

"Who do you think is the mastermind?" Marcos asked.

He and his brothers were sitting in Brenna's living room, and he couldn't stop himself from glancing around again. Just like her bedroom, it was painted with a bright pop of color. The furniture was bright and full of personality, too. It all felt like Brenna and yet, something was off, as if she wasn't fully settled in yet.

Her house was quiet now that his colleagues had cleared out, taking Carlton with them. Normally, Marcos would have insisted on going with them. He'd wanted to be involved in questioning the drug lord, but he knew his partner would do a good job. Jim had more than fifteen years of experience, and if anyone could get Carlton to spill everything, it was Jim.

Still, Marcos knew that wasn't going to be a quick process. He'd told Jim he was exhausted and needed rest. Jim had raised his eyebrows and glanced at Brenna, like he'd known there was more to Marcos staying away from the initial questioning. And he was right.

It didn't matter that the biggest threat to Brenna's safety was now behind bars. Because she shouldn't have been in danger in the first place. It was completely illogical for Carlton to venture anywhere near the home of an armed police officer when the entire law-enforcement community was searching for him. And right now, Marcos wasn't going to be at ease unless he had her in his sights.

The fact was, he wasn't sure he'd ever be at ease again whenever she was out of his sight.

The thought gave him pause. He was in law enforcement; he knew and accepted the risks he took every day. He knew and accepted those risks with both of his brothers. But the thought of Brenna out on the streets in her police blues, or undercover again, made his entire body clammy with fear.

He knew she was capable. Not as well trained as her department should have ensured before she was sent out on a mission that involved Carlton Wayne White, but she was resourceful and strong. So, why did the thought of her at risk make him want to follow her around?

Marcos glanced over at his brothers, realizing that for all their teasing earlier, they were right. He was falling in love with this woman. No, forget the *falling*. He'd already collapsed at her feet, and he'd probably never get up again.

When he swore under his breath, Brenna gave him a perplexed glance, but his brothers just smirked at him. They knew him too well, and Marcos could just bet they knew exactly what he'd realized.

He was in love with Brenna Hartwell. Now he just had to figure out what he was going to do about it.

"…knew," Brenna said, staring at him as if she expected a response.

"Sorry. What?" he asked, trying to shake himself out of his fog, to focus on truly closing this case instead of on how to convince Brenna to take a chance on him. In the mountains, she'd made a deal with him: she'd show him her house if he showed her his. She'd fulfilled her end of the bargain, intentionally or not. But there was no doubt she was wary of relationships; how did he deal with that? How did he come to terms with dating a woman in law enforcement, who put herself in as much danger as he did every single day? And how did he overcome what had always seemed to be his nature: to only stay in a relationship until it got too serious, and then bail before she could? Because truth be told, he was wary of relationships, too, probably for the same reason she was.

"I said, I wish I knew," Brenna repeated. "Maybe it's our foster father?" She sounded unconvinced.

"We looked into him. It looks like he stopped working at the factory about a decade ago," Marcos told her. "I can't find anything about him working elsewhere, but I assume he was. We'll have to take a lot closer look, but if he was the mastermind, why let Carlton take on the front role? How would he have gotten hooked up with the guy?"

"I've been wondering that myself," she said, then shrugged. "I don't know. Maybe I'm wrong. Maybe Carlton was confused for some other reason, but my gut is telling me there's more here than we're seeing."

"Well, some of the things he said up in the mountains did make me wonder if either there was a second in command we don't know about making a power play, or if Carlton could actually be reporting to someone. If he really isn't the one in charge, then it's somebody pretty brilliant, because it's not just law enforcement who thinks so, but everyone I've talked to in the drug world. And I just don't see our foster father in that role."

"Maybe we need to pay Mr. Pike a visit," Cole suggested.

Andre looked at his watch. "It's almost three in the morning. Why don't we all get some sleep first? We can do it tomorrow after work."

"Or Brenna and I can go in the morning," Marcos suggested, his gaze darting to Brenna's bandaged hand. One of the EMTs who'd shown up with the DEA had stitched up Carlton's head and then wrapped her hand. It wasn't bad, but things could have been so much worse. He wanted to end this, stop any possible threat still out there as soon as possible.

His brothers didn't look thrilled about not being included, but Marcos didn't want to wait a full day. The fact was, he wanted to charge over to his foster father's house now, but Andre was right about it being a bad time to go knocking on someone's door if they wanted answers, especially when they had no proof of his involvement. And they didn't even know where he lived anymore.

"I wish I could skip out tomorrow and come with you," Cole said, "but I trust you'll keep us updated as soon as you know anything?"

"Of course," Brenna replied before Marcos could answer.

"Good," Andre said, standing and yawning. "Then let's head out. Brenna, you need a bag?"

Brenna stared up at him in confusion. "What?"

"You're staying with Marcos tonight," Cole answered for him. "Even if Carlton is behind bars, he cut a hole in your window that you need replaced. And we kicked down your door to get in. Yes, it's temporarily boarded, but you shouldn't be staying here like that."

"I'm armed," Brenna reminded them.

This time, Marcos didn't let his brothers speak. "You pick. Either you come stay with me or I stay here. But I have to warn you, given the fact that Carlton was here tonight and you think he's got someone pulling his strings, neither of us will sleep much if I stay here because Cole and Andre will be calling all night."

They both nodded, and she rolled her eyes. "All right. I'll get a bag, but you should know that Carlton must have found my place following us from the parking lot after his guards were taken out. He said he followed you back to your house before returning to mine. He was going to go after you next."

His brothers were instantly frowning again, and Marcos didn't want to drive out to either of their places, so he said, "Okay, we'll be extra cautious and check into a hotel for the night."

Brenna flushed at his words, and Marcos wished either of them were in any shape to do anything besides get a solid eight hours of sleep. But the hours on the mountains were catching up to him fast.

"You sure?" Andre asked. "Because I have room—"

"I'm sure," Marcos cut him off, then stared after Brenna as she disappeared into her room to pack an overnight bag.

And suddenly, he felt twelve years old again, meeting a little girl he was just sure he was going to marry someday.

BRENNA STARED AT the king-size bed in the center of the hotel room, and her heart did a little flip-flop. It didn't matter that she was too tired to do any of the things that instantly came to mind as Marcos sank onto the edge of that bed. And yet, instead of backing away like she should have, she found herself moving toward him.

His head lifted at her movement, those blue-gray eyes locking on her, hypnotizing. Then his arms were up, reaching for her, and she couldn't help herself from climbing onto his lap and wrapping her arms around his neck.

She'd expected him to pull her head to his, to lock their lips together, for passion to spark instantly like it had that first night she'd seen him. Instead, he gave her a soft smile and cupped her cheek, his thumb stroking her somehow more of a turn-on than full-body contact with any other man.

"You didn't answer your phone, and I don't think I've ever felt so scared. I don't know why, but I just knew something was wrong."

She smiled back at him. "My not answering a phone call was probably the most normal thing that's happened to either of us in the past four days! But I'm glad you came when you did." She shivered, imagining how bad things could have gone if Marcos hadn't worried about her.

Imagine that. Someone worrying about her. It was almost as if they were a real couple, like she had someone in her life again to care what happened to her. The last time she could remember feeling protected and cared about this way was before her mom had died.

Or maybe that was unfair, because she had people in her life she mattered to. And she'd had other men who'd tried to get close, who'd fought for a real relationship with her. But even when she'd felt reciprocal attraction, none of them had offered her something she'd battle for. And now? After four days, she'd found someone worth any fight, because she couldn't imagine her life without Marcos.

As she stared at him with growing awareness, Marcos just kept stroking her cheek, his other hand low on her back. There was something both possessive and familiar about his touch, and Brenna laid her head on his shoulder before he saw panic spark in her eyes.

She'd promised him a trade-off: a look inside each other's houses. But what that really meant to her was much more complicated. She'd been offering him a relationship, a look inside her heart. And while only time would tell how things might work out between them, she was already involved.

What did she know about relationships? She'd avoided them most of her life. Not just the romantic type, but all connections that got too close. Was she even capable of letting someone in?

Growing up in foster care, bouncing from one place to another, always alone, she'd pushed back her fears that her mother's death had damaged her. She'd always figured that she had time to make changes, that eventually life would fall into place and those connections would, too.

But that hadn't happened, and fear rose up hard now that she would always be too broken to offer Marcos anything worth having.

"Hey." Marcos's soft voice penetrated her fears and he cupped her cheek, shifting her to face him. "What's wrong?"

How did she tell him her fears without scaring him off? Marcos had faced a lot of the same challenges she had, but he hadn't let them close him off. Instead, he'd formed a brotherly bond that was as strong as the blood bond she'd shared with her mom.

So, instead of answering, she pressed her lips to his and kissed him. She poured everything she was feeling into the kiss: her fear; her attraction to him; her admiration for who he'd become; even the love that shouldn't be possible after such a short time, but she could no longer deny. Once upon a time, it might have been a simple crush on a boy who'd shown her kindness when she needed it most in her life. But somehow, in the past few days, it had morphed into something much bigger, something she knew wasn't going to fade no matter what happened between them.

His fingers slid over her face, down the back of her neck, then glided up her arms. His lips caressed hers as though he was feeling the very same things, and hope exploded in Brenna's chest with such intensity that she had to pull back and gulp in a breath.

Then Marcos was scooting them both backward along the bed until they could lay on it, and Brenna suddenly didn't care how tired she was. She slid her fingers up underneath his sweater, loving the way his ab muscles tensed underneath her touch. She fused her lips back to his, and he growled in the back of his throat.

His hands locked on her hips as he pulled her tightly against him and kissed her with such an intensity that the room seemed to spin. Brenna grabbed fistfuls of his sweater and held on, letting the emotions crash over her, letting Marcos further into her heart.

When he finally lifted his head from hers, Brenna had lost all sense of time. He looked just as dazed, but then he gave her that big, dimpled grin that had sucked her in from the very first time she'd seen him.

"What do you say we get some sleep, then head out tomorrow and close this case, put this threat completely behind us? Then I want to come back here and finish this, when I have the strength to love you like you deserve."

Brenna's mouth went dry, and she nodded back at him until he tucked her against his chest. If this was Marcos without full strength, then she was going to need some sleep, too.

As she drifted off to sleep in his arms, she felt a smile tug her lips. Had his word choice been intentional? Because being loved by Marcos Costa was something she wanted desperately, and not just for one night.

For the rest of her life.

Chapter Twenty-One

Marcos woke slowly, becoming aware of bits of sunlight sneaking past the curtains, the unfamiliar bed, the woman curled up in his arms. His arms instinctively tightened, holding Brenna closer, and she stirred a little, only to snuggle closer still.

Every day should be like this. The thought shouldn't have caught him by surprise. He already knew he'd managed to fall in love with her. But it did surprise him. Love was one thing; forever was another. And yet…his heart was telling him Brenna should never have left his life in the first place.

He'd never thought he was a *forever* kind of guy. Marriage and family were fine for Andre and Cole—and he wanted that for both of his brothers. But he'd always figured that he'd spend his life spoiling nieces and nephews rotten, and chasing down bad guys in undercover roles across the world. He'd even applied to an open post in the Middle East a few months ago; now, he knew he'd be retracting it. Suddenly, nowhere seemed like it could possibly be more exciting than right beside Brenna.

Panic threatened and he shoved it down. He went unarmed into the remote hideouts of vicious drug lords. He could handle being in love with a commitment-phobic woman who ran headlong into danger herself.

"Mind over matter," he muttered to himself. He might not be able to change his natural wariness about relationships, but he could choose to jump into one anyway. Because if anyone was worth taking that chance for, it was Brenna Hartwell.

"What?" she mumbled sleepily.

"Nothing." He kissed the top of her head, then let himself hold her a minute longer before slipping out of bed.

Grabbing the cell phone he'd dropped on the dresser last night, Marcos opened the slider to the balcony, and a rush of cold air blasted into the room.

"Brrr," Brenna groaned, sitting up, but hauling the covers with her. "What are you doing?"

"Sorry. I was going to step outside and make a call." He grinned at the tangled mess of her hair, the sleepy half-mast of her eyes. "I didn't mean to wake you."

She made a face at him and finger-combed her hair. "Why are you smiling like that?" Not giving him a chance to answer, she added, "And close the door. I'm up."

He pushed it shut, then strode over to the bed, leaned across it and planted a kiss on her lips. "I'm smiling because you're ridiculously cute first thing in the morning." And she was.

As for him, he was practically giddy with happiness. His brothers were going to have a field day teasing him. He probably deserved it after the way he'd mercilessly teased them when they'd both fallen in love over the past few months.

She flushed and straightened her hair a little more, then said, "I'm pretty sure this is far from first thing in the morning, but thank you. Who are you calling?"

Marcos glanced at the time on his phone, realizing she was right. It was almost noon. But apparently no one had expected him in the office that morning, and even Jim was giving him a little breathing room. "I'm going to give Jim a call, see what the status is with Carlton."

She let the covers drop away and crawled across the bed toward him as he sat on the edge of the bed. "Speaker?"

"Sure." He let his gaze wander over her. She'd fallen asleep in jeans and a sweatshirt; he was still wearing what he'd had on in the mountains, and he realized he desperately needed a shower.

But she didn't seem to care as she looped her arms around his neck and rested her head against his back. "Maybe he's talking."

There wasn't a lot of hopefulness in her tone, and Marcos doubted Carlton had broken, either. But if he wasn't really in charge, would he be willing to risk going down for another man's empire? "Let's find out," he said, dialing Jim.

His partner picked up on the first ring. "Marcos? I wondered when you were gonna tear yourself away from your lady friend and call in."

Against his back, Marcos felt Brenna muffling her laughter. "You're on Speaker, man."

"Oh. Hi, Brenna. Sorry about that."

"No problem," she said, laughter in her voice.

Marcos got down to business. "So, what's the status?"

Jim sighed. "Well, the good news is that we caught Carlton's last bodyguard-slash-cook. The guy came after us with a butcher's knife, so he's in surgery right now, having a bullet taken out of his chest, but it looks like he'll pull through."

"And what about Carlton?"

"He's not talking. The guy knows he's going to be doing some major time. But I think he figures we've already got him on trying to kill a federal agent and a police officer, and maybe on killing his own guard— although we haven't found a body yet, which always makes a conviction challenging. So I'm sure he's decided, why hand over a drug charge, as well? Because we can try to get him on promises he made to you, but you know how that'll go."

"Yeah." In court, he'd claim that he was talking about some other kind of product, or that he was just joking. With no audio and video evidence like they would have had if the buy had actually gone through, it was unlikely to stick. "What about Jesse? Is he flipping on his uncle?"

"The kid is scared," Jim replied. "Scared of his uncle, scared of doing time, and honestly, at this point, he's scared of his own shadow. But I think you might get through to him. We know he thinks Carlton had his parents killed. That's pretty powerful motivation to turn on the guy."

Brenna's arms tightened around him at the mention of the car crash that had killed Jesse's family, and he didn't think she'd realized she'd done it. "Is there anything there?" Marcos asked. "Can we get that case reopened? Even if we can get Carlton life without parole on everything else, I'd still like him to pay for that, even if it's just a symbolic sentencing."

"We're going to talk to the local police about that.

What do you think about coming in and talking to Jesse?"

"Later today," Marcos promised. "First, I need to pay my old foster parents a visit. Did Carlton give any sense that he *wasn't* running the show?"

There was a long pause. "No. You have reason to think he wasn't?"

"Maybe."

When Marcos didn't say more, Jim replied, "All right, well, do what you need to do with your foster parents and then give me a call. Keep me in the loop on this. You taking backup?"

"Yeah, Brenna's coming with me."

"Good. Hey, Brenna?"

She lifted her head from his back. "Yeah?"

"Take care of him for me, will you?"

Marcos twisted his head to look at her, and she smiled at him. "You got it."

THIS WAS HOME ONCE. Sort of.

Marcos stared at the empty lot where their foster home had once stood. Beside him, Brenna folded her uninjured hand in his.

Apparently, their foster parents had never rebuilt here after the fire. Eighteen years later, there was no evidence a house had ever stood there at all, except that it was one bare lot in a row of little houses. The grass was overrun with weeds, but it stood waist-high, browning leaves sprinkled across it in places.

It was hard to picture the worn-down two-story building where he'd come when he was seven years old. His most vivid memories of those days were of his brothers. Meeting them on that very first day when he'd faltered in the doorway, his only belongings clutched in a small backpack. Following them to the backyard when they'd gone to play a game of catch, thinking they hadn't seen him. His surprise and uncertainty when they'd called him over to join them. And then a bond he'd never had in his short years on this Earth.

And then there were the memories of Brenna. He'd known her only a few months, but the time was stamped into his brain. He didn't think he'd ever forget the sight of her on the stoop, tears watering over her eyes, her hair in braids and a nasty gash on her cheek from the car crash. He knew he'd never forget the way it had felt when he'd reached out and taken her hand—as though she was his reason for existing.

He turned to find her staring contemplatively at the empty lot. "It's hard to believe this is where we met," she said softly.

He pressed a kiss to her lips. "Come on. Let's go see our old foster parents."

They'd known before coming here that their foster parents were long gone. But they hadn't moved far, and on the drive over, Marcos had felt his hands turning the wheel onto a familiar street. In the passenger seat, Brenna hadn't said a word, but he'd known she realized exactly where he was taking her.

Silently, they climbed back into his car, and he made the relatively short trip to their foster parents' new house. When he stopped in front of it, Marcos whistled and then double-checked the address he'd written down back at the hotel.

"Awfully nice place for someone who quit his factory job and supposedly just went to work in his son's business part-time," Brenna said, a hard edge to her voice as they climbed out of his car.

Marcos found it hard to believe that the man who'd taken him into his home for those five years was secretly a drug lord. But the house in front of them—easily five times the size of the little house where they'd crammed eight people back then—suggested he was into something more than he was officially reporting on his taxes. Especially since their foster mother had also quit her part-time work a few years later.

"Let's be ready for anything," Marcos said, and Brenna nodded, patting her hip. He knew that concealed under her sweatshirt was her service pistol. He was also carrying. Probably unnecessary with their foster parents, but if they were in league with Carlton in any way, they were more dangerous than they seemed.

They walked up the long entryway, and then Marcos knocked, hoping the Pikes would answer. The plan was to try to play it off as an innocent visit initially, in case their foster parents hadn't heard about Carlton. If necessary, he and Brenna would take a more official route, but right now, they had no evidence and nothing to get an arrest warrant.

The door swung open, and Marcos recognized their foster mother immediately. She'd aged gracefully, with streaks of silver through her light brown hair, and a regal stance to her that Marcos didn't remember from his childhood.

"Can I help you?" she asked.

"Uh, yes. I'm Marcos Costa. This is Brenna Hartwell. We were—"

"Oh my goodness," she cut him off. "From before

the fire. Of course! Come in." She held the door wider, letting them pass.

Inside, Marcos glanced around curiously. The house was a far cry from the small place they'd packed in six foster kids. The floors were expensive, patterned hardwood in the entryway, a huge chandelier overhead. Disappointment filled him at the mounting suspicion that they were involved even more than he'd expected. Passing on foster kid information was bad enough; actually being the mastermind took the betrayal he was feeling to a whole new level. Although he didn't have any real bond with them, he still had fond feelings for the home, because of all that it had given him in his life: Andre, Cole and Brenna.

Their foster mother led them into a huge living room with a wall of windows looking out over a man-made lake, then gestured for them to take a seat on the big white sectional couch.

Brenna sat gingerly at the edge of the couch, and he sat beside her. "Is Mr. Pike here?" he asked.

"Yes, he is. Let me just get him." She fiddled nervously with her hair, then shook her head. "I can't believe you two. All grown up." She glanced between them, and added, "And dating now? Or married? It's a good thing you two didn't stay in that house like siblings."

Brenna nodded noncommittally, and their foster mother backed out of the room. The truth was, none of the kids in that house had felt like siblings to him, except Andre and Cole, no matter how long he'd lived there. Brenna hadn't been there very long, but his connection to her certainly hadn't been familial.

When their foster mother was out of the room, Brenna whispered, "What do you think?"

"She's definitely nervous," he replied, watching the doorway carefully. Although he didn't expect their foster father to suddenly appear with a weapon, he wasn't taking any chances.

But when Mr. Pike did appear a minute later, Marcos worked to keep his jaw from dropping. Their foster mother was leading him into the room, with a supportive hand on his back. Physically, he looked pretty good. A little hunched over from his years of hard labor, but the years didn't show on him otherwise.

Mentally was a different story. Even before his eyes locked on Marcos's, he could tell the man wasn't entirely there.

"Dementia," their foster mother explained, a little teary eyed. "Started about a year ago. He's got good days and bad. Today he probably won't understand who you are, but we'll try." Then she smiled at him and said, "Honey, you remember Marcos Costa—he lived with us about five years, back before the fire? And little Brenna Hartwell? She was there a few months."

"Marcos," he repeated. "And Brenna. Nice to meet you."

Their foster mother shook her head at them, then helped her husband settle into a chair. Then she took a seat and leaned forward, twisting her hands in her lap. "So tell me how you've been. It's so nice to see you after all these years."

Marcos shared a glance with Brenna. If their foster father had ever masterminded anything, that time was long gone. But the house they lived in was nicer than Marcos would have expected for someone who was just passing names for a payoff.

They were missing something. But what?

Chapter Twenty-Two

"Marcos and I just recently ran into each other again," Brenna told them, watching carefully for any reaction. Because *someone* had blown their cover at that mansion with Carlton, and she might have recognized Sara Lansky's voice on the phone, but she doubted the woman would have recognized *her*. And if she had, she would have only known her as a fellow social worker. And she wouldn't have known Marcos at all.

The leak had come from somewhere, and if it wasn't Mr. Pike... Brenna turned her gaze on Mrs. Pike, who was fiddling with the hem of her sweater. She'd been nervous since the moment they'd arrived, but Brenna found it hard to believe she would have collaborated with her husband's mistress. Unless maybe her husband had been in charge until the past year, and then his wife had reluctantly taken over in order to keep up their lifestyle.

Brenna frowned at the idea. It could fit, but she sensed that wasn't right, either.

"Oh, yes?" their foster mother said. "How did you reconnect?" She looked from Brenna to Marcos, seeming genuinely curious.

"Up in the mountains," Marcos said, sounding purposely vague.

"Oh. That's...unusual." Their foster mother returned to fiddling with her sweater. "And what about those other boys, the ones you were so close to?"

"Cole and Andre?" Marcos said. "They went into law enforcement, just like me."

"Law enforcement?" Her voice went up half an octave, then she coughed. "That's great. So, you're a police officer? I never would have imagined that."

"No," Brenna replied. "He's not a police officer. I am. Marcos works for the DEA."

"I see," she replied, and the nervousness seemed to fade, replaced by a wary distrust that blanked the expression on her face.

Next to her, Marcos leaned forward, glancing from Mrs. Pike to her husband, who didn't seem to be following the conversation at all. "So, you know why we're here."

"No," she said, her voice suddenly hard and cold. "I can't say that I do."

"Carlton Wayne White," Brenna supplied.

She shook her head. "I'm not familiar with him."

"How about Sara Lansky?" Brenna asked, and this time she got a reaction.

Mrs. Pike visibly twitched, her gaze darted to her husband, then back to them as she stood. "I think it's time for you to go."

"If we leave now, we'll be back with a warrant and a whole lot more agents," Marcos promised.

She folded her arms over her chest. "Then I guess that's what you'll have to do."

Marcos stood and Brenna did the same, but before

Mrs. Pike shut the door behind them, Brenna told her, "Oh, in case you hadn't heard, we've got Carlton in custody."

The door didn't close fast enough to hide their foster mother's panicked expression.

Brenna stared at Marcos. "Well, she's involved."

"Yeah," Marcos agreed with a sigh. "I guess we'd better give Jim a call. I'm not sure how we're going to get that warrant, but we'd better figure something out before they run."

As they walked toward Marcos's car, Brenna glanced backward and saw their foster mother peeking through the shades, a phone pressed to her ear. When she spotted Brenna, she dropped the shades back into place.

"Something is off here, Marcos. I mean, she obviously recognized Carlton's name, but when we first showed up, she seemed to genuinely want to know how we'd reconnected."

Marcos nodded grimly as they climbed back into his car. "I know. And if she was the one who'd blown our covers, then she'd already know exactly how that had happened."

"I THINK JESSE is going to work with us," Jim announced as soon as Marcos called him.

"That's good news," Brenna said, listening over the speaker, one eye still on the Pikes' house behind them. Marcos hadn't started his car, but had decided to sit out front for a while and see how the investigation at the DEA office was going, then plan their next move.

And it really was going to be *their* next move. She knew Marcos wasn't comfortable working with her yet—that he was resisting his natural urge to keep her as far away from danger as possible—but she also knew that if things were going to go anywhere between them, he'd have to get used to her job.

She was going to stay. She'd realized it while they were inside the Pikes' house, working together. She didn't think she'd be going back undercover anytime soon, but *detective* was an idea that was gaining traction in her mind. Her mentor had been pushing her in that direction since the beginning, telling her that was where she belonged, and she was starting to think he was right.

As for the other place she belonged? She glanced at Marcos, looking serious as he listened to Jim explain that the kid hadn't made any promises, but had been asking about him. Jim felt confident he'd turn if Marcos could give him some guarantees. And she knew Marcos wanted to help the kid turn his life around.

She smiled and twined her hand with his, and he squeezed back as he told Jim, "We'll come into the office in a few minutes and talk to him then. We just got finished at our old foster parents' house."

"How'd that go?" Jim asked.

"Strange," Brenna supplied. "Our foster father has dementia. He wasn't following the conversation, but our foster mother definitely knew something. As for how much they were involved? We're not really sure."

"We're going to need to bring them both in," Marcos said.

"If he's sick—" Jim started.

"This man was up late at night, going over the names of foster kids he could sell out to a drug dealer in exchange for a cushy life. It may have been an accident, but he still started that fire."

In the pause that followed, Brenna could tell that Jim knew a lot about what had happened the night of the fire. How it had separated Marcos and his brothers, the scars it had left on his back.

But when he finally spoke, his words left her speechless. "It changed your life. You lost Brenna."

Marcos pressed his lips to her hand. "And now that I've found her again, I want to get some closure on the past. Whatever our foster father did, he still needs to pay for it."

"I understand," Jim said. "We're going to need more than a hunch, and Jesse never said anything about someone involved besides Carlton. But if we can flip Jesse…"

"It gives us leverage on Carlton," Marcos finished. "And he'll want to share the jail time if he can, rather than take the heat for everything himself."

"Exactly," Jim agreed.

"We're on our way," Marcos told him, disconnecting the call and pulling on his seat belt.

Brenna was doing the same when a Hummer squealed to a stop in front of them, blocking their exit. The driver got out, slammed the door and strode toward them, a furious expression on his face.

"He looks a lot like—" Brenna started.

"It's the Pikes' son," Marcos finished. "Trent."

"She must have called him when we left the house," Brenna said, watching Trent approach and doing the math. He'd be in his early forties now. He looked ageless, one of those guys who could be anywhere between thirty and fifty, with perfectly styled blond hair, chiseled cheekbones and an expensive wool coat. He'd managed to get the best of both parents' features, and apparently things had changed in eighteen years, because now he was showing up.

Trent stopped next to Marcos's window and knocked on it until Marcos rolled it down.

"What's wrong with you?" he yelled. "You come over here and harass my parents, accuse them of working with *drug dealers*? Are you crazy?"

"We're not harassing anyone," Marcos replied calmly. "We just needed explanations for some inconsistencies about your father's access to the foster care system."

"Foster care! Right. So, this is the thanks you give them for taking you into their home, raising you like you were actually their kids instead of street trash no one wanted?"

"Street trash?" Marcos repeated, sounding both offended and incredulous. "Is that what you think of foster kids? Is that why you think it's fine to use them however you want?"

Trent jerked backward, but recovered quickly. "I don't know what you're talking about, and I want you out of here, now."

"Let me ask you something, Trent. Does the name Sara Lanksy mean anything to you?"

"Yeah, my father's mistress. So my dad's not perfect. Guess what? No one is." He stabbed a finger toward Marcos's face. "You leave them alone. I just left my wife by herself at brunch to deal with this nonsense. If I have to do it again, you're going to regret it. And your little badge there isn't going to save you this time."

He stomped back to his vehicle and peeled away, leaving Brenna to stare at Marcos in disbelief. "Did he really just say *this time*?"

"Yeah, he did. And if Carlton sent pictures of us from the mansion to anyone in this family, they'd all be able to recognize us."

Brenna frowned. "And get access to what we really do?"

"Someone who's been secretly running a drug operation of this size for twenty years has connections."

Brenna considered that, mulling over the idea of Trent being involved—and whether he'd gotten pulled in because of his father, or vice versa. "He didn't even go inside to check if they were okay."

"Yeah," Marcos agreed, his gaze following the Hummer as it spun around a corner. "And yet, eighteen years ago, I'm not even sure he would have done this much. You think he's protecting them or protecting the business?"

"It sure seems like both," Brenna said. It had never occurred to her to consider Trent, but it made a lot of sense. He could get the information from his dad and pass it on to Carlton, then Carlton could use it to build his empire.

"I agree," Marcos said. "But is he doing Carlton's bidding or is Carlton a figurehead?"

"Hang on," Brenna replied, texting Victor at the station. Less than a minute later he came back with a reply.

"Victor says Trent's lifestyle doesn't come even close to matching his tax returns."

"That was fast," Marcos said.

She grinned. "Yeah, you'll like Victor. He's got a way with computers. And he's the one who convinced me to become a cop."

Marcos leaned toward her, dropping a kiss on her lips that made her anxious to wrap this case up and take him up on his promise from last night. A shiver of anticipation ran through her at the thought, and he grinned, his dimples on full display, like he could read her mind.

"Maybe they're partners," Marcos said. "Carlton is perfect for the front man. He's got the sort of personality that likes being feared. And remember eighteen years ago, the way Mrs. Pike talked about her son? All the bad influences he hung around?"

Brenna nodded. "And how he was a genius."

"Yeah, well, that might have been a bit of an exaggeration, but whoever ran this organization for the past twenty years is really savvy."

Brenna nodded back at him. "Probably savvier than Carlton Wayne White."

"I think we just found our mastermind."

"Then let's go and get him."

"Maybe you should think about making the leap over to DEA," Marcos suggested as he pulled away from the curb. "We could work together like this all the time."

"Yeah, I'm not sure undercover work is for me," Brenna replied.

"Carlton thought you were a natural," Marcos teased, shooting her a smile as he left the Pikes' neighborhood and turned onto the freeway.

"We just decided Carlton wasn't all that smart," Brenna joked. "Besides..." She squeezed his hand, still tucked in his as he drove one-handed. "Doesn't the DEA have rules about coworkers dating?"

"Not to mention spouses," Marcos added, and he said it so easily, so casually, as if it was a foregone conclusion.

Brenna's head spun at the idea, and panic tightened her chest. Marriage. Was she cut out for that?

Then she glanced over at Marcos's strong profile, and the panic started to subside. If anyone could make her want to promise her life to him, it was Marcos.

In fact, the more she thought about it, the more right it seemed. A smile started to bloom, and the panic in her chest exploded into unfettered joy. Marriage to Marcos. It might be a little scary, but there was suddenly no doubt. That's what she wanted for her future.

She probably should wait until they finished the investigation, until they were back in that hotel, making good on Marcos's promise, to tell him. Not driving on the freeway, knowing in their hearts who all the major players in this drug organization were, but still needing to prove it. But the words wanted to escape, and she couldn't hold them in one minute longer.

"Marcos, I lo—" she started, then her gaze darted up to the rearview mirror and she screamed as a huge dark vehicle raced toward them. "Watch out!" she screamed, but it was too late.

The Hummer slammed into the back of Marcos's car, and everything seemed to move in slow motion as the back end of the car lifted off the ground. Then they were spinning, out of control, heading for the concrete divider in the center of the freeway.

Chapter Twenty-Three

The air bag deployed, smacking her in the face hard enough to disorient her as Brenna clutched the armrests in a death grip and the car spun wildly.

Next to her, Marcos was grappling for control, trying to maneuver around his own airbag and pull the car out of the spin before it slammed into the divider.

It started to slow, and then she saw the Hummer, coming at them again. This time, when she looked behind her, she could actually see Trent behind the wheel, his face twisted in a nasty grimace as he barreled toward them.

The car lurched forward as Marcos gave it a little gas, trying to stop the spin and get out of the way at the same time, but Brenna knew it was too late. She braced for the next hit, but it didn't matter.

The Hummer smacked into them again, squishing her against the air bag before her seat belt yanked her back, making it hard to breathe. Beside her, Marcos made a sound of pain, and then the Hummer hit again.

This time, the car flipped. Her stomach dropped as up became down, and then they slammed back into the ground. She felt the jolt through her entire body, but only once in her life had she felt this helpless as the car slid forward on its roof.

Marcos dangled upside down next to her, his eyes closed, and when she heard a wailing sound, it took a minute to realize it was her. Instantly, she was transported back eighteen years to another car crash, to looking into the front seat and seeing her mom, already gone. She couldn't survive watching another person she loved die.

As the car finally came to a stop, Brenna struggled against her seat belt, but thought better of it just before she unsnapped it and fell on her head. Instead, she stretched left, trying to touch Marcos.

"Marcos? Marcos? Are you okay?"

Her voice sounded distant, and she blinked as he went blurry. Swiping her hand over her eyes to wipe away tears, she was surprised when it came back bloody. Her head pounded, and she realized she had a nasty gash in her hairline, but it didn't matter. All that mattered right now was Marcos opening his eyes.

"Marcos!" She grabbed his arm, shaking it, hoping for a response. When there was none, she fumbled to press her fingers to his wrist, searching for a pulse. But she couldn't tell over the thundering of her own heart, the pain exploding all over her body.

"Marcos!" she shouted, and this time he groaned in response.

Relief made it hard to breathe, and her hand shook as she took his. "Are you okay?"

His eyes opened and he stared back at her. Pain was reflected in those blue-gray depths, but he was alive.

This wasn't like eighteen years ago. Tears filled her

eyes instantly, the rush of them so heavy it was hard to see.

"It's okay," Marcos rasped. "We're okay."

Behind him, through the cracked side window, Brenna spotted cars swerving to a stop. But much closer, a pair of expensive loafers moved leisurely toward the vehicle and Brenna swore. "He's coming."

She braced her hand on the roof, now underneath her, to help break her fall, then pressed down on the seat-belt release. Nothing happened.

Tugging harder, Brenna tried again as Marcos did the same. Beside her, he slammed into the ceiling with a sickening thud, partially bracing his fall, and let out a groan. He was twisting to reach for the weapon he had holstered at his hip, but she could tell something was going wrong even before he lifted his sweatshirt and she could see that the gun had come free during the crash.

Then, Trent's face was filling the side window, a satisfied grin on his face. He mouthed a mocking *Sorry* as he pulled something from his pocket.

Expecting a gun, Brenna gave up on the seat belt and reached for her own weapon, but it was wedged between her and the seat belt, jammed tight.

Then, Trent's hand came back and Brenna's pulse took off. Instead of a gun, he held a match.

Yanking at the seat belt was useless, so Brenna shoved herself closer toward Marcos, her eyes watering at the intense pain that ripped through her side. Ignoring it, she yanked her gun free and swung it toward Trent, still grinning in the window.

Angling her arms in front of her awkwardly, she fired just as Trent struck the match and tossed it.

Then the front of the car went up in flames.

THE WORLD IN front of him was on fire.

Marcos reacted instinctively as smoke billowed toward him and flames sucked at the windshield. He jerked his feet away from the front of the car and grabbed the door handle, trying to shove it open.

It stuck, refusing to budge, and Marcos gasped in a desperate lungful of air, even though he knew he needed to try not to breathe the smoke. Through the window, he could see Trent on the ground, eyes wide but staring sightlessly at the sky.

But they were still in trouble. The people who'd stopped on the freeway had kept their distance—either because of the gunshot or the fire. The smoke was starting to turn gray, and he could feel the heat seeping in from the hood.

He tried to keep the panic at bay, tried not to remember the feeling when he'd lifted his head in that house all those years ago after falling on the stairs. But it came back to him, the sight of the flames blocking his exit, his brothers both gone.

At least in that terrifying moment, he'd known they'd made it out of the fire, even if he didn't. He turned to look at Brenna, and his fear seemed to quadruple. "Brenna, does your door open?"

She grabbed the handle, twisting awkwardly, still hanging upside down, tethered by her seat belt, trying to kick it when it only moved centimeters.

"I...can't...get...it," she wheezed.

Marcos swore and climbed into the back seat awkwardly, his head throbbing and his vision unsteady. "Come on. Move away from the fire. The back isn't as crumpled. Maybe these doors will...yes!" He shoved the door and it popped open.

"Brenna!" He glanced back, and she twisted her head to look at him, tears in her eyes.

"I'm stuck."

He pushed his head and chest through the small space between the two front seats, reaching around her and grabbing hold of her seat belt. Pressing hard on the release button, he yanked as hard as he could. Nothing.

Bracing his feet on the roof beneath him, Marcos tried again, and this time, Brenna wrapped her hands over his and tugged, too. He sucked in another breath, choking on smoke instead as he yanked again and again. But no matter how hard they pulled, the seat belt didn't come loose.

"Go," Brenna said, her gaze swiveling from the hood of the car, now engulfed in flames, a thick black smoke rising from it, back to him.

"No way," Marcos said, fighting the panic making it hard to breathe. Or maybe that was just the smoke. It no longer seemed to matter that the back door was open, letting in air, because smoke was filling the interior fast.

Way off in the distance, Marcos heard sirens approaching, but he knew they weren't going to make it in time.

"The car's going to blow," Brenna told him, her voice strangely calm, even though there was fear and sadness in her eyes. "You need to get out."

"I don't suppose you have another butter knife on you," he said, ignoring her ridiculous suggestion.

"Marcos, go!" Brenna shouted, then choked on the smoke. She coughed violently, then insisted, "I want you to go. You're not dying in here."

"Neither are you," he promised, searching the car

for something—anything—to saw through the seat belt and get her free. But there was nothing.

He kept searching, reaching past her to yank open the glove box, and swearing at the burning heat that seared through his hand. But the only things in his glove box were a compass, a map of the Appalachian Mountains and a spare cell phone.

"Marcos." She grabbed his hand in hers, holding on tight and effectively stopping his desperate search. "I love you. I've loved you since I was eleven years old."

He started to respond, but she kept going. "And I'll never forgive you if you don't get out of this car right now."

"Brenna," he whispered, tears clouding his vision because he knew she was right about one thing. The car was going to blow any second, and he couldn't get her out.

But he wasn't leaving without her, either. "We're a team," he told her, then scooted closer.

She lifted her other hand to shove him away from her, trying to force him to leave, and he spotted it: the gun still clutched in her hand.

Yanking it away from her, he tugged her toward him, then reached around her and aimed the gun at the seat-belt mechanism.

"No!" she yelled. "The fuel. It could spark!"

Marcos fired anyway, and then Brenna fell toward him and he grabbed hold of her and tugged her into the back seat. He could tell he was hurting her—something was wrong with her side—but he kept going, feeling blindly for the open back door as the thick smoke got even blacker.

And then, somehow, they were falling onto the cold,

hard pavement. But Marcos knew that wasn't good enough.

The car was going to go.

He shoved himself to his feet and ran, half carrying Brenna as she stumbled along beside him. Then he pushed them both to the ground and covered her body with his as an explosion *boomed* behind them, and pieces of metal and fire rained from the sky.

Beneath him, Brenna groaned and rolled so she was facing him, the pinched expression on her face telling him she'd broken at least one rib. Then her arms were around his neck as she choked out, "We're a good team."

"I love you, too," he said in return, then wiped soot away from her mouth and kissed her.

Epilogue

The boy in the doorway smiled at her. It was tentative, but understanding, and it made dimples pop on both cheeks. Then he held out his hand and Brenna took it, and somehow, she knew nothing would ever be the same again.

"Marcos."

"I'm here."

Brenna frowned, trying to make sense of what was happening as her past mingled with her present, and she opened her eyes. She was lying in a hospital bed, and Marcos was sitting in a chair beside her, his hand tucked in hers.

"What happened?"

He leaned closer, looking concerned, and she saw the hastily cleaned soot still clinging to the edges of his face and his clothes. "Trent hit our car and—"

"I know that," Brenna rasped. "Why am I in the hospital?" The last thing she remembered was being flattened to the pavement by Marcos, then him whispering something to her before he kissed her.

"You love me." She remembered his words.

He grinned, and there were those dimples. The man was so much more than she ever could have imagined in the eighteen years they'd been separated, and yet, he was exactly how she'd expected him to grow up on that very first day. Strong and kind and exactly who she needed.

"I do," he whispered, then he got serious and told her, "You passed out on the freeway after we hit the ground. They admitted you to check you out, but everything looks okay. You have a few cracked ribs and a lot of bruises. They stitched up a bad cut on your head, and they gave you oxygen because of the smoke inhalation, but you'll be out of here by tomorrow."

"And you?"

"I'm fine. Some burns on one hand, but I've been through this before. They're just covered in ointment and wrapped. Same deal with the smoke inhalation, but nothing that won't heal."

"When we were in that car, I was flashing back to the time with my mom..."

"I know," Marcos said softly. "I'm sorry."

"And then the fire..." It had to be his worst nightmare come back to life, too, and yet, he'd stayed with her.

"We got out," Marcos said simply. "And when Jim told Jesse what had happened to us, the kid spilled everything. He didn't want any part of that, said he knew we'd tried to help him get away."

"So, was Trent in charge or Carlton?"

Marcos shrugged. "Jesse wasn't sure, but he thought they had a dysfunctional partnership that was getting more and more uneven. It sounds like once upon a time, Trent had all the power, but Carlton was trying to make a play for it. And Carlton still isn't talking. Jim agrees with us that they were in it together from the very beginning. Carlton's power came from being the face of the organization, and Trent's came from his foster care connection. It's why Carlton was recruiting you. He knew Trent's connection through his father was retiring, so he wanted to grab some of that power for himself."

"What about the Pikes?"

"They're talking, too, since their son's death. They're claiming they didn't know what he was really doing with the names, but we're not buying it. I'm not sure what's going to happen because of Mr. Pike's medical needs, but they're going to face time."

"Good." She squeezed his hand, and he scooted his chair even closer to the bed. "They should pay for what they did to all those kids. And for what happened to us all those years ago."

"I'm glad we found our way back to each other," Marcos told her. "Because—"

A knock at the door cut him off, and then Cole and Andre peeked in. "How's she doing?"

"Awake," Marcos told them. "Come in."

"Thank goodness," Cole said, and Andre added, "We've got company."

Brenna shifted a little, pressing the button on the remote beside her to lift her bed so she was half sitting. She grimaced at the pain in her ribs, but it was worth it to see everyone right now. "Who?"

"The rest of the family," Cole said. "This is my fiancée, Shaye." He indicated a tall redhead with a friendly smile.

"And this is my fiancée, Juliette," Andre added, gesturing to the brunette holding his hand.

"Nice to meet you both," Brenna said. Normally, she'd be self-conscious about the fact that she was laid out from injuries and still feeling emotionally wrecked from being trapped in that car with Marcos. But somehow, this group made her feel instantly at ease. As if they were her family, too.

"We're glad you're awake," Andre said. "And that the case is finally over."

"Well, we've got all the major players in custody," Marcos corrected him. "But the investigation isn't over. I want the rest of his organization, too."

"And the kids he had running drugs for him," Brenna added. "I don't want them falling through the cracks again. I want to find a way to help them into normal lives, if we can."

Marcos smiled softly at her. "I've been thinking about that transition program you were pretending to set up for Carlton."

"What about it?"

"What if it was real?"

Brenna nodded back at him, knowing that she was going to find a way to do it. She had a lot of free time outside of the job. It wouldn't be easy, but she had a feeling the things most worth doing weren't easy.

"I think between the two of us, we can garner a lot of support for a program like that," Marcos said.

"Between the six of us," Cole spoke up. "That's how family works. We're a team."

Tears welled up so fast that Brenna couldn't stop them from spilling over. *Family.* It had been eighteen long years since she'd had anyone to call family.

"Hey," Marcos said, wiping the tears away. "Don't start crying yet. I haven't even gotten to tell you what I wanted to say before my brothers came in."

A surprised laugh snuck out. "You're going to make me cry?"

"Happy tears, I hope," Marcos said, suddenly looking nervous. And then he was reaching into his pocket and telling her, "So, I remember you telling Carlton that you liked diamonds…"

He flipped open a box and a ring was staring back at her.

Brenna's mouth dropped open, and she looked up into his eyes, surprised and scared and happier than she thought she'd ever felt in her life. "It's only been a few days," she whispered. "Are you sure?"

"I love you," he answered, as if it was the simplest thing in the world. "And after all these years, after thinking I might lose you in that car, there's one thing I know for sure. It's something I think I knew the minute I saw you in the doorway of that foster house. Home is always going to be wherever you are."

"I love you, too," she said, and she realized it didn't matter that it had been less than a week since she'd first seen him all grown up. She'd never stopped loving that boy with the dimples, and she was never going to stop loving the man he'd become.

She had a lifetime to learn all the little details about him. And she knew it was going to be the best journey she'd ever take.

She held out a shaky hand for the ring and Marcos grinned at her, his dimples popping. "So is that a *yes*?"

"Yes."

Then, the ring was on her finger and Marcos was kissing her and there was a loud *pop* behind him.

When she pulled back, she saw Andre holding up an open bottle of champagne and Cole pulling out glasses.

"To family," Marcos said, his gaze never leaving hers.

"To family," she agreed, and pulled him down for another kiss.

* * * * *

MILLS & BOON®

INTRIGUE
Romantic Suspense

A SEDUCTIVE COMBINATION OF DANGER AND DESIRE

0817/46

MILLS & BOON ®

Why shop at millsandboon.co.uk?

Each year, thousands of romance readers
find their perfect read at millsandboon.co.uk.
That's because we're passionate about
bringing you the very best romantic fiction.
Here are some of the advantages of
shopping at www.millsandboon.co.uk:

* **Get new books first**—you'll be able to buy
your favourite books one month before they
hit the shops

* **Get exclusive discounts**—you'll also be
able to buy our specially created monthly
collections, with up to 50% off the RRP

* **Find your favourite authors**—latest news,
interviews and new releases for all your
favourite authors and series on our website,
plus ideas for what to try next

* **Join in**—once you've bought your favourite
books, don't forget to register with us to rate,
review and join in the discussions

Visit **www.millsandboon.co.uk**
for all this and more today!